THE WOLF MILE

THE WOLF MILE

Book One of The Pantheon

C F Barrington

This edition first published in the United Kingdom in 2021 by Aries,
an imprint of Head of Zeus Ltd

A CIP catalogue record for this book is available from the
British Library.

ISBN PB 9781800246416
ISBN E 9781800244368

Typeset by Siliconchips Services Ltd UK

MIX
Paper from
responsible sources
FSC® C020471

Aries
c/o Head of Zeus
First Floor East
5–8 Hardwick Street
London EC1R 4RG

www.headofzeus.com

THE PANTHEON ORBAT (Order of Battle)

THE CAELESTIA (THE SEVEN)
Lord High Jupiter
Zeus
Odin
Kyzaghan
Xian
Tengri
Ördög

THE CURIATE

Europe Chapter
Russia Chapter
China Chapter
Far East Chapter
US Chapter

THE PALATINATES

The Legion ~ Caesar Imperator ~ HQ: Rome
The Sultanate ~ Mehmed The Conqueror ~ HQ: Istanbul
The Warring States ~ Zheng, Lord of Qin ~ HQ: Beijing
The Kheshig ~ Genghis, Great Khan ~ HQ: Khan Khenti
The Titans ~ Alexander of Macedon ~ HQ: Edinburgh
The Horde ~ Sveinn The Red ~ HQ: Edinburgh
The Huns ~ Attila, Scourge of God ~ HQ: Pannonian Plain

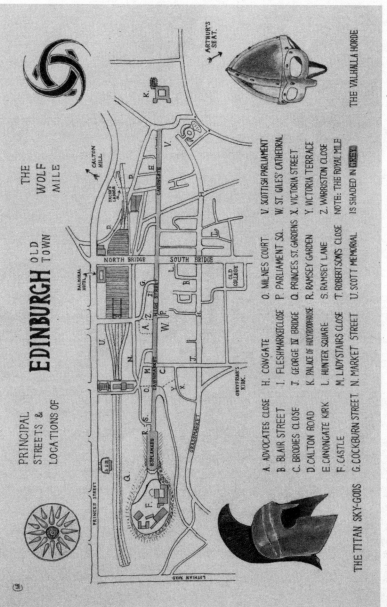

PRINCIPAL STREETS & LOCATIONS OF

EDINBURGH OLD TOWN

THE WOLF MILE

ARTHUR'S SEAT.

CALTON HILL

A. ADVOCATES CLOSE
B. BLAIR STREET
C. BRODIES CLOSE
D. CALTON ROAD
E. CANONGATE KIRK
F. CASTLE
G. COCKBURN STREET

H. COWGATE
I. FLESHMARKET CLOSE
J. GEORGE IV BRIDGE
K. PALACE OF HOLYROODHOUSE
L. HUNTER SQUARE
M. LADY STAIRS CLOSE
N. MARKET STREET

O. MILNES COURT
P. PARLIAMENT SQ.
Q. PRINCES ST. GARDENS
R. RAMSEY GARDEN
S. RAMSEY LANE
T. ROBERTSONS CLOSE
U. SCOTT MEMORIAL

V. SCOTTISH PARLIAMENT
W. ST. GILES' CATHEDRAL
X. VICTORIA STREET
Y. VICTORIA TERRACE
Z. WARRISTON CLOSE
NOTE: THE ROYAL MILE IS SHADED IN GREY

THE TITAN SKY-GODS

THE VALHALLA HORDE

Mark Clay (markclay.co.uk)

To Jackie and Oscar, for all the cakes and the walks.

Prologue

Pantheon Year – Eighteen

Season – Blood

A thin rain stole from the Forth, sullying the city, smearing its bright lights.

It was the third week of the Blood Season and Timanthes, Colonel of Companion Light Infantry in Edinburgh's Titan Palatinate – one of seven rival forces in the great game known as The Pantheon – waited on a terrace three storeys above Lawnmarket, his back straight against the wind and water seeping through his hair. He was a tall, lean, stoic figure and he made no outward movement to betray the tension in his gut. Only his eyes shifted constantly to the clock on the Balmoral hotel above Waverley station. It read one fifty-six in the morning, but Timanthes knew it was customary to keep this clock running three minutes fast to ensure travellers did not miss their trains. So there were still seven minutes until the appointed hour. He held his face to the rain and cursed softly.

Despite the inclement weather, he wore a short-sleeved tunic under a bronze corselet. On his hip was a sword sheathed in horn and from his shoulders hung a cloak of fine wool held in place by a Star of Macedon clasp. Behind him his troops squatted in silence and steeled themselves with skins of wine, their cloaks wrapped around them and their circular hoplon shields strapped to their backs.

It had been a typically hard Scottish winter and so – when the previous afternoon's sunshine brought a promise of spring – the city had cautiously unfurled. But then a fresh deluge arrived at dusk, sluicing the pavements clean of shoppers and stalling rush-hour traffic along the arteries of Leith Walk, Corstorphine and Queensferry until headlights trailed through the dark like diamond rosaries. Now the traffic was gone. The residents of New Town were sealed into their grandeur. The last bars in Leith had detached themselves from their more tenacious customers. The estates of Craigmillar, Niddrie and Muirhouse harboured only a handful of youths loitering over their phones. And among the snaking alleys either side of the Royal Mile, just a few itinerant souls scurried on their way.

No one looked up into the darkness. No one saw the figures on the roofs above Brodie's Close or spied the gleam of streetlight on bronze and iron.

'My lord, we must go.' Olena, Captain of Companion Bodyguard, stepped to Timanthes' shoulder. 'The doorway will be open for no more than fifteen minutes.'

'Are the Rope-Runts ready?'

'The whelps are all at their stations and briefed for our return.'

Timanthes nodded his approval and cast a final look

along the High Street. A lone taxi turned down Cockburn, but otherwise the pavements were clear. 'Rouse the troops.'

Olena handed him his helmet and Timanthes watched as she summoned the Companions to attention with a quiet order. As one, they donned helmets and straightened into two ranks, fifteen in each. The rain streamed through their horsehair plumes and their eyes glittered in the dark behind their bronze nasal protectors.

It was a critical moment in the Blood Season. A traitor had spoken of a secret Gate leading into tunnels that ran to the heart of the underground refuge of the Titan's main rivals, the Valhalla Horde. *Kill the King*. If the Titans could gain access to Sveinn's throne room and take him unawares, it would be a crucial victory before the Season's finale and a night when the fortunes of the Titan Palatinate might finally turn. But Timanthes was an old trooper, made shrewd by hardship and the loss of many friends, and he was uneasy about this opportunity thrown their way so readily.

He tugged on his helmet, signalled to Olena and the two ranks swivelled into columns and followed him between slanting roofs. The Titan Hoplites were sure-footed through the puddles. These rooftop balustrades were their aerial territory, their wind-scoured stronghold. They were the Sky-Gods, or the Sky-Rats as the media referred to them. They knew every foot of negotiable ground above the streets of Edinburgh's Old Town: where to assemble; where to drop; where to defend; where to disappear. They could move swiftly and silently, so that people below were lucky if they caught the movement of a cloak or the hint of a weapon and even the CCTV cameras rarely captured anything better. Those cameras which proved persistent irritants were simply dismantled and then dismantled again as soon as the engineers had righted them.

The columns reached the junction above Lawnmarket. Spread below, Edinburgh was a city of contrasts. Medieval, Georgian and Sixties, all shoved together, stirred and flung out, then scrawled over by alleyways, bridges, cycle paths and tramlines. In places the buildings had fallen in tightknit clumps, fighting for room, and in others great seams of green kept them at bay.

The Rope-Runts dropped their coils over the side. Without a word, Timanthes caught one and swung gracefully over the parapet. The Runts had done well for the twine was still dry. He curled his legs and let himself drop to the pavement. When all were down, the Runts heaved the ropes up and the Hoplites clustered into their two columns again. At the rear of the group, a new figure emerged. He was a broad man, wearing a leather tunic and wide linen trousers tied at the knees above boots. He bore the distinguishing red sash, pointed helmet and iron mask of a Vigilis – a Keeper of the Rules. Attached to his helmet was a tiny camera, so forthcoming events could be viewed in real time by those who really mattered.

Timanthes ignored the newcomer and instead stole another look down the High Street. Two pedestrians were working their way up, their stride lent a lilt by alcohol. He contemplated waiting to lose them, but time was disappearing. He glanced at Olena, then grunted an order and struck out at a fast jog.

*

As soon as they emerged, the rain embraced them, misting their faces and sluicing off their helmets. Timanthes hated being at street level and he could sense the tension in his troops. They were high, straining, just a whisper from breaking. But that was good. It meant they were primed for a fight. The two pedestrians hurled themselves into a doorway and he spied the glow of their phones as they filmed the progress of this Titan troop. On a less urgent night, he would have harried them into surrendering the devices, but this time it would have to be tolerated. Let them post their footage and the online masses have their moments of hysteria.

The Titans swept across the empty junction at George IV Bridge, skirted around St Giles' and crossed the street to Advocate's Close. He halted them with a hand and peered down steps, but nothing moved. With another gesture, they bounded forward. Two doors on their right were locked, but it was the third he was seeking. It had a metal grill which stood ajar and the door beyond was open.

He glanced at his Captain and there was a soft hum as thirty blades emerged from oiled scabbards.

'Use this opportunity, Companions. Take them by surprise and bleed them. Tonight we even the odds.'

He opened the grill and shouldered through the door. For a moment he could see nothing. The fresh air was replaced by a stale odour of damp stone and the acrid scent of piss. Steps dropped into darkness and he cocked his head to listen. Somewhere a vehicle hooted, but the shadows below yielded only yawning silence. He edged forward and began to descend. Within such confined space, the noise of their advance felt like a din. Men swore softly. Swords knocked corselets. Shields bumped on the wall. *For the love of Zeus, Sveinn will hear us coming from a league away!*

He could feel the fear of his Hoplites. They were Sky-Gods, born to bound across the rooftops, but now they were fumbling like moles, hemmed in by stone. And worse, they were in the terrain of the foe. This was the Horde's stronghold and its troops knew every inch of the tunnels and crypts and vaults that ran beneath Edinburgh. They were masters of its secrets. They had spent years burrowing and building, reinforcing, widening. It was said that a warrior could run the mile from the Castle to Holyrood Palace in ten minutes without once seeing the stars.

Inching down, Timanthes saw the flicker of flame. Olena had noticed it too and the whole company rounded a corner and emerged into a cellar, about forty yards in length, low-ceilinged, musty, frigid, with torches burning from sconces on each wall. There was a closed door on either side and another at the far end. He stepped forward and behind him the Hoplites fanned out.

'This doesn't feel right,' Olena whispered, because the room seemed to be awaiting their arrival.

'Aye,' Timanthes nodded as he eyed the doors. 'Titans, shields.'

In practised movements, the Hoplites swung their circular, leather-and-bronze-faced hoplons from their shoulders and locked their left forearms into the straps. Even as the movement died away, the returning silence was broken by a single howl, like that of a wolf. On its final note, it was joined by the rest of the pack.

'Titans to me!' Timanthes yelled and each figure stepped together, interlocked their shields and braced.

The cry died away and then the doors opened and the warriors of Valhalla stepped wordlessly into the room. In that closed space, they were a multitude. Booted, helmeted, mailed, some with heavy bearskins, many with silver arm-rings which shone in the torchlight. They carried war axes and broadswords. There were women among them too, their faces hidden behind the iron eyepieces worn by every player in the Pantheon to conceal their identity, but their figures betraying their gender. The Horde kept coming. Forty, fifty, sixty. They filled the room, arraying themselves in front of the Hoplites with just ten yards between the two lines and Timanthes knew this would be the killing ground.

At the fore was a huge man carrying an axe, his blond beard braided into forks and a tattoo creeping across his throat. He locked eyes on the Hoplite officer and Timanthes expected him to speak because this was the Viking Jarl – the pack leader – and it was custom to begin confrontations with ritual challenges to ignite the troops and give the watching Curiate something to salivate over. But not this time. This time the slaughter would be swift. The Jarl raised his battle-axe in one hand and hurled himself across the gap.

There was no space for tactics. The Titans were masters of battle formations – of line and phalanx, of feint and manoeuvre, of speed and leverage. Given the freedom of a field of conflict, their commanders could outthink far greater numbers. But now, here, stuck in this cellar, it was only kill or be killed.

The Horde rammed into the wall of hoplon shields. A warrior beat at Timanthes' shield, smashing his arm back against his corselet, and the man's thigh pressed intimately against his own, closer than lovers. A head appeared, a young face beneath a helm, mouth gritted in a teenage snarl. Timanthes shifted his weight and slipped his sword across the top of his shield in a short, precise thrust. The blade shattered the lad's teeth, sliced through his tongue and buried itself in the base of his skull. Blood erupted and his face froze in choked surprise. Timanthes yanked his weapon back and watched the boy sink from view.

The shortswords of the Titans were their one advantage, for the dreadful press of a battleline needed the kiss of a short blade and there was no room for the Horde's great broadswords. The Hoplite training kicked in. Absorb the impact on your shield, then push, step forward and stab low and fast. It was the way of the battleline. Time and again. Absorb, press, thrust, retract.

Timanthes jabbed once more, just as an axe arced towards his head, but his stab had taken him forward and the axe cleaved through his horse-hair plume where an instant before his neck had been. He knew it was the Jarl and he barely had time to react before the axe came again, buckling his hoplon. The Hoplite next to him was forced back by the impact and a gap opened, but the Jarl's attack had bent him forward and Timanthes caught sight of the tattoo where his opponent's neckline was revealed between mail and helmet. Keeping his shield low, he struck. It should have been a kill. The sword point drove towards the soft throat and the arteries beneath, but even as it prepared to embed itself, Timanthes was hit by a new blow from his unprotected right. It skewed his aim and his blade bit into bone and sinew on the giant's shoulder. The Jarl yelled and stumbled away from the fray.

Timanthes became mindful of the broader battle around him. His Titans were being forced back into a circle around the steps and already he could see Hoplite bodies down. The air was heavy with the tang of blood and hot as hell. Sweat was streaking his face and his left arm was still clinging to the remnants of his shield. He became conscious that his new assailant was standing back and waiting for his attention. He also realised that a gap was growing between him and his troops. Olena and another Hoplite were still wedged beside him, parrying and thrusting, but around them the Horde was massing.

'This is a trap!' he yelled at Olena. 'We're betrayed. Get as many out and send word to Alexander.'

She was gasping for breath and bleeding. She had a dent across her helmet's cheek protection and the right shoulder piece on her corselet had been cut open. 'With respect, lord, Companions don't run.'

'Olena, you fool! See them safely out. You must.' He pushed his Captain backwards and was startled to glimpse tears smearing her cheeks. She stared at him from behind her helm, her face creased and her eyes great pools of sorrow.

'I'm sorry, my lord. It was never meant to be like this.'

Oddly chosen words. What the hell did she mean? But there was no time to say more and he knocked her gruffly. 'Go.'

She seemed on the verge of reaching out to him, but then relented and began driving the troops up the stairs as he turned his attention back to the waiting warrior. This woman had long braided hair, almond eyes beneath her mask and lips that might even have seen balm within the hour. The incongruity struck him and he felt suddenly bereft. She was dressed in black leather, with high boots and a short coat of mail. She had dropped her shield and now held a sword and the thin seax knife favoured by the Vikings.

It was over in seconds. His eyes followed the sword and he moved to block, but she was so fast that even as he parried he felt the seax sneak beneath his breastplate, through his tunic, under his ribcage and up to his organs. Her braids whipped across his face as she swung away and they smelt of something too sweet for this place of death beneath the earth. He knew he was crumpling and he was angry because it had been a good life – a life of thrills and raw emotions and entitlement – and it should not be ending in a piss-smelling cellar. Vaguely he was conscious of another figure – the Vigilis – standing apart from the carnage and filming his demise.

Olena fought a rear-guard action up the steps. The tight stairwell was a huge advantage because it meant the Horde could follow only one at a time. She retreated slowly, giving the Hoplites opportunity to reach the surface and disperse to preordained rope points. At the top she slammed the gate on the lead Valhalla pursuer and dashed back up Advocate's Close. The rain had stopped, but she didn't notice. On the High Street the Titans split, racing apart, thankful to be out of the stone confines. A taxi was stationary at lights and the driver watched them fly around him, cloaked and helmeted figures, speeding like Sky-Gods. The Horde was on their tails now, but slower. They yelled in confused elation at their victory, but lost the momentum of organised pursuit.

In dark alleys up and down the Royal Mile, the Titans swooped onto ropes and flew skywards. Behind them, they left almost a third of their number.

The lights changed, but the taxi driver was too shocked to move. He stared through his windscreen as the Horde searched up and down the street, hooting and calling, swearing and laughing. Then gradually, in twos and fours, they too disappeared. Shaking, the driver put his car into gear and turned onto South Bridge. Edinburgh's Royal Mile once more resumed its night-time hush.

Part One

The Armatura

I

Pantheon Year – Nineteen

Season – Interregnum

Despite the gentility of their Comely Bank neighbourhood, Oliver Muir's parents brawled like baited beasts every chance they got. He could read the signs of an impending fight – a snap about condensation on the windowsills or brittle towels removed too early from their drying cycle – then the defensive response. He knew his father's homecomings were perversely late and his mother's Chardonnay indulgences indecently early. And, at thirteen years old, he was better versed in the aftermath grunts of reconciliation than he should be.

So, as offspring do in domains as tight as a bowstring, he took to retreating to his bedroom window on the corner of Learmonth Place, sitting cross-legged with his iPad, looking out at sloping communal gardens. He knew all the regular dog-walkers and could set his watch by the passing of old Calum on his way to Dean Bowling Club. He would shake his head at fat Mrs Hendrie jogging around the perimeter of the gardens each morning when she always looked so red and miserable. Even at night, after his parents had retired to bed and the flat was silent, Oliver would sit at the window, lit by an eerie glow from the hard-drives stacked above his desk, and tap his fingers lightly over his tablet screen like a maestro pianist, while other teenagers climbed the locked gates of the gardens and laughed among the shrubs.

So when one August evening an enigmatic new neighbour arrived to claim the empty flat across the hall, it was only natural that Oliver became rapidly and almost unconditionally besotted.

It was five-thirty when a wheezing battered van chugged down the street, braked hard and pulled into the parking space reserved for the Connaughts on the ground floor. The driver killed the engine and sat for several minutes smoking a cigarette. Then he emerged and limped across to the garden gates, where he turned on the spot and looked up and down the road. He was thin, in his early twenties, with long hair falling below a brimmed hat. He dragged on his cigarette, stamped it out, then retrieved a kit-bag from his van and entered the front door of Oliver's building. The boy listened to the irregular footsteps as they climbed the stairs to the third floor and heard the door slam opposite.

And that was that until next morning – a Saturday – when Oliver pulled back his curtains and was surprised to see the man smoking on one of the benches in the gardens, still wearing the hat, which nodded in response to curious good mornings from the dog-walkers. Oliver pulled on his clothes and watched as the man finally eased himself upright and limped back inside.

This time the door opposite didn't bang shut, so Oliver crept to his own front entrance – careful not to disturb his slumbering parents – and peered out. There were several boxes scattered down his neighbour's hallway and a big sack that looked heavy. The man stepped from a room and lifted one of the boxes. Oliver watched the way he leaned awkwardly to take his weight on his right side and held his left arm crooked at the elbow. He wore a blue shirt with the sleeves rolled up and his arms looked thin and pale, as though they had seen none of the summer sun.

'Morning to you, laddie,' the stranger said without looking up. His accent was from southern England, but had an Edinburgh inflection. He raised his head and for a moment his gaze was interrogative. 'You're quite the watcher. Seen you at that window almost every moment I've been here.' He disappeared with the box. 'The school holidays boring you or something?'

'I suppose.'

The man harrumphed from somewhere inside his flat. 'Well, there must be better things to do than watch me.' Oliver said nothing and the stranger returned. 'What's your name, neighbour?'

'Oliver, sir.'

'Sir?' There was a hollow laugh as he lit a fresh cigarette and leaned against the door. 'I don't think anyone's ever called me that.'

He had the palest blue eyes, like winter sky. Beneath his dark hair, he wore an earring in his left lobe. The trace of a moustache followed the contours of his upper lip and reached down to a shadow beard on the end of his chin. Beads of sweat hung on his forehead. Oliver decided he was an ill-looking musketeer – a D'Artagnan with malaria.

'I bet not much happens around here without you knowing about it, eh?'

'Not much happens around here to know about. Full stop.'

The man studied him for a few seconds, then stepped onto the landing with a smile and his hand extended. 'That's the way I like it. I'm Tyler.'

Oliver shook the hand awkwardly. Despite the cigarettes, the man smelt of soap and washing powder.

And that was the start of Oliver's fascination. Over the next few weeks, Tyler caused quite a stir in the community. His van remained unmoved in the Connaughts' parking space. Every morning, regardless of weather, he was to be found either sitting in the gardens or practising a series of slow stretching movements on the damp grass, and sometimes he would glance up at the window and nod his hat to the observer. Oliver's mother invented reasons to catch Tyler on the stairs and it turned out – disappointingly – that he was employed on the late-shift at the university library on George Square.

Then, in the second week of August, Oliver's perseverance elicited two discoveries. Firstly, Tyler spent whole nights in his van. Oliver would force himself awake in the small hours to study the vehicle and sometimes see a pinprick of light as its occupant smoked. The other discovery was that on certain evenings, while his parents watched television from their separate chairs, strange thumps emanated from Tyler's flat. Oliver would sit tense and listen. The thumps came in heavy bursts, followed by silence. Whack, whack, whack. Something hard on to something soft, as though Tyler were smashing the dust mites from his mattress.

II

Tyler Maitland made his way up Blair Street and into Hunter Square, his usual return route from his evening shift. The library had been hot and stuffy, so it did him good to wend his way back through the alleys of the medieval quarter, taking in the air and stretching his weak leg. It was nine-fifteen and the September light was fast disappearing.

He pulled a stick of gum from his pocket as he crossed the High Street, dropped into Cockburn and turned down the steps of Fleshmarket Close. There was graffiti scrawled on the walls, one big message advising, '*Chin up, you might see a Sky-Rat*'.

The Close was empty except for three men ascending from the bottom and he took no notice until he realised they had stopped and were looking up at him. He glanced behind and saw two more figures coming down. All were dressed in black hooded sweatshirts, lightweight trousers and stout boots. *Christ, how have they caught up with me already?* He toyed with rushing the three below, but two of them looked hard bastards. The central man was shorter, wiry and older. His cropped hair was the same length as the stubble coating his chin and his eyes were coals beneath a deep-set frown. He climbed up and brought himself close.

'Tyler Maitland?' he asked in a clipped voice.

'Who's asking?'

'Do you recognise this?' The man was holding something in the palm of his hand and Tyler bent to make it out in the gloom. It was a silver amulet shaped to represent three interlocking curved blades. *What the hell?* He had assumed these men were from one of the coke gangs on the estate he had fled, but why would they be showing him this?

He tried to sound dismissive. 'Those things are two a penny if you know where to look.'

The man's jaw tightened and he pocketed the piece. Now he pulled out a phone, retrieved a thin pair of reading spectacles and tapped the screen. 'Are you Tyler Maitland of Flat 6, 18 Learmonth Place? Information Assistant (Probationary) at Edinburgh University Library since last month. National Insurance number QN 345863 B. Driving licence number MAITD722398CS7TY. One Vauxhall Vivaro van, licence plate PL02 XSN. Bank account number 38577239. Funds in aforementioned account as of the end of yesterday: £4360.82. Favoured online password…' He raised his eyebrows in mock approval. 'Niflheim99.'

Tyler felt prickles across his back. 'Who wants to know?'

'My colleagues and I are a Venarii party tasked with the annual replenishment of troops. I have been given your name. Do you understand?'

Tyler stared, speechless for many moments. 'I think so,' he stuttered.

The man studied Tyler. He took in his pale features, his crooked arm, the fragility of his frame and the way he favoured one leg. The man was obviously unimpressed and his frown deepened. 'I require you to demonstrate a firmer acknowledgement. I repeat, do you understand what I have just said to you?'

'Yes. Yes I do.'

'You will find a token of our interest at your flat. Look at it. Consider it. Think about the implications. And if you want no more of this, ensure you deposit the item beneath the old yew tree at the west end of Greyfriars Kirk before midnight next Monday. No one but I knows your personal details, and so you will hear nothing more from us.' He paused, as if expecting Tyler to plead non-involvement there and then. 'If, however, you wish to continue, be on Lady Stair's Close at 10 p.m. next Wednesday evening. Your password is *runestone*.'

He waited for some late shoppers to pass, then nodded sharply and climbed up to Cockburn. The four men followed and Tyler was left alone, standing in the shadows, his gum forgotten.

Tyler's weaker limb was burning by the time he got back to Learmonth Place. He glanced up and saw Oliver at his darkened bedroom window, but this time the lad was tapping on the pane and stabbing his finger down towards the front door. Something – or someone – had alarmed him. Tyler waved assurance and entered the building. The stairway was empty. Mud-spattered boots sat outside the Connaughts' front door and their Miniature Schnauzer yapped at him from beyond. On the third floor everything looked normal. He could hear the television in the Muirs' and hoped the boy wouldn't come out.

His own door looked untouched. He had left a wilted

pot plant outside that morning, intending to bin it, and he had spilled some of the soil across the mat. Yet even that looked just as he had left it, none of it flattened by a stranger's boot. He unlocked and flipped the light switch in the hall.

Reaching the open-plan living room, he stood in the doorway scanning the scene. His lunchtime pasta bowl sat unwashed on the coffee table and there was whisky as always, discarded in a glass by the sink. With the lights all on and each room checked, his tread grew in confidence, but something felt different. It was in the air. The faintest smell of a different body, different clothing, like when you sit with a companion in a small place, then leave for a moment, only to return and realise how much it smells of their leather jacket or onion breath or cheap deodorant. He stepped into the bedroom and sat on the bed.

And that's when he felt something beneath the sheets and before he had even thrown back the bedclothes, he knew what it was. There, in the centre of his mattress, beneath sheets that had been diligently remade, was a second amulet on a thin chain. He cradled it in his palm. It was silver, each arm locked into the other in a never-ending cycle. The Triple Horn of Odin. The talisman of the Valhalla Horde. It was said the Viking warriors who roamed subterranean Edinburgh carried the Triple Horn around their throats and to lose it foretold of death.

Everyone knew about the emblem. Kids scrawled it on walls and in their exercise books. Tattoo parlours specialised in it. Local jewellers sold cheap and not so cheap versions. But this one was different. Its workmanship was beautiful. The horns had faint whorls etched into them.

On the underside there was a ruby embedded in the centre and the Roman numerals VI engraved.

Tyler unbuttoned his shirt and reached inside to retrieve a cord around his neck. On the end was a smaller, but identical symbol, this one carved from ivory. He had worn it every day for the past six months since she had left it for him in their Craigmillar flat on the last occasion he had ever seen her. On the reverse, instead of a ruby, was a tiny Star of Macedon – symbol of the foe – embedded expertly into the ivory. Reverently, he removed it from his neck and took it into the living room, where he hung it over a photograph on the dresser. Then he slipped the new amulet over his head, tears pricking at the corners of his eyes.

III

Lady Stair's Close was a small square with views north over New Town and beyond to the Forth. Every stone reeked of history. In the western corner was the turreted and balconied Writers' Museum. On the eastern side ancient steps led to original tenements and in the centre was an oil lamp, now electrified, but still casting a limp yellow light that only encouraged the darkness.

There was a breeze from the Forth and it was cold, but this wasn't the only reason Tyler shivered as he leaned smoking against the railings on the upper south side. He was dressed in jeans and a long coat, with his hat pulled low over his face. His left arm was feeling stronger and could almost straighten, but at night it still protested deep in the bone. People were drifting through the square towards the Royal Mile, but he had no interest in them. Instead he covertly studied the other figures around the edges of the Close. He counted ten, maybe more. They shuffled or leaned motionless, but each was careful to avoid the glow of the lamp.

Tyler checked his watch: 9.58 p.m. From beyond the tight alley which led onto the Mile, a woman laughed and several pairs of high heels clicked past. Ten o'clock. *Come on.* A figure appeared up the steps on the northern side, silhouetted against the distant lights of New Town. Despite a sweatshirt with the hood pulled up, Tyler could see by the gait that it was a man. The figure walked without pausing to the first of the waiting bystanders and there was a brief exchange. Then the man moved to the next one and the next. As he went, the figures detached themselves from the walls and shuffled after him. Eventually he came to Tyler.

'Your password?' he demanded from beneath his hood.

'Runestone.'

'And your number?'

Tyler had to think and suddenly remembered the Roman numerals on the back of the amulet. 'Six.'

The man grunted. 'Follow me.'

Tyler stamped out his cigarette and joined the silent group as they walked up the alley towards the Mile. He looked at the woman in front. She had a strong build, dark red hair cut short and plimsolls on her feet. For some reason he had an image of her as the captain of a racing yacht, hauling on the ropes and shouting orders through the spray.

They stepped onto the more brightly lit Mile and their host peered down the street. Three large cars pulled up and Tyler found himself crammed on the backseat of the second, between the short-haired sailing captain and a very tall man who smelt of tobacco. Another man got into the front passenger seat, smaller but wider, with cropped hair and a chubby band of flesh above the back of his collar. The hooded driver moved off, following the car in front, then turned in his seat and dropped a piece of material into each of their laps.

'Put these on.'

Tyler toyed with the length and glanced at the others. The chubby chap in the front had a cocky confidence and with a shrug he bound the material around his eyes. Tyler followed suit and he heard the others doing the same. Despite the moving vehicle, he felt the driver reach back and check his blindfold. Then they picked up speed and were jolted against each other's shoulders as the car was taken around tight corners. They drove for fifteen minutes, but Tyler had a good sense of direction and he had a suspicion that they kept cutting back on themselves and weren't travelling far.

The car came to a halt and a door was flung open. 'Final stop,' said a new voice, this time female. 'All out, but leave your blindfolds in place.' They struggled onto the pavement and felt themselves herded through an entrance. 'Steps down ahead. Feel the person in front of you and go slowly.'

Tyler pushed up against the tobacco-smelling man and counted fifteen steps until they levelled out. Hands placed him on one spot and there was movement as the others were sorted. Light flickered at the edges of his blindfold and he smelt burning wax and used matches. Eventually there was silence except for nervous breathing. He found himself wondering if the whole of the Valhalla Horde was standing before him, inspecting his hunched form.

'You may remove your blindfolds,' said a staccato voice Tyler recognised.

He found himself in the second row and the tall tobacco man obscured most of his view, but he could see there were twelve of them in three rows of four. They were in a basement with a window high up on the wall, through which he could hear buses. A table on a raised platform was covered in a white cloth, with two candles burning at either end and a large Triple Horn of Odin embroidered on the cloth in the centre.

Behind the table were three men. Two of them were standing, arms folded and grim. They both wore helmets which curved up to a point, with eyepieces that masked their identities. They had dark moustaches and broad necks. A red sash sloped from their left shoulders, above bright baggy trousers. Between them, Tyler recognised the bristly head, beaked nose and deep frown of the older man who had intercepted him on Fleshmarket steps.

'Welcome,' the man spoke. 'I apologise for the blindfolds, but I'm sure you understand.' He peered at the faces. 'You are twelve. We called eighteen. We found three amulets beneath the yew tree and we have three no-shows tonight. It is of no consequence. Twelve is enough.'

Tyler took a glance to his right. There was a woman in the front row next to the tall man. She was petite, with curling blonde hair tied in a ponytail. She wore a good quality coat and heeled ankle boots. The candlelight played on a pearl earring and a soft touch of make-up. Tyler had the impression she had come straight from work, perhaps even beautified herself in the staff bathroom before she departed. The image seemed at odds with this grim basement.

'I can see the question burning in your eyes,' the man said, gazing shrewdly at the newcomers. 'The question that has been tearing you up since you each encountered our Venarii parties. The one that has put you off your food, loosened your bowels, drenched your bedding with night sweats and laid siege to your minds. And I can confirm that the answer to this question is, aye. This is indeed the Pantheon. You have found us. Or, rather, we have found you, because no one ever finds the Pantheon. I am Radspakr, of the Horde of Valhalla. Thane of the Palatinate. Paymaster. Custodian of the Day Books. Counsellor of War. Lord Adjutant to High King Sveinn the Red. These gentlemen behind me are Vigiles. Keepers of the Rules. And you would do well to abide by any that we give you.'

Radspakr studied his audience, shifting his eyes from one face to another. 'And I ask myself, what else have you been feeling since you were handed your amulets? Elation? Terror? Animosity? Resolution? Why have you allowed yourselves to be blindfolded and herded into this basement? Is it because you wonder where this trip might take you? Where it could end? Whether it just might be so much more than what you hold in your lives already?'

He let the questions hang, then smiled humourlessly. 'Twenty years ago, I was present at the very start of this venture. When the first sums were invested, when the Palatinates were created and when the rules were being thrashed out over days of debate. It was a crazy, exciting time and I marvelled at the confidence of the seven Founders, their determination to see their grand project given life. But I always assumed it would be a project fated to be played out in the haunts of the underworld, constantly harassed by the forces of law and order, and loathed by the rest of humanity. I was wrong on both counts.'

Radspakr rose and stalked around the table. 'Firstly, I underestimated the power of money. You can do anything with enough wealth, it's just a question of quantity. Money buys acceptance. It averts scrutiny. It smooths feathers. It permits everything without interference, as long as the right palms are greased.

'And secondly, I never foresaw that this mad game of ours would actually enthral people. No matter the blood and violence, nor how hard we might try to keep our activities concealed, the world became obsessed with the Pantheon. If I could weave together all the conjecture – all the so-called opinion pieces, the wafer-thin facts, the grandiose assessments – I have no doubt it would stretch to the moon. Many condemn us. Still more fear us. But what I never saw for a moment was that so many would value us, even love us. It seems we all live in a soulless world. A place of routine and debt. Where every week is the same as the next. Where aspirations crumble. Where a person grows old just trying to find the keys to life. And so – perhaps inevitably – the Pantheon became a beacon amidst this grey, meaningless anonymity. We offer the glamour of the unknown. The thrill of the enigma. The blank canvas on which everyone can paint their dreams. People hear stories of danger and exploits and they are drawn by the romance.'

He pointed a bony finger at the high window. 'They're out there now, thinking about the Pantheon. The office workers. The school kids. The teenagers. The penniless. The homeless. The forgotten masses. All contemplating us. All asking if it's true there are adventures and fortunes to be won in the Pantheon. All wondering how to find us. So you should count yourselves very lucky that you are the chosen... *the Electi*. You are here because I have been given your names. You are here because every detail of your lives has been researched and passed to me. You are here because you have been selected. You each have certain... aptitudes... which may or may not prove to be of value to us.'

He paused to let his words sink in. The room was still,

save for the sound of the traffic, and he let the silence linger, then cleared his throat and continued more expeditiously.

'The summer Interregnum is drawing to a close. The city is quietening and we can once again go about our business more freely. September marks the first days of the Armatura Season, when each Palatinate – each team – is awarded the funds it has earned during the last Blood Season and may use them to recruit fresh troops. Edinburgh is blessed with two Palatinates and our foes, the Titan Hoplites, have fared miserably and hold barely a silver denarius to strengthen their numbers. We of the Horde, on the other hand, have won great victories and have been rewarded accordingly. We have filled our ranks with new blood from our training house – the Valhalla Schola – but we have also decided to seek a few select individuals from outside. *You* may be those individuals.

'The Pantheon uses Latin for its main terminology. Armatura means "*to arm*" – and that is the purpose of this season. Pass the tests, prove your worth and we may deem you Weapons Worthy and welcome you into our number. You will have read the drivel about the riches to be won in the Pantheon. Much of it is nonsense, but there are indeed great opportunities to gain reward. For those who enter the Pantheon, it is life-changing and the world out there,' he waved again at the window above them, 'will seem crass and meaningless by comparison. But the Pantheon is no place for the faint-hearted, nor for the uncommitted, and you would be wise to ponder this.'

He returned to his seat. 'You speak of this to *no one* outside this room, nor do you attempt to find out the identities of any of your companions here tonight. Believe me when I say that it's not through mere chance that we know everything about you that is worth knowing. The Pantheon has eyes and ears everywhere. We will be watching.' He gestured to the men behind him. 'And my Vigiles friends here don't want to learn of anything that displeases them.

'You are not yet under oath. You may step away from this process if you so wish. Each of your amulets has a number on the back. If we find it beneath the yew tree, we will forget we ever met you, just as we will expect you to forget you ever met us. Do you understand?' No one spoke. 'Do you *understand*?' he demanded.

Ludicrously, Tyler found himself shouting yes along with the others, as though they were an assembly of schoolchildren.

'Good. The cars will return you. If you still want to be a part of this by the end of the week, then you will gather at Bull's Close on Canongate next Saturday, again at 10 p.m. As a symbol of intent, you will wear your amulets around your necks like true warriors of Valhalla.' He glanced at both the Vigiles. Neither had moved, nor even changed expression. They were implacable behind their helmets and they scared Tyler more than anything else.

'You are dismissed.'

'Blindfolds on!' called the female voice and there was sudden bustle. As he brought the material up to his face, Tyler looked across to the girl with the ponytail. She had turned and she caught his eye before bending her face into her blindfold.

Soon they were squashed in the cars, hammering hard around corners. When they were told to remove their blindfolds and deposited on the pavement of the Mile, Tyler looked around at the others, trying to catch faces, but each dropped their eyes and walked away in separate directions. He waited and then cut through the alley and back across the square towards Waverley, stopping only once to shout exultantly at the moon.

IV

Lana Cameron had been in her final year reading for an MA in Linguistics in the School of Philosophy, Psychology and Language Sciences at Edinburgh University when she was raped at a student party on St Leonard's Street on the south-western fringes of Holyrood Park.

Until that night in early May – only weeks before her Finals – she had rejoiced in university life. It was a long-held ambition of hers to live in Edinburgh, a city that she first found intoxicating during teenage visits from Dumfries with her mother. She became a model student, immersing herself in lectures and tutorials, reading hungrily in her room in Hall. An already fine distance runner who had represented Scotland at the European Youth Games, she joined the University Athletics Club and pounded out laps of the cinder track in the sharp air of countless dawns.

In her third year she was awarded a place on the Erasmus Exchange Scheme to spend twelve months at the Aristotle University of Thessaloniki. She fell in love with Greece, and the golden light that touched everything. She became fluent in the language. She trained under the Mediterranean sun and spent endless balmy evenings feasting on fruit and wine. She met a man named Andreas who was reading Ancient

History and he shared with her the Roman, Byzantine and Ottoman remains around the upper town. They strolled in the harbour, hiked in Seich Sou forest, swam in the Thermaic Gulf at Peraia, ate *bougatsa* for breakfast and dwelt over *meze* in the tavernas of Ladadika.

She could have lost herself in Thessaloniki, but from the other side of the continent, she felt Edinburgh clawing her back. Her fourth year was spent focusing on her dissertation, becoming Secretary of LangSoc by popular demand, and researching a career as a translator. Andreas had inspired in her an appreciation of history and architecture, so she reconnected with Edinburgh through a new love of its twisted dark past.

Now, as Lana walked down the Mount towards the Scottish Academy and Princes Street, her ponytail swinging and her boots clicking on the paving, she struggled to analyse everything Radspakr had said and to understand how her life had taken such a calamitous turn and washed her up in that room beneath the road, listening fearfully to the Lord Adjutant of the Valhalla Horde.

She could remember the night five years earlier only in vague generalisations, but the attack itself she could recall in every sharp detail as though it were yesterday. The party was one of those usual student affairs. No rules of attendance. Friends of friends turned up, acquaintances of acquaintances. Anyone was admitted as long as they brought a bottle. Lana had gone with friends after an evening in a bar in nearby Newington. The downstairs rooms of the house were barely lit, stinking like a brewery and packed. A bass line throbbed somewhere beneath the conversation.

She remembered leaning against the doorframe of the living room, sipping from a bottled beer and talking to a man with smart jeans and hair so pale, it was almost white. Icelandic, she had thought, or perhaps Norwegian. Something about him called up the pristine sparkle of glaciers. The beat was loud and they had to tilt in to each other and shout. She was telling him about Thessaloniki, and he would nod and yell responses in her ear, but neither of them could really hear what the other was saying. Instead, they just kept speaking aimlessly and using the noise as an excuse to get closer. She could feel his breath on her cheek and he held his own beer against his chest in a way that caused his hand to brush hers. She could sense a lean physique beneath his shirt and when he looked at her, his eyes were ice blue and cocksure. At some point he raised his eyebrows in a question and she didn't need words to agree they should find somewhere more private.

She recalled that he was decisive and she found it attractive. He led her upstairs by the hand. He tried various doors, escorted her into an empty room and pushed the door closed. Even then, she always remembered, she was keen to be there. She wanted to kiss him and her arms came around his neck. She enjoyed the moment. His mouth tasted of hops and his body was strong against her. She broke the kiss with a laugh.

And that was when it changed. The pressure of his arm around her didn't ease and he began to walk her backwards. She stumbled and started to say something in protest. Her calves came up against a bed and she tried to twist around him, but he had her wrapped into him and, with a grunt, his momentum bore her over and his full weight was on her. She swore at him to get off, but he was hard against her. She worked her hands onto his shoulders and managed to push his head back. For a moment they looked at each other. His eyes retained their mesmeric blue glint even in the half-light. He was waiting for her to speak and she mustered every ounce of firm calm into her voice to state, *No*. He tilted his head at this, like a dog, then grinned and lunged back onto her. Brutally, he kneed her in the thighs and forced himself between. She punched him, but her cries were drowned by the music below and her resistance only aggravated his violence. He pawed expertly up her dress and she knew then that nothing would stop him.

Perhaps it didn't last long, for she had no real sense of time. Suddenly he was done and he pushed up to adjust his clothing. He ran his hands through his hair and sat still for several seconds, letting his eyes rove over her in the dark. Then he bent his face close to hers and nuzzled against her throat, as though smelling her fear. 'You know what you did wrong, girl?' He wound a finger in her hair and then jerked it. 'You gave up too soon. It's the fight that's so damn sexy.' He sat up, blew out his cheeks dismissively and left the room.

She lay on the bed for an age, getting cold, feeling a stickiness on the tops of her thighs. Traffic went by outside. The hubbub of voices continued. The Black Eyed Peas were pulsing from the music system. Even if someone had come in, she couldn't have moved or covered herself.

That night was the start of her collapse, yet also the beginning of something so truly incredible, so untouchably precious, that it would take her through a whirlwind of the greatest highs and lows that a woman could experience, and deliver her five years later into the arms of the Valhalla Horde.

As Lana reached Princes Street, her mobile rang.

'I'm in the Voodoo Rooms,' said the caller. 'Tom's pleaded fatigue and left. Want a nightcap?'

Her body cried out for a stiff drink, so she accepted, but she was soon regretting the decision. She wanted the alcohol, yes, but in the warm solitude of her bath at home, not with Justin in the fading hours of the night.

'Rum and coke?' he asked from one of the semi-circular booths when she arrived. 'Or, then again, you look pretty worn out. Maybe something a bit more special?'

He handed her the cocktail menu and she flipped through, avoiding his eyes. 'A Gin Palace Blush.'

'Crispy and elegant,' he said as he took back the menu and read the drink notes. 'Naturally!' He looked up at her and winked, thinking her fatigue sculpted her features and her eyes were pools of dark green mystery.

Then he walked away to begin a cheerful dialogue with the bartender and Lana was thankful that cocktails took time to make. She caught her reflection in giant mirrors above the bar and grimaced. Twenty minutes earlier she was being bundled unseeing out of a cellar and crammed into vehicles with strangers.

He was coming back, a champagne flute in one hand and a whisky tumbler in the other. She smiled her thanks and toyed with the glass, watching the blueberries bounce in the bubbles.

'You look beautiful,' he said, suddenly serious.

'You just told me I looked worn out.'

'Worn out and beautiful. You have eyes like no one I've ever met.'

She smiled limply and gave a slight shrug.

'So what did you get up to with Helen?' he asked.

'Oh, we had a couple of glasses in… Brodies.'

'Brodies? I wouldn't have thought that was your type of place.'

'It was fine.'

'And Helen?'

'She was fine. It was all fine.' She lied and glugged her drink. 'I'm sorry, I'm just tired. It's pretty late.'

Justin was replying, changing the subject, but all she could picture was Radspakr as he strode across the platform, and the expressionless men behind, and the thin man in the hat who had glanced at her just before she replaced her blindfold. What the hell had they all been doing?

She could sense her amulet in her pocket, the one with the Roman numerals VIII engraved on the reverse. It seemed to be throbbing and she thought that Justin must know it was there. Surely he would pull it from her any moment. She dropped a hand and touched it. She was a fool. She would take it to Greyfriars, bury it under the bloody yew tree and be shot of the lot of them.

She forced herself to focus on Justin, sipping from her glass and allowing it to hide her expression. He was handsome in a clean-cut way. The sort of man her mother in Dumfries would adore. A good job in a law firm not many blocks distant and a sense of style that was all well-fitting tweed and fashionably styled brogues. He could have his choice of women, but he seemed to want her. He would make someone a wonderful husband, but she knew indisputably that it wouldn't be her.

V

'The Three Pillars employed to bring the physical body to peak readiness are as relevant today, as they were in ancient times. Speed. Strength. Violence.'

Once more they were underground, but this time it was no ordinary cellar. The space was larger and the walls rose to meet an arched roof. The stones spoke of great age and Tyler wondered if they stood in one of the many vaults that had been abandoned, bricked up and forgotten either side of the spine of rock that formed the Royal Mile. He had studied what was written about Edinburgh's secret places. He had borrowed books and knew the basic facts. In the 1700s space on the bridges running up to the Mile was at a premium and so tenements were built into the great arches. They filled with artisans of every description, crammed into the tight confines: cutlers, milliners, victuallers, smelters, cobblers, and the other industries that flourished unofficially around them – distillers, smugglers, whores. More floors and ceilings were constructed and the sunlight was lost. They became damp and claustrophobic places.

And then the plague roared through them without prejudice or mercy and they deserted. But Edinburgh was too crowded for them to remain unused for long and they filled again with the dregs of society. No one knew what went on in the disease-ridden darkness after that. There were stories of new tunnels being dug and tales of ancient ways giving access to other parts of the city, but eventually the squalor forced the authorities to build over the vaults, brick them up, leave them to the ghosts of the past.

The twelve initiates remained. No one had returned their amulet. Once more they were lined up in three rows of four and Tyler found himself at the back. The arrival procedure had been the same. Collection from Bull's Close at ten, passwords, numbers, lurching sightless journeys, then herding down steps. This time he was next to another tall man, but not Mr Tobacco. This man had at least four inches on Tyler's six feet. He was about Tyler's age, with a shaven head and chin, which exaggerated the luxuriance of his eyebrows in the half-light. He had glanced across when the blindfolds were removed and Tyler was surprised to register warmth and even humour in his expression. In the row in front, Tyler could see the bulky red-haired girl with her plimsolls and at the end of the front row he could just see Miss Pearl Earrings, looking pensive and meagre compared to the rest of the burly figures.

This time there was no Radspakr and no Vigiles. Instead there were two newcomers, who had informed them solemnly that they were Housecarls in the Valhalla Palatinate and were here to instruct them. The woman had introduced herself as Freyja and added without pausing that she was so-named after the goddess of beauty, love, war and death in Norse mythology. She was of Indian origin, slim, ochre-skinned, with braided hair and wearing a T-shirt, leather leggings and knee-length boots. Her fine features combined with an expression of such intensity that every person in the room found her at once striking and intimidating. Her partner was Halvar – *defender of the rock* – a man-mountain. His face looked as though it had been punched relentlessly for more than a decade and a scar ran from his left eye to his upper lip. His hair was cropped short and matted, and his chin hadn't seen a razor for a week. He too was dressed in a black T-shirt which flaunted his huge arms and on his right bicep three triangles, separate and yet all interconnected, had been tattooed.

He walked through the rows, repeating Freyja's words in a slow Lowland Scots accent. 'Speed. Strength. Violence.' He glanced at Tyler and for a heartbeat his eyes held and his fierce expression faltered. Puzzlement flickered across his features and his lips tightened, but then he controlled himself and his gaze swung away.

Freyja spoke again from her place in front of the candles. 'Over the next weeks of the Armatura, we'll equip you with the skills you'll need to enter the ranks of the Valhalla Horde. Only some of you will make it. Those who succeed will then come up against our foe – Alexander's Titans – in the Raiding Season. The Sky-Rats are many things, but they're not poor warriors. If you fail to possess the necessary skills when the Season begins, they'll destroy you.'

'Aye, and it's not simply a matter of skill,' Halvar interjected. 'It's also about resolve, the bloody will to win whatever it takes, you wet-arsed mares.' He halted and spun around glaring at them all. 'Will you do whatever it takes?' No one answered and he swore loudly, but let his question drop.

'Along the wall behind you there are boxes each marked with a number,' Freyja continued. 'Find yours and change into the contents. Go!' Everyone looked at each other uncertainly. 'Now!' she commanded.

The twelve strangers found themselves stripping to their underwear. White bodies, fumbling and trembling as though they were primary children getting ready for gym class. They found sleeveless black T-shirts, soft leggings and sports shoes, all correctly sized. Each of them wore their numbered amulet around their neck. They returned to their original places and Halvar walked between them with a large marker pen and wrote their respective number in Roman numerals on each arm.

'Your names in the real world are irrelevant and never to be used,' said Freyja. 'For the present, you are all *Thralls* – those who occupy the lowest rank in Viking society – and we will know you by your numbers. *Thrall I, Thrall II*, etc. I trust that I'm understood. Those of you who can take the pace will meet with us three times a week, always from ten until midnight.'

'That's late for a weeknight,' said a brave voice further along Tyler's row.

Halvar glared in the direction of the speaker. 'Do you have something more important to attend?'

'No,' conceded the speaker weakly.

'In the first weeks we'll alternate between speed and strength, for you are nothing if you're not agile and overpowering. And then, if you get that far, we'll combine these and hone them into combat skills. Let me be plain – you'll not succeed if you limit your efforts to these sessions alone. Learn what we teach you, then take away the knowledge and train every minute the gods provide until you cannot fail.'

'Now hear me,' Halvar bellowed. 'Even-numbered Thralls to my left, odd to my right.'

The room burst into disorder. Tyler looked at the numbers of those around him and found himself with his bald-headed neighbour (II), Miss Pearl Earrings (VIII) and the big sailing woman (X), along with two others, both men. One (XII), he thought, looked like the thick-set man who had sat in the front of the vehicle on the first night.

Halvar strode over to them and directed them out of the vault, while Freyja remained with the others. They found themselves in a passage with doors along one side. He led them to the last one and they entered another torchlit room with an arched ceiling.

'Line up there.' He pointed to the back wall and advanced to the other end where he picked up a drum and looped the strap over his head. 'We'll begin slowly. Start by walking in a line towards me. When you reach me, I'll beat the drum and you'll turn and walk back and I'll beat the drum once more. You'll repeat this again and again, but – be warned – you must reach the end wall each time *before* I beat the drum. When you fail to reach the wall before you hear the drum, drop out. Do you understand?' The six of them nodded. 'Wordless whelps.'

He struck the drum and they began walking. Tyler had *Thrall VIII* beside him, her ponytail bouncing and her face strained. He noticed that tonight she wore no make-up and it struck him how vulnerable she looked. They reached

Halvar and he hit the drum. They turned and walked back. The tall bald man, *Thrall II*, strode ahead, forcing the pace. His shoulders were thrown back and his posture was ramrod-straight. The others copied this new speed and the drum echoed around the stones when they reached the far end. Back again, this time a very fast walk. Tyler's weak leg began to complain. By the time they turned, they had shifted into a steady jog following the lead of *Thrall II* and Tyler had to grit his teeth against the pain licking up his thigh. He could hear the breathing of the stocky man on his other side, *Thrall XII*.

The beats came ever more speedily. They were running now and Tyler stumbled, trying to take the impact on his stronger side. Number *XII* began wheezing and he could hear *Thrall VIII* panting as well, although she was moving smoothly. *Thrall II* was out in front and reaching the walls well before Halvar hit the drum. Another length and turn and accelerate. The girl next to him had lost a yard and, for some strange reason, he felt bad about it.

'Drop out,' Halvar shouted and Tyler knew the stocky man had failed to reach the end of the room.

Faster. Tyler's knee was starting to scream and his breathing was making ragged piping sounds. He hit the wall full-on and had to push himself away with raw willpower.

'Drop out,' Halvar pointed to Tyler's left. 'And you as well.' There was just three of them now. The girl had rallied and was overtaking him with every step. Tyler wanted to heave but even as the wall came within touching distance the inevitable crash of the drum broke through his agony.

'*Thrall VI*, drop out!'

He hit the cold stone and stood with his face pressed

against it, sucking in the air and holding his weak leg bent forwards. Behind him the race continued until the girl finally had to yield and only number *II* sprinted back and forth, his bald head flung back and his long legs thrown out. Halvar accelerated the beat to an impossible speed and the Thrall crashed out, leaning hands on knees and dragging in the air.

'By the end of this period,' Halvar spoke as he deposited the drum, 'you'll all achieve that or leave the process.' He let the statement hang and walked into the centre of the room. 'Now, star jumps.'

For the next ninety minutes he kept at them and it was torture for Tyler. They jogged holding heavy stone balls. They dodged around sandbags. They even tried to shadow box. And then they did it all again. There was no chance to converse, so instead they just caught each other's expressions and asked the same silent questions. Then, when their bodies longed for respite, they were told to retrieve their personal items and were escorted blindfolded back to the cars.

When Tyler returned to Learmonth Place in the small hours, his leg was agony. He poured a slug of whisky, flung himself on the sofa and tried to marshal what he already knew about the Pantheon. He started with the basics.

There were seven Palatinates. Everyone knew that. The Horde and the Titans in Edinburgh. The Sultanate in Istanbul led by Mehmed The Conqueror. Caesar's mighty Legion in Rome. The Kheshig troops of Genghis Khan with training camps somewhere on the Mongolian grasslands. And Zheng, King of the Qin, who ruled the Warring States Palatinate from his powerhouse within Beijing's Forbidden City. Tyler counted on his fingers. Horde, Titans, Sultanate, Legion, Kheshig, Warring States. That made six. He tapped his forehead in frustration. Of course – the Huns. Who could forget them? The wild kids of the Pantheon. The bad seeds. Attila led his lines from the flatlands east of Budapest and their reputation attracted huge fan bases around the world. Never trust the Huns, it was said, and never ever get captured alive by them.

Although each Palatinate was led by a King, true power lay with the Caelestia, a body made up of seven gods. It was said that these gods were the real owners of their respective Palatinates and perhaps also they were the seven original founders of the Pantheon. Rumours of their true identities blazed like wildfires. A common theory was that they had all been friends and contemporaries in their younger days as they began to build their legendary wealth. Perhaps colleagues in the same firm. Perhaps students at the same institution. Oxford had the audacity to claim them. Harvard too. But no one was any the wiser.

Okay, what else? Tyler knew the Pantheon was nineteen years old and there were two Conflict Seasons each year – Raiding and Blood – but Radspakr's reference to a third Season – the Armatura – was the first Tyler had heard of this. Each Palatinate seemed to have a regular adversary. The Kheshig battled the Warring States. The Sultanate took on the Huns. And, of course, the Horde faced off against the Titans in the streets of Edinburgh. Though now he thought about it, Tyler was uncertain where that left the Legion. He scowled and tried to think. Who the hell opposed the Legion?

No one seemed to know why Edinburgh hosted two Palatinates. Theories abounded. Blood feuds. Broken hearts. Unpaid debts. Passionate affairs. Whatever the true reason, the Titans had upped sticks from Athens years ago and settled across the rooftops of the Old Town, glaring down at the Horde in its subterranean lairs.

Tyler swallowed his whisky and rose to pour another. What else did he know? Well, there was something called the Curiate. This was a secondary body, nowhere near as important as the Caelestia, and supposedly comprising wealthy friends and associates who loved to bet on the outcomes of each Pantheon contest. They were sometimes referred to as the Watchers, because it was believed they paid vast sums to enjoy the action on live feeds and to place their bets in real time. People said the Curiate numbered hundreds, others even suggested thousands, and this led to a minefield of rumours. Every millionaire, every billionaire, every CEO, every national leader, every significant figure in public life had been linked to the Curiate at one time or another by online gossipmongers. Accusations of membership were hurled across the internet, often resulting in more than one legal proceeding. But no one really knew. If the Curiate did exist, it was something of which the politicians, the police and the official media never spoke. The Pantheon guarded its secrets jealously.

Tyler opened his laptop and began to trawl the internet for 'Pantheon' and 'Valhalla Horde' and 'Sky-God'. He had done this countless times in the months since she had disappeared from his life, but tonight, after the remonstrations of the Housecarls in the cellars, he probed with renewed conviction. Pages of finds were returned – but none of them amounted to more than the usual conjecture. Most of the sites were constructed by fan boys and girls with nothing better to do than salivate over battle tactics or argue about the routes taken by the rooftop Titans or the subterranean Horde. Idiots debating every detail of worlds they could never know. There were Facebook fan sites too: Star of Macedon. Valhalla Hordettes. And interminable YouTube footage. But all of it was just crap. Sensationalised nonsense. No one caught anything of substance on camera. People claiming to be 'ex-Titans' or 'ex-Vikings' sometimes gave interviews about life in the Palatinates, but they were invariably exposed as frauds or simply disappeared.

Tyler found plenty of naysayers too. *The Pantheon is legitimised violence – The tribal aggression of football fans taken to a different extreme – This is evidence that beneath the fabric of our twenty-first-century social order lies a primordial heart where blood for money is the only mantra – How do we protect our children from this brutality? – Where are the forces of law and order? – Where is the democratic government of this country?*

Questions indeed, Tyler thought. Where *were* the government and the police? No one disputed that the warriors existed in the cities, nor that at certain defined points in the year they fought each other. So, in a world of constant surveillance, why had no unequivocal footage been captured? Why no multiple arrests? Why no Palatinate strongholds raided by Special Forces?

The answer according to the online forums – and corroborated by Radspakr when he had first gathered the year's new intake – was money. Real money. Riches of a magnitude beyond anyone's dreams. The kind of wealth that bought governments, smothered security forces and made the courts impotent. Of course, Holyrood and Westminster talked the talk whenever necessary. There were discussions at First Minister's Question Time. Senior ministers and police commissioners ensured they chose the right career-enhancing moments to describe how much they were doing to crush the Palatinates. There were occasional much-hyped raids that showed everyone busy achieving nothing. Even the odd arrest with some poor individual paraded before the cameras. But the conspiracy theorists were adamant such actions were pre-agreed with the Pantheon.

He pushed the laptop aside and let his gaze drift across the room to his framed photographs on the sideboard. The central one was his dearest possession and around it he had hung his special ivory Odin amulet. The picture showed him in close-up, a shockingly clear-skinned fifteen-year-old wearing his school tie, and on either side of him were his mother and sister, both as beautiful as he had ever seen them. It was his sister's graduation from Leith College of Art and they stood on the lawns with a crowd of families. He knew he romanticised the image. In reality, the tension between his mother and sister by that point was almost unbearable and the shouting was only made worse by the endless silences. That was why he clung to the photo. It represented a shining moment, a smiling happy family.

When Tyler and his sister were younger, they used to gossip together about the Pantheon. They would return from school armed with the latest rumours and would gawp at snippets of videos online. He remembered one infamous piece of footage that caused a sensation. *Angels of Mercy?* the papers had asked in the subsequent furore. The video had shown a group of posturing short-sleeved youths on the southern end of North Bridge. It was late, after closing time, and they were obviously inebriated. A fight broke out. One man was punched to the ground by the others, then repeatedly kicked. He was dragged semi-conscious to the side of the bridge and hauled onto the parapet high above Waverley station. In moments, he would have been pushed into oblivion, but in those same moments cloaked figures swung into the video. They came from above and at such graceful speed it was almost impossible to capture the detail in the footage. Three took the attackers and sent them sprawling backwards. Another disappeared over the edge of the parapet and then returned to the pavement with the victim in his arms. The drunken aggressors ran for their lives and the cloaked figures trotted into the street, forced a car to stop and placed the victim onto the backseat. With that, they were gone.

'Titans. That is *so* cool,' said Tyler's sister in a husky voice as she watched.

And she wasn't alone in that sentiment. In houses across the land other children gossiped about their favourite characters, while their parents hosted Palatinate dressing-up parties or wine and warrior appreciation evenings. So politicians had to tread a thin line. Make the people think their leaders were in charge. Make them feel safe in their beds, secure in the knowledge that their leaders could maintain all appropriate levels of law and order. But never destroy the people's fantasies, their belief in something amazing beyond the norms of society.

And now – if Radspakr was to be believed – the Pantheon wanted him: Tyler Maitland. He twisted the top back onto the whisky bottle and stretched his leg. This was an opportunity he wasn't about to let slip. The next morning, dressed in his new kit, with his day clothes stowed in a rucksack on his back, he forced himself to jog all the way to the university, even accelerating on the ups.

VI

Over the coming weeks, the twelve initiates found their training alternating between stamina and strength. The vaults were set up with a variety of equipment – some hi-spec, some primitive – and they came to recognise the apparatus and to anticipate the exercises. When their blindfolds were removed, Freyja and Halvar were always solemnly waiting for them in the central vault and Tyler wondered if the two of them prepared everything beforehand, although he could not imagine these two stern Housecarls lighting candles and hoisting hanging sandbags. Perhaps night elves scurried up from hidden depths and set everything to rights before each session.

In the second week *Thralls IV* and *IX* left the process. Freyja pronounced their departure in matter-of-fact tones at the start of one session, saying that their amulets had been found beneath the yew tree. In week four, she stated, '*Thrall III* will no longer be with us. She was foolish enough to email her parents about her experiences and the Vigiles were not amused.' Everyone glanced at one another, wondering what the Vigiles did when they were not amused.

So there were nine of them. They always began with running and stretching exercises and Tyler's leg burned.

Then on those nights when the focus turned to strength, it was his crooked arm that bore the brunt. They used stone dumbbells of varying weights for biceps curls. They carried even heavier pairs on slow walks across the vaults or clasped them as they stepped forward in alternating lunges. They balanced sandbags on their shoulders and bent their knees into gradual squats until their thighs screamed. They used parallel bars to practise lateral raises, sometimes forcing the upward motion to be excruciatingly slow and sometimes the downward. They dropped into push-ups and crunches and the cold flagstones were a relief in the sweat-soaked fug.

Their torturers-in-chief retained a parade ground mix of iron discipline and oath-ridden exhortations at the hopelessness of their charges. Yet Tyler also noted quieter touches in the detail of their approach – encouragement and even tenderness. When the ponytailed girl, *Thrall VIII*, struggled with the push-ups, Halvar patted her shoulder and explained gently that doing them from a kneeling position was much easier. When bald *Thrall II* continued to complete the challenges with ease, Tyler saw the admiring nods between the instructors. He realised that while they might shout and curse and prod and kick, these Housecarls were on their side. They wanted them to succeed. And the knowledge helped sustain him through the dark waves of pain.

But he also recognised that if there was one of their number who was consistently falling short, it was him.

What do I have to offer? he asked himself repeatedly. *The others are all so naturally good at this. Some strong, some fast, some agile. Why am I here?*

Four months before, on a rain-swept concrete stairway

deep in the Craigmillar estate, he had been kicked unconscious by three youths in his first and final warning that it was one thing to eviscerate his meaningless life snorting coke, but it was quite another to attempt his own pathetic dealing of the little packages without proper permission. With a newly contrite fear, he had taken stock, sworn to himself that he would never touch the shit again, and found a new flat in Comely Bank. It seemed a world away from the hand-by-mouth benefits existence on the estates, but he still looked over his shoulder and stole out to sleep fitfully in his van where he felt more secure.

He thought his limbs would never recover from the attack, but he had purchased a punch bag and evening after evening he'd worked at it – whack, whack, whack – praying for improvement. Now, in the Valhalla training vaults, his face was a grimaced scream of pain as he bobbed awkwardly on the lateral bars and attempted to haul himself up ropes hung from old iron hooks.

One night Halvar knelt beside him as he struggled with press-ups. 'In a Valhalla shieldwall your left arm will be strapped into your shield, and when the Titan Hoplites come at you it'll be your primary means of defence against their shortswords. And when their Phalanx advances onto you with their eighteen-foot sarissas, well then, it will be the *only* thing that saves your life.'

After he fell exhausted from the lateral bars on one occasion, bald, smiling *Thrall II*, who eased through everything that was thrown at him, slapped Tyler on the back and gave him a quiet nod of encouragement. When he dropped the stone dumbbells, Halvar and Freyja glanced grimly at each other, and when he descended a barely climbed rope, he caught ponytailed *Thrall VIII* watching him with her wide unfathomable eyes.

Despite her slight frame, she performed better at the tasks than most expected. Her aerobic fitness soared and she bobbed on the bars and shinned up the ropes with balletic grace. On one night they were introduced to heavy corn sacks suspended from ropes and told to help each other bind their hands with strips of cloth. They took it in turns to punch the bags. Little *Thrall VIII* barely moved the sack and she reddened with frustration. Staccato seabird cries burst from her as she slapped and hit to no effect. She turned away with a look of embarrassed outrage. Then, in a blur of movement, she launched herself into the air, spun through 180 degrees, brought her right leg out so that it was level with her shoulder and hit the bag side-on with her heel. She completed her turn full-circle as the bag swung backwards, landing with perfect poise with her back once more to the apparatus. There was stunned silence as she walked away and then Halvar began a slow clap and, before they knew it, they were all clapping and laughing, and she was looking around torn between anger and bewilderment.

'Not what we asked for,' Halvar called above the noise. 'But thank you for the demonstration, miss.'

When it was *Thrall II*'s turn, he shoulder-barged into the bag, almost tearing it from the rope. An impressed Halvar returned his grin. 'Army rugby,' *Thrall II* said.

Freyja stepped towards him with a raised hand. 'Have a care. You may offer up stories and thoughts that can help us develop as a group, but not details that could reveal your identities. No one shares their true selves in the Pantheon. Choose your words wisely.'

Thrall II nodded and it was the first time Tyler had seen him with shoulders sunk and hurt in his eyes. Usually he strutted about with such supremacy. No, that was an unfair description. He didn't strut, for that suggested arrogance and *Thrall II* was anything but arrogant. Self-assured, that was it. The self-assurance and competitive streak of an athlete. But also, Tyler now noted as he watched the shiny bowed head of the tall man, beneath the confidence was an altogether more delicate character.

Tyler Maitland was four and his sister, Morgan, seven, when their mother led their escape from London. Tyler had sensed the tension the day before, but he was dazed when she shook him awake and struggled to dress him in the middle of the night. He didn't know why she needed him out of his pyjamas so rapidly in the cold February dark with the rain on the windows, but he knew she was frightened and he must be good and get into his trousers and try not to shiver too much or cry. Then his mother marched them down the stairs from their spacious apartment in Kensington. Morgan had her own small bag and clung bravely to her favourite teddy as they climbed into the waiting taxi.

It was an endless journey. The lights of London sank behind and the rain clawed at the windows. The fan pumped heated stale air under their feet and dried their throats. The windscreen wipers seesawed back and forth and the radio played tinny songs interrupted by static. The driver smelt of aftershave and whenever they stopped at wet, fluorescent service stations, he sucked on two or three roll-ups, ignoring the signs when filling up with petrol.

Morgan slept on one side of Tyler with her head against the door, and his mother's own head nodded on the other side of him as she held his hand, but she kept forcing herself awake as though not trusting that it was safe to slip into unconsciousness. Tyler couldn't sleep, even though the hum of the engine never let up and the miles kept passing unseen. He understood that what they did that night was of utmost importance and he stared wide-eyed at the motorway lights.

Perhaps he did sleep eventually, for suddenly they were driving over gravel and pulling up beside a rural semi that belonged to his mother's sister. He was struck by the silence as he was helped from the car. The rain had stopped, but everywhere dripped like a million clocks and the air had been washed clean and smelt of such fresh newness after the stuffiness of the taxi. His mother handed over great wads of notes to the driver and he backed out of the drive with just a shrugged farewell. It was still dark. They had hot chocolate and biscuits at his auntie's kitchen table and then he and Morgan were escorted to a cold little bedroom with bunk beds and heavy blankets. As they were left to sleep, she informed him solemnly from the top bunk that they were in Scotland now and would never *ever* go back to London.

They must have spent a few weeks with his aunt, although he could recall little of them except her home-baked teabread, his uncle's pipe smoke and the cat that stole onto his bunk and left a warm, hair-strewn indentation on his pillow. His mother disappeared for long spells and she would exchange significant looks with his aunt whenever her mobile phone rang and she left it unanswered. At night he heard them talking from the kitchen and he knew it was about his father.

His father. In all honesty, Tyler could barely picture him. He hovered at the corner of his mind. He used to appear at their London apartment and very rarely stay the night, although in Tyler's earliest memories his mother seemed pleased to see the man and would embrace him earnestly. He smelt strange. Heavy-scented, musky. Not unpleasant. He had long smooth hands and pretty cufflinks. He would sit Tyler on his knee and study him and search his face for something, but he didn't play with him or seem to offer the love that his mother provided.

There were nights when he raised his voice at her and the children lay rigid in their beds. Morgan would say that he had been drinking, although Tyler didn't really understand. His mother too seemed to drink increasingly – a tiny amber liquid during the day and tall glasses of clear liquid at night with lemon and ice fighting for space. She would make long, rambling emotional phone calls and they knew she was speaking to their father during his long absences. Sometimes she would call him horrible names and then sweep them up in her arms and cry and say she was sorry, and they would cry too.

One evening not long before their hurried departure, she drank heavily and came out of her bedroom in a sleek black dress. Her hair was brushed loose down her back, her heels clicked on the floor and her lips were painted scarlet and fixed in a tight pinched line. She gave them sandwiches and said she would be back in two hours, then strode out the large flat with silent purpose and even Tyler knew she possessed a terrible beauty that night.

When she returned, her make-up was smeared and she had been crying. She hugged them and got them bathed and into bed, kissing them with a breath of liquor fumes. Then they were woken by the voice of their father. He was shouting and their mother shouted even louder in return. There was heavy movement. The kitchen table screeched on the floor. One of them backed into their bedroom wall. A glass broke. Morgan climbed out of her bed and padded across the carpet to get in with Tyler and hold him. The yelling climaxed and they heard the front door slam. There was a long silence, although they thought they heard a muffled, keening sob. Then their mother came and looked at them from the bedroom door, but she said nothing and simply closed it again and her heels echoed away along the oak-floored landing.

Five days later, they made the journey to Scotland and several weeks after that they left their aunt's house in the country and took a taxi into a city of spires and colonnades and battlements and hills. They arrived at a small ground-floor flat just a few minutes' walk from the sea. The air had a salty, fishy tang and they shared hot-dogs by the sand, but the flat itself was cramped, cold and spartan. Without realising it, time drifted and it became their home for over a year. Official-looking strangers visited and quizzed their mother and filled out forms and asked the children if they were happy. Morgan went to school and had a different uniform from the one she had worn in London. Tyler found himself in playgroups for most of the weekdays in a hall that smelt of bleach and toast. Morgan told him that his mother now went to work, which was something she had never done in London. She picked him up each afternoon in a green uniform with a supermarket logo.

At weekends they played on the beach and watched the

great ships ease past. After a few months, their mother bought a little second-hand Peugeot and they drove north to see hills with snow and vast wild tracts of land. And perhaps they were happy. Certainly Tyler didn't think about London, nor remember his father.

VII

'Violence,' said Freyja, 'is the art of knowing when to add speed to strength.'

It was late October. Winter's bite was just around the corner and the evenings were once more darkening early. Seven weeks had passed since they had first stood before Radspakr, and they had shared much and grown as attached as a group can when they know each other only as numerals. They had dwindled to six as some of their number had been overcome by the expectations and given up their amulets under the yew.

Thrall X, the chunky woman whom Tyler imagined a yachter, had proved herself a fine all-rounder. She was faster and more agile than her physique suggested, and powerful on the strength tasks. She had short, unprepossessing, red hair and a small gold stud in her nose. She rarely spoke and seemed more comfortable with actions than words, and Tyler liked her.

Thrall XII, the broad man with the thick neck, remained one of the group, much to Tyler's surprise. His fitness was an issue and he still sounded like a steam locomotive when asked to run, but he was built to use his arms and he could heave and pull and lift almost anything. Give him something to charge into and he was unstoppable.

They were joined by the single remaining odd numbered initiate, *Thrall VII*, a mousey-haired lad of only seventeen with a long horse face that seemed too large for his neck and a sullen, insolent demeanour. His physique was lean, hard and knotted, diligently honed, and he knew it. He strutted cockily and cursed when his performance placed below top spot. He liked to leer at ponytailed number *VIII* and even dared to give Freyja lascivious looks, which she ignored with glorious contempt.

Tyler felt a kinship with *Thrall II*. The tall man outperformed everyone, but he did it with gracious humility and warm comradeship.

Thrall VIII was the one Tyler found most enigmatic. She rarely spoke or partook in the sense of growing bonds between the group. She related a little with *Thrall II*, blossoming imperceptibly under his gentlemanly demeanour, but she avoided communication with Tyler and imposed a particular distance on him. She took care to miss his glance, but just occasionally he caught her big eyes on him and felt vulnerable under her scrutiny.

Without question they had all hardened after almost two months of arduous training. They were muscular, trim and fast. Only Tyler still felt like an interloper. Everyone could see that he was the one among them who wasn't a natural athlete. His arm was improving, but it still throbbed with the demands placed on it, and his leg hampered him. He was slow on the ropes and dropped out of the press-up challenges. He imagined he could see surprise in the eyes of

Freyja and Halvar when he returned for each session and he feared daily that he would be evicted from the process.

This evening the central vault was laid out differently. There was no apparatus. No stones placed at the edge of the room, no sandbags strung from ropes. Instead there was a giant hexagon chalked across the floor, with little bowls containing flaming oil at each of the corners. It was perfectly symmetrical and Tyler wondered how it had been created. Halvar was seated on a bench against one wall and Freyja was standing in the centre of the hexagon, facing them as they waited in a single line.

'Without strength, you are but a leaf tossed on the storm. Without speed, you are but a rock whose foe will wash around you. If, however, you can hone your mind and body until you know precisely when to contain and when to release these two qualities, then you can let the violence within you burst over your foe.' She walked in a slow circle around the inside of the hexagon, her boots tapping on the stone. The candles at the end of the room silhouetted her body. She was a tigress. 'In pairs,' she continued. 'One on one. The first one to leave the hexagon loses. *II* and *XII* first. Then *VIII* and *X*. Then *VII* and *VI*.' She paused and looked at them. 'No rules.'

They were split into their pairs and required to remove their boots and bind each other's hands with several wrappings of cloth until their knuckles were padded and blunted. Then Freyja directed *II* and *XII* into the hexagon. They stood opposite one another at the chalked edges, leaving about twenty feet between them. Halvar stepped between them holding a five-foot length of rope and beckoned them closer. He took their left arms and bound one end of the rope to each of their wrists, so that it hung between them.

They were powerful men and the other initiates watched mesmerised. Freyja had placed herself beyond the hexagon, hands on hips. Halvar stood between the opponents. 'It ends when one of you is no longer within the hexagon,' he said simply. 'Begin.'

The word had barely passed Halvar's lips before *Thrall XII* exploded towards his opponent. He held his broad neck low with his arms wide and bent like horns. He hit number *II* full in the chest with his head, and his hands grabbed at the other man's shoulders. His tall opponent was taken three steps back by the impact and was only just able to arrest his momentum before he would have been driven from the hexagon. They swung precariously by the edge and became locked in a grunting, gasping embrace.

With an almighty shove *Thrall II* managed to push his opponent away and escape his grip. Then they began to circle each other, hands raised in classic fist-fighting pose with the stronger arm in front of the face and the other hovering just below the chin. They seemed to have forgotten the rope, which hung uselessly between them. Number *XII* shifted his weight onto his leading leg and launched a punch to the face. His opponent parried it with his forearm, knocking it away and striking forward himself.

These were practised moves, flowing and natural, and Tyler realised with shock that these men hadn't been selected by the Valhalla Venarii party because they could do press-ups or lateral raises or bicep curls. These men were in this vault because they knew how to fight.

XII came again. A left punch which made contact with the other man's ribs and then an immediate strike with the right aimed at his opponent's nose. At the last moment, number *II* swung his shoulders to the side and the blow passed harmlessly beyond his ear. It took his attacker forward and off-balance and in the same flowing movement, the taller man spun around him and lifted the rope so that it looped around his opponent's torso. As he dragged it tight, it clamped number *XII*'s left arm against him and dragged him even further off-balance. In the same instant, the taller man barged into him with the force of a bus and in four rapid steps his opponent was outside the hexagon.

The movement stopped. The room held its breath. For a split-second anger washed over the face of the defeated fighter and then it was gone and they embraced and Tyler saw Halvar nodding approvingly. The big man stepped over to them and began to untie the rope. 'A good start. You fight to win at all costs, but when it's over you respect your opponent.'

Freyja hadn't moved. 'Next pair.'

The girls stepped forward. The one with the nose stud and honest face, and the small one with her thoughtful eyes and golden hair. She pulled her ponytail tight and then stood in silence looking somewhere into the middle distance.

'Go girls, you can do it,' *Thrall II* reassured and took himself forward to the edge of the hexagon, clapping his hands a couple of times in encouragement. Number *XII* followed his lead and stepped up as well, muttering words of confidence.

'Begin.' The girls started to walk around each other. They had watched the earlier fight and they copied the men's

67

stance with their hands curled into loose fists and held up to protect their faces. The vault was silent except for the soft padding of their bare feet. Somewhere above there was a hum of traffic. The candles and bowls of flaming oil cast shadows across the walls.

In a sudden flurry, number *X* stepped forward and struck a blow. It had none of the power of the earlier duel, but it was direct enough and it broke straight through the other's defences and caught her hard on the shoulder. She let out a little cry and stumbled backwards. *Thrall X* came again, using the moment to her advantage. She pushed into her opponent and struck with both fists. Number *VIII* defended herself with open palms, soaking up the hits with her hands. She moved quicker than her watching audience had expected and none of the punches landed. She took a step back and then swung her right leg in a graceful wide arc that brought her tibia hard against her opponent's lateral thigh muscle. It was a powerful strike and number *X*'s face crunched with pain. Her leading leg collapsed under her and she went down on one knee.

Thrall VIII danced away, still holding her fists locked in front of her face and watching her downed opponent. Tyler noticed Halvar make an instinctive motion to urge the little blonde back on the attack while she had the advantage. Number *X* recovered and stood. Now *Thrall VIII* stepped in again and spun around in a rising circle with her leg extended. It would have been a huge blow, but she had forgotten about the rope which curled with her as she spun. It slowed her attack and with a grunt number *X* grasped the leg as it came towards her. In moments the advantage had changed. Now *Thrall VIII* was standing uselessly on one leg and her other foot was held by her opponent. With a single pull, she fell onto her rump and without further ado, number X dragged her out of the hexagon.

The fight was won. *Thrall X* stooped with her hands on her knees, catching her breath. Her opponent sat unceremoniously on the floor and stared at the stones above her. *Thrall II* stepped over and offered her his arm. She took it with a flicker of a smile and he raised her to her feet. Then the spell was broken and the two opponents hugged each other.

Halvar unbound their wrists. 'When you have the advantage, never give your foe the opportunity to recover,' he chided, but then added more softly, 'You'll learn.'

Freyja was still a motionless observer. '*VII* and *VI*. Take your positions.'

Tyler found himself following his neighbour into the centre of attention. He sensed Halvar in front of him, saying something and binding the rope around his wrist. There were words of encouragement from the periphery, but he could make out none of them. He could see the rope leading away to the vague figure of his opponent and he could recognise that the man was springing from side to side, pumping himself up. But it was all a blur. Blood was rushing through his ears. He should be moving, he thought, but his legs were locked in place under the spotlight.

Halvar must have said begin because the voices renewed in volume. Tyler compelled himself to shift to the right. Yet even as he did, the figure of his opponent flew towards him and suddenly *Thrall VII*'s long horsey face was right in front of him. Tyler felt a hand gripping his shoulder, but worse, there was another hand striking his groin. This was a streetfighter's move. Fast, hard and without mercy. The palm of *VII*'s hand struck his testicles and the cloth-bound fingers found purchase. A white light exploded in his groin and he shouted in pain.

It was a mockery of a fight. His hands were down and trying to tear at his opponent's grip and *Thrall VII* raised him onto his toes and dragged him by the balls out of the hexagon. It was over in moments and Tyler found himself on his knees, heaving into the stone floor as he cradled his groin.

With the pairings complete, Halvar spent the rest of the session showing them what they had done wrong, using Freyja to demonstrate the moves.

'Some golden rules,' he said, standing in the centre of the hexagon with the candlelight playing on his oak-tree arms. 'Get your stance right. Legs shoulder-width apart, with your strong foot in front. Bent at the knees. Never locked, but also not so bent that you feel the strain in your thighs.

'Keep your chin down, pushed into your neck. Don't give your attacker a chance to hit this area. A chin or neck punch will fell you.

'Keep moving. Not bloody dancing about like a monkey, but not a stationary target either. Little light steps, always in balance and not too high off the ground.

'Hooks, jabs and uppercuts – only use these if you're very confident they'll work. They can be slow or wild or risk counterattack. A straight-on direct punch is always the best option.

'Likewise, kicking.' He looked at *Thrall VIII*. 'Never kick higher than an opponent's thigh, unless you are very, very good. Any higher and you risk having your foot caught exactly as we saw. Believe me, in a full-out fight you really don't want to find yourself in that position.

'If you can't avoid a punch, step into it. This may seem counterintuitive, but the real power in a blow is when the elbow has extended. Step forward so that your attacker's strike hits you before the arm has fully extended and it'll soften the impact.

'Finally, attitude. Show confidence at *all* times. No matter the odds, bristle with confidence. Your opponent may be a gigantic piece of horseshit, but you need to worry him. Make the bastard wonder if you can win.'

The group were silent as he spoke. Stilled. Half-listening, but also lost in their own thoughts. Perhaps that was why Halvar made sure he filled the quiet with his voice. There had been violence here tonight and they had stepped across a boundary. It was one thing to lift and hit bags, but over the last hour they had gone at one another. They had punched and kicked and hurt. And they had done it unquestioningly because they had been commanded. Some had won. Some had lost. Some felt quietly exhilarated. Some chastened.

But the same question played in all their minds: *What have I just done?*

They departed blindfolded and wordless, and the cars drove them to the Royal Mile. Behind them, Freyja approached Halvar as he extinguished the candles with his fingers.

'I'm worried about number *VI*.'

'I know, but he keeps coming back for more. That's a lad with some serious demons to banish.'

'If he doesn't improve fast, I'll be recommending his expulsion to Radspakr.'

Halvar sighed. 'Aye, but not yet. Give him a chance, Freyja. See what he's got. I think it's important.'

VIII

Lana walked up the Mile after the cars had dropped them off, steering wide of people still out enjoying the night. She made her way to the junction beyond St Giles' and stood on the corner. In her pocket she gripped her amulet, which she turned over and over as she peered down St Georges. A sickness rolled through her stomach.

Ten minutes down there to Greyfriars. That's all. Ten minutes to the graveyard. People drifted passed her. There was a spot of rain in the air. *Come on, girl. Go to the tree. Leave them the bloody amulet. It's time to get out.*

She churned through the events of the evening, replaying the movements of their bodies as they had fought. Then – unbidden – her mind began to stretch further back, reaching for memories, trying to plot once more her journey to that vault.

For the first few weeks after it happened, Lana had told no one about the attack at the party. She took herself back to her university room and showered, letting the water cascade over her for an age and shaking uncontrollably. She continued going to lectures and revising for her exams, but a silence descended upon her. She stopped running, gave up studying in the department library and instead sat in her room, staring at her papers. She could read the information dozens of times, but none of it went in. The more she screwed up her face and burned a sentence onto her cornea, the more the words escaped and floated away, uncatchable, like dust.

As the dates of her Finals reared closer, she went to see her tutor and told him in bare, matter-of-fact terms about the attack. He passed her to the College Dean and she passed her to Student Welfare and they strongly advised that she contact the police, and by that point she was sick of the lot of them. She took the one option left to her and escaped home to Dumfries. Her mother tried to understand, but Lana would overhear her on the phone to her aunt railing at the injustice and dismayed about what her daughter would do with her life now. After the exams, various letters arrived from the university and she found herself classed as DNC – Did Not Complete. There was an option to take her final year again, but the idea physically sickened her, made worse because her mother clung to this possibility like a floating spar after a shipwreck.

For six weeks Lana festered in Kirkcudbright, rotting in the summer heat. The numbness within her, she realised, was loss of faith. Not with her attacker. Not even with the university. Rather, with herself. For a few minutes in that bedroom in Newington, she had been forced to become a victim. Someone else had held control over her body. And she hated herself for it. She would look at her image in the mirror and see something which was pathetic, and she swore that no one would ever control her again. So she began to research martial arts and was drawn to the Eastern traditions, especially the grace of kickboxing. She toyed with this, practised a few movements in her bedroom and looked into the details of joining clubs. Of course, there were few in rural Dumfries. But there were more than enough to choose from back in Edinburgh and she started to wonder whether the city still offered a form of escape.

Then one muggy day in August, tacitly accompanying her mother to a farmers' market in Castle Douglas, she felt uncomfortable and queasy. It got worse the following day and she was barely able to leave the bathroom. Examining herself naked in the mirror above the washbasin, she found a new realisation dawning on her like the coming of a slow winter's morning across a black sea, that the true legacy of her ordeal might just be beginning.

As Lana stood on her street corner, Tyler walked down the long stairway of Warriston's Close, drawing shakily on a cigarette. He was still simmering and trying to fight off the urge to tell the whole damn Pantheon to go fuck itself. His groin hurt and his arm protested, but it was his sense of purpose which was truly undermined. As he emerged near the junction with Market Street, another set of footsteps fell in beside him. 'How're you doing?'

It was *Thrall II*. He had his hands thrust into the pockets of his coat and had pulled on a beanie to protect his bald head from the night temperature. Tyler looked over both shoulders. 'We shouldn't be speaking.'

'I've already checked and we're not being followed. You looked pretty broken tonight. The little bastard fought dirty with you.'

'The little bastard beat me fair and square. He knew how to win.'

'So you'll learn and you won't let anyone do it next time.'

'Maybe.' Tyler walked on. A hen-party careered towards them with balloons, tartan caps and short skirts. They whooped around them and the two men had to shoulder their way through. 'The problem is, I don't think there's going to be a next time. My leg kills me. I can't keep up with the strength exercises. I can't climb the ropes. If I get beyond fifteen press-ups it's a major victory. And tonight… watching you all fight… watching *you*. Your skill. I can't do that. I'm no fighter.'

They walked in silence for a few paces, then the taller man spoke again. 'I don't think they've picked us as their Electi because we can fight. If they had, if it were just physical prowess, then there are always other lads who are stronger and harder than any of us. So they'd be first on the list.'

'Then why us?'

'I keep asking myself that. Perhaps because they need people who are going to flourish in their ranks. People who can take orders, who can work as a team, who can be trusted. Perhaps you're blessed with those attributes and you're unaware…?' He trailed off, head bowed as he thought. 'I'll tell you this – I, for one, *trust* in their choices. I think they've strong reasons for selecting us. Although Christ knows why… because I'm a washed-up reject and there's no reason on god's earth to select me for this opportunity.'

Tyler halted and stared at *Thrall II*. 'You're a reject?'

'In the eyes of my family.' He was well-spoken. An upper-class Edinburgh accent, with a hint of east coast Highland.

They hovered beneath the Scott Memorial. It seemed wrong to go any further together. Better not to know more about where the other lived. Tyler framed his next question. 'So why are you doing this?'

Thrall II smiled thinly. 'The million-dollar question. Why am I doing this? Why are any of us doing it? Do you want the short or medium or long answer?'

Tyler peered up and down the street, wondering what eyes were on them. 'Better make it the short.'

'Okay. I'm unemployed, directionless, without motivation. The Pantheon comes along and says, *Do you want to be a part of this?* And I think, *Why not?* It's an opportunity. Rumour has it there's good money to be made. So I think of these weeks as an extended and very selective interview process. Got to be worth a try.'

Tyler puffed out his cheeks. 'Right, we both know that's bollocks.'

'For some people that might be enough. A chance to break the cycle and make some money. Lead a more exciting life. I suspect even one or two of our fellow Electi think that's enough. Look at *Thrall VII* tonight. He can fight, and he put you down hard. But he's a street punk and he knows he won't get far in normal life if that's all he can offer.'

'Want to give me your medium reason?'

Thrall II looked at him for a few seconds, then nodded, checked along the pavement and ushered the other man through a nearby gate into Princes Street Gardens. They wandered over to a large tree and stood close under it where they were shielded from the streetlights.

'My family's always been a military one. From when I was a nipper, my father drilled into me a respect for the

– quote – *unity of the regiment, the unbreakable bonds between men who stand shoulder-to-shoulder against a common enemy* –unquote.' He tapped his foot against the tree trunk. 'When I was eight, like all the boys in my family before me, I was sent to boarding school. Believe me when I tell you, there is no place more capable of destroying unity than a boarding school. It's every sod for himself. Even the gangs have no bonds, they just exist because it's the survival of the many against the one.

'I think that place damn near did for me. I couldn't speak to my parents about it because it was the same venerable institution my father had attended before me, and his father before him, and the natural stepping stone into the regiment. So instead I just brought down the shutters. I might have spent my nights in crowded dormitories and my days in busy classes, but you'd be amazed how alone you can become inside.

'One February weekend, I came into the centre of Edinburgh. I was supposed to be shopping for a gift for my mum's birthday, but I ended up walking the streets. God knows what I was thinking, I just remember letting my legs take me anywhere. It got late. I was hungry, but I kept going – great arcs out of the centre and back again. I think I was waiting to see if anyone would miss me. Pupils were required to be back in the school grounds by six on weekend nights, but I was still walking at eleven. I probably wondered if the alarm had been raised in my dormitory, whether my parents had been called and were even then fretting and wringing their hands and jumping in the bloody car to come find me. And that's when I saw him on the roofs above Cockburn Street, a little after midnight...

a Titan. I was the only person on the street at the time and he looked back at me. Probably wondering about this kid out on his own. He was... *magnificent*. The armour, the cloak, the helmet, the shield, the spear. I remember him so clearly. He was like a god looking down on my stupid life.'

'What did you do?'

'Nothing. Eventually he moved. One moment he was there and the next he was gone. But that was a turning point for me. I went back to that damn school and I devoted what private time I had to finding out more about the Pantheon. The internet was more limited back then, but it was enough to have me hooked. I borrowed books from the school library about history's ancient warrior societies. The three hundred Spartans at Thermopylae; that was the ultimate classic. Three hundred, shoulder-to-shoulder against the hordes of Persia. It reignited something in me, some of the early teachings of my father about the unity of military comradeship. I loved the underdogs the most. Always the great warrior units that defeated the odds. Because that was me in that bloody school. The underdog.'

He stopped, chewing his lip. 'So now this opportunity has come along and I guess I'm running with it even if I don't know where it's leading.' He looked at Tyler. 'And I like what I see of our group. There's unity there too. Common purpose.'

He trailed off into silence. For a long moment Tyler could find no words and then he ventured, flippantly, 'If that's your medium reason, I sure don't need the long one tonight.'

'No, you don't.'

'Aren't you going to ask me why I'm doing this?'

Thrall II shook his head. 'No.'

'Why not?'

'Because your reasons are strong enough without needing explanation.'

'What's that supposed to mean?'

'You might think you're failing, but that's not the way the rest of us see it. We see a man pushing himself through the pain barrier every session. A man fighting each screaming muscle to make that one final pull-up. A man who won't stop until he literally drops the weights. A man who – perhaps – wants this more than all the rest of us.'

Tyler stared at his companion, but before he could find a response *Thrall II* moved and spoke again.

'I think we've said enough.' He began to walk back to the gate, but then stopped and spoke over his shoulder. 'Don't give up now. Let it play out a little more. And stop beating yourself up about being good enough. Instead, ask yourself this – if I'm such a bad selection, such a weak recruit – what can have happened in my life, what have I got, who *am* I – that made the Pantheon select me? Think about it, *Thrall VI*. Goodnight.'

Tyler left his flat in the near silence of a Sunday morning twilight and jogged gingerly through the cobbled streets of New Town, feeling his weaker leg respond. His objective was the summit of Arthur's Seat. A few early morning starters poked around on Princes Street, while the rough sleepers still lay wrapped in shop doorways. The great buildings of Old Town presented a solid wall along the spine of the hill with no discernible routes through and the castle squatted on its rock outcrop, rinsed of colour in the morning light. He thought, why shouldn't there be men of sword and shield in this place?

It was cold and he was wearing gloves despite the exertion. When the November sun finally broke over Whinny Hill and lit his face, he was already well above St Margaret's Loch and the ruins of St Anthony's Chapel. He crested a rise and could at last see his goal of the summit. At any other time there would be a smattering of figures on it, busy taking selfies, but now it was deserted. It could have been a forgotten eagle's eyrie above an empty glen, but instead the vagaries of history had determined it should become surrounded by a capital city of over half a million sleeping souls. Adrenaline drove him up the final few steps and he hauled himself to the white summit cairn, where he stood heaving in the cold air and spitting. What a view. The sea hung to his right, lit by the rising sun. The Forth estuary ran lazily across the northern horizon, with the Fife coastline and Ochil Hills beyond. Spots of snow lay across the far peaks, as though god had been carelessly white-washing the ceiling. Below him the city was just waking, propping up its pillows, having a first sip of tea and thinking about the day ahead. The Palace, the castle, Morningside to his left, it all lay there before him.

There was a cold breeze that sought out the sweat on the back of his neck, but he barely noticed. He was thinking about the past few weeks and what *Thrall II* had said. He had needed those words. Someone assuring him he wasn't failing; that they could see the pain he was forcing himself through and his will to succeed.

Because he really *did* want to succeed. Underneath

the aloofness, the injuries, the nicotine and the liquor, he remembered all those times he and his sister had chattered about the Pantheon. They had loved the idea that the Palatinates existed somewhere beyond the law, exotic and god-like. The Pantheon was something to dream about on the housing estate, something to follow. Together they had bonded over it.

IX

The punch stunned him. It came from nowhere, hammer blowing into the side of his head. If the knuckles hadn't been so heavily bound, they would surely have cracked through his skull and pulped the soft tissue of his brain. He was as defenceless as a toddler when the next strike caught him in the midriff and doubled him over. If cocky young *Thrall VII* had chosen to follow up the attack with a knee to his lowered face, it would have felled Tyler and he would not have been getting up again. Instead, *Thrall VII* stepped in beside him, threw an arm about his neck and clamped him in a headlock. But then he seemed uncertain of his next move and the two of them stood clasped together for a few seconds, panting and sweating. The pause gave Tyler a chance to take a few lungfuls of air and consider his options.

The other initiates were spread around the perimeter of the hexagon. Freyja was stationed as ever at the head of the room, while Halvar prowled within touching distance, studying their every move as though he were a referee made redundant by a fight with no rules. It was mid-November, three weeks since their first attempts at the hexagon challenge, and Edinburgh had succumbed to the dark of winter. The far corners of the vault seemed colder and damper than before, so that while the antagonists sweated, the onlookers froze.

During the three weeks, they had learned the dark arts of hand-to-hand combat. Halvar and Freyja had demonstrated complex new techniques, then got the group to practise in slow motion or against the hanging corn sacks. They had mastered the straight punch, the side swipe, the upper cut. They had worked at hip throws, leg takedowns, shin kicks, knee hits and elbow strikes. They had spent hours struggling on the stone floor in grapples and they had been taught the techniques that would bring opponents to their knees – straight-fingered throat strikes and eye gouging. At the end of each week, they took the hexagon challenge and Tyler had become acclimatised to the sudden serious violence with which each of them approached this test.

Thrall II demonstrated a particular skill for boxing and shared his techniques and tips with the group. Bulky *Thrall XII* became expert in holds and lifts and showed a special fondness for smashing his opponent down onto the floor. Little *Thrall VIII* was encouraged to use more of her Muay Thai kickboxing moves and they clumsily copied her. The two Housecarls cast satisfied looks between each other as they saw an *esprit de corps* maturing. Tyler too had improved and grown stronger. His arm hurt less and he no longer moved with such an awkward gait. Every muscle on him had hardened.

One night, he found himself paired with *Thrall VIII* for the first time and she seemed so delicate in his arms. There was nothing to her. A tiny waist and stick-thin arms. Up close, he could see the remnants of make-up around her eyes and he wondered what she did during the days, how she made her living, whom she spoke to, what she wore. As she turned in a hold, her ponytail brushed across his face and he inhaled rosemary and juniper, and as she tugged at his neck her bare arms smelt of coconut. It felt wrong to knock her down and he found himself gripping her in a strange irresolute manner. But when she kicked at his calves and threw him across her hip, there was power enough in her movements, and it took him four tumbles onto the cold floor before he realised he needed to fight back.

Now Tyler tried to clear his eyes, caught in *Thrall VII*'s headlock. He found himself being dragged by the neck towards the hexagon's perimeter and he knew he had to resist or he would be defeated yet again. They had already been trading punches for some minutes and both men were hurting and tiring. Tyler forced his thumped brain to think. What had Halvar said?

'When you find yourself caught in a headlock, you think your attacker has got you good and proper. Wrong. Listen to me when I say that *you* are actually in the position of dominance.'

Tyler grasped at the half-forgotten advice. The natural desire would be to pull away, but this would put his neck under unacceptable pressure. So instead he hunkered in close to the other man and burst into action. With his free right fist, he struck onto *Thrall VII*'s knee, pounding three times at it in quick succession. His left arm was already behind his opponent, and now he brought it up and over *Thrall VII*'s near shoulder, so that he could grab his face. The skinny youngster was responding by using his own free left arm to punch up into Tyler's abdomen, but Tyler was beyond feeling it. With a roar, he rammed his left leg against the back of his attacker's knees and simultaneously pushed the man's face rearwards with his left hand. The speed and power of both actions swept *Thrall VII*'s torso back and his legs up into the air. With a thump he hit the floor belly up and lost his grip on Tyler's head.

Tyler threw himself on the man. He grabbed both of the outstretched arms and brought his shin across his opponent's throat in an attempt to lock him down into a choke hold. But *Thrall VII* was fast. His legs came up in a graceful rolling motion and caught Tyler's head pincer-like between his calves. Tyler was forced back and had to break the hold. Both men escaped and struggled to their feet. They were breathing raggedly and bleeding. Tyler could feel a cut beneath his eye and *Thrall VII* had blood running from the corner of his mouth. They could hear the voices of the onlookers in the corner of their minds, but none of the words.

They went in again. Direct, tight punches. *Thrall VII* got him twice on the right side of his head and then Tyler landed a full hit on his opponent's cheek, sending him sprawling backwards a few steps. There were shouted words of encouragement. They circled each other, searching for openings. Tyler struck again, but this time *Thrall VII* dodged the blow and a two-step jig took him to Tyler's undefended shoulder. They closed into a grapple and Tyler fought to keep his footing, but the man's fingers were around his face and his body was inching behind Tyler's until he could wrap his arms around the other's torso in a bear hug. Tyler found his arms trapped in the embrace and he could feel himself being lifted onto his toes. He knew what was coming. His opponent would shove him forward and charge him over the hexagon perimeter. He had only moments. He worked at his arms, struggling to break them out of the grip.

Then, with cold clarity, he knew his next move. He could feel number *VII*'s ragged breath on the back of his neck and could hear him grunting as he began to drive them both forward. Tyler steadied himself and then threw his head back full into the other man's face. He felt the nose implode and heard a sharp crack as it broke. With a cry, *Thrall VII* released his hold and stumbled away gripping his face. There was blood pouring through his fingers and his stare was wild and amazed. Tyler didn't even pause to consider the injury, but grabbed the other man by the neck and threw him from the hexagon. He landed in a sobbing heap, still clinging to his nose, and *Thrall X* dropped to her knees beside him.

The only other movement was from Halvar who began a slow handclap. 'We have a victor.' He stepped over to *Thrall VII* to examine him. 'Hmm... your mother won't be pleased, laddie. We'll call it a night, everyone. Thor here and I have a date at A&E.'

Tyler realised the others were staring at him and there was a new look in their eyes. The bout had lasted ten exhausting minutes, during which time neither man had given an inch. Tyler's face was beaten, scratched and bloodied. His elbows were raw from hitting the floor and the sleeve of his T-shirt was torn. Nevertheless, he stood victorious at the centre of the hexagon and his glare dared anyone to set foot in it.

X

Within moments of climbing into the cars, they knew they were being taken somewhere new. It was Wednesday evening and the six Thralls had gathered as usual at Bull's Close on the lower end of the Mile. The cars had arrived just before ten. There were only two vehicles now, with space for three Thralls in each. The silent drivers no longer bothered with passwords, but the blindfolds were still a requirement before the cars moved off. By now each of the Thralls knew the route by feel alone. Up the Mile, left, then right, then straight on, then another left and another. So when they didn't turn right as expected, a new tension grew behind the cloth over each set of eyes.

The vehicles purred into higher gears. Tyler had a sense of longer roads and space, of moving away from the jumble of the Old Town. His face still felt raw from his combat bout. His lower lip was split in several places. He had a swollen right eye and a cut under the other one which he had bathed and plastered. His supervisor at the library had looked at him aghast and summoned him into his office. Although Tyler had concocted a story about an attempted mugging and found himself wading deeper and deeper into the fiction, the man could see his bruised knuckles and offered little sympathy.

Eventually Tyler had been excused with a veiled warning about taking more care. He slunk back to the information desk and attempted to ghost through his shift. At the best of times he had no inkling that he was quite a celebrity among the regular students. The girls loved his flickering blue eyes and the sadness that hung around his shoulders. A man who had experienced tragedy, they whispered to each other. But over those next few nights, his beaten and broken face sent them into fascinated palpitations and he was inundated with enquiries to look up obscure reference numbers on the database so that they could peer at him more closely.

It was twenty minutes before the cars pulled up and they were ordered out but told to maintain their blindfolds. A wind whipped at them as they were herded over tarmac and then onto rougher ground with stones and gravel underfoot. They must have passed through an entrance because the wind died and the fresh air gave way to something colder and staler. They were on concrete now, but there was still loose gravel and the crunch of glass fragments under their boots. They were positioned together and left motionless for a few moments.

'Welcome, Thralls. You may remove your bindings.'

It was Radspakr. They found themselves standing in a large derelict warehouse. It would have been an impressive building in its heyday. The walls were split on all sides by great arched windows on the lower level, then rows of round windows above like portholes. Columns ran down the length of the building, holding up a roof of metal and glass. Moonlight was pouring through, bringing a lunar glow to the interior. Graffiti was plastered on every available surface and the windows along the sides were broken. The floor was strewn with wooden spars, stones, grass and wild plants. Outside, Tyler could just make out other buildings, but they were distant.

Radspakr was standing on a raised platform at one end of the building, in front of a door leaning off its hinges. There were candles around him once again, but they did little more than cast a light on his legs. Without the moon they would have been in pitch dark. He wore a long, well-cut coat with the collar up to guard against the cold and his hands shoved deep into the pockets. Halvar and Freyja were beside him.

'My apologies for the choice of venue. It's hardly luxurious, but it serves our purposes from time to time.' He stepped off the platform and walked over to them and they could see his eyes above his coat collar, luminous in the twilight like those of a cat. 'From the eighteen who were called, six remain. You are the last ones standing and you should congratulate yourselves. This Armatura is nigh complete. We are but weeks from the commencement of the Nineteenth Raiding Season and the cycle of the Pantheon begins again. Succeed at the final challenges and you shall be deemed Weapons Worthy and welcomed into the Horde of Valhalla as Thegns.'

Radspakr paused. It was ten weeks since he had last spoken with them and he could see they had changed. They exuded strength, even confidence. No longer did they fidget with unease and stare at the walls. Now they returned his look openly and waited for their next orders. He liked what he saw.

'The Housecarls tell me you show promise. You have each passed the tests for Speed, Strength and Violence. You have each overcome obstacles both physical and emotional. You have absented yourselves from none of the instruction sessions. I have been informed of no transgression of the rules. You have spoken to no one of your experiences and you have not attempted to interact beyond the confines of the group sessions.' He nodded approvingly. 'You please me, Thralls.'

He signalled to Freyja and she strode across to him, her braided hair resplendent in the moonlight. She handed him a small leather-bound notebook and he fidgeted in his inner pocket for a pair of reading spectacles. As he attempted to angle the notebook to catch the moon's rays, with the glasses perched on the end of his nose, he resembled more a tutor in mathematics than Lord Adjutant to Sveinn the Red. He tutted and muttered something to Freyja, who scuttled back to the platform and retrieved one of the candles to help him read. It was a tiny, endearing glitch in the otherwise carefully scripted theatre.

'It is time for you to receive your first Palatinate identities. Step forward, *Thrall II*.'

Tyler watched the Thrall take a pace in front of the group and stand to attention. He held his arms straight with hands clenched and thumbs pointed down, his back ramrod and his chin raised, and it struck Tyler that this was a military stance. *Perhaps his father would be proud of him.*

'You shall be Brante,' said Radspakr. 'It means *sword*.'

'Yes, sir. Thank you.'

Radspakr waved him back. '*Thrall VI*, step forward.'

Tyler came out of the group and found himself mimicking Brante. He threw his shoulders back and stared over Radspakr's bald head.

'You shall be Punnr.'

'Yes, sir.'

'*Thrall VII*. Next.'

Thrall VII's nose was encased in bandages and his lips were swollen. Radspakr observed him wryly. 'It pleases me to see that your training is taken so seriously. You shall be Erland, the outsider. *Thrall VIII*, step forward.'

The little blonde took her turn. Radspakr studied her for several seconds, taking in her slight frame and sculpted features. 'You have done well,' he said. 'You shall be Calder.'

'Yes, sir. May I ask what it means?'

'It is ancient Norse for *cold waters*.'

She considered the description. 'Is there a reason for that choice?'

Radspakr had been about to call the next number, but her question arrested him and he peered at her. 'I receive the naming options from higher levels in the Pantheon, from which I may make my choice. I understand in your case that my selection is not unapt.'

She stepped back and *Thrall X* was called. 'You shall be Hertha. *Powerful woman*.'

Finally, bull-necked *Thrall XII*. 'You shall be Vidar, the *fighter in the woods*.

'Learn these names,' he commanded once they were back in line. He returned the notebook to Freyja and dropped his spectacles into his pocket. 'Henceforth you will forget your numbers and use only these new titles. It is an honour I bestow.' He turned and strode back to the platform. 'You are the final few in this process. The true Electi. You are not, however, the *only* ones seeking recruitment to the rank of Valhalla Thegn. There are others who will challenge you for a place at the officers' table. Others who will seek to surpass you. Halvar, signal that they may enter.'

Halvar stepped to the broken door and beckoned impatiently into the shadows. The six Thralls stood transfixed. From the darkness emerged new figures. One, two. They kept coming. Six, seven. They walked in a line off the platform and down the centre of the warehouse, stopping across from the newly named Thralls. There were eight in total. It was hard to see them clearly, but they looked young, perhaps between fifteen and eighteen. Seven males and one female. They were dressed in the same black T-shirts, trousers and boots which appeared to be the regulation garb for trainees during the Armatura, but their appearance differed in one dramatic way. Each carried a wooden sword and circular shield.

They faced the group of six. They had grim, hard faces and sinewy bodies. They stood with swords and shields lowered, at ease with the implements, holding them with casual confidence. There was a brooding silence and Radspakr let it extend. He was enjoying this new surprise.

'Let me introduce you to your competition. Please welcome the best graduates from our Valhalla Schola,' he said eventually. 'They are Perpetuals. The Disappeared. The Lost Children.'

Tyler felt prickles along his spine. *Lost Children!* Each of them knew what that meant. Across Britain statistics suggested a child disappeared every three minutes. Tens of thousands a year, mostly aged between ten and fourteen. The cases with higher profiles were those where youngsters ran away from otherwise 'normal' families, but much less was known about the thousands lost from deep within the bowels of the care system, from residential homes, temporary placements, foster families. The majority were found quickly, but there were many others who slipped between the cracks and were never seen again, at least under their old identities.

The online rumour-mongers were rife with speculation that some of these youngsters ended up in the Pantheon. Those with the best aptitudes, they said, were whisked away to secret Scholae. The media called them the Lost Children, although in truth many were already adolescents. There were unproven accusations that the care sector colluded with Pantheon Venarii parties in their search for viable new recruits, or at least that it did little to prevent the loss of these individuals from an already broken system. At the Pantheon Scholae, it was said, the Lost Children spent their formative years closeted from the outside world in an environment of discipline, learning and training. Those who didn't reach the required standards were released back into the community, often with far better prospects than if they hadn't been taken in the first place. Those deemed of suitable quality were put through rigorous selection criteria in the hope of joining the ranks of one of the Palatinates. The Scholae were the Pantheon's academies. The breeding grounds for each successive wave of warriors.

Tyler stared across at the motionless figures. They seemed almost mystical. The manifestation of so many rumours.

'I don't have a good feeling about this,' Brante said quietly.

'Perpetuals!' Freyja shouted with a parade-ground voice. 'Present arms!'

Eight shields locked into place and eight sword arms swept up. The figures hunched as one, took a single unified step forward on their leading foot and then held motionless again. Their eyes bore into the six Thralls from above their shield rims. The wooden swords looked clumsy, but they held them without so much as a quiver.

'Perpetuals! Advance!'

The figures marched in unison across the warehouse floor. Eight moonlit shadows coming straight at the six Thralls. 'Halt and brace!' They stopped dead ten paces away and hunched into their shields as if preparing to spring.

'I *really* don't have a good feeling,' whispered Brante, although the tall man stood strong and proud at the centre of the Thralls.

Freyja stepped down from the platform and placed herself at the end of the line. 'Perpetuals! Left present!' They spun towards her and brought their swords down in swift sweeps. 'Right present!' They turned on their rear foot, raised their sword arms and swept again in the opposite direction. Each motion was timed to perfection. 'Advance face! Flank right strike!' The sword arms swung out to the right, but at the same instant they each raised their shields across their left shoulder, so that the swinging sword of their neighbour struck the wood. There was a single resounding crack as the weapons hit as one.

'Advance face. Advance attack!' The eight figures spun back to face the Thralls, then came at them across the ten paces, cutting left, right, high, low with their sword arms, and letting out a single cry. Just before the moment of impact with the Thralls, they halted, presented their swords to attention and stopped motionless. To Radspakr's esteem, not one of the newly named Thralls had taken a step back. They stood rigid and faced the advance, and now both lines were a hair's breadth from each other.

There was silence.

Tyler found himself eyeball to eyeball with a youth of about eighteen. He had a small effeminate mouth with lips that almost pursed, a weak chin, a crop of crudely cut black hair, thick eyebrows and pimples on his neck. There was a hint of a moustache forlornly growing on his upper lip, like moss on a moon-baked stone. He seemed an unlikely warrior were it not for the sneering flash in his black eyes.

Tyler couldn't resist the unspoken challenge. 'Is that all you got?' he whispered.

Surprise flashed through the other man's face and then he took in Tyler's wounds. 'Your mum give you a thrashing?'

'Silence!' Freyja ordered from the end of the line. 'Perpetuals! Slope weapons!'

The eight figures stepped back one step and brought their swords up so they rested on their shoulders. The man hadn't taken his eyes from Tyler. 'Look out for me,' he said just loud enough for Tyler to catch the threat in his words.

'Perpetuals, retire!' Still facing the Thralls, they walked smartly backwards and halted. 'And stand easy!' Once more they lowered their shields into a casual hold and waited motionless.

Radspakr strolled between the lines with deliberate steps. 'So, my young ones, introductions over. I trust you are all now bosom companions. I will make this simple for you to understand. There are fourteen of you standing here tonight. Thralls and Perpetuals. When the Armatura is over at the end of next month, there will be but seven of you presented to Charon the Ferryman for the Oath-Taking and for the crossing of the River Styx. That is the number permitted by Valhalla's Blood Funds this season. So you each know the odds. You must each be stronger than your neighbour. Faster. Better. More ruthless. Only seven will make it.

'Thralls,' he continued, turning to the group of six. 'You will train with wooden weapons like those you have seen the Perpetuals demonstrate tonight. You will learn to use them in single combat and as a unit. You will practise until the shield and sword and stake are parts of your own bodies, until you do not feel their weight, until they are extensions of your own limbs. And then you will face the Perpetuals. And we will care not whether you are Thrall or Perpetual, only which of you is stronger than your neighbour. Which seven will stand and which seven will fall.'

He dropped into silence and let it hang in the air. A candle spluttered. Something flapped high up in the ceiling. He waved his hand towards Freyja.

'Perpetuals!' she called. 'Left face!' They spun towards her on their heels. 'And dismiss.' They strode back to the platform, filed through the broken door and were gone.

Radspakr turned his attention on the Thralls. 'As I have already said, you have done well to reach this point and in recognition I have given you names tonight. The Armatura is reaching its climax, but in the time remaining your training will become much more testing. And there will be great challenges to surmount. However, you are not yet

Oathsworn. If any in your number is doubtful, I urge you to listen to that voice and dispose of your amulet before it becomes impossible.' He studied them, but no one stirred. They were like granite in their wordless response. 'So be it.' He strode away to the platform. '*Some* of you I will see again. May Odin fortify you.'

He disappeared through the doorway and the group stirred. Halvar came over. 'Okay, you heard the man. We move to sword and shield practice now.' He grinned unexpectedly. 'Don't worry about those turds,' he waved towards the door. 'By the time Freyja and I have finished with you, you'll whip their arses!'

As the Thralls began to head to the opposite entrance where the drivers waited with blindfolds, Tyler dropped back next to Halvar. 'Radspakr never defined my name.'

'Defined?'

'Punnr. He never explained the meaning.'

Halvar peered at him. 'It's old Norse for *weakling*.'

Tyler stopped in his tracks. 'Are you winding me up?'

'Your arm. It's been holding you back. Giving you trouble. So Radspakr thought it a suitable name.'

'On Monday, in case you've forgotten, I broke *Thrall VII*'s nose.'

'Aye, you did laddie. And he's called Erland now.'

'I don't give a fuck what he's called. Radspakr had no right to name me that!'

Halvar squared up to him. He was several inches taller and he peered down into Tyler's eyes, but with a certain grim amusement. 'So what you going to do, Punnr The Weakling? Cry about it, or prove the bastard wrong?'

XI

On the next occasion they entered the vault, the room was empty except for Freyja sitting on a stool, waiting for them. Her braids were tied back and her burnt-cinnamon eyes glinted in the candlelight.

'Sit,' she said extending her arms to indicate the circle she expected them to form on the floor in front of her. They glanced at each other, but obeyed wordlessly, dropping down and crossing their legs like a class ready for a story. There was none of the usual equipment. No hanging punch bags, dumbbells, lateral bars. No hexagon drawn across the flagstones. Only Freyja looking at them and waiting for them to settle.

'It's just me tonight,' she said eventually. 'Halvar's excused himself because he's no good at this stuff. This evening I have a few things to say and you're going to listen. This isn't an open forum. I won't be fielding questions. But what I have to say is a vital part of the process. So I will speak, you will listen, then you will depart and each do as your conscience demands.'

She focused on a flagstone in front of her as she thought about her next words. No one stirred.

'People die in the Pantheon. Let's not pretend otherwise.' She said it simply and raised her eyes to look around the circle. 'I think you know that. I think most of the world out there—' she waved towards the ceiling to indicate the city above '—knows that. But there is the romance of death; and there is the reality of death. And they are two very different things.

'You saw the Perpetuals. You watched their skill with the training swords. You heard Radspakr and Halvar telling you it's time for your own weapons training to begin. And you're not fools. You know that although you may start with a blunt wooden stick, you'll graduate to razor-sharp iron. And when your foe also grasps such a weapon – well, that'll be the moment you fight for your life.'

She dropped her eyes again and the Thralls could see her trying to structure her words. 'When Radspakr had you all gathered in the cellar at the start of this Season and he gave his speech about how people seem to love the Pantheon, I was standing at the back and his words resonated with me. Over the last two decades, the world has got used to living with the Pantheon, especially in those cities where we operate most – Rome, Istanbul, Beijing, Budapest, Edinburgh. These populations have grown accustomed to our activities. They know on winter nights the Palatinates may roam between the hours of Conflict and they have learned to avoid us and get on with their lives.

'Many of them still dislike us and some are vocal in their opposition, but for others we have become something they welcome. A seam of excitement running beneath the surface of their lives. They follow us like they would a sports team – researching the results of our confrontations, surmising on the team strengths, debating who will be victorious at the end of each Season. Hell, we've even become tourist attractions. The cities brag about hosting their Palatinates, hoping to fleece visitors for every buck they own. And we ask ourselves why? Why does the world put us on pedestals? Why are people excited by our violence? Why do kids play Pantheon and why do their parents let them?

'We find these questions hard to answer because we're too involved. We're unable to step back and remember what the Pantheon looked like from afar. But if we could step back, we would see an irony – that it's not in the Pantheon where death is an obsession, it's outside in the everyday world. There's barely a film in the cinema or a drama on television or even a plot in a book which doesn't include death. We're all fixated by it. It fascinates us as much as it scares us. And when it passes us at arm's length – when it's part of a story, part of something bigger – well, we romanticise it. We make it glorious.'

She looked up once more and searched their faces. 'The reality of facing death is very different when it's coming right at you. And that's why I am tasked with giving you this talk. Next time you enter this vault you'll be given your training swords and you will begin your final journey towards becoming Weapons Worthy. We don't intend to waste our time on Electi who haven't understood the reality of death. If you aren't comfortable with this, then don't come back. We'll give your places to the Perpetuals and we can all move on.'

She took a deep breath and bit the bottom of her lip in a manner that made her look vulnerable. 'When I reached this point in my own selection many years ago, I was given this speech by my instructors and I went away and I found it hard to come to terms with what had been said. I almost left the process because I didn't think I should be forced to face danger.

'But then I had a revelation. I was raised among the orchards and terraced hills of the Kullu Valley in Himachal Pradesh, northern India, and in my teens I began to look higher and took to climbing in the Parvati Himalayas. After graduating from Delhi University, I came to Edinburgh to study, but what I really discovered were your mountains. Every weekend I packed off to a crag somewhere. In the summers I'd climb the warm faces of Rannoch Wall, Polldubh Crags, even the Cioch on Skye, until the last of the daylight was stretching the world into shadow. And in the winters you would find me on the ice walls of Glencoe and the Northern Corries of Ben Nevis. I loved it, but one loose piton, one weak rope, one broken handhold, one ice axe not properly embedded – and it would have been over. In climbing circles they say, *If you don't watch your step, the biggest obstacle to your ambition will be the fact that you're dead*. So there was my revelation. I discovered I had already faced the reality of death on innumerable occasions.

'And that got me thinking. I realised many ordinary people voluntarily place themselves in harm's way. It happens all around us, all the time. Every recruit to the Armed Forces. Every fireman. Every mountain or lifeboat rescuer. Every deep-water fisherman. And then there are the adrenaline sports junkies for whom the risk of death only makes their experience sweeter – motor racers, parachutists, white-water kayakers, big wave surfers. The list goes on.

We strain every sinew to take us to the very edges of life, because that's where we most keenly feel its fragility.

'So – I suppose I am trying to say to you – that what the Pantheon asks of us is not so exceptional.

'A thousand years ago, our ancient Viking forebears lived by a creed called the Havamal – the sayings of the High One – and the eighty verses are as relevant today as they were then. *A cowardly man thinks he will ever live, if warfare he avoids; but old age will give him no peace, only spears may spare him.*' She let the words hang in the air. 'Think on this.'

She was silent for many moments and when she spoke again, she was once more steely and regal. 'You may stand.' They fumbled to rise and kept their eyes averted from one another.

'The cars are waiting. Depart in silence and I suggest that if you're not at peace with what I've said or what we will expect of you – then don't return. Goodnight, Electi.'

After a year accommodated near the seafront in Edinburgh's Portobello, the Maitlands moved again, although their mother had seemed reluctant. The sea air disappeared and they moved closer to a strange shaped hill near the centre of the city, but this time their new home was many floors up in a grey concrete block. Their front door opened onto a shared walkway and when Tyler peered over the parapet, the ground would yawn up at him from an infinite distance below. There were many children here. His sister met new friends and spent hours absent after school. Tyler got to know other youngsters and they ran lawless up and down the blocks, playing, joking, boasting and fighting.

His mother worked longer and longer hours and she seemed to fade before them. She still drank and her slim figure became shapeless and no longer filled her clothes. She strove to provide a hot meal every evening, even though Morgan and Tyler rarely cared about it. She introduced touches of vintage, and even antique, furniture to the tiny flat and tried to create a space that resisted the concrete brutalism of the building around.

The years passed. Tyler grew tall and girls began to notice him. He started at the local secondary, making the commute each morning with gangs of other youths from the same estate. He kicked balls in the playground and supported Hibs and got into brawls. He played truant on Duddingston golf course, loitered in packs in the city centre at weekends, and kissed girls with bubble-gum-flavoured mouths on the edges of Holyrood Park. And he learned about the Pantheon. Kids talked about it in the playground and doodled images of Vikings and Hoplites in their maths books. They bought the stickers on sale at newsagents and offered themselves in tribal allegiance to one or other of the Palatinates. Tyler would write Valhalla on his hand and his mother would react with fury and slap him and try to scrub it off.

Morgan moved further into her teens and Tyler and his mother started to lose her. She grew unaccountably angry about everything. She would speak to their mother like dirt and stay out late every night. Swaggering boys collected her at the door and when she returned to their shared bedroom, Tyler would lie awake listening to her bang around and he knew she had been drinking. She smoked wantonly even when their mother shouted at her to do it out on the walkway and one time the police escorted her home. She could hardly stand and her mother whispered her apologies to the officers.

'Please forgive her,' she said, although they were already leaving.

When Morgan reached sixteen, she changed again and her estrangement took on a new ominous note. She had hung around with boys her own age on the estate for long enough already, drinking and copulating, but now she started to meet new men. Older, quieter, more powerful. She stopped drinking. Became serious and earnest. Spoke with new condescension to her mother. Disappeared for entire nights and returned with bruising which she flaunted. She chattered furtively to her girlfriends and they treated her with awe.

Tyler himself grew wilder in response. At twelve he was smoking and playing truant from school. By thirteen his evenings were fuelled with cheap lager. By fourteen he lived for hard spirits, soft drugs and older girls. He stayed away from the flat most of his waking hours, roaming the estate with his gang, torn between endless tracts of boredom and occasional explosions of violence.

Morgan left school, but didn't bother with a job. She seemed to have money without the need to work and she spoiled Tyler with gifts. A widescreen television, a games console, a new laptop. Whenever a purchase materialised, their mother would steadfastly ignore it and refuse to allow Morgan to contribute to the household's general expenses, saying she wanted none of her dirty money. So instead Morgan surreptitiously began a monthly payment of £500 into Tyler's account.

A year slipped by and Tyler first began to notice that

there was a new presence in his sister's life. She became more effusive and would tease him over breakfast and even hum as she flitted around the flat. Some evenings she departed not in her usual black garb, but dressed in smart clothes and smelling of perfume, and occasionally when she returned in the early hours he would lie in his bed and hear her speaking to a companion on the walkway outside in a tone he had never heard her use before.

One evening he was wandering back from a neighbouring block, when he caught sight of her outside their building. The light above the entrance had long ago been smashed, so he could only just make out the figure hovering in front of her, but he saw the kiss clearly enough. He made his way towards them, but when he called out she pushed the man away and he dissolved into the night.

Later that year, Morgan decided to begin a Foundation course at Leith College of Art. She appeared to take some pleasure in it and would show Tyler photos of her paintings on her phone. Then came the day of her graduation. It was an island of serenity amidst the usual strife and Tyler would always remember how beautiful his mother and sister looked in their finery. Ladies, both of them. He felt stupid in his tie and jacket, but he was swept up by the whole occasion and they celebrated Morgan's artistic creations over champagne and speeches and photographs and family embraces.

But the hostility resumed and as Morgan grew fiercer and more defiant, their mother wilted. Her natural beauty became hollowed out. Her skin dried and cracked like the bed of a stream in drought. Her eyes spoke of long-lost hurt and dark fears.

One afternoon Morgan used a felt-tip to draw a circular symbol on Tyler's hand and whispered about Valhalla in the same thrilled manner they had used when they were young. Their mother caught her doing it and became hysterical, swearing she would go to the police. 'Someone has to do something to save you!'

Morgan reacted with fury, grabbing her mother's arms and pushing her back against the wall. 'Don't ever threaten me with the police,' she shouted. 'You don't know what you're saying.'

Morgan didn't return that night and their mother paced until dawn, drinking gin. She tried to kiss him when he rose, but he was hurt and angry about everything and pushed her away. 'I made a call last night, Tyler. To the one person who can help your sister. She mustn't be allowed to carry on this way. It has to stop before someone gets hurt. It *must* stop.'

She took her coat and stepped out into the grey morning light.

'Where are you going?'

'I have a meeting with someone.'

'Not the police?'

'No, not the police. Don't worry, I'll be back soon.'

But she never was.

XII

As Tyler walked down The Mile to the usual meeting point at Bull's Close, he peered ahead through the darkness and his breath billowed in the bitter air. In truth he hadn't needed Freyja's pep talk, though her words and her effort had surprised him. He had returned to his flat and found the Havamal sayings online and sat until the early hours reading them and pondering these pearls of wisdom calling from across the centuries. During the course of the Armatura he had doubted much about his abilities, his resilience, his very presence among the Electi, but he had never doubted his willingness to risk life and limb. He instinctively knew what was coming and – he supposed – he had always been ready for it.

But now he looked ahead to the meeting point and could see only three figures. No *Thrall II* – Brante, and no little *Thrall VIII* – Calder. *9.59 p.m.* The cars would be pulling up in moments. *Where are they? Not those two, surely?*

He joined the other three and they nodded from under their layers. He could feel their eyes on him and realised that they all thought *he* might be the one not to show. He stared beyond them and spotted Brante striding up from the direction of Holyrood. *Thank god*, he thought and was surprised by the relief flooding through him. *I don't think I can do this without that man.*

The Mercs pulled around the corner at the bottom of The Mile and came towards them. Tyler caught Brante's eye and they both looked up the street, searching for the figure they hoped would materialise. The lead car pulled up beside them and the doors swung open. The others began stepping in.

Don't do this. Not now, Tyler found himself mouthing to himself. *Where are you?*

The first vehicle pulled away and the second drew up. He refused to take his eyes from the street rising westward because she always came from that direction.

'We have to go,' Brante said grimly. 'It is what it is.'

Tyler turned to the taller man. 'Fuck,' he whispered and the other man nodded his agreement. Tyler hunched and lowered himself into the back seat of the Merc.

Brante made to join him, then stopped himself. 'Wait!'

Tyler sat forward and stared over the driver's shoulder. She was coming at a half-run, blonde hair picking up the streetlights. Brante held the door for her and she dropped onto the seat next to Tyler, breathing rapidly. *Thrall II* closed the door and took the front seat.

As they moved away, Tyler glanced over at her. She looked back at him, eyes wide and serious, but neither spoke.

True to their word, during those final two weeks of November, Halvar and Freyja drilled the Thralls in the art of weapons handling. Each found themself provided with a hardened leather jerkin, gauntlets, a wooden sword and circular shield. In the first week, they practised only with the swords, learning how to grip the hilt, how to stand, how to step in and out, and how to thrust. The one now named Calder was dismayed by the weight of her weapon and Freyja explained that they were designed to be almost twice as heavy as the real things.

'Learn to wield these burdensome instruments until you can strike without flaw and parry every blow brought against you, and when a true iron weapon is placed in your hand it will be to you as light as air.'

The corn sacks were again suspended from the ceiling and they trained hour after hour. Then they were split into pairs and taught to feint and parry, and the crack of wood hitting wood reverberated around the stone walls. The weight of the weapons exhausted them. Calder found she could barely lift her arm beyond the first thirty minutes of each session and they all left the vaults with shoulders that burned.

At the end of each night, Freyja and Halvar gave them a demonstration. The Thralls watched in silent wonder as their trainers each took a clumsy wooden sword and became in that moment a breed of warrior that their class hadn't seen before, attacking without hesitation or reserve. There was a flowing beauty, as well as a latent ferocity. Halvar exhibited a grace none of the watching Thralls could have imagined as his booted feet danced, but Freyja was the true revelation. Her stern reserve dissolved and her face was lit with wild delight as she skipped around Halvar, dodging his blows and parrying his sword arm with such strength that it belied the sheer power of his strikes. Despite his own size and speed, it was she who was in control, stepping beyond his thrusts and stabbing at leisure, then jumping away again. Halvar was like a bear enraged by a wasp and it wasn't lost on the Thralls just how many times the wood of Freyja's weapon made contact with his exposed torso and just how much blood would have been spilt had her blade been iron and honed to a brilliant cutting edge.

The second week, they were introduced to their shields. These were circular and designed in varying sizes to ensure each warrior – tall or short – could be protected from chin to knee. They were made from lime wood, with an iron boss in the centre of the face and an iron grip riveted to the reverse. They were practice shields. The real things would be covered in hardened leather, rimmed in iron, and painted. First they were taught to soak up blows. They would stand braced while a partner used their wooden sword to strike the shield. A hefty hit often smashed the shield back into their bodies and Halvar would bellow at them to hold firm until their arms were blue and ready to drop. Then they learned how to move and circle while holding the shield and how to manoeuvre it to defend attacks from differing angles. Finally, they were presented with their swords again and shown how to thrust over, under and around the rims. It was torture. They were shaken and bruised as they staggered home, but each time they returned a little stronger, a little faster and a little more deadly.

They no longer carried the Roman numerals on their shoulders. Instead, each was referred to by their new name and treated as though they had been given these at birth. Tyler had to make a physical effort to remember them and would recite each under his breath. Tall Brante, taking to the skills of sword handling like a duck to water; Erland, formerly *Thrall VII*, with his broken and bandaged nose, who maintained a new deeper sullenness; hefty *Thrall X*, now Hertha, throwing herself into the tasks; bull-necked *Thrall XII* – Vidar, crashing into the duels bereft of finesse but with the force of a bus; and then remote little *cold water* Calder, pale, beautiful, delicate, agile, fleet, tough, wordless, and utterly enigmatic.

And what of Punnr the Weakling? He approached the training with a new indignant anger, determined to show Halvar that the sobriquet was poorly chosen. He was thankful that the others hadn't learned the meaning and didn't think to ask. They had enough on their minds and simply accepted that thin *Thrall VI*, who had battled to a standstill against his feeble limbs and overcome every challenge thrown at him, was now to be known as Punnr.

XIII

Princes Street Gardens and St Andrew Square were filled with the bustle of Christmas Markets. Wooden stalls spawned everywhere, hung with lanterns and filled with trinkets. Ice rinks were laid over the grass, spruce arrayed in regimented lines and a huge Ferris wheel given leave to shoot upwards beside the Scott Memorial, like a vast alien weed seeking to smother the carefully nurtured architecture around it. The night air became redolent with the heavy scents of mulled wine, spice candles and fried onions. On cue, the weather also joined the festive spirit and saturated everything with heavy squalls.

On the first Thursday of the month, the six Thralls were given new joining instructions. Gather on Waverley Bridge at four in the afternoon.

'If any of you whelps have commitments,' Halvar said, 'get yourselves excused. We'll wait for no one.'

The daylight was just dissolving beyond Corstorphine, washed away by the rain, when they assembled on the Bridge a few dozen yards from the fumes of the ever-present tourist buses. Brante had a huge maroon and turquoise striped scarf coiled around his neck and he was growing his own small musketeer beard to match Punnr's, but set against his shaved head, the effect was more Ali Baba. Punnr's cuts were healing and he no longer sported a plaster beneath his eye, but his lips remained tender. Vidar was smoking, his bulk hunched into a leather jacket. Calder peeked from the recesses of a fur-lined hood and nudged closer to Hertha who had opened a large umbrella and was trying to shield them both from the blustery wind. Erland stood a few steps detached, his coat collar zipped up to his bandaged nose and his usual hoodie pulled over his head.

'Well, well,' said Halvar as he approached from the Old Town. 'Don't you lot look the spitting image of battle-hardened soldiers. I love the umbrella. Essential piece of kit. You must remember to take that with you into a shieldwall.' He wore a bomber jacket and a cigarette hung from the corner of his mouth. 'Follow me.'

They crossed the road and strode down the sloping entrance to Waverley Station. The concourse was filled with evening commuters and smelt of warm doughnuts. Freyja was waiting for them. 'Platform 20,' she said simply.

Punnr twisted his head up to the boards and located platform 20. It showed only two destinations: Stirling and Inverness.

Halvar stopped beside a wall and stubbed out his cigarette. 'Got any more of those?' he asked Vidar. The Thrall pulled out a pack and offered it to Halvar. He took it, then dropped it and ground the box under his boot.

'What the...?' Vidar exclaimed hotly.

'What about you?' Halvar demanded of Punnr and stamped on that box as well. 'Both of you take a last drag on the one in your mouth and then get rid of it.'

'Why?'

Halvar glared at Punnr. 'You ever heard of a ninth-century Viking with a Camel in his gob? In the Horde we find other, more direct methods to kill ourselves. Smoke them in your own time. In the Pantheon you're clean.'

Freyja led the way down the platform. She wore boots with higher heels than usual, which rapped out a staccato tattoo as she strode. She had a tartan woollen shawl around her shoulders and a small leather bag, and she looked every inch the affluent lady-about-town. The train was already waiting. It was twelve carriages long and they had to walk the whole length of the platform to board the rearmost. It was the last of three first-class carriages and it was empty. They filed through the sliding door into the quiet, air-conditioned interior and then hovered in the gangway as Halvar and Freyja seated themselves together at a table halfway down. The Thralls didn't know whether they were supposed to sit as a group or maintain the careful separation they had cultured over the preceding weeks.

'So who's with me?' Brante asked as he made a decision and sat himself down at one table of four. Calder placed herself next to him, Punnr took the window seat opposite and Hertha pushed her large frame down beside him. Vidar and Erland took the two seats across the aisle. It seemed right. They had been through much together and it was time they were allowed to act as a group.

Halvar eased himself along the aisle and they were half expecting him to scatter them to the far ends of the train. 'So ladies, you've no doubt noticed that this isn't our usual routine. We're going on a little trip out of the city. This carriage is ours. No one else will be joining us. Food and drink will be coming round shortly, so I suggest you relax and enjoy the journey while you can.'

'Where are we going?' Erland asked.

'Now, you hardly expect me to answer that, do you?'

'Is it just for this evening?' said Hertha.

'We'll be away for six days.'

'Six days?'

Halvar nodded. 'It's time for the final challenges of the Armatura.'

'But what about our jobs?' demanded Calder. 'I'm expected in the office tomorrow morning.'

'Everything's been sorted. You are all excused for a week and no one will miss you.'

'But I have clients...' She trailed off when she saw the look in his eye.

'I'll repeat for your benefit, madam. *Everything* is sorted.'

A new thought occurred to her. 'I've nothing with me. Only the clothes I'm wearing.'

Halvar put his head to one side, as if daring her to require him to repeat a third time and she lapsed into sulky silence.

'That reminds me,' he said. 'Your phones and watches, please. They'll be returned to you at the end of the week.'

A few minutes later, the train doors beeped closed and the platform began to ease away. They broke from Waverley's long concrete tentacles and peered up at the nettle-strewn cliff that reared above them, with the castle perched atop. A little commuter train rattled alongside as they picked up speed, crammed with passengers so that its windows were already steaming up. The faces were tired, surly, sad, all lost in their own routine worlds. One or two glanced back at them and must have envied the empty comfort of the carriage.

There was a clatter as a staff member pushed a drinks trolley through the door at the far end. He stopped at the table beside Halvar and Freyja and they heard her ordering a bottle of white. The man busied himself opening it and placing glasses, then he came on down to the six Thralls and threw out a cheery smile.

'Just you tonight. Nice and quiet. Are you heading to Stirling or Inverness?'

The question caught them out and no one answered. A voice in Punnr's head, however, made him certain of the answer. 'Inverness.'

'Okay. We're due there at 7.31 p.m. Would you like some refreshments?'

Calder twisted in her seat and peered down the aisle to Halvar. He raised a glass to her, the vessel looking ridiculously dainty in his huge paw. 'Like I said, relax and enjoy.'

She ordered a Chilean Merlot and a Marlborough Sauvignon for the table. Erland and Vidar plumped for Tennent's. As the train slid through Haymarket, past the golf courses and Murrayfield rugby stadium and then on through Broomhouse, the Gyle business park and finally across the ring road to the blackening fields beyond, the alcohol began to soften them.

Brante eased back in his seat and looked over at Punnr. 'Why did you sound so certain about Inverness?'

'I don't know. Just this feeling that the Pantheon is removing us from the city because it needs places which are wilder, more... ageless. Landscapes that have barely changed since the Vikings locked shieldwalls. I reckon we're going to lose ourselves somewhere in the Highlands, and isn't Inverness the gateway to the Highlands?'

'I wonder what they have planned for six days?' Hertha asked.

'Training. But it's going to be different, I think. Harder.'

Brante was still watching him. 'A lot more mud, I expect.'

'Mud?' Calder demanded.

'I doubt they're taking us all the way to the Highlands to lock us in another bloody vault.'

There was a spurt as Vidar opened a second can of lager. 'They'd better not be thinking I'm running up any fucking hills,' he said gruffly.

'And I've a feeling,' continued Punnr, 'that we won't be alone either.'

Calder's huge eyes fixed him with a stare. 'You mean the Perpetuals?'

'Seems to me there has to be a reckoning with them and my money says it's this week.'

'We're not ready,' Calder said softly.

'We're going to have to be.'

They were served salmon fillet with minted new potatoes and peas, followed by chocolate sponge and coffee. They ate quietly, still unsure how to break the barriers and communicate with each other. Outside, night descended. They travelled along the southern shore of the Forth, catching the lights of the refineries, and then headed into deeper country. Vidar closed his eyes after the food and was soon snoring. Erland dozed fitfully.

'Why are you here?' Calder asked unexpectedly, turning

to Brante beside her. He looked at her in surprise and she stammered her apology. 'I'm sorry, I spoke before I thought.'

Brante relaxed. 'Perhaps we shouldn't be asking *why* we're here, but whether we're prepared to do whatever it takes to succeed.'

Each of them looked searchingly into the faces of the others. Calder sipped her sauvignon and then said solemnly, 'I am.' Punnr believed her.

They dropped into an awkward silence again. The train pulled into Stirling and they saw figures come and go on the platform, but their carriage remained undisturbed. Later Hertha spoke up. 'The Vikings never made it into the heartland of Scotland.'

'What's your point?' Brante asked.

'Punnr said we were going to the Highlands because those landscapes haven't changed since the Vikings. But actually, although the Danish Vikings built a commanding empire in huge swathes of England, they were only ever coastal raiders in Scotland.' Everyone looked at her and a hint of indignation crept into her voice. 'Hey, I've been reading about the period. Seems to me that if the Horde wants me, I'd better know about their Viking traditions.'

'Too right,' Brante nodded. 'We should all be better informed.'

Punnr was itching for a cigarette. 'You realise if we get to the Oath-Taking, there won't be any turning back after that. No chance to return the amulets and say thanks very much, not for me.'

'I think we all understand that,' said Calder.

'It's said that once a warrior reaches the requisite number

of Blood Funds or Blood Kills,' said Hertha, 'he or she may then depart the Pantheon for a new life with all the wealth they've earned.'

'But that's a long way off,' said Calder. 'Is that the only way to leave?'

'I understand you can leave on the end of a sword point,' said Punnr maliciously. Calder shot him a hard glance, but refused to rise to a response.

'I don't think they'd let us walk away with all the secrets of the Horde,' Brante pondered. 'Their numbers, locations, strategies. The Vigiles – whoever the hell they actually are – would never allow it.'

'The Keepers of the Rules,' Hertha interrupted. 'That's what they are. Impartial overseers with no loyalty to one Palatinate or another. Their role is to observe the activities of the Palatinates, to punish any transgression and to report back to the Caelestia.'

'The Caelestia,' Brante said dismissively. 'I've read so much nonsense about them, but I still don't get how they're supposed to fit with the Curiate.'

'I find a football analogy simplifies it. The Palatinates are the well-paid teams, that's obvious. The Vigiles are the referees. The Kings – well, they're the managers, training their players and working on formations. The general public are the fans in the poor seats. They have bad views of the action, but they love their teams and support them through thick and thin. Then you have those who pay extortionate amounts to occupy the best vantage points, to dine on lobster and champagne in warm dining rooms while the game plays out below and to upstage each other with more and more excessive bets on the outcome of the match.

So those are like the Curiate. Ultimately, above it all, you have the chairmen and owners. Individuals who've lost track of how to spend their vast wealth, so they purchased football clubs to amuse themselves. They may seem distant from the action on the field, but behind the scenes nothing happens without their agreement.'

'And they're the Caelestes?'

Hertha shrugged. 'It seems that way to me.'

Erland had woken long enough to hear Hertha's explanation and now he snorted derisively. 'Football? Bollocks.'

Hertha turned on him. 'The Pantheon has rules, funds, seasons, competition and teams. You got a better analogy?'

Erland's eyes soured, but he held his tongue.

It was Calder who spoke next. 'Imagine,' she said thoughtfully, dragging the word out. 'Imagine riches beyond your wildest dreams. Now times them by ten. A hundred. We're talking mega-wealth. The kind that buys governments, shapes economies, enervates security forces and makes a mockery of justice systems. What would you do with it? What's next on the list when you're bored of the parties and premieres, the cars, the houses, the planes? When you've had all the sex and drugs you'll ever need? When you've owned every sports team, every horse, every gambling syndicate you could ever want? What's going to excite you all over again? Make your heart thump?'

'Behold, the Pantheon,' said Punnr.

'Aye,' nodded Brante. 'One night twenty years ago, seven bastards just like that sat down and invented a blood sports competition because they needed something to get their rocks off to.'

'It's no different from how the Ancient Romans amused themselves,' commented Hertha.

'And so the wheel of time turns,' said Calder.

No one responded and they sat wordlessly digesting these points as the train sped through the darkness. Punnr had a sense of high places rising to the east and he guessed they were skirting the Cairngorm plateau.

He shifted to look down the carriage and could see Halvar and Freyja in conversation. She had her back to him, but Halvar was drinking wine and smiling with a warm mischief that Punnr had never spied on his face before. On impulse he bid Hertha excuse him and walked down the aisle with his wine in hand until he reached their table. For a few moments they ignored him, then Halvar turned his head. 'May we be of service?'

'Can I join you?'

The two of them looked at each other in genuine surprise and then Freyja shrugged, so Halvar beckoned him gruffly. 'Be our guest.'

Punnr sat beside Freyja, but she continued to look ahead and sip her wine. Despite all their hours in the same vault, he hadn't been in such close proximity to her before. Now he found himself looking at her hands on the glass. She had long, slim fingers with gold nail varnish that complemented her umber skin, and on both thumbs were silver rings with intricate swirling designs. On her left wrist was a thick silver bracelet which partially covered a labyrinthine tattoo flowing across her forearm, and the sleeves of her shirt were pulled up revealing arms rippling with tendon and muscle. A furtive glance at her profile revealed high cheekbones and lips painted in the same gold as her nails. There were hints of crow's feet spreading from her lids and he wondered at her age. She wore no perfume, but the air around her called up distant orchards.

'Have you been in the Pantheon for long?' he found himself asking her, but it was Halvar who sucked his teeth and responded.

'For as long as I can remember. I'm like the ones you saw in the warehouse.'

'The Perpetuals?'

'Aye, a Lost Child. Taken by a Venarii party when I was young.'

'How old were you?'

Halvar's eyes caught Freyja's. 'I don't know.'

'Too young to remember your life before?'

Halvar glared at him. 'I *said* I don't know.'

Punnr knew he should shut up, but the wine was getting the better of him. 'Were you trained at the Valhalla Schola?'

The Housecarl studied him irritably, then relented. 'Aye. Turned from a brawler into a soldier. And schooled. Taught to read, to count, to appreciate some of the finer things in life. Much more than I would have known in the real world.'

'How many Lost Children are in the Schola?'

Halvar glanced again at Freyja as though seeking her permission to continue. 'Here's the way of it. No one knows how many apprentices graduate into the ranks of the Pantheon Palatinates, but in each Schola there are dozens of Lost Children living, learning and training. Some fail and are returned to the outside world. Those who make the grade are called up and enter the Pantheon at the most basic rank of trooper. In the Horde these troopers are called Drengr. How many are recruited in any one Season depends on the Blood Funds won by each Palatinate. Valhalla's success last year against the Sky-Rats means that we have already initiated twenty-six new Drengr into our ranks in readiness for this new Season.'

'And what of the eight in the warehouse?'

Halvar's face twisted into a grim smile. 'They are the best of the Schola graduates and seek a different way into Valhalla. Not content to be rank-and-file Drengr, they strive to be Thegns. Young officers. The Housecarls of the future.' The big man fixed Punnr with a glare. 'But they're not going to make it, are they? Because you and your friends stand in their way.'

Punnr mulled the information and the other two sat in silence. They seemed unwilling to offer up anything more and so Punnr thought he had better leave.

Then Freyja spoke unexpectedly. 'I'm like you.'

She turned and looked at Punnr. Her eyes were copper, exaggerated by heavy mascara. She stared right into his soul, opening it up, assessing it and weighing whether to continue. 'It was eight Seasons ago. I was twenty-four, and ten months earlier I had returned to India with my Glaswegian fiancé. I wanted to show him the land of my birth, wanted him to see my village and meet my parents, so he would understand my humble beginnings. We took a climbing trip into Nepal. We were on the Lhotse face in the Himalaya when I watched the pins above me come out one by one and my fiancé fall past me. The rope snapped and he fell three thousand metres to his death. I searched for seventeen days, but I could not find his body and I swore I would never climb – or love – again.

'When I returned to Edinburgh I never expected Radspakr

to track me down and give me the amulet. I was taken to the same vaults as you and shown my new competition. There were fourteen of us that year. Fourteen Electi. But the Horde's Blood Funds were limited and only allowed for one Thegn to join. I was the last Thrall standing.'

Punnr stared at her, imagining this warrior in her moment of victory. He tried to frame his thoughts. 'Why… why do they need people like us if they have all these Lost Children already?'

'I wondered that and I asked Radspakr before my Oath-Taking. His answer has stayed with me. He said, *It is the very fact that Electi forsake their lives in the outside world voluntarily, which makes them so prized*. People like you and me, Punnr, *choose* this path. Such choice is a powerful force. Used wisely, it can make us better warriors – better leaders. The Pantheon knows this.'

Halvar harrumphed. 'Better leaders, my arse. Someone's stupid theory. What it does do is make Thegns expensive. Four Blood Credits for every one Credit a Drengr costs!'

'Just ignore him,' Freyja said. 'But he tells the truth. Thegns are expensive. That is why you must compete with the Perpetuals. King Sveinn has chosen to call just seven Thegns into his service this Season, when he could have used the Credits to buy a further twenty-eight Drengr from the Schola.'

'So you'd better be worth it!' interjected Halvar.

Punnr drained his wine and decided to push his luck. 'What's Sveinn like?'

'That's enough, laddie.'

'He's a good man,' said Freyja simply, but then turned away.

Punnr ran his tongue along the sores on his lips. 'Can we beat the Perpetuals?'

Halvar glared at him. 'No.'

Punnr was taken aback by the reply. 'Then why are you pitting us against them with so little training? They've been schooled for years!'

'You won't *all* beat the Perpetuals. Just as they won't all beat you. Some from each of you will win and some will fail. It's the way of the Armatura.'

'When will we face them?'

'I think, laddie, it's time you returned to the other whelps. They've been staring at you for long enough.'

It was true. When Punnr rose, he could see Brante, Calder, Hertha and Erland all looking down the carriage. Only Vidar continued to snore.

They arrived at a windblown but dry Inverness at 7.45 p.m. and found themselves transferred to waiting Range Rovers. They drove beside the brightly lit river at the centre of the town and then into an absolute darkness that eliminated the need for blindfolds. Punnr sat with Hertha and Erland in one vehicle, Brante, Calder and Vidar in another, and Halvar with Freyja in the lead one. The vehicles' headlights revealed twisting single-track roads, sudden deep puddles and heather verges which dropped away into nothing. At one point they passed a huge black expanse of water. Often they saw pinprick eyes in the night and guessed there were herds of deer roaming by the roadside. The clouds parted above and Punnr could make out stars and looming crags. Something in him quickened. He remembered his trips with Morgan and their mother during their early days in Edinburgh as they sought out the wild places of the north.

The cars moved fast. The drivers knew these roads and were practised in their switchbacks and steep inclines. Punnr couldn't tell if they went north, south or west. He guessed it wasn't east because they would have found the sea and lost the mountains, and he thought it wasn't south because they would have run along the endless shoreline of Loch Ness. So he decided it must be west, deep into the Highland glens, seeking the remote emptiness of the interior.

When it seemed they had left the world behind forever, the vehicles braked and lurched onto a rough track which they banged along for an age before lights appeared ahead. The cars drove through a pillared gateway and the occupants could make out gardens. They sat open-mouthed as a castle materialised from the night and the vehicles pulled to a halt. They stepped out and the cold clarity of the air took their breath away. The silence too. It felt as though the whole universe was listening to the crunch of their footfalls.

They could sense an ancient keep lying in wait, but it was wreathed in darkness. Walls led away and to their right was the bulk of a medieval hall with flickering light playing at the windows. Halvar led the way up steps to oak doors which he shouldered open and they entered a high-ceilinged entrance hall with thick rugs underfoot and a roaring fire. Deer heads, swords and pikes lined the walls, as well as a circular shield above the fireplace. No one was present to greet them and it was as though the fire had burned alone for eternity.

'Come,' Halvar ordered and they trooped after him

through a small doorway next to the fire, down a cold corridor and then right, through another doorway into the main hall. It was a huge room, almost a hundred feet long. The walls spoke of antiquity and stars peeked through high arched windows. Mighty beams crossed the ceiling, decorated with ancient coats of arms. The stone floor was littered with furs and benches ran along both sides. At the far end was a dais with a long table, above which hung a wooden carving of the Triple Horn of Odin. In the centre of the hall was a circular stone hearth and a fire burned ferociously, the flames licking up towards a hole in the roof.

'Welcome to Sveinn's Mead Hall,' Halvar said solemnly. 'The Heart of the Horde.'

The six Thralls worked their way down, staring up at the roof, touching the walls, feeling the heat of the fire and gathering below the great Triple Horn.

'It's magnificent,' said Brante.

'Aye, that it is, laddie.'

Freyja walked to the centre and let the light play on her. 'You'll have plenty of time to take it all in later. For now, follow me and I'll show you to the tower where you'll find everything you need for your stay here. We'll give you thirty minutes to freshen up before you gather back here.'

'What then?' asked Vidar.

Halvar reached down beside a bench and retrieved a large horn, edged with ornate silver. 'This is the Mead Hall. So we'll drink with Odin until we can no longer stand.'

XIV

In the upper floors of the tower, Freyja showed them to their rooms and they discovered chests with their names engraved on brass plaques containing items they would require for the week's stay. There were boots, trousers, T-shirts and fur jerkins, all in the correct sizes. There was also soap and wash cloths, but no deodorant, toothpaste or any other cosmetic.

Calder was disgusted. 'It would seem we're literally living in the Dark Ages this week.'

These inconveniences were forgotten when they returned to the hall. Clay mugs had appeared and leather beakers filled with ale, cider or mead. The benches had been pulled around the fire and covered with furs. There was bread to dip in saucers of walnut oil, crumbly goat's cheese and fruit. Halvar used stones in the hearth to bake flatbreads and slavered them with honey. The ale was foul, the cider head-blowing and the sweet mead addictive. When they had eaten and drunk their fill, Halvar sat on a central bench and began to tell them stories in a deep, mesmeric voice. He spoke of the Nine Worlds of ancient Norse mythology, which are each held in the branches of Yggdrasil, the World Tree. He told them of the Norn Sisters who weave all men's lives. He described Asgard, the world of the Aesir gods; Niflheim, the primordial world of ice; Vanaheim, the world of the Vanir gods; and Hel, the place of the dead.

They listened rapt as he told of Odin's journey to the Well of Urd in the roots of the World Tree, where he traded an eye for a taste of the well's water which could give knowledge of all things to the drinker. Halvar recounted how Loki was chained in his cave by Thor, how his struggles sent earthquakes through Midgard, the world of men, and how – as destined – Loki's eventual escape led to the destruction of the cosmos.

The Thralls swaddled themselves in furs and lost themselves in the words of the Housecarl and gradually, one by one, they fell asleep close together.

At dawn Halvar called reveille, pacing around the still hot embers and kicking them awake. The first grey light was just creeping through the windows in the east and the hall was frigid. They shivered and sat close to the hearth as Halvar began baking thick crumpets. There was lashings of butter and more goat's cheese, but their thirst could only be quenched by hot water sweetened with honey.

'I don't function without coffee,' said Calder.

'You want coffee, you'd better shift your arse to Inverness Starbucks, missy, but don't bother coming back.'

She bit morosely into a crumpet and whispered to Punnr beside her, 'Christ, I'd kill for an espresso.'

'And I'd murder for a ciggie.'

Breakfast over, Halvar led them outside and around the crumbling walls to the back of the castle. Although the sun was rising, the castle grounds were shadowed by a crag jutting above and the cold cut through them. The grass cracked and broke beneath their boots and steam plumed from their jittering breath. Formal gardens dropped away to bog and heather which sloped for half a mile to a loch, above which a layer of mist floated. Mountains reared on all sides, their flanks orange and their summits studded with snow. The sky was winter-white and cloudless.

'You're lucky bastards,' said Halvar. 'I've known this place when the rain lashes your face so hard that you cry for your mother, and I've still sent Thralls like you out into it.'

He took them around the keep and they found Freyja laying out items beside six goatskin sacks. 'Good morning, Thralls. Select a sack and check each item before packing it. You'll carry everything you need for the next two days.'

They worked through the piles. For each, there was a wooden spoon and bowl, leather beaker, flint and kindling, fur jacket and fur hat, flatbreads, cooked sausage, beans and millet. Once loaded up, they were presented with heavy wooden training swords and shields. They shoved the swords through their belts, used the leather straps around the goatskin sacks to secure them to their backs, and shouldered the shields. Weighed down, shivering with cold and still half asleep, they followed the Housecarls up the flank of the nearest hill.

The ground underfoot was frozen. Halvar maintained a murderous pace, which Brante matched, but the others became strung out. Freyja walked at the rear and watched those flagging, but didn't offer to help. It was mid-morning before the sun reached them, but by then they were sweating from exertion and its rays were unwelcome. The ground thawed and became sodden, and they squelched and slipped and sank. They found mountain burns and used their beakers to quench their thirst, not caring about the sediment. When they reached the summit ridge, a wind surprised them and froze their sweat. They pulled on the fur jerkins and hats and struggled, heads down, into the gale.

By midday they had dropped into another glen and were climbing the far side. They had covered six miles when Halvar stopped them among a nest of rocks and let them eat flatbread and sausage. They were out of the wind and lay on the rocks, soaking up the sun. In the afternoon Halvar's pace was unrelenting. They crossed two more ridges and toiled along the floor of a giant glen, following a stream upriver. Hertha fell far behind and so Punnr dropped back and argued with her until she allowed him to take her sack and shield. Less encumbered, she walked silently with him and occasionally summoned the energy to thank him and bless him.

By mid-afternoon Vidar had fallen back as well. He stamped and blew like a buffalo, forcing his stout legs to keep stepping forward, but soon even Punnr and Hertha overtook him. Brante waited for him on a rise and took his shield and sack. Vidar was red-faced with frustration, but he yielded the items and walked wordlessly beside him. Erland strode alone at the front and didn't look back and Punnr felt an irrational anger towards him, as he himself laboured under the weight of two shields.

As dusk fell, they had covered sixteen miles of upland terrain. They were each lost in hell, sightless, unmoved by the magnificent scenery. Their feet were ribbons. Their bellies were full of gritty water yet their bodies were dried to a husk. Their skin was raw and salty, their clothing wet and mud-strewn. They walked now only because their legs knew no other motion. With the coming of evening, the temperature plummeted and they froze even under their extra layers of fur.

Finally, at the head of the glen, they saw firelight. It looked so fragile and minuscule among the hulking black crags and they were fearful that the vastness of the valley must surely extinguish it. They kept their salt-filled eyes upon its tiny light and didn't dare blink lest they mislay the beacon. Punnr heard Hertha whispering gratitude to the gods and he summoned the energy to find encouraging words for her. Finally they were close enough to make out low stone walls surrounding the fire. They dreamed of collapsing on furs and eating hot stews and sleeping forever.

It was when they were almost upon the walls that Punnr's exhausted brain began to register the figures beyond. They were unmoving, watching the approach of the group, and with sinking heart he counted eight. Brante had come to the same realisation.

'Shit,' he swore and glanced at Punnr through the gloom. 'Not now, surely!'

They entered the enclosure and they could feel the welcome warmth of the fire. Calder walked towards it in a trance, but the motionless figures didn't part for her and a rough hand arrested her motion. 'This fire isn't for Thralls.'

She was beyond understanding and stood mutely with the firm hand on her shoulder, until Halvar came over and wheeled her away. 'You want a hearth, you have to make it yourself.'

Without Halvar's aid they would have failed in the task of creating fire on a damp Scottish mountainside.

They spent their last reserves of energy finding bunches of heather and trying to generate a spark from flint and tinder. Halvar leaned in and showed them how, but even then they could only create a smoking smog of foliage. They were on the point of total mental collapse, when he finally relented and took charge. At last they had flame. They circled round, removed their boots for drying and took out their clay pots. Under the tutelage of Halvar, they cooked a bean and sausage stew, swallowing it ravenously with chunks of bread, washed down with fortifying wine which Freyja produced from her sack.

Only then did they swathe themselves in furs and begin to take notice of the other fire. The Perpetuals were eating their own stew and talking quietly, and their movement appeared unhindered by fatigue.

'Why are they here?' Brante asked.

'To test you,' Halvar replied, chewing on a piece of sausage. 'To see if they need to worry about you, or whether you're as horseshit as you look.'

With warm food in their bellies the Thralls wished only to nod off into oblivion, but Halvar wouldn't permit it. He shook them. 'Come. Your night's work isn't done yet. Leave your swords and shields, just bring your wits.'

They trooped out of the enclosure, watched by the Perpetuals, and followed him into the darkness. He stopped on the opposite hill flank and looked back at the fires. 'Imagine that's the stronghold of the Titan Sky-Rats. Imagine Alexander himself awaits capture within and all that's needed is for one of you to evade the guards and breach the wall. How will you accomplish it?' No one answered.

They were shivering again and only half listening. 'Rouse yourselves, you pathetic excuses for turds!'

'We'll select an individual defender and attack him as a group,' said Brante. 'Overpower him before the others can react.'

'There are two fires within those walls. The guards will see you coming.'

'We'll blacken our faces, come at a rush.'

'Anyone else still with us?'

'We split into pairs,' said Punnr. 'Two pairs rush the guards, draw their attention, while the final pair uses the dark as cover.'

'That sounds like a plan, laddie. I suggest you get to it if you want any sleep tonight.'

It was Punnr's idea and he found the others looking to him for leadership. They circled him and awaited his direction. He chose the bigger ones as the decoys – Brante and Hertha, Vidar and Erland. Once spotted, they would need to take the counterpunch of the Perpetuals. The final pair required stealth and lightness of foot, and it seemed natural that it should be himself and Calder.

He sent the other pairs left and right of the fires, telling them to circle wide and then come in from opposite directions, and they set off obediently, adrenaline dispersing the final vestiges of fatigue. The last he saw of them was Brante's bald head glowing in the starlight. He looked at Calder next to him. 'All set?'

She was wearing a fur hat and she tucked her hair into it as best she could, then dropped down and found damp earth to spread across her face. He copied her and then they walked shoulder to shoulder back towards the lights. As they got closer, Punnr realised two things. The Perpetuals were armed with wooden swords and shields. And he could only see six of them. He touched Calder's shoulder and they knelt. The visible defenders ringed the walled enclosure, black against the firelight, but they were bunched into two groups of three. One set patrolled the side facing down the valley and the other looked uphill. They had left a yawning gap in the path of Punnr and Calder. It looked so easy to rush through the heather and break into an unstoppable sprint for the wall.

'Where are the other two?' Calder whispered.

'I think they may be hiding in the shadow of the wall, waiting for us to make a run for it. Let's go forward, but very slowly.'

They progressed on hands and knees, listening and straining their eyes to make out movements by the wall. But their care meant their progress was slow and they were still fifty yards from the enclosure when they heard yells and saw the other Thralls attack. It was Brante and Hertha first, racing downhill out of the night, but they were clearly visible in the firelight and the three defenders locked shields and hurled into them. Brante knocked one almost flat, but the second one caught him with a blow from his wooden sword. The other three defenders didn't react to the commotion and remained staring downhill, so that when Vidar and Erland rushed at them, they too had time to brace. The combatants struck each other with an almighty clatter that echoed around the silent glen. Vidar was an unstoppable rhino and almost made it to the wall with two Perpetuals on either shoulder, but they beat at him and his momentum stalled. They collapsed in a pile of writhing, cursing bodies.

'We have to go,' Punnr whispered. 'In moments we'll have all of them recovered and looking for us.'

They rose to a crouch and crept forward. The enclosure looked so empty and inviting ahead. Another forty yards and they would be there.

'Welcome, arsehole.' The voice was no more than a whisper and so close to Punnr's ear that he felt its breath. He turned in bewilderment and looked straight into the face of the man with the effeminate mouth and black eyes whom he had goaded in the warehouse. He was unencumbered by sword and shield, a noiseless wraith in the night. 'We've been hunting you.'

Before Punnr could react, the man stepped back and threw him a punch that sent him sprawling. It was followed by the full weight of the man. Punnr felt his long hair grabbed and his skull thumped against the mountainside. Fingers found purchase on his face and sought his eyes. Desperately he forced his knee beneath his assailant and kicked. The man was knocked to the side and Punnr rolled on top, but before he could steady himself, his attacker coiled like a snake and rolled him again. A fist slammed into his face and then hands found his throat. He kicked and hit and squirmed, but it was no use. The hands clung on and crushed his windpipe. He saw stars and heard blood roaring in his ears. He tried to drag a breath but nothing came. The night grew deeper and he was falling and spinning and then it started to feel pleasant, like dropping through endless layers of leaves to a warm embracing mattress.

He was almost gone, when there was a voice. 'That's

enough children! Game over. We have a winner.' Punnr felt the man yanked from him and Halvar's rough hands were shaking his shoulder. 'Are you still with us, laddie?'

Punnr took a savage, hoarse breath, sucking the mountain air into his lungs, and his vision returned, along with an almighty pain across his face. He blinked up at Halvar and tried to nod. The Perpetual stood behind Halvar, rigid with anger, his jaw clenching and his hands still balled into fists. He stared at Punnr with raw hatred. Punnr shook his head and looked to his left where the female Perpetual was sprawled, holding her stomach. He forced himself to focus and twisted to stare over his shoulder. There, on the wall, silhouetted by the fires, arms raised in victory, stood Calder.

Halvar chuckled. 'Not a bad little missy, is she?'

Punnr wanted to laugh, but his face hurt too much. Halvar grabbed his arm and pulled him onto watery legs. 'Now shake and make up, ladies.'

The Perpetual approached and regarded Punnr with cold interest. He held out a slim hand and as Punnr took it he thought how those same fingers had moments earlier been around his throat.

'What are you called?' the Perpetual asked.

'Punnr.'

The man considered this. 'And I am Ulf, *the Wolf*.'

'You almost killed me.'

'That was my plan.'

XV

Dawn arrived with freezing inevitability and they were kicked awake. Calder's victory had invigorated the Thralls and they had celebrated long around their fire, sharing Freyja's wine and catcalling across to the sullen Perpetuals at the other fire. At last they had fallen into a dead slumber, wrapped in furs and watched over by Halvar.

Punnr stirred in the early light and looked over to see Brante grinning at him. Erland was already prodding at the fire. Hertha coughed and groaned somewhere to his right. Calder peeked at Punnr from her furs. Clouds had rolled in overnight and the morning was a damp grey monotone. Freyja showed them how to make a porridge from their millet. It was disgusting, but they wolfed it down and drank more of the sweetened wine. The two parties packed silently and then Halvar led the Thralls out onto the mountainside. They tracked through the wet grass and prayed that it wouldn't snow. When Punnr looked back at the enclosure, the Perpetuals had disappeared and all that remained were two limp smudges of smoke.

He had enough sense of direction to know Halvar took them in a much wider loop this time. They climbed west and pushed across new glens. By midday they were once more in the zone of the dead, walking without thought, spread out in a long line, muddied, and parched despite a thin rain that dripped from the cloud blanket. Again he and Brante took extra loads from Hertha and Vidar. Vidar refused to give them anything until he fell flat in a bog and then he limply allowed them to unburden him. Halvar forced them to take a high line along ridges with views of endless folds of grey land sweeping away north and west. They surprised deer and saw buzzards and even, once, an eagle just below the cloud base.

By dusk they had walked fifteen miles. Their bodies were greased, their hair matted and their clothing so caked they doubted it could even be peeled off. They pushed over a final rise and below them was the castle. There was firelight in the windows of the hall and now there were also lights in the keep and two silver Range Rovers parked at the front. As they stumbled downhill, Punnr felt Brante's arm come around his shoulder and then Vidar had an arm around his waist and Hertha and Calder joined too. They strode as a single unified line back to the Heart of the Horde. If they had looked, they would have seen Halvar grinning at Freyja, and realised that the whole exercise had been about team spirit. Throw every physical hardship at a group and see how they bond. Only Erland walked alone.

Once again Sveinn's Mead Hall was deserted and the fire burned unattended, but they sensed other company hidden somewhere in the heights of the keep. They washed in bowls of hot water they discovered in their rooms and returned to find a feast laid out. Nettle soup, roast venison and duck, chicken poached in wine, honey crumpets, warm bread. They drank mead and ale and wine, and one by one dropped into unconsciousness around the fire.

The next day, Halvar let them rest. There was no kick at dawn and when Punnr opened his eyes daylight was streaming through the windows, accompanied by the clatter of rain. They stirred slowly and let the morning drift. Halvar finally roused them to begin sword and shield training in a line down the hall. Later he showed them how to lock shields with their neighbour and how to advance as a unit. They practised and he cuffed them when they got it wrong, but they could see he was pleased with their progress. They continued the following day, glad not to be hiking in the rain. Freyja demonstrated how they should stab to the right in a shieldwall, rather than ahead. The whole formation relied on teamwork. Each individual stabbed at the foe to the right of his shield, thus protecting his neighbour in the line, while his companion on the left also struck right, so protecting his own front. They worked at it hour after hour and at the back of all their minds was a conviction that they would soon be facing the Perpetuals again.

His mother had been hit by the van as she walked from their estate. Eyewitnesses said it was a non-descript white Ford Transit which mounted the pavement and flung her against a wall, but no one had the presence of mind to obtain the number plate before it roared away.

The first Tyler knew of anything amiss was when his form teacher pulled him aside to tell him that his sister was waiting in the Headmistress' office. Wild horses would never drag Morgan back to that school, so Tyler knew something was dreadfully wrong and his fears were confirmed when he saw her perched on the little sofa opposite the secretary's desk, with shaking hands and wordless defeat in her eyes.

Morgan, he learned, had already been at the coroner's for two hours waiting to identify the body in advance of a post-mortem examination. Early conclusions were that their mother had died of massive internal bleeding in the ambulance at the site of the hit and run. Tyler accompanied his sister home and they drank sweet tea while they awaited the arrival of their aunt and uncle. Morgan quizzed him about what had been said before their mother's departure, but other than that she was quiet, mechanically clearing up kitchen things and tidying the sitting room, as though getting it ready for their mother's return.

It took four days to complete the autopsy and then Morgan – as the formal adult next-of-kin – received the death certificate and was able to agree the release of the body to a local funeral director's. They all went in their uncle's car to the funeral parlour and were escorted into the chapel of rest which was cold, and some distant part of Tyler's brain told him this was necessary because of the dead flesh. His mother's face looked surprisingly peaceful, but there was a sheen on her skin, as if it had been varnished, and the colour was yellowy white, like gloss paint left too many years without a fresh coat.

They refused to go with their aunt to her house in the Borders. The police visited on two occasions to ask background questions and to state that their enquiries hadn't yet led them to identify the driver of the van. Tyler spent his time out on the estate walking alone, letting his legs take him where they willed.

The funeral took place on a slate-grey Monday. A blustery wind whipped at the coattails of the undertakers and a few spots of rain sought out the downturned faces of the mourners as they filed into the chapel alongside the funeral parlour. It was a small group, just colleagues from the supermarket where their mother had manned the checkout and a smattering of friends from the estate. Morgan exuded tragic strength, but there was a vulnerability to Tyler which he had striven to hide as he gave the reading. His voice had cracked twice and he had been forced to pause, staring at the bible verses, never looking up from the lectern at the faces before him.

Over the coming weeks, Morgan dealt with the many legal details without fuss. They received visits from Social Services who questioned Tyler. They looked into his schooling and Morgan dispatched herself to the Job Centre. Eventually, after interminable bureaucracy, she was able to sign a new tenancy agreement with the local council which allowed them to remain in the flat.

Tyler reached sixteen and thrust a departing finger at a school that was just as pleased to see the back of him. He signed on and made half-hearted attempts at employment, but he could stick at nothing for long and the money his sister provided only encouraged him to grow desultory and wanton, and to lose sight of any direction that his life might have hoped to take.

The one activity that did arouse an interest in him was dabbling in soft drug deals around the estate. Such transactions were closely controlled by the local gangs and if they caught him he would be beaten to a pulp, yet the threat of this very real danger was his only natural high, the stimulus that got his heart beating and forced him out of the front door each night.

XVI

Calder hunched by the glowing embers of the fire in the Mead Hall. It was the fourth morning of their stay and she felt like hell without her coffee. Her body protested against the hardships, not only the rigours of training but also the unremitting pressure of the stone floor they lay on each night, the cold of which no quantity of furs could alleviate. She stretched her neck muscles. In these bitter dawns she would rather be anywhere than this lonely castle.

Brante passed her a cup of warm water with honey and she sipped gratefully, watching the smoke from the fire loop up to the hole in the ceiling. She liked the tall man. A quiet care radiated from him and she found herself drawn to him, perhaps even pleased that this mad adventure had sent her life colliding into his. She hadn't felt that way for many years about a man – certainly not Justin – and it frightened her that she might be letting a barrier down.

Halvar was inspecting their wooden weapons stacked by one wall, but he seemed in no hurry to rouse the Thralls. She watched his hulking frame. His head was bent over a shield, his cropped hair matted and uncombed. His chin was covered in its usual stubble and it struck her that in all the months she had known him his beard had never grown longer, yet neither had it been shaved clean. She decided his unkempt look was, in fact, carefully cultivated. She studied the swirling tattoos on his massive arms and found herself wondering about his personal life.

The Perpetuals had joined them around the flames the previous night. Together they had shared meat, bread and fruit and eased their fatigue with alcohol, but there had been no conversation. She could see from their hardened bodies and the way they nibbled their food that these Lost Children had endured regimes of discipline, asceticism and sacrifice. They took their lead from Ulf, who sat cross-legged and stared belligerently at the Thralls. At the end of the evening, the Perpetuals rose as one and departed and the remaining six settled in their furs and talked quietly, although mostly they were silent and, one by one, drifted off to sleep.

They spent the morning outside duelling with wooden swords and shields under the watchful eyes of the Housecarls. At midday they stopped to eat bread and cheese and wash it down with cold water. Then Halvar led them back into the hall and they saw they were no longer alone. The fire had been raked and the benches cleared to the sides to leave a large area of empty stone floor. On the raised dais were three new figures. Two of them were Vigiles, helmeted to hide their faces. The third was clean-shaven, with short grey hair, fleshy cheeks and soft eyes, and dressed in purple robes like a priest. He sat on a chair on one side of the dais with a goblet of wine resting in his hand.

'Welcome,' he said as they lined up in front of the dais. 'My name is Atilius, Praetor of the Pantheon. I have heard a great deal about the six of you.' Then he waved to Halvar and sat back with a smile twitching on his lips.

'Right, you bunch of clods, look sharp. Place your weapons where I'm standing. Then split yourselves in a circle.'

Calder felt nervous adrenaline tickling up her spine as she complied. She noticed two tripods set up at opposite corners with video cameras mounted on them. They were being filmed.

Punnr was next to her, unstrapping his shield. 'Forget about the cameras,' he murmured.

'I will,' she replied under her breath.

The six of them sorted themselves and stood in a ring, facing the pile of weapons at the centre. Calder could sense the seated man behind her and, despite Punnr's advice, she found herself wondering who was watching from beyond the cameras. She had Vidar on one side and Hertha on the other. Erland was across from her, with Brante and Punnr either side of him. She took a deep breath and steeled herself.

Halvar strode around the wooden weapons. 'If you receive a strike anywhere on your torso, you are out. Last one standing wins. Any questions?' His expression dared them to venture any. 'Good. You've an audience today, so don't disappoint them.' He strode to the edge of the circle, then turned to the seated man, who waved magnanimously. 'Alright, you maggots,' the Housecarl bellowed. 'Begin!'

Before she could react, Calder sensed Vidar and Hertha fly forward. Brante was already there, shouldering against Erland. Too late, her legs released her and she dashed after them, only then understanding what everyone else seemed to know, that half the battle would be won before weapons were even in hand.

She caught movement at the corner of her eye and knew

Hertha already had her wooden sword and was arcing it down onto her. Without thinking Calder hauled her shield above her stooping frame. She only had a half-hold on the grip, but it was enough to catch the blow. She grabbed her sword and sprang backwards from the melee. Hertha braced and came towards her and Calder realised Vidar was also singling her out. Both approached her with shields raised to their chins.

Hertha launched herself and Calder had only an instant to bring her sword to parry. They locked together and pushed. Calder looked at the other girl's face inches from her own. Over the weeks they had developed a quiet bond of friendship – of sisterhood among the men – but that didn't hinder the competitive spirit driving them both. She shoved Hertha away and then crashed after her, pushing her several yards across the stones. The larger girl was off-balance and Calder knew she had her. She brought her sword arm through in a flowing stab, aiming below the raised shield and driving the point into her opponent's stomach. Hertha grunted in exasperation.

'A hit!' Halvar bellowed. 'Get yourself out of the fight, missy.'

Calder didn't even pause, she turned and brought her shield up, knowing already that Vidar must be taking his chance. His sword clattered against the wood and she scuttled backwards to give herself a moment of respite. They circled each other. Around them, she sensed the others struggling, and she heard Halvar calling again. Vidar stepped forward and lunged. He was so strong and she knew that any blow from him would seriously hurt, but he was also slow. She managed to bring her shield down and knock the wooden blade's trajectory to one side. He tried again, stabbing at her right side, then bringing his shield forward in a punch. She gasped and back-pedalled.

The motion brought her near Punnr. He was locked in a struggle with Erland and their momentum took them between her and Vidar. The pair seemed to have renewed their duel from the vault when Erland's nose had been crushed. They had managed to wrap their shields around each other and were pressed so close that neither could find space to bring their swords to bear. They were snarling, teeth gritted. In her seconds of respite, she wondered where Brante was and realised with surprise that he was already beaten and leaning disconsolately against the far wall.

In the same moment, Punnr pushed Erland away from him and with his sword arm free, he prepared to strike. But he was so focused on his opponent that he failed even to consider the remaining Thralls. Almost apologetically, Vidar took one step forward to Punnr's back and poked him in the lower kidney with the end of his sword. Punnr turned with a look of surprise. The hall held its breath.

'That's a hit,' said Halvar. 'Get out of there, laddie.'

Punnr kept his feet rooted in place. The adrenaline was still surging through him and he seemed unable to compute what had just happened. Erland had hit Brante right from the off, before the taller man had even picked up his weapon, and Punnr had been struggling with the bastard for all the rest of the exercise. He wasn't prepared for it to be over so quickly – in this way. He gulped and tried to control the fire in his belly.

Perhaps Erland should have contained his own fire. Instead he gloated at his conquered adversary. 'You heard the Housecarl. Go on, piss off.'

Something snapped in Punnr. With a yell, he launched once more into the man, lunging with his sword. Erland was taken backwards, but stayed on his feet. Punnr struck again and again, swearing aloud, not caring about the others, just wanting to hurt him. He felt Halvar's bulk driving in to separate them and began striking Halvar instead. Thump, thump. He swung at Halvar, his sword hitting him on both shoulders.

'Bastard!' he found himself yelling.

Then Halvar was in his face, a huge fist blocking his next strike and the other one grabbing him by the throat. 'Stand down!' he bellowed in Punnr's face. 'Stand. Down!'

Punnr pushed himself away, but lowered his weapon. 'Why should I?' he spat back. 'We play your bloody games again and again. Never questioning. Just doing whatever *Lord* Halvar says! I'm sick of it! All you ever tell us is we're going to have to fight the Perpetuals and only seven of us will succeed. If that's what all these months have been about, just to get us ready to fight those fucking Perpetuals, then I'm sick of your bloody games. Just let us get on with it!'

'Why, you little runt…' Halvar stepped towards him.

'Perhaps a moment of calm?' The voice was soft, yet it cut through the hall and stilled everyone. The purple-robed figure had walked to the edge of the dais and was watching proceedings, still with a slight smile on his lips. 'Well, well, Punnr.' His smile broadened, though it was glacial. 'So now we meet. And I must say I'm not disappointed.'

Punnr stood motionless, breathing heavily. He could

sense Halvar glaring at him and Erland standing against the wall, rocking from side to side. It was obvious from the young man's body language that in those last few seconds, any loyalty he felt to his fellow Thralls lay shredded like a rabbit's carcass beneath the crows.

'You are frightened,' said Atilius. 'It is natural. You are frightened and you want to know what the future brings. I understand. So ask me what you wish.'

Punnr looked around him uncertainly. Brante was rigid. Calder paler than new snow. He turned back to the Praetor. 'Will we face our deaths against the Perpetuals?'

'Only time and circumstance will determine that.'

'When?'

'Tomorrow.'

The hall was still. None of them had expected the answer to be so direct. Punnr sought for words. 'How will we face them?'

'That has yet to be confirmed. The rules of the *Sine Missione* are fluid and change each year depending on the number of initiates. Some seasons Valhalla may only have one or two Thralls, sometimes none at all, depending on their Blood Funds. But I'll tell you this. Tomorrow at dawn you will enter the field of the *Sine Missione* and you'll be expected to seek out a tower. When dusk comes we will collect you, and the seven who are in the tower will be taken forward to the Oath-Taking.'

'Will we be armed when we enter the field? With real blades?'

'No.'

'Will the Perpetuals?'

'No.'

Punnr felt his exasperation rising again, but could find no words for another question. Atilius watched him, then spoke again. 'All warriors are frightened before conflict. Even our most experienced warlords. But that is no sign of weakness. I've monitored your progress over these weeks and I've watched you today. You are ready to face what lies ahead. You all are. You have come this far readily enough without turning back. So don't falter now. Have faith. You have fire in your bellies. You are ready.'

He stepped awkwardly down from the dais and suddenly beamed and clapped his hands. 'Enough talk. You are fine warriors. Bring them wine!'

The spell broke. Freyja disappeared through the door at the end of the hall and returned with a tray of beakers and a clay jug. She began distributing the wine among the group, serving the robed man first. The two Vigiles seemed unmoved by what they had seen and went about dismantling the cameras without eye contact.

Halvar approached Punnr, his eyes hard but his voice low. 'You know what you just felt, boy? Battle rage. It's powerful stuff and I suggest you bottle it, ready for tomorrow.'

Very slowly the tension leaked from the room and Calder felt herself begin to tremble as the waves of adrenaline that had flooded her body receded. Hertha approached her and smiled cautiously. 'Well done.'

'Thanks,' Calder replied dully, sinking onto a bench.

Hertha hesitated, then sat next to her. 'How have we got ourselves to this point?'

'By turning up every night, by getting in the cars. We've allowed it to happen.'

'Are we fools?'

Calder looked at her friend. She could see the girl was frightened, but she herself felt strangely calm. 'No, we're not. We've taken this path with open minds and they've made no secret of the risks. I think we know it's right to be here, otherwise we would have stepped away already.' She reached out and squeezed the girl's arm. 'You stick with me tomorrow and you'll be okay. We'll all stick together.'

Hertha nodded and smiled, bringing her hand up to clasp Calder's. 'I'd like that.'

'Drink,' said Halvar approaching and handing beakers to them.

Calder gulped at the liquid and kept dragging it down her throat until the beaker was empty. She noticed the purple-robed man speaking seriously with Freyja, who looked flustered. She was trying to make points, but being overruled. There was sunshine peeping through the western windows and a hint of blue sky, and Calder suddenly needed to get away. She passed her beaker to Hertha, patted her on the knee, then rose and strode out of the hall.

The air outside hit her with its freshness and she realised how much the interior stank of smoke and sweat. She breathed in and tried to calm her shaking. The sky was blanketed with low cloud, but in places it was broken, as though eaten away by moths, and sunlight flooded through these holes, spotlighting sections of hillside, here and there setting a mountain afire. There was sunshine on the loch as well, sparkling the rippled surface and colouring it an exquisite blue. She walked down and found a small pebbly beach where she could crouch and study the water.

Something jumped and splashed further out. A grebe appeared from some reeds and bobbed before her, oblivious of her presence.

She heard a sound behind and turned to see Punnr. He was carrying a fur wrap and he placed it over her shoulders, then settled himself on a rock a few yards along the shore. Brante was making his way down the slope as well. She picked up a pebble and tossed it into the loch, forcing the grebe to make a rapid retreat. Brante arrived with beakers and a jug.

'I've probably had enough,' said Calder.

'A bit more won't do you any harm.'

She took a beaker and sipped at it as she watched the loch.

'I'm sorry about all that,' Punnr said without looking at them.

'Erland deserved it,' said Brante.

Calder contemplated the loch. 'I told Hertha we'd all stick together tomorrow.'

'All except Erland,' Brante replied.

'We'll keep a wary eye on him. But, if the rest of us stay together, we'll get through.'

Brante lobbed a stone. 'It sounds to me like we just have to get to some tower before the Perpetuals and then hold it until we're collected at dusk. So, as soon as we enter the field tomorrow, we grab Hertha and Vidar and the five of us make for high ground to locate the tower, then speed march direct to it. We don't stop for anything, we don't divert and we don't let those bastard Perpetuals try any stunts. Agreed?'

The other two nodded. 'Agreed.'

There was movement and they were startled to see Freyja join them on the beach and squat down too. 'That was an interesting demonstration,' she said. 'Not what we were expecting.'

'Who was the man in the robes?' Brante asked.

'As he said, he is called Atilius, Praetor of the Pantheon. He's important. You'll learn more after the *Sine Missione* tomorrow.'

'Without Mercy,' said Calder thoughtfully. 'Why are so many things in Latin?'

'It's the way of the Pantheon. They say that the Pantheon first began with Caesar and the Legion. So the rules were drawn up on a Roman basis and Latin is used for all the key events which are common across the Palatinates. We then add our own Valhalla Viking flourishes. Hence, if you join the Horde, you'll find we're structured as a true Viking army and we have our Viking customs and ancient Norse names, yet our actions are ordered around major Pantheon ceremonies which are Roman in essence.' She looked at each of them and they could see she wanted to say more, but was trying to hold back. They waited and eventually she spoke. 'I've just been informed that the rules tomorrow have been changed.'

'What's that supposed to mean?' Brante demanded.

'You will go into the field in pairs – and you are likely to find your companion is a Perpetual.'

'Shit,' Brante swore.

'It just gets better and better,' Punnr smiled thinly, staring out across the water.

Freyja continued. 'It's highly unusual to change the rules. Normally they send everyone into the field together and in that scenario my advice would be to keep it that way, work together and get to the tower. But this time it's going to be different, so don't trust your partner. Get yourself on your own as soon as you can and stay that way until you can find another Thrall.' She cut herself off. 'I've said as much as I should.'

Calder looked at her for several long moments and then said, 'Tell us this, Freyja, and tell us truthfully. Is the Pantheon worth it?'

'Yes. I believe it is. If you become Oathsworn, you'll have many, many occasions when your lives are at risk. Such sacrifice is expected of you. But the rewards outweigh those risks. In the Pantheon there is honour; there is valour; there is adventure; and, above all, there is comradeship. You will stand shoulder-to-shoulder with comrades in arms.'

'Unity,' breathed Brante.

'Yes, unity. Like nothing you find in the real world.' She let her words sink in, then said in a new tone, 'But you can still step away. You are not yet Oathsworn. You need only give me your amulets.'

Calder stared out across the loch and thought about her little flat by the banks of the Leith and about Justin in his office somewhere in the city and her mother in Kirkcudbright.

'I'm in,' she said.

Punnr looked at her. 'Me too.'

'Aye,' said Brante.

Freyja stood. 'So be it. Go carefully tomorrow. Don't trust the Perpetuals. By day's end you will have aged, you will be wiser – and you may be crueller. But you're all good enough for this and soon we will welcome you into the Horde.'

*

The arrival of the Valhalla Caelestis at the castle was understated. No helicopter landing on the front lawn. No underlings rushing to their positions. No procession up the grand steps. Instead a single Range Rover bore him through the dark and drew up at a little noticed side door to the keep. Wearing a hooded cowl over his head, he slipped from the vehicle's comfortable interior and crossed the few metres of gravel.

A lone figure waited for him. 'My lord Odin.'

'Atilius. I might have known you'd be here.'

'Tomorrow is an important day. I would be negligent in my duties if I wasn't present to ensure its smooth running.'

Odin brushed past him, ascended the stairs and entered his quarters at the top of the keep. The lighting, heat, bed linen and bathroom fittings were all the best money could buy, but these modern embellishments were subtle. In all other respects, the rooms retained their ancient ambience. Thick stone walls, tiny windows, oak flooring, deep hearths alight with flame, tapestries, rugs, simple wooden furniture.

'So it begins,' he said over his shoulder, pulling off his cowl and taking it into the bedroom.

'It does indeed, lord,' Atilius replied. 'The Nineteenth Season.'

'Is that goddamn Radspakr here?'

'He is delayed. But will be with us before tomorrow's events are over.'

Odin strode back into the main room. There was wine

and coffee left on the table. He poured a single goblet of wine and drank deeply. 'Is everything set?'

'It is, lord. Halvar and Freyja have your Valhalla Thralls in the main hall. And the Perpetuals are in the further wing.'

He took his goblet over to the fire to warm himself. 'Six Thralls and eight Perpetuals,' he said, staring at the flames. 'And at the end I take seven. I assume the sensible money's on the Perpetuals?'

'Perhaps, lord, and perhaps not. The Thralls are an interesting bunch.'

'They'd better make it worth my damn time.'

'I believe they will.' Atilius paused. He still stood in the doorway, his purple robes shimmering under a spotlight embedded in the ceiling. 'The Lord High Caelestis has suggested a change to the usual groupings... to make it more interesting.'

'Oh really?'

'Only with your blessing, naturally. You are the Valhalla Caelestis. This is your *Sine Missione*.'

'And what, pray, has our bloody Lord High Caelestis suggested?'

'Pairings. One Thrall to one Perpetual. It will add to the tension of the day.'

'It will add to the number of goddamn unfortunate incidents, that's what it will do.'

'Indeed, lord.'

Odin poured another drink and seated himself at the end of the table. 'Do it. As long as I have seven at the end.'

'You will, my lord. You may rest assured.'

'Now bugger off, Atilius. I wish to shower.'

XVII

The vehicles bounced along a stony track in the half light of dawn. The sky was just pale enough to make out the black masses of hills on either side and the headlights captured glimpses of moorland rolling away into nothingness. It had snowed overnight, little more than a dusting, but enough to lend a ghostly eeriness. The going was rough and the vehicles threw their passengers around as they lurched through potholes and forded gushing mountain burns.

The convoy comprised four mud-streaked Land Rovers, and Punnr sat with Calder, Vidar and Brante in the third. They had breakfasted in the hall and Freyja had encouraged them to eat heartily of the porridge, sausages, crumpets and warm wine, but, in truth, none of them had found the appetite to force much down their throats. It had been a subdued affair, lit only by a small fire in the hearth. Halvar and Freyja were studious in speaking with each of them, giving them quiet words of encouragement and patting them on the shoulders as they passed, but their actions only served to heighten the tension. It was obvious that their journey with these Housecarls was coming to an end of some kind that day and the ending was as yet unwritten.

They were dressed in their usual boots and black trousers, along with woollen fleeces and fur hats. In addition, each wore a body length cloak which had been placed upon their shoulders by Halvar and then fastened around their necks with a silver clasp in the shape of the Triple Horn of Odin. That was all. None of them had been provided with provisions, tools or spare garments, and Calder stared out at the cold darkness beyond the windows and fiddled nervously with her Odin clasp.

To their left was a high deer fence which had been running alongside the track for most of the hour they had been travelling. Every mile or so they came to a tower with a gate beneath it. The edges of the towers bristled with wire and Calder doubted such defences were needed simply to stop roaming deer. They were there to enclose something else and she wondered what awaited within.

They reached another of the towers and this time the convoy ground to a halt. Two more 4x4s were waiting just off the track, their headlights illuminating the fence, and Calder thought she could see someone standing at the top of the tower. A figure detached itself from the darkness and pulled open the passenger door. It was a Vigilis, not helmeted on this occasion, but with a thick scarf and a fur hat pulled so far down that they could see little more than his moustache and the black eyes above.

'Which of you is Brante?' he asked brusquely, craning his neck to look into the back.

'Here.'

'Get out.'

Brante opened his door and dropped to the ground,

hugging his cloak around him in the chill. Punnr made to step out as well.

'Just him,' said the Vigilis and then stalked along to the vehicle in front. After a few more words they saw one of the Perpetuals alight as well.

Brante looked back at them and nodded grimly. 'This seems to be where we part company.' He held the door and the steam from his breath swirled in.

On an impulse, Punnr offered his hand.

Brante grasped it. 'Whatever they throw at us, stay safe all of you. And let's find each other in there as soon as we can.'

He slammed the door and the vehicle began to bump away. Punnr watched him from the back window and saw him walking over to the Perpetual before the figures disappeared from his view.

Every mile they came to another tower and they found more vehicles waiting and the procedure repeated itself. A different Vigilis came to the cars and two individuals were ordered to alight. At the third stop their door was wrenched open and Vidar was told to step out. In the growing light of dawn, Punnr saw that the other figure was Ulf. A bleak sense of foreboding rolled through his stomach.

'Be careful my friend,' he said to Vidar. 'That one is a snake.'

'I won't take my eyes from him, Punnr.'

A mile further and it was Punnr's turn to be called. He looked at Calder and felt a surge of reluctance to abandon her. 'Good luck,' was all he could think to say.

'You too.' She looked fragile and wan, and he could see her pale face watching him as the car bumped away.

Once the convoy had been lost along the track, an intense silence descended. The song of countless miles of empty land muffled by snow. One of the Perpetuals was standing a short distance away, cloak wrapped around him, and the Vigilis who had called them was striding back to a parked car. Punnr heard a noise above him and saw another figure in the tower pointing a video camera right back at him.

Irritated, Punnr headed to the Perpetual. He was of a similar height and build, with scraggy ginger hair and a thin beard, sallow complexion, and calculating blue eyes. He looked Punnr up and down, taking the measure of him.

'We're on film again,' Punnr commented, but the other man didn't reply. 'I'm Punnr.' He held out his hand.

The Perpetual paused, then took it. 'I know. I'm called Gulbrand.'

Punnr looked at the fence and the land beyond. The growing visibility was beginning to reveal a vast valley cosseted by icy mountain flanks. There were patches of heather moorland, white in the dim light and surrounded by forest. The trees began not far from the fence line, sterile ranks of conifer through which no light could penetrate and under which only carpets of dropped needles would be found. But lower down towards a river, it seemed as though the trees became much less tightly packed and were larger, with vegetation clumped around them. Far beyond the river a single hill struggled from the grips of the forest and on its summit was a tower.

'What happens now?'

'Your guess is as good as mine,' said Gulbrand, but Punnr sensed he knew more than he was choosing to say.

The Vigilis emerged again from the car and walked over

to them. 'Follow,' he snapped and led them to the gate. He unlocked it, but didn't pull it open. Instead, he looked at the two of them, his long moustache damp in the morning air. 'You have until dusk. Be at the tower then and you'll be collected.'

He lapsed into silence again, one hand still on the handle of the gate. Punnr stamped his feet and listened to the man coughing in the tower above. Then the peace was shattered by a single long mournful horn which reverberated off the distant faces of the mountains. The Vigilis yanked open the gate and herded them through.

'Go,' he commanded, waving them towards the forest. 'Go!'

Calder was the last from her vehicle. She had watched Punnr's figure disappear from view, then sat rigid in the back as the driver took her a further mile along the track. When he stopped she didn't wait for the Vigilis, but stepped out into the cold and looked across to where the final Perpetual was also alighting. He stood next to the car and returned her look. With much noise and bumping, the vehicles turned and headed back along the track, leaving the two cloaked figures alone with a Vigilis who emerged from a parked car.

The snow was soft beneath her boots and would soon turn to slush as it melted. She shivered under her cloak and saw a man in the tower leaning forward and aiming a video camera straight at her. She gave him an imperious look and walked across to the Perpetual.

'Hello,' she said. He had removed his fur hat and she

could see his curly black hair and pimples. No more than a boy. 'What are you called?'

'Einar.'

'And what does Einar mean.'

'The one who fights alone.'

Calder wasn't certain she liked the idea of that. 'I'm Calder, which I am told means *cold waters*.'

'I know,' he replied stiffly.

The Vigilis approached, gave them their instructions and took them over to the gate. The man above was leaning right over the parapet to ensure he captured their every move on film. Then the horn echoed across the valley and the Vigilis began pushing them through the gate.

'That way,' he said, pointing down the obvious path between the ranks of pine, then he stalked back to the warmth of his waiting car, his duty performed.

Calder and Einar began to walk. The trees closed in and despite the growing daylight, they could only see past the first two or three trunks before darkness prevailed once more. The snow was slippery underfoot and their breath plumed around them. On a tree to their right, Calder noticed a camera fixed to the trunk with a large battery pack strapped next to it. It turned as they walked by, following their progress. She didn't know if Einar had noticed, but she decided not to say.

There was absolute quiet except for the squelch of their boots. No birdsong danced through the branches, no forest resident ferreted in the needles beneath. Even the slight breeze she had felt beside the cars couldn't pierce this far onto the path. She listened to Einar breathing near her and thought about Freyja's warning. *Get yourself on your own as quickly as you can.* But the forest was impenetrable. There was nowhere to go but ahead. She stole a glance at her companion. He looked young and strained and she thought he should be in school uniform. His hands were inside the folds of his cloak and she wondered if he concealed anything.

'What do you think we should be doing?' She put voice to her questions.

'Just keep walking.'

'Did they tell you much about the *Sine Missione*?'

'Only that if we look carefully, we'll find all we need.'

He stopped. They had reached a fork in the trail. There was another camera perched on a trunk and Calder stared at it, again wondering what eyes lay behind.

'Which way?' the boy asked. 'You can choose.'

Both paths looked identical, angling away from each other through the trees and thinning so that they would be forced to progress in single file. She feared their empty stillness. 'Perhaps we should each take a different one? If we find anything we can shout to the other.'

Einar looked at her uneasily. 'No,' he said slowly. 'We stay together.'

'If we split, we'll be more able to cover the ground. We could agree to meet back here in fifteen minutes once we've scouted both routes.'

Einar shifted his gaze between each path. 'Safer to remain together.'

Calder wanted desperately to get away from him, but dared not flee down one of them in case he pursued. 'Okay,' she said, trying to sound resolute. 'Let's take the left, it's leading in the direction of where the others must be.'

They stepped off and as the trees tightened around them, he stood aside and waved his arm to let her lead. She tried to make him go first, but he wouldn't move and so she walked steadfastly ahead. Now she no longer looked to the side or worried about what perils might lie in front, she only listened for his tread behind and thought of his hands beneath his cloak, and her neck burned where she imagined his eyes upon her.

Punnr and Gulbrand had been walking for almost an hour. What little snow had managed to fall through the trees was now turning to slush and the path was treacherous underfoot. They reached a place where the woods opened out, but the ground between was boggy and sucked at their boots. Punnr swore as his leg sank up to the knee, but to his surprise, Gulbrand grabbed his arm and pulled him out. They made it to the other side and the trees arranged themselves back around a single path. Gulbrand strode ahead and Punnr followed.

'Why does Ulf hate us Thralls so much?' he found himself asking aloud.

'Ulf is a friend to no one.'

'But he's detested us from the moment he set eyes on us in the abandoned warehouse.'

'Isn't the reason obvious?'

Punnr thought about it. 'I goaded him that night.'

'Ulf hates you because he's spent years under the yoke of the Valhalla Schola, years of discipline and training. And what for? So he can get to this point – here and now – with a chance to enter Valhalla as a Thegn. And then you six Thralls turn up with a few months' preparation and you're offered the same opportunity. Do you think he finds that fair? Do you think he's going to let you take his chance away?' He shot Punnr a brief look. 'Do you think any of us is?'

They came upon a stream and they had to track along the bank until they could find rocks to step across. It was precarious, but both made it to the other side dry. They walked back to the path where the trees were thinning. Punnr was watching his footing and didn't notice that Gulbrand had stopped until he almost walked right into him. He froze behind the stationary figure and peered passed him. Ahead the track led into a clearing, where an ancient tree rose, its trunk the breadth of two men and its roots contorting across the ground. Laid out against the base of the trunk was a sack, two shields and two swords. But these weren't the ponderous wooden training tools they had been using. They were iron, real and razor sharp.

Gulbrand looked from side to side, checking that the forest remained silent. Without a word, he began walking towards the tree. Punnr followed, quickening his pace. Gulbrand strode even faster and Punnr felt a sudden panic. They reached the tree together and both snatched a sword and faced each other. Punnr thought how weightless the blade felt compared to the wooden ones, but also how perfectly balanced and brilliantly sharp.

'So are we supposed to kill each other now?' he asked. 'Is that how we get down to seven?'

Gulbrand nodded grimly. 'Yes. Why do you think there's a camera above your head?'

Christ. Punnr gripped his weapon and tried to think, not daring to take his eyes from his adversary.

'However,' Gulbrand continued cautiously, 'I'm not sure it would be the most sensible course of action.'

'What's that supposed to mean?'

'With shields and working as a pair, we can defend ourselves effectively if we meet the others.'

'And how long do you suggest we work as a pair? Just until my back's turned?'

Gulbrand didn't answer, but instead he straightened slowly, never taking his eyes from Punnr, and lowered his blade. 'It's our best chance of making it to the tower.'

Punnr struggled with his panicked mind. *Get yourself on your own*, Freyja had told them, but what Gulbrand was saying made sense. Better, at least, than a one-on-one life battle right there beneath that bloody camera.

'Okay.' He tried to sound confident and lowered his blade. The two men studied each other warily. 'What's in the sack?'

Gulbrand pulled at the cord, still watching Punnr, then took a quick look inside. 'Provisions,' he said. He hunched down on a root and placed his sword close beside him. Then he pulled out a flatbread and flung it over to Punnr. 'There's cheese as well. We eat a little now and take the rest with us. We don't know if it will be our last.'

Brante had been following his companion at a distance for over an hour. They had exchanged no words since the gate, when Brante had introduced himself and even offered his hand. The man had replied to say he was Eluf, but he had been nervous and hostile, refusing to shake hands and wanting only to get through the gate. He was shorter than

Brante, but broad at the shoulder and waist, and had a habit of clearing his throat and spitting.

When the horn cut through the silence, the Perpetual strode off at pace in the direction of the far hill. The land in this sector wasn't forested for the first part and they had a clear line of progress down through the heather moorland towards the sloping valley bottom. Brante had been uncertain about his strategy. Should he angle away from the figure in front, put distance between them and then lose him altogether once they reached the treeline, or was it better to keep the man in sight? He went for the second option and followed Eluf down the slope, leaving about thirty yards between them.

Occasionally the Perpetual looked back, but mostly he peered from side to side as though searching for something, his cloak brushing the snow powder from the low heather. They crossed a stream and then an area strewn with boulders. The daylight strengthened, but the sun was lost behind a blanket of cloud which leached the land of colour, painting the whole scene in the black, white and grey pallet of an old photograph. Their russet-red cloaks were the only splash of contrast.

As time passed, Brante became more apprehensive. He felt exposed on the open hillside and didn't like the way Eluf kept looking around. His companion was slanting northwards across the slope towards a forested area where the next pair had probably been let loose. On this open ground, the two of them would be spotted easily by the other group. Did that matter? He made up his mind that once they reached the trees, he would let the man get well ahead and then set off in a different direction. Better to be alone.

The stocky Perpetual was almost to the trees and was peering into them. Then he checked back at Brante and made a sudden change of direction, veering down the slope. Brante also altered his course and when the man realised he was still being followed, he broke into a run. *What the hell?* Brante thought, his heart spiking. He stared into the woods and checked behind, but he could see nothing untoward. *What's the bastard up to?* He broke into a jog, tracking after the receding figure.

The man was moving faster, angling towards the trees further down the slope, wanting to get somewhere before his adversary. Brante threw himself forward. *What the hell is he doing?*

And then it was clear. Spears! Shields too. Positioned against a trunk so that anyone coming from the open land should detect them. *Oh my sweet god!* He accelerated. His long legs churned up the yards. *Feet don't fail me now. Don't catch on the heather and send me sprawling.* The other man was labouring heavily across the ground, but he had a twenty-five-yard lead.

If the weapons had been a dozen paces further, Brante would have caught him. But they were not. He was too far behind. The Perpetual would get there seconds before him. Brante hit the brakes, his feet pedalling frantically on the slope. *Got to get out of here, off this open ground!* His ankles screamed as he veered towards the wood. Eluf reached the tree, slammed right into the trunk and grabbed both spears, then spun around and brought his right arm up ready to throw.

Brante fled across the last few metres of open ground, but it seemed to him now that his legs were as heavy as stone and his entire cloaked back stretched wide. Any moment the spear would thrust into his spine. There was a rush of air behind his neck and the smack of something into the heather upslope, and he knew the man had missed. The world rushed back to him and he flew into the forest. He ran blindly, crashing into trunks and slipping on the needle carpet. Spiky pine branches whipped at his face. His cloak slowed him and he wrenched at it, tearing the Odin clasp and leaving the garment caught on the branches. He thought the Perpetual would let him flee into the thick fastness of the woods, but then he heard the man in pursuit. He was coming at him low between the trunks, carrying the other spear.

'Eluf, this is madness! Let's take a spear and shield each and we can go together to the tower.' But the time for bonding had been on the walk in.

Brante altered direction, crashed through a low-hung section of pine and weaved around more trees, but the mass of the forest flowed ahead. He grabbed a trunk and spun around. Eluf could never throw the spear in such conditions, but he could gut him if he got within stabbing range. Then something caught his eye at the edge of the trees.

He turned and fled deeper. Eluf came with him. He was breathing heavily, but his smaller stature made it easier for him under the canopy. Brante subtly changed direction and angled uphill, then began to head back towards the light. He peered through the trunks and panicked because he had lost sight of what he had seen a few moments before. He must find it. He couldn't risk heading out onto the open hillside at the wrong spot.

Yes. There it is! The man was cutting back across his

path, closing in towards him. Fifteen yards. Ten. They would be together in moments and the Perpetual could drive his blade through Brante's back. But the object was still there. The discarded cloak, hanging in the tree like a beacon in the black shadows of the forest, telling him exactly where he was on the hillside. He tore past it and out into the vast openness of the heather moorland. *Please god, let me be right.* Eluf was only steps behind him, his breath wheezing and panting. *Where is it? Where the hell is it?*

And then he saw it. He flung himself onto the heather and rolled up onto one knee facing his charging assailant. A camera on a tree nearby monitored everything in unblinking silence. It saw the fleshy young face of the Perpetual frozen in surprise. It saw the thin rivulet of scarlet blood slip from the corner of his mouth, bright against the monotone glen. And it saw the first spear embedded blade-deep in his gut.

It was late morning and Calder had been walking with Einar for several hours. They had broken free of the plantation pines and were moving down the hillside through a more open area. It was beautiful and in different circumstances Calder would have wanted to dally and soak in the views. Ancient Caledonian pines stood scattered at wide intervals, more like oaks than conifers. Heather and blaeberry grew in abundance, perfect habitat for a range of Highland wildlife such as grouse, capercaillie, pine marten and wildcat. There were birds now. Groups of tiny crested tits milling from one tree to the next. The snow was gone and the place had come to life after the still of the forest.

In this more open space she tried to keep a distance from

Einar, but he stayed never more than a dozen yards away and if she shifted direction, he changed as well. When his eyes weren't on her, they were shifting across the landscape. They reached the river at the valley bottom and found it was full with meltwater and much wider than they had expected.

'Left or right?' he asked.

Right led to the valley head and the slope steepened. Left seemed flatter and easier. She indicated in that direction and they walked along the bank, looking for an opportunity to cross. The water was loud and the tumult added an edge to her fear because now she couldn't even hear him. She tried to keep him in the corner of her eye, but whenever she lost him, she panicked that the water's rush would smother the sound of his approach.

They must have covered almost a mile along the bank and Calder was starting to feel weak from hunger. It had been many hours since breakfast in the castle and she needed sustenance. Looking across the river, she could see the forest was thickening again. Not the rigid rows of plantation, but a mixed woodland of ash, alder and rowan, gloomy beneath the bare boughs but giving enough room for passage.

Ahead of them was a wooden footbridge. It looked dilapidated and insecure, but it was preferable to an attempt across the rocks, and Calder felt thankful for this small boon. When they reached it, they realised there was a camera at either end, giving clear images of the bridge and the land on both sides. Einar refused to cross first and so she stepped carefully out over the water, sensing him close in behind her as the river churned below.

When she was halfway across she realised there was a

giant ash ahead, set back from the bank. And against its trunk rested a row of weapons. A shield, two swords and a longbow, along with a sack and what could be a quiver. The forest grew in a semi-circle around the bridge, with twenty yards of open ground in each direction. Had he seen? If she rushed to the weapons, what would she do then?

'At last,' he said from her shoulder and she knew he had spotted the cache.

They dropped off the far end and Calder stood rooted to the spot. Einar paused next to her, then started to walk towards the tree. In moments he would be there. In seconds he would be armed. She thought to flee back across the bridge, but the ground was too open on the other side. She looked left at the treeline and saw gaps under the bare branches and felt them calling her.

Knowing the sound of the river covered her movement, she began to pace away. He was focused on the tree and it was the first time all morning that he wasn't watching her. She quickened as he reached the ash and bent to inspect the sword, and then she was at the edge of the forest, the first tendrils of woody boughs catching at her. She ducked beneath them and ran, seeking the deeper darker parts of the forest. The ground rose and then dropped away and she leapt down into this groove and fell to her knees. The river's tumult had dimmed and she could hear her heart pounding against her temple. She crawled back to the top of the slope and peered in the direction she'd come from.

There was no movement. She could see the clearing and the weapons beside the ash, but not him. She held her breath. Then he appeared from behind a large alder, staring into the trees, searching for her.

'Calder! Where the hell are you? There's food here. Bread and cheese in the sack. Come and eat.' His face showed concern, but he was holding one of the swords, the point hanging loosely against his leg. 'Calder! You need to have something to eat to keep you going. Don't be stupid.'

He turned towards her hiding place and she dropped her head below the slope. The soil was cold and iron-hard against her chin. She counted to ten, then looked again. He had the shield now as well and was walking into the trees.

'Calder? Don't be foolish. I'm not going to hurt you. We arm ourselves and we'll be fine.' He stopped and listened and turned on the spot. 'We can share the weapons and the food. Here, you can have this sword if you want.' He stalked towards her and she dropped down again, not daring to breathe. She thought he would appear above her, but when she peeked again, he had changed direction and was groping through the trees further off to her left. 'Goddamn, Calder. Just come out wherever you are.'

Slowly he returned to the clearing and then his attention was drawn across the river. She followed his gaze. *No, no, no.* Hertha was running along the far bank. She was bright red with exertion, panting and stumbling. She had seen the bridge and also Einar in the clearing.

'It's okay,' he called and pointed at the bridge. 'Come over. I have food.' Hertha paused in confusion, then looked back fearfully along the bank as Einar started walking towards his side of the bridge. 'Come over.'

She looked at him, hesitant and afraid, then stared again along the bank. 'They're coming for me.' Her words made up her mind. She pulled herself onto the bridge and ran over.

Einar strode across the clearing. 'Who's coming for you?' he asked, four paces from her.

He dropped the shield and held out a hand in reassurance, but the other still grasped the sword. Hertha started to speak and point towards the far bank, and something in Calder knew already what was about to happen. She rose to one knee and drew a breath to yell at her friend, but even as she did, Einar drove the sword into Hertha's belly so hard that it took her back three steps.

'No!' Calder screamed. It tore from her and Einar's head whipped round. Hertha had fallen onto her back and he stood over her, trying to pull the blade from the body. It was stuck and he had to yank with both hands. Survival instinct kicked into Calder and she fled. She ran blindly, hitting branches, tripping over roots, not daring to look back.

No, no, no! Finally, exhausted, she stumbled into an area of juniper and blaeberry bushes and fell to the ground. *Hertha!* She sobbed into the earth. *My friend.*

XVIII

Punnr and Gulbrand reached the river a mile downstream from Calder. They had eaten and had made good progress over the last few hours. Each had a sword thrust through his belt and carried a shield, and Gulbrand had the sack with the remaining provisions slung over his shoulder. They had seen no one since leaving the Vigilis at the gate, but they had spied several cameras. The day was reaching afternoon and the snow had melted. Occasional shafts of sunlight energised the valley, but were quickly closed down by regiments of cloud.

They walked along the bank, brushing through knee-high yellow grasses and clambering over boulders. The dark waters flowed fearsomely and each time they thought they had found somewhere to leap across, they were forced to reconsider. At last they came to a place where fingers of rock crept out from both banks, catching the water between them and making it broil through the narrower channel. The gap looked jumpable and Gulbrand led the way onto the rocks. He looked back at Punnr and considered his next words. 'I won't make it if I'm holding this stuff, so here...' He drew his sword, reversed it and presented the pommel to Punnr. 'Take it.'

Punnr accepted and watched as Gulbrand scanned the far side, then jumped hard and hit the far rocks with his leading leg. The momentum carried him on to dry land and he was over. 'Right,' he said, turning back and perching as far out as he could. 'Give me the weapons. Then you can jump.' The two men stood facing each other from opposite rocks for long seconds, until Gulbrand shrugged. 'I trust we're both still honouring our pact. If not, you had ample opportunity to spit me like a pig just moments ago.'

Punnr stepped back and threw both swords, shields and the sack onto the far bank. Then he returned to the leading rock and jumped. There was nothing for it. If he met a sword blade as he landed, then he had miscalculated. He landed heavily, but Gulbrand steadied him, then picked up Punnr's sword and handed it back to him.

They walked off into the trees. There were no obvious paths now, but the wider spaced mixed woodland gave ample room for them to infiltrate. The sound of the river receded and the ground beneath the trunks became rolling, creating myriad dips. They began to climb and eventually broke out of the trees onto a small windblown summit. They could see the opposite side of the valley which they had spent the morning descending and above them the mixed woodland continued, rising until in the distance there stood the tower.

'I wonder if anyone's made it there yet,' Punnr said.

'And if so, how many? Let's go, we need to get there fast.'

Punnr was about to follow when movement caught his eye down by the river. 'Wait.' He crouched on the summit, scanning the ground below.

Gulbrand joined him. 'What is it?'

'Something over there. About three hundred yards downriver on the far bank.'

They watched intently, but there was no further movement. The land was as empty as they had seen it all day. 'Your eyes are playing tricks on you.' Gulbrand began to move.

'Maybe... No, wait! There!' A figure detached itself from the trees and loped across the grass. It was cloaked and armed with a spear and shield and it still wore a fur hat despite the warming day, so they couldn't discern an identity. It moved fast and then disappeared into the trees again. The two watchers sank lower onto the rocky summit. Long seconds dragged by.

'Who was it?' Gulbrand whispered.

'No telling, but if they keep going they'll find the rocks where we crossed. Does our pact extend to a threesome?'

Gulbrand looked at him. 'If it's one of your Thralls, you'll outnumber me.'

'And if it's one of your Perpetuals, I sure won't feel I'm in good company.'

'Then I suggest we go now. Head to the tower. Take our chances there.'

'Wait! Look.'

The figure had appeared again, moving quickly along the far bank, and there was a second one coming from trees behind. Then a third and a fourth and a fifth. All of them armed, cloaked and trotting along the bank, searching for a point to cross.

'Shit,' said Gulbrand.

They flattened themselves to the summit and waited to

see if the figures would spy the rock fingers. Sure enough, the leading one halted at the place and stooped to inspect the options. Then he waved to the others and they assembled. One stepped forward and dropped onto the rocks to check the span of the river, using the spear shaft to balance. The watchers had a clearer view of their faces.

'Shit indeed,' said Punnr. 'That's Ulf. I really don't need that bastard on my tail.'

'Three of the others are my colleagues – Dagfinn, Havaldr and the woman, Signe. I can't make out the one in the hat.'

As Gulbrand spoke, the figure they had first seen swiped his hat off and rubbed a hand through his hair. He raised his face to the sky and Punnr caught a glimpse of the bandaging. 'It's Erland. The bastard's got himself in with the Perpetuals. If he's made a pact with them, then it's only five Thralls against nine of you.' He said it without thinking and Gulbrand looked at him.

Ulf had stood back as one of the others prepared to jump first. 'So what are we going to do?' Gulbrand asked.

Punnr was silent for a few seconds, watching the man make it successfully to the near bank. 'That depends on where your loyalties lie. You can wait here and join up with them. The six of you would make a pretty powerful force, almost certainly a winning number. But you'd have to let me go right now.'

Gulbrand studied the figures below. Three were across and Ulf was preparing to jump. 'I've already said Ulf is a snake. I'll take my chances with you.'

'Then we'd better get out of here bloody fast.'

They crawled backwards until they were hidden and were about to dash up the hill, when a disturbance to their left arrested their movement. Another figure broke out onto the summit and drew up sharply when he saw them, levelling his spear. He wore no cloak and he was breathing heavily.

It was Brante.

He looked haggard and for several seconds he barely seemed to recognise Punnr. The three men faced each other.

'Brante, it's me!' Punnr took a step towards his friend. The tall man's eyes saw him properly for the first time and he gave a relieved sigh, but he kept his spear pointing at Gulbrand.

'Hail, Punnr. I knew you'd still be standing.'

'Are you alone?'

'Aye. Have been for a long time. But then I saw those bastards on the other side and I've been tracking them from above.' He looked at Gulbrand. The Perpetual hadn't moved and still had his weapon pointed at Brante. 'Why are you with this one?'

'We've been together since the start,' Punnr said. 'We haven't seen anyone until just now.'

'Don't trust him. He's a filthy Perpetual.'

Punnr took a step towards Brante and held out a calming hand. 'Gulbrand's okay. He trusts Ulf even less than we do. I have a pact with him.'

'Don't trust any words of his,' Brante hissed. 'They're all out to get us. They already knew about the weapons caches, must have been told in advance. And their only game-plan is to stick all of us Thralls through the guts the first chance they get!'

'No, you're wrong.'

'Listen Punnr, his mates are just minutes away. Watch how worthless your pact is once they get here. Two against six? I don't fancy our chances. We have to finish him here before the others arrive.'

Punnr glanced back at Gulbrand and realised he was retreating, eyes still on Brante and sword held level. 'Where are you going, you fool?'

'I'll take my chances alone. Your friend doesn't like me. Sorry, Punnr. It was good while it lasted, but from now on I'm doing it alone.'

'Wait!'

'Let him go,' said Brante.

Gulbrand backed to the trees, turned and headed into the woodland, still carrying the sack of provisions. Punnr watched his cloaked figure recede and disappear over a rise.

He sighed. 'Bloody hell, Brante. We'd have been better with three. We could have formed a shieldwall like we practised in the hall. Knocked Ulf and his friends about a bit.'

Brante leaned on his spear shaft. 'Don't you get it? Half of us are expected to die out here and the Perpetuals have known the score all along. *Sine Missione*. Without Mercy. They'll stop at nothing to eliminate us six first, then turn on each other if they have to.'

There was no time to say more. Punnr walked back to the crest and looked down towards the river crossing. It was empty. The pack must be over and working its way up through the trees towards them. 'Erland's with them.'

'I know. The little lump of goat shit! Well, I've taken care of one already.'

Punnr looked at the tall man. 'Really?'

'I had to, otherwise I'd have this spear in the ribs.'

'So you've made your first kill for the Pantheon.'

'Fuck the Pantheon. I made my first kill to stop myself being gutted and left as a carcass for the crows. And if Ulf and his companions find us, the carrion feeders will have a bloody feast.'

Together they ran up the hill and vanished into the arms of the trees.

Calder had lain in the juniper bushes for thirty minutes after she had witnessed Hertha's death, too petrified to move. But as the time stretched out and the forest around remained undisturbed, her fear subsided and a new feeling crept into her gut. Her mind kept replaying the image of Einar leaning over Hertha's body and the way he had been yanking at the sword to release it, as though she was nothing more than a hog run to ground.

She rose from her spot in the bushes and followed the river back to the clearing. Einar was gone. Only Hertha's body remained sprawled several yards from the bridge. Calder stood respectfully next to her and looked at the face which had smiled and flushed throughout their training. She hadn't deserved to die like this. Calder wondered whether to do anything with the body, but knew she could never dig a hole in the hard ground. Then she remembered the camera on the end of the bridge. It was pointing straight at her and with a surge of anger she swore she wouldn't entertain them by trying to move Hertha. So in the end she said a few simple words of farewell and then stepped away to look around the clearing.

What she saw held her gaze and in that second it determined her next plan. Einar had left the longbow and quiver. With the two swords, shield and provisions sack, he must have decided he already had enough to carry. He was a fool. At the very least, he should have hidden them. She picked up the bow and ran her finger down the string and along the curve of the arm. She had never held one before. She positioned herself and tried to pull back on it. The string was incredibly taut. She could barely bring it halfway back towards her ear. She took an arrow, fitted it clumsily and aimed at the tree about fifteen feet away. She drew the bow as best she could and let go. The arrow hit the tree with a resounding thud and pierced the bark enough to remain hanging.

Calder looked again at the bow. She knew she could never hope to use the weapon proficiently without training, but this first shot had shown her that if a target was close enough, the arrow could do damage. She pulled the strap of the quiver over her head, yanked the arrow from the tree and returned it to the quiver. There was a tiny pencil thin track leading off into the woods. She took one last look back at Hertha, held a single finger up towards the camera, then ran up the path.

It took her twenty minutes to catch sight of his cloaked figure. He carried the shield and one sword and had the other tucked in his belt. She followed cautiously until he disappeared over a rise, then she ran headlong up the path until she too reached the rise. Checking over it, she saw he was still walking ahead, but now closer. She knew she needed to get within fifteen feet, but didn't dare follow further on the path. He only needed to turn and she would be spotted. In a full-on attack, she doubted her rudimentary archery would be any match for his own charge. So she slunk into the bushes on one side. The deciduous trees were winter bare, but there were plenty of scraggy bushes and clumps of long yellow grass growing between the trunks, and the rising ground was still broken by little dips and bumps. She ran uphill. Her months of fitness training were paying off. Her heart beat firmly, but her breathing was regular and contained. She felt strong now. A hunter.

He was looking from side to side and once he turned and checked back down the tiny path. She threw herself to her knees and waited motionless. If he had seen her, he showed no sign. The ground steepened and he began to lean into the climb, less able to look around. He reached a stony section and the rocks were like natural steps taking him upwards. She could see that once he reached the top of these the land flattened again and it would take him from view. So she angled her run in towards the path, timing it to reach the rock steps just as he disappeared over the brow. She drew an arrow from her quiver, fitted it as best she could, then padded lightly and rapidly to the top of the steps. As soon as she reached the top, he came into full view. He was still walking away from her, but she had made up so much ground that he was only twenty feet ahead. She took three steps forward, braced, positioned and took aim, pulling back on the bowstring with all her remaining strength.

She must have stepped on something, or perhaps he simply sensed a new presence in that lonely place, for he swung around. She loosed the arrow in the split second before he could bring his shield across to cover him. Its flight had little power, but it hit him in the stomach and he doubled over, dropping the sword and grabbing at the shaft in front of him, then sank to his knees and looked back up at her with astonishment. She could see that the iron head of the arrow had pierced his flesh.

She lowered the bow. He was still kneeling, pawing at the shaft, staring at her and starting to make small mewing noises. All her anger drained away, replaced by horror at her actions. She stumbled backwards and fled down the rocky steps.

It was minutes before she forced herself to stop and bent double retching. What had she done? He was no more than a boy! She closed her eyes and forced deep breaths. The forest air was cool and damp in her lungs, like that of a cave's when there seems a deeper undertone, a lower octave, to the very oxygen.

She opened her eyes.

Two hundred yards below, a cloaked figure was looking up at her. It was another one of the Perpetuals and he held a shield and spear slung across his shoulder. Then two more emerged from the trees behind him and she realised another two shadows loomed at the edges of the track. She reached for her Odin clasp and undid it, letting her cloak drop to the ground. Its warmth was of no consequence now and it would hinder her. She took a single long breath and exhaled slowly. *Now girl, run like the wind.* She spun on her heel and leapt uphill. Even as she did, she heard an excited howl below and the yip of other voices joining the call, something between hyenas and chimps, the primeval sound of pursuit.

She rose onto her toes and let her legs pound in short fast steps up the incline. She was confident she had the endurance to make this a long chase, but she didn't know if she had the pace. She reached the rocky steps and took them two at a time. With a shock she reached Einar again. He lay unmoving on the grass. She rushed to him and looked into his face, then with a small cry, she tore on.

As she reached a bend, she risked a quick glance back. The five figures were just coming over the rise and they let out a combined yell as they came across Einar. One of them gave him a testing kick. As she ran into the bend, she saw them do the one thing she feared most. They split. The middle figure threw out his arms to right and left, and she saw his companions break into two pairs and disappear either side of him, while he continued rampaging towards her.

She reached another steep rocky section which then levelled out onto a shelf. From this she was able to see out over the trees below, back down to the river and the opposite side of the valley. She wondered whether the other Thralls still lived. Perhaps she was alone in this vast landscape, with no hope and nowhere to run from this pack who had her scent. She was tiring now. Her pace was becoming laboured and even her terror couldn't keep her from slowing to a walk.

Looking up the hill, she realised the tower was much closer. She could even see a camera high on it, pointing down towards her. The day was dying. Dusk was approaching. What should she do? If she headed to the tower, they would find her in minutes. She walked to the edge of the shelf and peered down. The man on the path was still climbing fast, approaching the steeper ascent below the shelf. With a sinking heart she saw it was Ulf. There would be no reasoning with him.

And then it struck her that they would all have to return to the path to ascend onto the shelf because it was the only way up. Even as her brain mapped this out, she saw a figure in the woods come towards the rock face and curve back towards Ulf on the path. Then the second one appeared and did the same. They bounded away to her right, back to the path. There would be a few precious seconds when they were all hidden from view as they climbed the rocky section and then they would be on the shelf with her. She leaned over the edge and studied the terrain. She had just one chance or they would hound her all the way to the tower and there would be no escape.

She thrust the bow over her head, dropped to a crouch and swung her legs out over the void. Then she turned on her stomach, explored with her feet until they found purchase and eased herself over the edge. The rock was damp, slippery and loose. Feeling with her boots and scrabbling with her fingers for holds, she took herself lower. She peeked down and grimaced as her right leg sought a niche. For terrifying seconds she could find nothing and thought she would lose her grip, but then her boot caught in a cleft and gingerly she took the weight. It held and she moved her left leg down to the spot she was seeking. Over eons a great branch from the nearest tree had extended its embrace towards the rock, pushing into it and then caressed its way along the face. She placed her foot onto the branch, shifted her weight and then froze still as a voice spoke above her.

'No sign, but she must still be on the path. It's the only route.'

If they looked over, they would have her. But they kept running.

She waited until she knew they were gone, then worked her way along the branch to the trunk. Thankfully there were enough lower branches for her to grab and make a clumsy descent. She landed heavily and pain licked up her spine, but she was down and she was away from them. She looked around. She didn't dare return to the path, so she must head across the slope below the shelf and work her way through the trees. She set off at a cautious run, heart still in her mouth, not quite believing she had fooled them, and then there was a whoop and she jerked to a halt and looked upwards to see Ulf watching her a hundred yards above. Frantically she threw herself across the hillside, but this time they had the advantage of height and they came tearing through the trees.

She broke from the forest onto a bare rise and the whole valley opened before her. Blankets of grey cloud. Iced black mountains glowering beneath. The river. Even the fence line on the far side. She wondered if the men in the towers could reach her with their cameras. Was her flight being relayed to the hidden watchers for their afternoon amusement?

In that moment, halfway across the bare slope, knowing she could run no further, a late beam of sunlight caught her, ready to illuminate her final act, and even as she slowed and prepared to turn for the confrontation, she saw two figures coming towards her from the further treeline. One was cloaked, one was not. Both were armed. Both were running towards her, calling her name. She fell onto her knees and Brante was suddenly there, sweeping her up, pulling her into his strong chest, and Punnr was springing past them both and placing himself on the summit with sword levelled and shield across him.

'We got you,' Brante whispered into her ear.

The five pursuers reached the edge of the woods and fanned out.

'Don't take another step,' Punnr challenged.

There was something lordly about him as he bestrode the summit, cloak caught in the upland breeze, long hair streaked across his cheeks, the clasp of Odin dazzling in the sunbeam, and the pursuers did indeed halt in the face of his anger. Brante joined him and Calder notched an arrow from behind them. If this was the end, they would face it together.

'Erland, you faithless arsehole,' Brante shouted. 'You're a marked man.'

From somewhere on the distant wind came the whir of helicopters, but no one noticed. The sunbeam dimmed and the summit was thrown once more into cold grey.

Ulf stepped forward. He held his spear low and he had one of the provision sacks over his shoulder. 'Now then, let's all keep calm. Only one of you needs to die.'

'Fuck off, you snake,' Brante answered.

Ulf smiled smugly and made a play of looking around at his companions and then back at the cluster of Thralls. 'I count eight of us. The challenge ends when there are seven. So we require only one of you and this tiresome game is over. Who will it be? I'd prefer the little blonde who's been giving us such a run around, but the choice is yours.'

'What about the others?'

'We came across the body of your female Thrall – Hertha. And I think your little archer over there did for Einar. Seeing you here, Brante, I can only assume you dispatched Eluf, who is no loss. And our new friend Erland gutted Torvald, for which I've forgiven him.'

'What of Vidar and Gulbrand?' demanded Brante.

Ulf sighed theatrically and heaved the provision sack from his shoulder. He pulled the strap open and shook two severed heads onto the soggy ground.

'I killed Vidar within moments of discovering our weapons cache. He screamed like a pig. Gulbrand had more class when we came across him. But I've always thought he had outstayed his welcome. So come now, maths was never my strong point, but I believe we eight are all that remains of those fourteen brave souls that began the day. So I only need one of you. Which shall it be?'

Punnr looked at the heads and felt a new fury rising in him. He raised his face to the group before him. 'We are the remaining Valhalla Thralls, Ulf, you bastard. If you come for us now, I'll bury this blade in your brain.'

Ulf's expression fluttered. Punnr looked mighty before him and he suddenly doubted that his superior numbers were enough to overcome these opponents. He tried to smile. 'So we have a predicament.'

He was about to say more, when there was a thud behind him and a low gasp. All eyes swung to the source of the sound. The one called Dagfinn was looking in openmouthed surprise down at his belly where the point of a sword had broken out, as though bursting from hibernation in his stomach. He released his spear and cupped the tip of the protruding blade as his lifeblood began to spill over his fingers. Erland stepped away, dragging his sword from the Perpetual with a mighty heave. He had lost the bandages on his nose during the course of the day and it looked healed, but wide and crooked, and somehow at odds with his long face. Dagfinn sank to his knees and then collapsed.

Ulf turned on Erland. 'What the hell are you doing?' he demanded incredulously.

'Solving the predicament. Now we're seven.'

'Are you mad?' Ulf glared at him for interminable moments and then a look of knowing stole into his eyes. 'I hadn't thought you capable of such vision, but I won't make that mistake again.'

The helicopters were much closer, coming in from the north. Ulf looked up and waved. 'Let's end this thing.' He grinned wolfishly at Punnr, then swung around and jogged away across the slope in the direction of the tower. Signe and Havaldr, his two remaining Perpetuals went with him. Erland gave Punnr a long stare, then followed.

The helicopters lowered and the trees began to churn with the draft from their blades. Punnr turned to the others. Calder had sunk to her knees, tears in her eyes, but there was a ferocity in her expression. Brante's shoulders sagged and he was pale.

Punnr planted his shield rim on the ground and his cloak swept out behind him as it was convulsed by the helicopters. 'It's over,' he said simply.

XIX

'Pairs, my lord?' Radspakr said, keeping his voice level.

The Thane of the Valhalla Palatinate had arrived at the castle by helicopter an hour earlier when the *Sine Missione* had already been drawing to a close. He had been greeted by a worried Halvar who informed him that he should see the live feeds from the valley. Radspakr stalked to his office in the lower keep where, surrounded by computers and CCTV screens, he was in time to watch the Perpetuals' pursuit of Calder and the confrontation on the hilltop. Another screen showed him edited highlights of what had already happened and he had sworn and sent the helicopters early lest he have no one left to initiate that evening.

Then he had made his way up the steps to the quarters of the Caelestis.

'Yes, Radspakr, pairs. Stop worrying about it, man. We decided to play loose with the rules.'

'With respect, lord, we do usually keep the initiates in larger groups for each *Sine Missione* because when they are grouped and armed with shields, they can defend themselves effectively and once one group has reached the tower it is relatively easy to keep the other group at bay. It tends to keep the body count down, which is no bad thing when they aren't even Oathsworn yet.'

'Well, this time we didn't. Goddamn it man, we've had fatalities before. We wouldn't arm them with iron blades if we only wanted them to bloody well tickle each other.'

'Agreed lord, but we don't usually have *seven* dead at this stage. I was expecting to return at least some of the losing Thralls to their old lives – sworn to secrecy on pain of death – and the losing Perpetuals would have gone back to the Schola for another year.'

'You're uncommonly full of qualms, Thane.'

'Experience shows that killing off Thralls before the Oath-Taking necessitates a tangle of diplomatic delicacies. They tend to have jobs and colleagues and friends who will ask tricky questions about their disappearance.'

'From what I saw, that one called Ulf was a real hothead, but his plan backfired.'

'How so?'

'Of the seven corpses the Vigiles are disposing of as we speak, I believe five of them were Perpetuals.'

Radspakr murmured his agreement. 'Probably just as well. The loss of Perpetuals is not noticed beyond the Pantheon. They are, after all, Lost Children, and have been forgotten by society for years already. But those two Thralls will be missed. If the media get hold of this, they'll have a field day.'

'I don't need a bloody commentary from you, Radspakr. The media isn't your problem. Atilius will handle all that. The two Thralls will disappear quietly enough. Sad accidents.'

'Yes, lord.'

'Now I must leave. I'll take your helicopter. Are you staying?'

'I will remain for the Oath-Taking.'

'So be it.'

Radspakr stalked back down the steps, chewing furiously on his lip. If truth be told, it wasn't the body count which worried him. There had been plenty of fatalities in previous years and the Pantheon authorities always smoothed everything. No, it was the fact that the rules had been changed on a whim. This was unprecedented. At every previous *Sine Missione* the Thrall and Perpetual rivals were herded through the fence as a group and left to get on with it. It worked well enough. They usually split themselves into trusted parties and once the weapons caches were discovered, the action always kicked off.

So why meddle with the rules this year? Why the pairs and the separate starts? And why, oh why, would the meddler-in-chief be the Lord High Caelestis? Radspakr strode angrily towards his rooms, a frisson of anxiety licking up his spine.

In the months leading up to Morgan's disappearance, Tyler guessed the unknown man must have left her life or, at least, the romance collapsed. He watched his sister and noted the changes in her. She became sombre and spent more time at the flat. She was physically fitter than he had ever known her and any curves she once displayed had long since morphed into muscle. She ate carefully, no longer drank and even started to manage the little household with more precision. Disciplined, was the word that sprang to his mind. Morgan had become disciplined in a way he would never have imagined.

But he saw something else too. A new fear that rippled around her eyes, that made her pick at her food, that dropped her into bouts of silence, that painted her face with blotches of fatigue, that forced her out of the door each night even when he knew she wanted to stay. Perhaps he should have said something or followed her into the city. Maybe he might have been able to intercede in the direction her life was taking, but his own emptiness prevented him.

Then one inevitable morning in March he stumbled back from a night around the estate to find a huge home-cooked lasagne awaiting him, along with a short note and something next to it wrapped in tissue paper.

Tyler. I must go away and I don't know when I'll be back. I can't explain why, but you have to trust me. I've raised the monthly amount into your account to £2,000. Use it to get a fucking grip on your life. Get off the estate before those coke-dealing scumbags beat the crap out of you. Rent a place somewhere else and try to be somebody.

I love you, little brother.

There were smudges on the note, as though it had been raining, and the last line had been written lower down the page at an angle, like a last-minute addition scrawled as she raced from his life. He picked up the object and eased away the tissue paper. Inside was an ivory amulet fastened to a length of cord. He knew the design. He had seen it across

Edinburgh. And actually, if he was truthful, he had known about his sister's secret life all along, ever since those early years when her face looked so full of wonder. It had been toying with her and now it had come to claim her.

He had lost his sister to the Horde.

Calder looked at herself in the mirror above the washbasin. Her face felt like leather, parched and baked by the Highland air. Blotches ringed her eyes and streaks of grime criss-crossed her cheeks. She had a graze on her chin that wanted to bleed. She had untied her hair and it fell in frizzy neglected curls to her shoulders. She leaned forward and examined the pools of her eyes. Something about them had changed. What had Freyja said? *By day's end you will have aged, you will be wiser and you may be crueller.*

And you will be a murderer too, she thought. She had killed another human being and not in the heat of the moment. She didn't even have that small consolation to cling to. She had planned and stalked and looked him in the eye in the calculated moments before she loosed her arrow and now he was no more and she wondered if he once had a family who would have mourned him and what his life could have been if it hadn't set him on an unstoppable trajectory to the *Sine Missione*.

Her hands wouldn't stop trembling. They had shaken all through the helicopter flight back to the castle, when she had been squashed against Ulf and she had squirmed as far away from him as her strap would allow, but no contortion would remove the pressure of his shoulder. She had hated the idea that he would notice the weakness in her hands, but with the completion of the *Sine Missione* he had sunk into his own thoughts and stared out the window at the passing scenery. There had been another helicopter on the lawn behind Sveinn's Mead Hall and two expensive cars around the front, but the returning group had seen no one new as a subdued Halvar led them into the corner tower and showed them up the stairs to the rooms they had barely used.

Calder's eyes dropped to her thin shoulders and the delicate lines of her collarbones. She had always been petite, but now the months of training had hardened her contours and burned away every last scrap of surplus flesh. A young girl from the Schola had been waiting in her room and had set about removing her greased and brittle clothing. Then she had used a sponge to wet her all over and applied a revolting mix of pumice and ash. Calder had been too exhausted even to comment and surrendered herself to the girl's good intentions. Next had come olive oil, dribbled over the ash mix until she looked as if she had emerged blackened from an oil slick. But the girl was an expert. She picked up a curved metal implement and scraped the mix from her arms, legs, buttocks, neck, back and chest, then sponged her once more with warm water, and even in Calder's dazed state, she could feel the pores of her skin rejoicing in a cleanliness they had rarely known.

The girl had left her and Calder spent an interminable time inspecting the detail of her still dirty face in the mirror. It told the outward story of the last twelve hours, but not the inner. There were fluffy white towels waiting for her on a chair next to the wash basin and their promise of comfort, of refinement, of civilisation itself, overwhelmed her. Somewhere out there across the hills, there were seven bodies being collected by the Vigiles in their role as *libitinarii*, removers of the slain, and here she was with fluffy towels and a tub behind her filled with hot water infused with bay, laurel and juniper. She ran a wet hand across her graze and through the grime on her cheeks and she tried to recognise the Lana Cameron she had once been. Unprompted, tears pricked at the corners of her eyes and broke their own trails through the dirt on her cheeks and then she couldn't hold back and she gripped the edge of the washbasin as her body was wracked with shudders from her core.

Next door, Punnr lay in his bath and stared at the vaulted ceiling of his tower quarters. The boy had already gone through the ash ritual with him and then left him to his ablutions. He had sunk his head below the water and kept it there for an eternity, as though hoping the cleansing bay and juniper would ooze into his orifices and seek out his soul. He pummelled his long hair until it squeaked and scrubbed at his beard, then lapsed again into vacant stillness as the water steamed around his face.

Halvar and Freyja had been different on the return journey. Gentler. More respectful. The Housecarls knew the exercise had played out bloodily this year and they left them at peace with their thoughts. Now they were being provided with luxuries which they could never have expected, nor really wanted, as though the Pantheon was saying, *Sorry, old chap, for making you do all those ghastly things.*

And that was the catch picking at Punnr's thoughts. Had he really done such ghastly things? Actually, he was somehow alive and in the final seven without having done much of anything. The fates had conspired to make him watch his friends either fall or find themselves forced to take blood. Brante and Calder had both killed to survive and he knew already that it had changed them. He had seen it in their faces. They had crossed a line. They could never return to being the people they were before that first night on Lady Stair's Close. Through their actions, the Pantheon had already claimed them far more than any facile Oath-Taking could. And Punnr didn't know how this made him feel. Should he rejoice that he had come through it still an innocent? Surely no man would lie in this bath and truly wish he had been forced to kill. Yet would his Thrall friends think differently of him now? The one who had cheated the ultimate challenge.

He stepped out of the tub, towelled himself dry and dressed in the grey leggings and black tunic the boy had left draped over a stool. The tunic had gold swirls embroidered on the hem, cuffs and collar. Then he trod barefoot to the door and opened it, peeking down the corridor. It was empty. Leaving the door ajar, he stole across to the room opposite and knocked.

She was covered only in a towel when she opened it and he could see she had been crying.

'Hi,' was all he could think to say.

She didn't reply, but eventually she stepped back and let him enter. Her room was fashioned identically to his, yet it smelt of peppermint oil and somehow felt entirely feminine. She sat on the stool in front of her washbasin and Punnr couldn't help looking at her legs as the towel rode up her thighs. He dragged his eyes away and perched on the edge of her tub.

'Are you okay?' He knew it was a stupid question and regretted it immediately.

She stared at him with huge, reddened eyes. 'Freyja told us we'd be crueller.' She gave a dry laugh. 'She was right.'

'You did what you had to do – to survive.'

'Live and let die, and all that, eh?'

'I suppose.'

Punnr could see the back of her head in the mirror behind her, the wet tresses of her hair sticking to her naked shoulders. She was looking vacantly towards the window, lost somewhere. He waited until she spoke.

'Once before I held a life in my hands. Someone so precious to me. And despite everything I tried to do, every journey I made, every prayer I gave, every tiny piece of information I researched, every night I sat awake, I watched that life ebb away and I was powerless to stop it leaving. I decided there was no god in the universe, no great force of good, and I raged silently at the world.' She pulled the towel tighter around her breasts and hunched in on herself as the chill of the room reached for her. 'I've carried that anger for many years. It's always been there, somewhere inside me, making me who I am. Defining me. And you know what, it was that anger that propelled me through all those nights in the vault. Radspakr had selected me and perhaps he was right – perhaps the Pantheon was the answer for me.'

She was shivering and Punnr thought he should look for something to put around her, but he didn't dare move.

'Today, all that anger came to a critical point and instead

of trying to save a life, instead of doing everything to preserve it – I took one. And now… now the anger's gone and there's just emptiness.'

'Are you going to leave?' Punnr asked quietly.

She looked at him, startled by the question. 'Leave?' She shook her head. 'No. Of course not. How can I leave now? I can't go back, I can't undo what's been done. If you'd handed me a crystal ball on the first night in the cellar and shown me where this journey would lead, then yes, I would have walked out that place and never returned. But now? Punnr, I've already abandoned the person I was. Whether I want to fight it or not, the Pantheon has me.'

They sat in silence.

'You're cold,' Punnr said eventually and she smiled thinly.

'Yes, I am.'

'I must leave you to dress.'

He rose and walked to the door. She followed him and she was very close when he turned with the door half open.

'I'm glad you're staying,' he said.

'You are?'

'I think – probably – if you or Brante left now, I wouldn't be able to go through with it myself.'

She sighed. 'I know. Go get dressed, Punnr.'

The boy was waiting when he returned to his room. He had brought new garments. First he produced a corselet of chainmail from a roll of sheepskin, oiled to prevent rusting.

'You must put this on without my help,' he said.

'Why?' asked Punnr, shocked at its weight when he took it from the boy.

'No warrior can wear a *brynjar* if they can't put it on alone. It is the Viking way.'

Punnr grunted, holding the corselet up by the shoulders and then began to pull it over his head. The rings were so heavy and seemed to snag on everything. He dropped the garment with an oath and felt the boy's eyes on him. 'How is anyone supposed to move in this?'

He tried again and this time he got his head through and his arms came out flailing above his head. The boy stepped forward then and strapped the *brynjar* to him with a wide belt. Then he helped Punnr pull on knee-length boots. The leather was soft and the fitting perfect. Finally, a new russet-red cloak was draped over his shoulders and fastened with a Triple Horn of Odin clasp. Punnr stepped awkwardly to the mirror and looked at this unrecognisable man before him. It was a Viking warrior. Armoured, hardened and inscrutable.

XX

They gathered on the stairway, dressed in their Valhalla finery. Brante looked glorious in his mail and there was an imperial calm about his expression, like someone who had wrestled in private with every emotion and found a resolution. Likewise, it wasn't Calder's clothing that took Punnr's breath away – although her silver mail sparkled – it was the rigid ethereal set of her face. The three of them stood together, keeping their distance from the other four. The Horde might be receiving them as a group of seven, but there was little on earth that could bridge the divide between these two parties.

Halvar came up the stairs. He too was dressed as they had never seen him. He wore a full knee-length ring-mail *brynjar* under his cloak, edged with fine silver thread. A broadsword clung to his hip, sheathed in a scabbard of wood, lined with sheepskin and covered in purple velvet, and under one arm he held an iron helmet, polished until it shone. He looked at them grimly, then led them downstairs and out into the dark of the rear lawn. There he paused and pointed to one of the helicopters. 'That will fly you to Inverness right now if you choose.' Then he pointed in the opposite direction to the far outer corner of the hall, just visible in the night, where they could see shadowed figures waiting. 'And that way will take you to Valhalla.'

Punnr glanced at Calder, but she was looking away into the night.

'So be it,' Halvar said.

Radspakr awaited them, along with two Vigiles. He was dressed in a simple grey woollen robe that dropped to his feet. It was buttoned diagonally across his chest from his left shoulder and belted by a black sash. A plain gold band circled his brow and a large Odin amulet hung from a sturdy silver chain around his neck. The Vigiles were once again helmeted to hide their identities, moustaches oiled and combed, and great curved swords hung from their belts. In addition to their baggy pantaloons and boots, they too wore chainmail.

The group was illuminated by three burning braziers, and more of these stretched in pairs down the slope to the shore of the loch. Halvar left them and strode away through the braziers until they lost him from view.

Radspakr looked angry and wasted no time on preliminaries. 'These are your last moments as Thralls and Perpetuals. Soon you will be recognised as Thegns of the Horde of Valhalla, junior officers, assigned to one of the regiments. Do not hold grudges for the deeds that have been done. Do not look back at those no longer with us. Look only forward and dedicate yourselves to the Horde.'

The group said nothing. Eyes were drifting from Radspakr down the slope where they could see more figures by the shore and something else which was looming out of the darkness of the water.

'You are about to take the Oath. This is your oath of fidelity to the Pantheon itself, not to the Horde. Thus, as with all official Pantheon rites, it is a Greco-Roman ceremony and will be led by the Praetor of the Pantheon himself. Do as he commands. You will then be addressed by our own High King Sveinn, who will assign you to your regiments.' He reached into his pocket and retrieved a small sack. 'Hold out your hands.' Into each he placed a single silver coin. 'These are *denarii*. You will need them to pay your passage. Be warned, the point you give these up marks the moment of no return. Now follow me.'

They trooped after him down the slope between the braziers. The sky held no stars and the air threatened rain, but they were warm in their cloaks. Brante led the way with Calder alongside him. Punnr walked behind, heavy under his mail. Then came Ulf and Signe, Havaldr, and Erland, who refused to look at anyone. As they approached the shore, they could see the waiting figures more clearly. It was the same little beach which the three Thralls had clustered on before the *Sine Missione*, where they had thrown stones into the calm waters of the loch. Now braziers burned on it, flames licking up towards the cloud, crackling and sending shadows bounding across the surrounding slope. There were more Vigiles positioned in a semi-circle around the edge of the beach and two figures standing together between a pair of smaller braziers. Beside these two was yet another camera mounted on a tripod. But the eyes of the group were drawn inescapably to the shoreline of the loch, where a vast figure loomed silhouetted in front of a final fire, and behind him, magnificent in the glow of the flames, waited a Viking longship. Its square sail was furled, but the mast disappeared into the black sky and a beaten gold dragon's head roared from the prow. Shields lined the sides, oars sat to attention in the water and seated bodies waited in silence on the benches.

Radspakr led them onto the pebbly beach and ordered them into a row facing the two figures beside the smaller fires. Then he stepped away and joined the watching Vigiles. One of the men came forward so that he was more clearly illuminated and they realised he was the chubby, grey-haired man they had seen before, still wearing his purple robe and still with his soft eyes. He too wore a circlet of gold around his brow and a gold sash.

'Welcome, I am Atilius, Praetor of the Pantheon, High Keeper of the Rules, Praefectus of the Vigiles, answerable only to the Caelestia. You are to be congratulated. Thirty-one began this process, a mixture of newly identified Thralls and the strongest Perpetual graduates from our Schola. Now only seven remain.' He rubbed his fleshy, clean-shaven chin and smiled. His voice was high, strangely out of place among the huge warriors. 'At the end of the last Blood Season, Valhalla was awarded Blood Funds amounting to fifty-four credits to spend on additional troops. High King Sveinn and his Council of War decided to use twenty-six of these credits on twenty-six new Drengrs, the backbone of the Valhalla Grand Heathen Army, chosen from our Schola. However, they decided to expend the remaining twenty-eight credits on recruiting just seven new Thegns. I am sure you can do the arithmetic. Each of you has cost the Horde four Blood Fund credits. They could instead have chosen a further twenty-eight Drengr, but they chose to gamble, judging the worth of you seven to be greater. So you are indeed to be congratulated, the new cream of the Valhalla intake.'

Atilius looked over towards Radspakr and his smile thinned. 'Only time and the Titan Palatinate will determine whether the Horde has gambled correctly.'

He held out a hand and one of the Vigiles came forward with a scroll. Opening it, he peered at the contents for several seconds, then spoke again to Radspakr. 'Shall we do this alphabetically?'

'Yes, lord.' Radspakr cleared his throat from the sidelines. 'Brante, step forward.'

Brante looked sidelong at Punnr, then set his jaw and walked to stand in front of Atilius. The Praetor inspected him. 'A fine-looking man. Review this, then read it aloud.' He handed the open scroll to Brante.

For a few seconds there was quiet as Brante scanned the contents. In the night sky above, the clouds hung low, drawing down a black ceiling on proceedings. Perhaps in some corner of his brain, Brante was thinking about his lonely, bitter schooldays, lying on his dormitory bed dreaming about the three hundred Spartans and about his military father, so enslaved by the chains of his ancestry.

Clearing his throat, Brante spoke with resolution. 'I – that am known as Brante – swear by the great gods of the Pantheon – Jupiter, Zeus, Odin, Xian, Tengri, Kyzaghan and Ördög – that I will be forever loyal to the Pantheon in thought and word and deed, until such time as I am released from this bond. I will hold as friends those that they hold as friends and consider those as enemies whom they judge to be such, and I will not be sparing of my body or my soul, but will face every peril which they deem to cast at me. I will not speak of the Pantheon, nor any of its Palatinates, strongholds, activities or plans, to anyone who has not also given this oath. If I should hear of anything spoken, plotted or done contrary to this, I will report this and be an enemy of the person speaking, plotting or doing. If I should do anything contrary to this oath, I impose a curse upon myself encompassing the destruction and total extinction of my body, soul and life. May neither earth nor sea receive my body, nor bear fruit from it.'

He stopped. The words hung in the air for the other six initiates to grasp. It was as though Brante had taken a vast step across a ravine and waited beyond it, far from them.

'Thank you,' said Atilius, with another of his odd smiles. 'Well recited. You have just read the words of the Sacramentum. You are now one of the Oathsworn, Thegn Brante. Stand over there.' He retrieved the scroll, waved Brante aside and peered at Radspakr. 'Next please, my dear Thane.'

'Calder, step forward.'

Punnr felt her depart from his side. Her hair was golden in the firelight and her chin raised in defiance. It seemed an age before she began to speak the words in an empty voice, imposing the curse upon herself that could lead to the destruction and total extinction of her body, soul and life.

After Erland and Havaldr, it was Punnr's turn. By then the words had settled in his brain and he was thankful he hadn't been first. He wondered, *did my sister give this same pledge?* Afterwards he stood to one side as Signe and then Ulf completed the process. Ulf was earnest, embracing the words enthusiastically in front of Atilius, but Punnr wished the snake would curl up and die.

Atilius looked once more at the combined group. 'New members of the Pantheon – Thegns of Valhalla – I give you your High King, Sveinn the Red.'

The second figure stepped around the braziers and into the light. Sveinn. The gathered Thegns gawped at him. This was the man who would now be their High King, whom they were expected to serve with devotion. He approached with slow, purposeful movements and stood in front of them. He wasn't a man who needed words to command an audience. He was probably in his early fifties and his shoulder-length hair, parted at his temple and falling loosely, was streaked with silver, like comet trails. His beard too was silver, except on his chin and upper lip, where it retained its lustrous black. He had hazelnut eyes, oddly peaceful, and wore a silken black undershirt, silver mail trimmed with gold, and a wolfskin across his shoulders, held by a chain with the Triple Horn of Odin at its centre. Earrings made from what appeared to be predator teeth hung from leather cords below his lobes and in his belt was a hunting knife and a broadsword, the scabbard of which was a pale blue and decorated with rune snakes. He wore nothing on his head. No crown or other symbol of his office. It was unneeded.

When he eventually spoke, his voice was soft, but unlike Atilius' high pitch, Sveinn's was gravelly and drawn out. This wasn't a man who hurried his speech for he was unused to interruptions. 'Welcome, my troops. My new Thegns. I am told you have endured a great deal to be here and news of your deeds has already spread through my Horde. They are gathered in your honour and tonight we shall feast. The season of the Armatura is so called because each Palatinate devotes it to training their new warriors in the use of arms.

This night you become Weapons Worthy and you will be furnished with the arms of Valhalla.'

He stopped speaking and made no outward motion, but the circling Vigiles understood the signal. They positioned themselves behind him and the Thegns saw they carried between them a host of weapons and shields. They followed Sveinn as he stopped before Brante, and the first Vigilis passed him a broadsword.

'Thegn Brante, this is your sword of Valhalla. Honour it.' He held out the weapon. It was exquisite. The scabbard was deep crimson velvet and wreathed in silver. The hilt was curved with delicate runes etched upon it. The grip was leather, bound with gold thread, and the large round pommel was made of polished bone. Brante took it speechlessly in both hands and gripped it before him.

Sveinn reached an arm out again and the Vigilis placed another weapon in his glove. 'And this is your seax, your Viking dagger. Use it to seek out the hearts of our enemies.' The seax was a foot long, thin, encased in a black and silver scabbard, and whereas the sword had been magnificent, this looked deadly.

Next came a shield with an iron boss polished until the brazier flames danced upon it. On the reverse were three iron bands which came together to form a handgrip bound in leather. The shield was painted crimson like his scabbard and emblazoned across the front was a wolf's head in black.

Sveinn looked him up and down and nodded. 'Good,' he said, then turned his gaze upon Calder and the hazelnut eyes lit. 'Thegn Calder, you are a goddess this night.'

She wouldn't touch the proffered weapons for several moments and tried to return his piercing look. Then she relented and took the broadsword and seax. Her crimson shield had a raven's head on it.

Sveinn dragged himself from her and made his way down the line. When it was Punnr's turn, the High King studied his face. 'Thegn Punnr, Radspakr named you the Weakling.' He handed him the sword. 'I think not. You are made of sterner mettle. I believe you will prove my Thane wrong.'

When the weapons had all been distributed, Sveinn returned to the space between the small braziers. 'I have assigned you to the regiments as follows. Thegn Brante, litter number three, Wolf Company House Troop under Housecarl Halvar. Thegn Calder, litter number one, Raven Company House Troop, under Housecarl Freyja. Thegn Erland, litter number twelve, Hammer Regiment, under the Jarl Bjarke. Thegn Havaldr, litter number seven, Hammer Regiment, under the Jarl Bjarke. Thegn Punnr, litter number four, Wolf Company House Troop, under the Housecarl Halvar. Thegn Signe, litter number three, Arrow Company, Storm Regiment under the Jarl Asmund. Thegn Ulf, litter number five, Hammer Regiment under the Jarl Bjarke.'

'Thank you High King,' said Atilius. 'I note your selections with great interest and sense we will have some fun during this Raiding Season.' He walked in front of the group. 'Thegns of Valhalla! The time is upon you. Every new initiate to the Pantheon must symbolically cross the great River Styx that divides the world we know from the underworld. Charon, Ferryman of the Dead, awaits his payment. Go now. Cross to the Pantheon.'

A vast figure stood by the water's edge. He wore faded breeches and boots, but was naked from the waist up despite the Scottish winter. His enormous belly broke across his belt and hair matted his chest, shoulders and arms. His head was encased in a rimmed iron helmet, and the air holes punched through the visor were the only indication that something living could be found within. Over one shoulder he carried a hammer. He waited motionless as the group shuffled towards him.

'If you should ever turn back from the Pantheon now,' Atilius said with an offhand tone, 'you will answer to Charon.'

Brante took a position in front of the monster. Even at his full height, Brante's eyes barely reached Charon's shoulders. 'Payment,' a voice growled beneath the helmet.

Brante reached inside his tunic for the *denarius* and offered it to the Ferryman, who flung it into the burning brazier beside him. 'Pass.'

Brante walked around the giant and out into the water towards the longship. Hands beckoned him and helped him over the side. One by one, the Thegns each proffered their *denarii* and followed. Punnr flapped and struggled as he tried to get purchase on the straked sides of the ship with the water sucking at his mail, but hands hauled him aboard. Ahead of him Havaldr was working his way over the benches and down the central length of the vessel, and so Punnr followed, feeling his way past the shadowed rowers. The keel curved up beneath his boots as he approached the far end. He pushed past Havaldr and circled the silent Erland, until he reached his companions. They clustered together and looked back to the shore. An ornate wooden chair was being manhandled into place on a platform at the prow of the ship. Although the dragonhead was the front of the vessel, it seemed on this occasion that it had been hauled onto the beach headfirst for effect and they would be crossing to the underworld in reverse. Sveinn climbed on board and seated himself in the chair and Radspakr came beside him. Atilius, Charon and the Vigiles stayed on the shore.

Some of the unseen boatmen had jumped into the water and could be heard pushing the vessel off the stony beach. The keel shuddered and then they were free. The men hauled themselves aboard again and the oars settled into a rhythm. The Thegns looked out across the dark loch. The mountains were invisible on this cloud-blackened night and the water too was almost impossible to see when nothing reflected on its surface. They could have been flying across space and the completeness of the dark made it seem to their exhausted brains that they were indeed crossing to Hades.

There were new lights coming from the far shore. At first they were just a smear of yellow across the horizon, but as the longship continued on its silent journey, they broke into a myriad of separate flaming torches and braziers, dozens of them, even hundreds. The shoreline came closer and they could see banners raised into the night. There were figures now too. Lines of them. Waiting and wordless. Light danced on shields and gleamed from mail.

Sveinn's voice growled from behind. 'Behold! My Horde.'

The boat approached the shore and the oars which had been dipping in unison, ceased as one and were raised. The keel rumbled across pebbles and juddered to a halt and the oarsmen again jumped over the side and secured it. Sveinn rose and walked imperiously up the length of the boat and the Thegns parted for him. With practised ease, he vaulted over the side and strode through the water to the shore.

'I think that's our cue,' Brante said and jumped into the water too, followed by the others. The drop was greater than Punnr expected and his knees jarred on impact and almost sent him sprawling into the water in front of the ranks of warriors, but he just steadied himself and joined the others in a little bewildered cluster on the beach.

Sveinn was already in front of the centre ranks and speaking with a beast of a man, a huge bearded warrior, helmeted and carrying an axe and a crimson shield depicting a hammer. Punnr spied Freyja at the head of a troop to their right. She was wreathed in black, with a short silver mail *brynjar* and a necklace sparkling around her throat. Her hair was untied and the braids flowed over her shoulders. A raven decorated her shield.

Sveinn returned to them and he was accompanied by the warrior. 'Bjarke, these are my Thegns. And this, my Thegns, is the mighty Bjarke – the *bear*. Jarl of Hammer Regiment, the Heavy Infantry Shieldmen. The core of the Horde and the heart of our shieldwall in any battle. Bjarke leads the *berserkers* at the centre of our line.'

The giant harrumphed and barely looked at them. He had a thatch of unkempt blond hair that fell to his shoulders, matched by an equally unruly blond beard. His face in the half-light was creased and bunched into a scowl. His arms were bare except for leather wrist protectors and silver rings around his huge biceps. He wore a studded leather jerkin that dropped to his thighs, leather leggings and boots, and a bearskin tied across his shoulders which hung almost to the ground. An evil-looking dagger was thrust through his belt and he held his axe casually across his shoulder as though it were merely a spade. On the side of his neck, Punnr noticed a tattoo running across his throat until it disappeared under the collar of his jerkin.

Despite the bulk of the man behind him, the High King exuded quiet authority. 'Now, let me recall. Thegns Ulf and Havaldr, you are assigned to Hammer Regiment. My Valhalla Horde numbers 220 warriors this Nineteenth Season, and the Hammer Regiment accounts for 119 of them, fifteen litters of eight, each commanded by a Hersir to whom you will report.'

'Asmund.' Sveinn raised his voice and another warrior approached. He was short, but lean and light on his feet, clean-shaven, young and with long dark hair which was carefully combed. He carried a crimson shield with a lightning flash across it, similar to the one the female Perpetual had been given, and over his shoulder hung a longbow. 'Thegn Signe, you will go with Asmund. He is Jarl of Storm Regiment, Light Infantry, comprising forty-seven. Four litters of eight in Arrow Company and two litters in Spear Company.'

Signe stepped over to Asmund and Sveinn regarded the remaining four. 'Now we have the ex-Thralls. The truly new recruits. Those found by the Venarii Parties. You have been much tested today. Thegn Erland, you too will be joining Hammer Regiment under Jarl Bjarke. As for the remaining three of you, I think you are acquainted with your commanders already. Halvar! Freyja! Come forward.'

The two Housecarls approached from opposite ends of the massed ranks.

'Thegn Calder, I have placed you under Housecarl Freyja in Raven Company House Troop, the elite Squadron of Scouts, numbering sixteen. You will go with her and learn from her in the coming weeks. You will be the Horde's eyes and ears.'

Calder looked emptily at her two companions, then walked with Freyja back to her troop under a giant raven banner.

'And finally, Thegns Brante and Punnr. What am I to do with you two?' Sveinn mused in his low rumble. 'You will both be joining Wolf Company House Troop, my elite Kill Squads, numbering thirty-two in four litters. Halvar is your captain. I wish to see if you have the mettle to be my assassins. Bjarke and his Shieldmen make all the noise in battle and are unbreakable at my centre, but my Wolf Company wields death in a much more refined manner. Halvar speaks well of you both. Learn from him. Go now.'

Sveinn brushed them away and they followed Halvar's great cloaked form up the shore. Sveinn stood alone on the beach in front of the combined regiments of the Valhalla Horde. 'Now my warriors, we feast with Odin!'

As one, the ranks burst into howls and cheers, and the noise rolled out in a great wave across the empty loch.

XXI

On their return to the castle, Sveinn's Mead Hall had been transformed and Punnr stood spellbound at the entrance, while all two hundred and twenty warriors of the Valhalla Palatinate deposited their weapons outside and pushed their way through the door, laughing and calling and posturing. Gone were the benches and scattered furs and the remains of the simple breakfast that the Thralls had hurried to eat early that morning. The central hearth had been swept clean of ash and a new mighty fire licked up towards the hole in the ceiling.

On either side of this, tables ran seventy foot down the length of the hall ready to seat every member of the Palatinate. But these weren't oak tables, darkened with age and befitting of the ancient space. They were glass, spotless and sleek. The benches that ran under them were of burnished steel, with cream cushions. Silver cutlery was laid and fine stemmed glasses. Along the centre of each table ran a solid wall of cut glass, dividing each table into two sides, but at a foot high, low enough for the revellers to speak to those opposite, and down the entire length of this glass were fixed candles, more than a hundred on each table, so close they too almost created a second barrier of wax and flame.

But what really took Punnr's breath away was the lighting. He had believed the hall had no electricity and for the last week they had laboured by burning torchlight to heat food over the fire. Yet now, jets of aqua-blue shot heavenwards from points on the floor near the walls, illuminating the coats-of-arms on the vaulted ceiling. The entire back wall behind the dais was awash with blue rays. The modernity of the glass and the steel and the spotlights should have been jarringly out of place in this medieval hall, but in fact it was wondrous. As Punnr followed his new Wolf Company to their allotted places, he thought the scene summed up everything he understood about the Pantheon. The blood and violence of the ancient world, conjured into this modern age by the unconstrained power of money.

He was seated with his litter of eight, one of the four Kill Squads comprising Wolf Company, and he could see Brante a few places down on the other side of the table with his own litter. Punnr looked further, searching around the hall at the many faces, believing he must at last see the one he had been missing for so long.

He was interrupted by the man next to him. 'I hear there are seven corpses burning on fires beside the loch.'

'Is that so?'

'That's a violent day's work for someone so wet behind the ears.'

The other members of the litter had ignored Punnr so far, but now they peered at him.

'If you're attacked,' Punnr shrugged, 'there's no other option.'

'So you're a man who will spill blood just to get a seat at this table.'

'If that's what it takes.'

'But how do you know we're worth it?'

'I don't, but I'll have a better idea when I've tasted your wine.'

It was a good response and there were muted grins. The man grabbed a flagon from a passing server and filled Punnr's glass. 'My name's Leiv. Hersir of Litter Four, Wolf Regiment.' He waved an arm at the group around them. 'It's my misfortune to be in charge of these bastards.'

'We are the Wolves!' smirked a bearded fellow across the glass barricade. Legions of youngsters were serving mead and wine now and the warriors' voices were becoming oiled into life. 'Hunt them; trap them; devour them. We are the Wolves!'

There was a chorus of cheers up and down the table and Punnr gulped down his drink. It was good. Expensive. Food arrived and he realised how famished he was. He had endured the whole *Sine Missione* and the Oath-Taking with only the mid-morning bread he had shared with Gulbrand. Gulbrand, who was now a corpse. His glass was refilled by a boy and he drank again. Platters of duck and venison arrived, steaming potatoes, fried fish, sausages, goat's cheese and more flatbreads. The troops gorged themselves.

Punnr looked up to the high table on the dais. Sveinn sat on a glass throne, sipping from his wineglass and scanning the length of the room, while Radspakr whispered into his ear. Freyja was seated on his other side, and Halvar, Bjarke and Asmund were the other occupants.

'The Council of War,' Leiv said through a mouthful. 'Those are the five who work with Sveinn and Odin on all strategic decisions for the Palatinate – recruitment, training, deployment, tactics in battle. Our seniors and our betters.'

'You say that with sarcasm.'

'Let's just say they're a mixed bunch.'

Further down the table, Brante was raising his glass to the men opposite, and on the far table Calder perched stiffly listening to her new Raven Company. Punnr thought she looked flushed and incredibly tired. His eyes moved on, running along the length of both tables, searching again the faces of all the warriors. *She* must be here. Sveinn had said his entire Horde was present. *So why the hell couldn't he spot her?* He leaned forward and looked up and down his own row. A sick dread rolled in his stomach and he forced himself to ignore it.

He tried to change his line of thought and focused back on Leiv. 'Tell me about the Kill Squads. "Hunt them, trap them, devour them"?'

'We're Sveinn's specialists, the ones he sends to eliminate targets. On a battlefield we wait on the flanks of Bjarke's shieldwall until a pivotal moment and then we go hunting.'

'Who are your targets?'

'Maybe a unit of the foe that's performing strongly, or an individual trooper if he's leading the line. We go for the officers or stalk the banner bearers. But mostly it's the same overriding order. Get to Alexander. Take him, kill him.'

'Have you ever managed that?'

Leiv eyed him. He was late thirties, tall and beardless.

'Almost. Last season. We broke behind the Titan line and came in from the flank, sixteen of us. We were hidden in the melee and the foe didn't notice us. Alexander was there, in the middle behind the line, and for that moment he had only his immediate attendants around him. We could have killed him with a thrown spear, but we were too bloody ambitious and thought he would perish on our swords.'

'So what happened?'

'We didn't reach him. We were maybe thirty feet away when he saw us coming from the flank. In that moment, I don't think he had an answer. His bodyguard had deserted him and advanced into the battleline. He looked utterly shocked to see us that close. But then Agape and her Sacred Band came from nowhere. They're the elite Hoplite Light Infantry. A match even for us. They numbered only fifteen last season, but it was enough to blunt our attack and hold us until Alexander's bodyguard began to return in numbers. We had just seconds before we would be surrounded and massacred, so we had to fight a costly withdrawal.' He ate a small piece of duck. 'But we were close that day.'

'What would have happened if you'd been successful?'

'To kill the King? That depends. If a King is felled by an arrow or a thrown spear, or by any other missile from distance, it's a reward of fifty Blood Fund credits to the attacking Palatinate. A hefty amount. Perhaps fifty new Drengr warriors for the death of one King. It's rare, but it's happened before.'

'Does the losing Palatinate get a new King?'

'Aye. Kings are replaced and the Pantheon continues. There will always be another Alexander and another Sveinn when one is killed.' He chewed on his duck. 'But kill a King with a sword in your hand, get close enough to drive it directly into him, that's a different matter. To my knowledge, it's never been done in the history of the Pantheon. Kill the King face-to-face – get to him before he can take his own life, before his bodyguards can cut you down, and stand over his fallen body – well, do that, and the entire Palatinate falls.'

'You mean no more Titans?'

'Aye, no more Titans. Or Turk, Roman, Mongol, Hun, depending which King has the blade in his belly. It's one of the sacred Rules of the Pantheon and the golden prize. It's said that vast sums are gambled on this before every Blood Season. Business empires could crumble on the outcome of this one wager. Kill the King in direct sword combat and his Palatinate falls and becomes part of your own.'

'Then what happens?'

'The victorious and hugely strengthened force moves up a level and takes on a new Palatinate as foe.'

'Which is?'

Leiv shrugged. 'Any of the remaining five. Could be the Qin in China, the Sultanate in Istanbul, the Huns in Budapest, the Kheshig on the Mongolian grasslands or maybe even the Legion at the Palatine. I don't care. Just point the Wolves at the enemy and we'll eliminate them. Anyway, it's never been done, so you only need to worry yourself about the Titans.'

The hall was buzzing now as the ale made them rowdy and argumentative. There were catcalls and shouted warnings amidst the laughter. Drink was thrown. Scuffles broke out and wrestling contests began over the glass divides.

'Last year, during the Blood Season before the Battle, the Titans came for Sveinn,' said Leiv, sipping his wine grimly and oblivious of the noise around them. 'They really believed they had a chance to kill him in his own tunnels and they sent some of their best troops, the Companion Hoplites. But we already knew they were coming and we'd laid a trap. They lost many of their best warriors, including Timanthes, their Colonel. The losses of such fighters blew their chances in the subsequent Battle and they ended the Season severely weakened. The success of that ambush is the main reason Sveinn was able to recruit seven new Thegns like you, as well as twenty-six Drengrs. We are stronger than ever this year. It should be celebrated.' He raised his glass and Punnr repeated the gesture, but Leiv still looked serious. 'The whole thing was wrong though.'

'Why?'

'It was such a damn risk they took. That was no battlefield fight, they brought their elite troops to a raid beneath the streets in Valhalla territory. They must have been truly fooled by Sveinn's trap.'

'What had he done?'

Leiv thought for a moment then shrugged. 'I don't know. Above my pay grade.'

He looked towards the High Table, where Sveinn was standing, holding a huge horn cup. The King raised it in front of him and the hall fell silent. Troopers kicked their more boorish colleagues into silence and all heads swung to their High King.

'My troops of Valhalla, we gather again for the first time since the glorious ending of the last Blood Season.' Sveinn's voice was soft, low and measured. 'We welcome new Oathsworn to our ranks tonight, both Drengr and Thegn, and we will share Odin's mead with them.' There was a murmur of approval. He waited until quiet returned. 'After Yuletide, we will meet at New Year and raise our Hammer, Raven, Wolf and Lightning banners on the field of the *Agonium Martiale*. We will parade our strength to the Titan Palatinate and challenge them once again, in the Nineteenth Year of the Pantheon.'

There was a roar. Glasses broke as they were thumped on the tables. 'I can tell you now, my troops, that Atilius, Praetor of the Pantheon, has this day shared with me the rules for this year's Raiding Season. The Pantheon law-givers have excelled themselves this time and I can promise you there will be many adventures to be had in these next few weeks.' Another howl of approval greeted this. 'I will consult with my Council of War and we will determine the approaches, the formations and the tactics to ensure victories for the Horde of Valhalla.'

Bjarke hauled himself to his feet and thrust his glass into the air. 'Odin, High King Sveinn and the Horde of Valhalla!' The hall erupted and everyone's drink was held high and then emptied.

Sveinn remained unmoved and the hall eventually returned to silence. 'So,' he said, as though there had been no interruption. 'We will share Odin's Mead.'

He raised the great horn high above his head, then took a reverent sip from it. He handed the horn to Radspakr first, who held it in turn as Sveinn dipped his hands into the mead and ran his wet fingers through his hair and forehead. The ritual performed, Radspakr raised the horn above his head, sipped and handed it to Freyja. She held it as he too dunked his hands and wet his almost bald head. The pageant continued along the high table accompanied by total silence from the floor, then Halvar walked with the horn down to the end of Punnr's table and offered it to the first warrior.

It took fifteen minutes for the horn to travel up and down the full length of both tables. Punnr drank of the sweet mead and Leiv held the horn for him to sprinkle more mead through his hair. Later Brante wetted his shaven and polished head so that it gleamed, and later still on the far side, Calder drank with an intense seriousness and applied the mead to her golden locks, so that strands curled down over her eyes. Throughout it all the hall remained silent and disappointment welled in Punnr's stomach again because the procession of drinkers gave him ample opportunity to observe each and every one, and proved to him that his sister, Morgan, wasn't present.

The horn finally returned to Sveinn and he carried it regally down the centre of the hall to the fire, where he flung it onto the flames. A mighty cheer rolled around the room and it seemed it was a signal for the feasting to end. Warriors stood and began to weave among each other, bantering, laughing, bragging and playfully punching comrades.

Punnr wandered into the centre of the hall, shouldering his way through the crowd. Already the doors were being opened and warriors were beginning to head out into the night. He circled the groups, staring at faces. Of the two hundred or more fighters, he counted forty women, but none of them was the one he sought. He closed in on Sveinn, who was listening to a group of five Hammer Regiment Shieldmen. Then he saw Halvar and wheeled towards him.

But before he could, he found himself facing Radspakr. 'Well, well and what does Thegn Punnr think of his first Valhalla feast?'

Punnr didn't even bother to answer the question. 'My lord, am I correct in understanding that every member of the Horde is present tonight?'

'You are. Our city stronghold is empty save for Vigiles sentries. This is the gathering of the Palatinate.'

'Is it possible that some aren't here?'

'No.' Radspakr did not elaborate, but the simplicity of his answer was enough to convince Punnr that all were indeed present. He tried to consider his next words, but his brain was frazzled with alcohol.

'I'm looking for someone who I thought was a warrior of the Horde, but I can't find her here.'

Radspakr had been glancing beyond Punnr, already bored of the conversation, but now his eyes came back and they could have been the only two men in the hall, such was the intensity of his stare. 'And why would you think you know the identity of any warrior of Valhalla before tonight?'

In sober daylight, perhaps Punnr would have stopped himself saying the next words. 'She's my sister. She joined the ranks of the Horde several years ago and now, as you can imagine, I'm desperate to see her.'

A weight descended on the older man, an immovable glacier that froze him. After an age he spoke in a flat voice. 'You are very much mistaken, Punnr the Weakling. Firstly, no person from beyond the Pantheon has ever known the identity of any single Valhalla warrior. Secondly, the Pantheon enforces a strict rule that no family member of a Pantheon trooper is *ever* recruited. It runs contrary to every rule of selection. Family ties from the real world are never brought into the Pantheon.'

'But this time there must have been an oversight.'

'I'm not party to the decisions of the Pantheon Selection Committees. I don't have a say in who is recruited. But I can assure you that the research and resources available to the Selection Committees is second to none and if you ever had a sister in the Pantheon – in any of the Palatinates – your name would not even have made it to the shortlist. So you are mistaken. I am sorry your search has proved fruitless. You are nevertheless now Oathsworn to Valhalla.' He broke his gaze and looked down the hall. 'I believe you have private quarters and a proper bed tonight. It is a rare privilege for our new Thegns after the *Sine Missione* and will never be offered again. So I suggest you go and enjoy it. You will feel better in the morning.'

He left him and Punnr realised the hall was already emptying. Only small groups of warriors still idled at the tables. Sveinn had gone. So too had Calder and Brante, probably up to the beds they had been honoured with. Punnr stumbled morosely to the inner door. He climbed the stairs and found his way to his room. True enough, there was now a great oak bed with white pillows and a thick white duvet, covered with a fur for extra warmth. He stalked over to it, looking down at the infinite softness. He could collapse into that and sleep until only the gods could wake him.

But even as his knees began to give way, he could hear the voices of the troops outside. He forced himself to stay upright and went over to the tiny window. Below him, stretching from the hall to the loch, an army settled itself around campfires. He took the fur from the bed and wrapped it around him, then padded back down the stairs and out into the night. He walked around the fires and at last spied Halvar, seated on a spread of furs with the men of his Wolf Kill Squads.

'May I join you?'

Halvar contemplated him. 'You have a warm bed in the castle tonight to mark your success in the *Sine Missione*, and instead you wish to sit here?'

The eyes of Wolf Company were upon Punnr. 'Yes,' he said simply.

Halvar ground his jaw and then his face broke into a craggy smile. 'After the day you've had, you would honour me by joining our fire.'

In the keep, Radspakr settled into his office. His giant desk was surrounded by screens. Televisions showed an assortment of live pictures from some of the cameras on site – the few stragglers still in the hall, an aerial shot of the night fires outside, the stairs leading up to the sleeping quarters in the tower. Other screens flicked through live images of all the Horde's underground strongholds beneath Edinburgh's Old Town. The places were quiet for now, awaiting the return of the troops. Another screen was freeze-framed on edited highlights from footage taken during the *Sine Missione*. The computers in front of him gave him instant access to the Horde's funds and resources, to the details of the manpower and to an inventory of weapons and clothing. He could look at the payments made into each warrior's bank account and edit the records of those who were promoted, injured or slain.

He called up Punnr's record and reminded himself of his background. Tyler Maitland, that was it. Flat 6, 18 Learmonth Place. Information Assistant at Edinburgh University Library. He scanned the rest of the data. The Pantheon Selection Committees didn't provide him with any family details, nor any reasons for their decisions. He switched to a second screen and tapped in a quick online search for Tyler Maitland. After several minutes of clicking through different pages he found the old newspaper report about his mother's death in a hit and run and a reference in the same article to a sister, Morgan Maitland.

The name rang no bells. He ran a query through the Valhalla database, but no one of that name, or indeed even of just the Christian or surname alone, showed up in the records for the whole nineteen years of the Palatinate.

He sat back. The lad was obviously mistaken. But the wily politician in Radspakr still felt uneasy. There had been something in Maitland's conviction. And more than that, everything about Tyler Maitland seemed wrong. The flirtations with cocaine dealing that showed on his record. The arm he could hardly use when Radspakr had first propositioned him on the steps of Fleshmarket Close. The weak leg. Reasons enough for the Pantheon to overlook such an individual.

Radspakr picked at his lip. And why had the rules been changed this time?

He didn't like anything about this day, nor about Tyler Maitland's presence in his Valhalla Horde.

He reached for his phone and pulled up a number. It was time to make some calls.

Part Two

The Raiding Season

Part Two

The Raiding Season

XXII

The Water of Leith was running fast and full as it twisted its way through Stockbridge towards the docks on the Forth. It was a grey, monotone Saturday morning and Lana was contemplating the river from the grassy bank in front of her flat on Reid Terrace when he came around the corner.

Eleven o'clock. As always, he was punctual. When she had called him the night before, he had been reserved, but had agreed after a few clipped sentences to come over the next morning. So here he was, striding towards her, blue jumper over white shirt, fitted tweed jacket, cream corduroys and burgundy brogues. Every inch the off-duty Edinburgh lawyer.

'It's cold to be waiting outside,' he said brusquely.

'I thought we could go for a walk.'

'Ah, "*a walk*".' He thrust his hands into his jacket pockets and maintained a careful distance as she led him back out the terrace and north along Arboretum Avenue. 'How's your mother?'

Her mother, yes. That had been the lie the Pantheon had created to cover for her week's absence. When Halvar had returned their phones and watches, Lana had discovered an email conversation on her work account.

On the first Friday, as she was breakfasting on honeyed flatbreads around the fire in Sveinn's Mead Hall, someone had hacked into her work email and sent her estate agent employers on Nelson Street a message to say that her mother had been taken ill and she had felt obliged to race to Kirkcudbright overnight. Her boss had replied that they would have to redistribute Lana's viewing appointments, but this could all be sorted in her absence and did she have an address to which flowers could be sent? With some panache, the hacker had thanked her boss and suggested that flowers could be addressed to Mrs D Cameron, Cedar Ward at the Dumfries & Galloway Royal Infirmary. Lana could only wonder how many times the flowers had been passed around the hospital in confusion.

'She's improving, thanks.'

It had been Thursday evening when the Pantheon released Lana and she returned to a flat which she had never been expecting to desert for a week. There were still dishes in the sink and her bedcovers were thrown back and the heating was high. The emailed conversation was not the only discovery on her phone. There were seven messages from Justin, starting concerned, turning mildly hysterical, then moving through anger, hurt and finally suggesting that if she couldn't be bothered to get in touch then perhaps she should go to hell.

They wandered through the gates of Inverleith Park to the sounds of children on the swings and dogs barking. She looked up at the bare winter trees. They were an unwelcome reminder of the Highland valley and of Hertha and Einar, who were no more, and Lana wondered how she could be expected to come back to this normal life. The city continued in its usual lethargic Saturday morning routine of coffee, papers, shopping, dog-walking, perhaps a bit of jogging, but she was a woman utterly changed and she thought Justin must see it.

'I'm sorry for not getting in touch,' she said at last.

'Just a text would have sufficed. Enough to know you were okay.'

'I withdraw when I'm stressed, drop communication. It's just the way I'm wired. And it's best for everyone because you really don't want to see me during the darker moments.'

'But that's precisely when I want to see you, because I hope I can make a difference. Any boyfriend would.'

Boyfriend. He had never used that term before and the sound of it on his lips appalled her. 'Oh Justin.'

'*Oh Justin* – is that all you can say? Five months, it's been. Five months during which you've seen me only when it's convenient, rarely confided in me about anything in your life and lavished about as much physical affection on me as you would a plague victim. But you know what? I've stuck with it. I've hung in there. I've ignored the voice in my head telling me it's useless. I've kept convincing myself there might be a thaw one day, and why? Because despite every indication to the contrary, I can't help hoping that maybe one day the two of us could have something.'

She looked into his eyes. He was handsome and honest. Reliable. Steadfast. A beacon of integrity. She shook her head sadly. 'We won't, Justin. I'm sorry.'

'I'm in love with you.'

'Don't say that.'

'I have to. I'm not stupid. I can see what's coming and if I don't say it now, then I'll never have another chance.'

He had reached for her hand and he thought that in that moment Michelangelo could not have improved on her gaunt cheekbones and the rigid line of her lips. She said nothing and fixed her gaze on the ground with her hand limply in his. Eventually he exhaled and released her. 'Well, at least we both know our position. I'm sorry that loving you is such a crime. It shouldn't have to be. But I won't bother you again, Lana.'

Christmas. A groggy, stale, impenetrable celebration of loneliness, Tyler thought, sealed behind his curtains, lazing in his own spent air and tobacco smoke. Mornings of black and white films, afternoons of chocolate and evenings of whisky and Netflix. His duvet had migrated from the bed to the sofa. His phone hadn't rung, his email not beeped. The radiators clicked and the gas heater wheezed. Books lay scattered, open at the page when his eyes had glazed over.

Jol, the Vikings called it before the Christians stole it. Yule. A feast of pork and beer traditionally held in mid-January. Sacrifices made to the gods to guard against the dark of winter, and toasts given again and again to bring good fortune in the year ahead.

When his mother had been alive, Christmas had always been a special occasion. Even in the hardest times in their small apartment, she had never stinted on the celebrations and together the three of them reminded themselves that beneath all the angst, they loved each other fiercely. They would wear hats and drink sparkling wine from antique flutes. The crockery was bone china, Edwardian, collected assiduously by his mother at car boot sales.

Tyler thought about his sister and glanced over at her ivory amulet hanging from the photo on the dresser. She had left it for him surely as an unequivocal sign that she had joined the Horde. Yet when he had spoken of her to Radspakr, the Thane had denied all knowledge. It made no sense.

On Christmas Eve he had found Oliver sitting on the stairs outside, hunched over his iPad.

'Hey, lad.'

'Hey.'

'Why are you out here?'

'We're supposed to be off to Grandma's, but Mum and Dad are fighting.' He was scrolling through lists of names and transactions.

'What are you doing?'

'Accessing the customer database of a chain of hotels.'

Tyler sat next to him on the step and peered at the screen. 'You are? Why?'

'Dad says he stayed at one of them last week.' Oliver looked sternly at Tyler, daring him to comment further. 'I want to check if he did.'

'I see... I thought that sort of information was confidential.'

'Nothing's confidential if you know where to look.'

'If you say so, lad.' He watched as Oliver closed down the lists. 'Well, thanks for keeping an eye on the place while I was away. Have I had any visitors?'

'All quiet. Where'd you go?'

'North. I wanted to do some walking in big country. I've never explored up there.'

'Did you fall over a lot?'

'No. Why?'

'Your face.'

Tyler ran a hand over his features and realised his cheek, lips and chin were still grazed. He pushed his fingers self-consciously through his long hair. 'I did have a couple of tumbles.'

Oliver looked up from his screen and eyed Tyler with a sceptical half-grin. 'Yeah sure. It's so easy to fall on your face.' He swiped up a drawing app and produced a stylus from his shirt pocket. 'I've got a little bet riding on you. Want to know what it is?' He wrote in large letters *Is Tyler…*

'Am I what?'

But Oliver was already absorbed in drawing a series of triangular arms below the words. They all went into a central hub. An eight-pointed star. Tyler felt his neck tingle. The boy continued, filling in another set of arms behind the first, so that it became sixteen-pointed.

'Or…' Oliver said as he began to draw something next to the star. A horn. Then another behind, and a third, locking them into a tight knot. He finished and leaned back, admiring his handiwork. Tyler was wordless.

'So?' demanded the boy. 'Which one are you?'

'I'm not sure what you mean.'

Oliver used his stylus to stab at the emblem on the right. 'The Triple Horn of Odin, symbol of the Horde of Valhalla,' he said as if explaining a simple problem to a very slow student. 'And the Star of Macedon. Although some say it's the Sun of Macedon and it can be drawn with eight or sixteen rays.' He looked up at Tyler. 'It's the symbol of Alexander's Titans.'

'And you're asking which one I like best?'

'No. I'm asking which one you belong to.'

Tyler forced a laugh. 'How come you know so much about these?'

'Everyone does. I read up about them all the time. Did you know Alexander's resources have allowed him to recruit only one Electus this Season?'

'No, I didn't.'

'But they say Sveinn has recruited as many as seven.'

'Who's *they*?'

'Some of the experts online.'

'Experts? Really, Oliver, you shouldn't believe everything you read online. Does your Mum know you look at all this?'

'She doesn't care.' He stared obstinately at Tyler. 'Well?'

Tyler sighed theatrically. 'I don't really understand your question. I can promise you I'm not part of either Alexander's Titans or the Horde of Valhalla. I'm sorry to disappoint, but I just work in a library. It's not very interesting.'

'Supposing you *did* belong to one, which would it be?'

'Well theoretically – probably Valhalla.'

'I like the Titans. They're Sky-Gods. They can appear on any rooftop and drop on their enemy. The Sacred Band are their best fighters. Look.' Within seconds he had pulled up lists of saved videos. 'Here they are coming into Hunter Square.' The jolting film showed distant shadowy figures flying down ropes from the roofs above the Square and turning towards the camera before the film ended. 'And here's them crossing Castle Esplanade.'

Something caught Tyler's eye among Oliver's list of files. 'What's that one?'

Oliver clicked on it. 'They're the Caelestia. Which is Latin for *of the sky, heavenly.*'

An image opened. It was an illustration showing the head

and shoulders of a man whose head was encased in a mask of gold. Features had been painstakingly engraved into the gold, along with small holes for the mouth and eyes. Curling hair had been designed to flow around the head of the mask and four sun rays broke from its top. 'That's Zeus, the Caelestis of the Titan Palatinate,' continued Oliver. 'And this one's Odin, the Valhalla Caelestis.' He flicked a new image onto the screen. Again it was an illustration of a masked man. This time the mask was silver and had horns, but it was also beautifully made to depict the strong, lined face of a bearded warrior, complete with ear-piercings, an eye patch and scars on the glittering cheeks.

'Who's drawn these?'

'I don't know. Just someone online. Aren't they great?'

'And what do *the experts* say about the Caelestia?'

'To the Ancient Romans, the Caelestia were lesser gods who fell from heaven. Today, they're the true rulers of each Palatinate. No ordinary person has ever seen them and it's rumoured they never reveal themselves from behind their masks.' Oliver swiped the images away, then pulled up another. 'Now check this out.'

The next picture was obviously taken using a telephoto from a great distance and was too blurry to decipher individual features, but it showed a large group of people – a hundred or more – dressed in formal evening wear and ranged on the lawns in front of a grand house.

'What's this?' asked Tyler, scrunching his eyes as though that would make the photo clearer.

'This,' said Oliver with a dramatic pause, 'is one of the few known images of the Curiate. Or, at least, some of the Curiate, snapped at a gathering in Bordeaux.'

'Jesus, are you serious? Where did you get this?'

'It's easy to find if you're on the right forums. The picture's old now anyway and everyone's seen it.'

Tyler brought his fingers to the screen. 'Can you zoom in?'

'It makes no difference. You can't see any faces.' Oliver demonstrated, then pondered the image. 'Such a pity.'

Tyler was fascinated. 'I wonder who they are.'

Oliver shrugged. 'Billionaires. Trillionaires.'

'I don't think anyone's actually a trillionaire.'

'Whatever. You name the top ten multinationals and try telling me their majority owners aren't neck-deep in the Pantheon.'

'I think you need to treat what you read online with caution.'

Oliver jabbed a finger at the photo. 'Oh come on. Google, Apple, Facebook, Gazprom, Exxon, all those Chinese banks. You can't tell me they're not in that picture. It's all about money. That's all it takes to be in the Curiate. Odin and Zeus and the other Caelestes may be the rulers, but these people are the elite gamblers whose money oils the whole enterprise. If the Pantheon was a sport, they'd be the punters.'

'Someone else once likened the Pantheon to a sport,' Tyler said reflectively, then caught himself. He stood with as much nonchalance as he could muster and rubbed the boy's head. 'Well, don't get cold out here, lad. And wish your parents a merry Christmas from me. Have a good one.'

It was on Christmas afternoon, as Tyler digested a festive meal of steak pie, mash, ice cream and half a bottle of Glenfiddich, when he reached for his laptop, logged into his bank account and discovered a deposit, dated 22nd December, for £4,338. He stared at the transaction. *It must be a mistake. My god, could it be from Morgan? Is this her way of telling me she's okay?* The only information provided was a six-digit reference number which refused to yield up any further clues no matter how often he tried clicking on it. Gradually a new realisation seeped into his stuffed and tipsy body. This wasn't Morgan. This was the Pantheon. *They own me now.*

He wondered if it was a monthly sum. *Fifty grand a year, if so. And that's just for being a new Thegn.* He had done none of it for the money, yet remembered Brante's facetious comments all those weeks ago about the Armatura being an extended job interview and he felt oddly gratified to see the sum in his account. It was evidence of his success. Payment. Weregild. Blood Funds for the winning candidate.

XXIII

It was two nights before Hogmanay and the old year was seeing itself out on a wave of blustery, bitter drizzle. Punnr hunched against the wet and made his way along Victoria Terrace, an elegant walkway that curved along the southern slope of the Old Town below the Royal Mile, with views extending over Grassmarket. It was almost midnight and the restaurants along the Terrace were quietening. In warmer months crowded tables would span the walkway, but now it was empty and the puddles lay deep.

At the far western end, where the Terrace turned a corner into a quieter non-descript stretch, Punnr could see Calder sheltering against the tall frame of Brante, and a few yards away Erland stood with his nose buried in the collar of his coat and hands thrust into pockets. Brante gave Punnr a small wave as he approached and Calder turned to look at him. It felt good to see them both again and he pulled himself in close to them in an attempt to hide from the rain, but no one spoke.

A hooded figure materialised further along the Terrace and a second one appeared from the shadows at the other end. They loitered for a few moments and looked around, spoke quietly into phones and then pointed to a small metal door near to where Erland stood. It was grubby, rusted and covered in graffiti, but there was a high-spec camera fixed to the wall above. The door opened into darkness and no one emerged, so the foursome pushed cautiously inside.

'Hurry up and close it,' said a thin, nasal voice which they recognised. Brante pushed it shut.

There was a click and a spotlight illuminated them. They blinked and looked about. They were in a stone tunnel, blocked ten yards further in by a full height iron grille. In front of this stood Ulf, dressed in an emerald tunic that dropped to his knees, with black leggings and boots. A fine leather belt was fixed around his waist, but no weapons hung from it. He looked pale and he eyed them coldly as they dripped in a huddle under the spotlight.

'This is the South West Gate. You'll learn that each Gate has an outer and an inner door. The outer one is always basic and absent of anything that would draw a casual eye.' He indicated the iron grille behind him. 'This one's a bit more sophisticated. It has a fingerprint scanner for access.' He reached to the side and pressed his thumb onto a small unit in the wall. They saw the light on the top change from red to green. He pulled the barrier open and stepped back to beckon them through. As they passed him, Calder pulled away involuntarily. Ulf noticed and smiled at her coolly. 'A pleasure to see you, too.'

'Why are you here?' Punnr demanded.

'They needed someone to welcome you to the stronghold of Valhalla and I very kindly volunteered.'

'But you're a new Thegn just like us.'

'I was also a Perpetual. Schola trainees provide a variety of support tasks for the warriors, so over the years I've spent a lot of time here. Who better to show you around? It's so nice to get reacquainted. I trust you all enjoyed your Christmas breaks with your loved ones.'

'Just shut up,' Brante snarled. 'And get on with what you've been tasked.'

Ulf's sneer faded. 'The outer door is open day and night, although you should take great care to enter unobserved. The second barrier is locked throughout the Interregnum and the Armatura and you can only access it via the scanner. During the two Conflict Seasons – Raiding and Blood – this second barrier will be open every night between the hours of one and four as per the Pantheon Rules, and won't require thumb scans.'

'Why?' asked Punnr.

'Those are the Conflict Hours and each Palatinate stronghold must – in principle – be accessible to the foe. You'll be told more when it's deemed necessary.' He began to walk down the tunnel at a pace. 'Follow me.'

They filed away from the spotlight and passed a small room in which two figures sat. One of them watched a screen showing alternating camera images of Victoria Terrace. They both stared at the new arrivals.

'Gate Keepers,' Ulf said as he led them along the tunnel in the dark.

'How many Gates are there?' asked Brante.

'Five. Each with an outer and inner, and each with the same hours of accessibility. You will be fingerprinted later tonight.'

The tunnel turned a corner and they found another door blocking their way, which Ulf pushed through. Light burst upon them and they stood in the entrance open-mouthed.

The tunnel continued ahead, but now it was spot-lit all the way and the air was no longer musty; instead there was an air-conditioned warmth. Along one side, for as far as the eye could see, the wall had been covered with sheet silver and on it were engraved detailed scenes showing ancient Viking villages nestled on the banks of fjords, longships cresting Atlantic waves, and victorious armies sweeping all before them. The scenes continued as they followed Ulf and the silver was dazzling in the lights.

'The South West Tunnel,' Ulf called over his shoulder. 'There's a North West Tunnel which mirrors this and exits behind the Divinity School, at a door below Milne's Court. Both tunnels lead into the rock beneath the Royal Mile. They are hundreds of years old, although the Horde has spent fortunes enhancing and widening during the last twenty.'

He had reached a point where doorways led off from the left-hand wall. The first one opened onto a large room bathed in blue light. There were benches and more doors in the far wall.

'The Reception Area. Washing and changing facilities. After tonight, you won't progress beyond this point until you've discarded your phones, watches and the clothes you arrived in, and then dressed appropriately for the Halls of Valhalla.' He pointed to the next door, which was closed. 'The Western Armouries. Unless specified by a superior officer, you'll not carry weapons in the Halls.' He strode onwards and the others followed, Erland bringing up the rear. They reached steps leading down and Ulf stood back to let them pass. 'Welcome to the Western Hall.'

They walked into a great flagstoned space. The walls

to left and right were dominated by fireplaces, alight and crackling. Banners of Raven, Wolf, Storm and Hammer Regiments hung from the ceiling and inlaid into the floor in the centre was a sandstone Horn of Odin. There were more silver panels on the walls covered in ancient Norse text, and tables scattered around the perimeter. Groups of warriors were seated, talking, drinking and playing a game that looked similar to chess but had unusual figures carved in ebony and ivory. To the left the North West tunnel led back towards the Divinity School. Punnr glanced at the fires and wondered where the smoke went in this deep place.

They followed Ulf along a new and wider tunnel exiting the hall on the far side. Punnr guessed they were heading due east and estimated they must be somewhere under Lawnmarket at the top of the Royal Mile. Rooms tumbled from the corridor on both sides and they could see troops training with wooden swords, punch bags and staves of varying length.

'The Practice Rooms. You'll be required to maintain and improve your fighting skills at all times.' Ulf gave Punnr a sly sidelong look, but said nothing further. He strode onwards. To their left another tunnel disappeared. 'The North Tunnel to North Gate on Warriston's Close. The South Gate lies on Blair Street, under South Bridge. The East Gate takes you into the rear of one of the vaults on Market Street. You can enter and exit by any of these. Indeed, it's encouraged to alter your routine so that you're not spotted.'

Brante spoke up. 'Are we expected to believe that in nineteen Seasons the Titans haven't discovered these gates?'

'You can believe what you like. The fact is that the Sky-Rats know full well about them. But they can only raid during the Conflict Hours when the second barrier is open, and taking the decision to attack through small doorways and into tight tunnels, at times when we're armed and ready, is something they dare not do for risk of too many casualties. Instead they watch and wait for us to emerge.' Ulf stopped and turned back to Brante. 'It's the *secret* passages that are the real prize.'

'So where are those?'

'They wouldn't be secret if every new halfwit got to know of them, would they?'

'In other words, you don't know either.'

'Only senior officers and a few trusted warriors are privy to their location. It's said that one runs to the Castle and one even to the Palace, but they're never used and you would be wise to forget about them. Now, here we are. The Throne Room of Sveinn. The heart of the stronghold.'

The tunnel opened into an even grander hall, with colonnades supporting a vaulted stone ceiling. Two more great fireplaces warmed the air and thick rugs lay over the floor. Braziers burned alongside ancient faded tapestries. On the right, the tunnel to South Gate led away and other doorways opened onto vaults from which could be heard the voices of troopers drinking and conversing. At the far end was an intricately carved wooden throne, behind which, rearing together to form a high arch, were two longboat prows with golden dragon heads similar to the one on the vessel that had borne the new Oathsworn across the loch.

'The prows of the High King of Valhalla,' said Ulf, following their eyes. 'The symbol of his office, as they were once the symbol of every Viking lord's Hall.' He walked on. 'Come. We'll go to the Reception Area at East Gate where you'll be fingerprinted and your clothing is waiting. Once changed, you are free to explore. Don't go beyond the Gate Keeper posts in any of the tunnels. The Council Chamber up there,' Ulf pointed to steps leading above the Throne Room, 'is off limits at all times. Follow me.'

As he led them into the East Tunnel, Punnr glanced into an open door and spied Radspakr seated behind a mahogany desk, surrounded by computer screens. Impulsively he dropped behind the group and stepped into the room. 'My lord Thane, may I speak?'

Radspakr looked up from a file he was consulting. He had his reading glasses perched on the end of his hawk nose. For a moment he stared at Punnr, then he exploded. 'No one enters the Quartermaster's Office without my express permission!'

'I apologise, lord, I didn't know.'

Radspakr came around the desk and marched across the floor until he blocked Punnr's path by the door. 'What do you want?'

'To ask you again about my sister because I'm sure there's been a mistake. Whether or not the Pantheon forbids siblings to join, I know she was a member of this Horde. Her name is Morgan Maitland.' He sought something in his pocket. 'And look, I've brought a photo of her in the hope someone must know of her.'

Punnr held out a small image of Morgan at the kitchen table in their old flat, drinking from a mug and smiling for the camera. Radspakr refused to glance at the photo. 'As I have told you, I don't know your sister and she has never been a member of this Palatinate.'

'Please look at it. I won't leave until you do.'

With a slow sigh, Radspakr took the photo and squinted down at it. He didn't move. Long seconds passed and still he did not respond.

'Do you recognise her, lord?'

With an effort the Thane pulled himself from the image and levelled steely eyes on the young Wolf. 'Never seen her before in my life,' he said rigidly. 'But I will keep this and show it to a few colleagues, if that will stop your yapping.'

'I'd be grateful. Thank you, lord.'

XXIV

It was the third hour of New Year and the streets far above were still alive with people struggling home from a raucous Hogmanay. Punnr had been happy to spend the celebratory hours deep in the womb of Valhalla and had shared a toast of ale with Brante, Leiv and other members of Wolf Company in one of the vaults off Sveinn's Throne Room. The Wolves never tired of remembering their battles and he was enjoying sipping his drink and listening to them when Freyja appeared in the doorway.

'Thegn Punnr, your presence is required.'

He followed her up the spiralled stairs and entered a room that sat atop most of the other vaults. It was higher-ceilinged and at one end, in the apex of the arch, there was a small barred window, which during daytime perhaps provided a relief of natural light. Braziers burned on the walls and coals glowed in an ornate hearth. The flagstone floor was dominated by a great rectangular table, around which stood Sveinn, Radspakr, Bjarke, Asmund and Halvar, the Horde's Council of War.

Freyja pointed Punnr to a place opposite Sveinn and took up station alongside him. Spotlights set the tabletop ablaze and across the entire surface had been painted an intricate map of Edinburgh's city centre. It was exquisite. The parks were redolent in green, each road given its name in careful black oil. The key buildings were marked in purple and gold, and some of the most important even illustrated to show their architectural splendour. It stretched from the Meadows in the south, up to the Botanic Gardens in the north, and ran from Haymarket in the west to the rugged contours of Arthur's Seat in the east. But this was no tourist map. This was a map of war. Shaded in red were the Gates to Valhalla's underground kingdom and shaded in blue were the primary rooftop strongholds of the Titans.

'Welcome Punnr to this War Council,' Sveinn said in his slow gravel voice. 'Thane Radspakr recommended that you should join us.'

'Yes, lord.'

'The Nineteenth Raiding Season – this year known as the Season of the White – will begin with the annual assembling of the Palatinates for the *Agonium Martiale*. As the Council knows – but I will elaborate for Punnr's benefit – from April through December each year, during the Interregnum and the Armatura, no blood is spilt in the Pantheon. The *Agonium Martiale* symbolises the point of change, the formal start of the two Conflict Seasons – Raiding and Blood. From tomorrow night, for a period of six weeks, the normal laws of the first of these – the Raiding Season – will come into force.'

The High King began to pace in a circle around the backs of the Council, his hands thrust behind him. 'The Raiding Season is only a precursor to the Blood Season, but it does serve two vital purposes in its own right:

'Firstly, it provides ample opportunity for the Caelestia

and the Curiate to place wagers on the Season outcomes. Let us not overlook the significance of this. We stand here today because we are paid handsomely. And why do our betters pay us to do this? Because it gives them pleasure. Between them, they have the means to ensure no force on earth can deny them this pleasure. So keep this at the forefront of your minds. Your individual actions – and those actions of your troops – will almost certainly have direct consequences on the myriad gambles that will be made. Money will flow constantly and inexorably. So they will be watching our actions not only with pleasure, but with the earnest interest of investors, competitors and paymasters.

'Secondly, the Raiding Season provides us with the opportunity to consolidate our strength before the Grand Battle.' He was enjoying holding the Council's attention. 'Success in warfare depends upon a series of key factors. The first and most obvious of these is the number of troops that can be put into the field. We know our Horde considerably outnumbers the Titan Palatinate. However, this advantage doesn't guarantee success. Previous Pantheon Seasons – and indeed many of the great battles of the ancient world – tell us that troop numbers alone rarely determine victory. We need only look at Hannibal at Cannae, Caesar at Alesia, and Alexander at Gaugamela to see that history is rife with forces that have defeated far greater armies through better deployment, discipline and sheer leadership verve. The art of all successful warfare, my Council members, is preparation, knowledge, deception, speed, the capitalisation of the landscape and the audacity to strike with maximum violence at the exact point where your enemy is weakest.'

Sveinn let his words hang in the air and walked again

to his place at the table. 'Radspakr will now enlighten the Council about the Pantheon's plans for this Season. The floor is yours, Thane.'

Punnr shot a glance around. The others were studying the map. Like him, they were dressed in belted tunics. Sveinn had a wolfskin fastened around his shoulders and Bjarke wore his usual bearskin. Radspakr was in his woollen robe with the diagonal buttoning and the silver Odin amulet hanging from his neck.

'My lord. As we all know, the rules of each Raiding Season are drawn up afresh every year and the objectives are always different. It is this fluidity that characterises the Season and sets it apart from its more rigid sister – Blood. Every year we must master these new rules from scratch and play the game that is set for us. So here are the details of this Nineteenth Raiding Season:

'Within a radius of one mile of the Tron Kirk above our very heads, Atilius' Pantheon planners have concealed four Assets. As my Lord King Sveinn has just been explaining, victory in the Grand Battle will be determined by more than just our warrior numbers. These four Assets will be critical success factors for each Palatinate and so we must compete with the Titans to find them.'

Punnr sensed movement around the table, eyes catching each other. There was palpable excitement. After Sveinn's extensive introduction, they were finally getting to the crux of the matter.

'Here are the rules. In this – the Season of the White – each Palatinate will have what will be known as a White Warrior. High King Sveinn has decreed that this year the

White Warrior will be Punnr, hence his presence at our Council.'

Punnr could feel the gaze of the others on him.

'It will be the task of the White Warrior to find each Asset. It will be the task of the rest of us to protect him in his quest, to confuse and hamper the enemy, and to seek out their own White Warrior. Likewise the Titans will array their forces to best find the Assets and kill our White Warrior.'

Punnr's head jerked up. Radspakr was looking at him, his eyes as black as the burning coals in the hearth behind. The others too were staring his way, all except Sveinn who studied the map.

'Your selection for this role, Thegn Punnr, is a great honour,' Radspakr continued. 'The King believes you have the necessary courage and aptitude.'

'And he's expendable,' growled Halvar, shooting a piercing glance at Radspakr.

'If you wish to put it that way, Captain, then I will concur. In our considered view, Thegn Punnr is courageous, committed and, in the unfortunate event of failure, he is of a rank that would not prove a grave loss to our forces.' The Thane stared steadfastly at Halvar and for several tense seconds Halvar returned his hostile look. 'May I continue, Captain?'

Halvar grunted and dropped his eyes.

'Thank you. The four Assets are as follows: One – Time. Find this Asset and the Palatinate will have two weeks' notice of the Grand Battle during which to plan its deployment. Fail and we'll learn of the battle only twenty-four hours in advance.

'Two – Field. Hold this Asset and we'll be told where the battle will take place and will be able to study the terrain. Failure will mean we arrive on the field with no more information than our scouts can hurriedly identify.

'Three – Supplies. Water and rations. Enough to maintain our army on full rations for as long as we are in the field. Failure to find this Asset will mean we march with empty stomachs and face our foe wracked with thirst.

'Four – Distance. Obtain this Asset and we'll be deployed close to the field of battle with time to set it to our advantage. Lose and we'll be deposited a day's hard march away.'

Sveinn interrupted his Thane. 'I hardly think I need to expound upon the seriousness of these challenges. The Council will be experienced enough to see that if we fail in this task, our greater troop numbers could count for nothing. We may arrive on an unknown field, exhausted, hungry, cold and unprepared. And then we will face the sarissas of Alexander's phalanx. Continue please, Thane.'

'Thank you, lord. The Raids will take place on four separate nights, with a week between each. One o'clock to four are the hours of operation. So we have an overall total of twelve hours to collect the Assets. And let me be clear – this is not a case of he who finds an Asset owns it. The Titans may find the same Asset within the four nights and claim it as well. The most certain way of winning this task, therefore, is to slay the enemy's White Warrior. Fell him and the foe can find no further Assets.'

'At which point,' Freyja interrupted him, 'they are free to focus entirely on disrupting our own attempts.'

'Precisely, Captain. If the White Warriors from both

Palatinates are felled, the challenge is over. I believe that explains the rules. Questions?'

'How does Punnr find the Assets?' Halvar asked.

'At the *Agonium Martiale* tomorrow night we'll be provided with a clue to the first location, which is for the eyes of this Council only. Find the Asset and Punnr will also find a clue to the next location. We don't know the order of the clues. Likewise, we don't know what the Titans will be given.'

Sveinn leaned forward. 'So this is an exercise in understanding our foe; in always being one step ahead of his thinking; in acting – first and foremost – to *deceive* him. The Titans are no fools. They will have their scouts arrayed across the rooftops and if we solve our first clue and stampede straight to our first location, we will have solved it for them also. So instead we will take them in the wrong directions. Lead them a merry dance.'

Radspakr waited until he was sure Sveinn had finished. 'The Council will meet after the *Agonium Martiale* when we have the first clue. In the meantime, you may brief your Regiments. Jarl Bjarke, Hammer Regiment will defend the Valhalla Gates, but you will also handpick a group of Shieldmen to act as close bodyguard for Thegn Punnr.'

The huge warrior looked across the table at Punnr. 'Aye, I can do that.'

'Good,' Sveinn said with finality. 'We have two days to prepare. I suggest you assemble your litters and brief them. Thank you for your attention.'

It was their signal to leave. Punnr followed Freyja as they descended back down the steps to the Throne Room.

She stopped at the bottom and touched him to pull him aside. They waited as first Bjarke passed without so much as a look, and then Asmund, who smiled and gave Punnr a quick wink. Halvar brought up the rear and he joined the two of them.

'Are you okay with this?' Freyja asked Punnr quietly.

'Do I have a choice?'

Halvar bent in close to his face. 'Every shield of the Horde will protect you. Every arrow, sword and spear will fight for you. You just focus on finding the Assets, getting the next clue, and staying alive.'

XXV

The Horde waited in South Tunnel. All two hundred and twenty warriors, lined in their litters, companies and regiments.

The tunnel's walls allowed for no more than two abreast and the tightly packed space felt hot and claustrophobic. There was a murmur of low voices and the movement of impatient bodies flushed through with adrenaline. The time was almost three in the morning on the second night of the new year and the city above was still sleeping off the excesses of Hogmanay.

Punnr waited nervously towards the rear, behind Sveinn, Radspakr and Bjarke, and surrounded by household shieldmen from Bjarke's Hammer Regiment who acted as Royal Bodyguard. They were strong men, heavily bearded and smelling of ale. They wore mail *brynjars*, iron vambraces on their forearms and bearskins across their shoulders to indicate their status. They carried broadswords at their hip and giant war axes, and each held a circular crimson shield with the hammer insignia.

They eyed the slim figure of Punnr curiously. And well they might, for he was clothed like no other warrior that night. While the rest of the Horde had gone through their dressing rituals in the Reception Areas, transforming themselves from their arrival garb into their full battle regalia with regimental colours, Punnr was escorted to a small room off the Central Tunnel where a boy from the Schola waited with his panoply. Punnr had pulled on a grey long-sleeve tunic, black breeches and knee-length boots, then turned in silent wonder to the armour. There were two iron vambraces with ancient designs inscribed across them, a front-and-rear iron corselet engraved with rune snakes, and a curved helmet with eyepieces, ornate cheekguards and chainmail hanging from the back to protect his neck. Each item was rendered in spotless white. The boy helped strap on the armour, then gave him the helmet to tuck under his arm. Next came the sword and seax he had been presented beside the loch, belted tight across his corselet, and finally a cloak and shield, also both white. Instead of his Wolf Company insignia, his shield bore a simple black image of the Triple Horn of Odin curving around the iron boss. Only Sveinn carried a similar design.

He sensed change far ahead of him in the tunnel. It was time. The South Gate Keepers would be checking movement outside and folding back the non-descript steel doors at the foot of an iron ladder that ran down from street level. The first of the troopers would be slipping up into the night air and Punnr knew this would be the elite litters of Freyja's scouts and Calder would be among their number. Not a moment too soon, he thought. The tunnel was beginning to reek of sweat and leather and oil.

'Helmets on!' came the whispered order down the line. Every helm was designed to hide the nose and eyes and, once above ground, no face was ever revealed consciously. Ahead of him, Sveinn pushed on his silver helmet. It was banded with gold and curved up to a gold spike on the top. He too had chainmail to protect the nape of his neck, but his was silver.

Punnr forced his head into the white helmet. He thought it too tight as he crammed it down, but once it was in place he realised it fitted perfectly. He had no memory of anyone ever measuring his head, but the helm clung to him like a glove, the inside softly padded and the eyepieces just wide enough to give him a good field of vision. Sveinn and Radspakr were moving and he followed them along the tunnel.

On that second night of January the Horde was arrayed in its customary order of march. In the vanguard, Raven Company scouts formed into their two litters of eight and armed with bows. Followed by one half of Storm Regiment light troops, twenty-four in all, armed with eight-foot spears. Then came Halvar and his four Wolf Company Kill Squads. Next was the might of the Hammer Regiment Shieldmen. They numbered ninety-six and carried an assortment of spears, warhammers and axes. Then came Sveinn and Radspakr, with Punnr stepping up through the opening and breathing in the night air. Around them were the sixteen-strong Royal Bodyguard with Bjarke, and the rear of the Horde was brought up by the second half of Asmund's Storm troops: another twenty-four, lightly armed with bows.

They dropped down the slope to the long road of Cowgate, which ran parallel with the Royal Mile, but sat deep in the bowels of the original valley. South Bridge crossed above their heads and over the centuries vast tenement blocks had grown up either side, like writhing plants fighting each other for sun. Even during the day, Cowgate was wreathed in half-light. Now it was pitch dark. Pantheon runners had earlier ensured the main streetlights were knocked out and CCTV had also been dismantled at the last minute. The Horde would progress east towards Holyrood, but Punnr glanced the other way as he emerged and thought he saw figures standing further up the road ensuring no unwanted traffic or pedestrians got through.

Calder and her scout teams were already loping far down the street and Punnr wondered where within the helmeted Wolf squads Brante was striding. This was no parade. The purpose was to get to the agreed destination as unobtrusively as possible and so silence reigned. Even the largest warriors were practised in the art of stealth. They moved lightly on their feet and their armour and weaponry had been oiled silent. Little did the residents high above know that Valhalla's Grand Heathen army passed them by that night.

There was, however, one exception to this rule, and as Punnr walked silently behind his King, he looked at his iron clad arms and comprehended that Cowgate might be as black as death, but he stood out like a spectral apparition. With grim realisation, he understood that the White Warrior wasn't simply symbolic. He was clothed to ensure that even the most short-sighted Titan could single him out as the primary target.

The column dropped down Cowgate for almost a mile and Punnr noticed more groups of figures at each junction. This was an important night in the Pantheon and he guessed

Atilius' men were out in force, cordoning off the route, ensuring the Horde progressed undisturbed. He began to wonder about the numbers of souls that must work behind the scenes of the Pantheon, in the shadowy wings, rarely seen, never highlighted, but each a vital cog in the whole machine and each as embedded in the secret bloody drama as any frontline Palatinate trooper.

They reached the empty taxi ranks behind the Scottish Parliament and wheeled right along The Mall until they broke away from the buildings and found themselves on a road that circumnavigated Arthur's Seat. Such transitions were a magical part of Edinburgh. Still deep within the heart of the capital city, they were nevertheless now facing swathes of rough open ground. The lead scouts left the road and began to move up a rising slope of grass. Punnr looked up and realised the sky was starlit. He could see the granite buttresses ahead and he thought he could make out small groups of figures on the crags. To his left the partially lit towers of Holyrood Palace came into view.

They rounded the northern point of Salisbury Crags, where these dropped to meet the road near the Palace, and Freyja brought her Raven Company to a halt. The rest of the troops fell into column behind and a calm settled. Ahead of them the Crags rose away to the right. On the other side, the even higher walls of Arthur's Seat reached for the sky. In the centre, however, the land remained lower, inviting them up into a wide bowl, a windswept grassy valley, and from within the bowl there was the glow of fires.

'Colours,' Bjarke growled to the sergeant of his Bodyguard.

The man pulled away wrappings from what Punnr had

thought was a long spear shaft. He hoisted it above his head and the great royal banner of Valhalla unfurled. It was red, black and white, with the Triple Horn at its centre and crimson ribbons that rustled in the slight breeze. From further up the line other banners rose: Hammer, Storm, Wolf and Raven. Punnr noticed more of the silent figures in the wings and realised some carried cameras. Once again, the actions of the Horde were being relayed to an unseen audience.

The scouts moved off and the rest of the column followed. They rose steadily over the brow and dropped into the wide valley of Hunter's Bog. The land around was dark, but the starlight was enough to show that it comprised open treeless scrubby ground. In the deepest section at the far end there was a small loch and the column set a course higher and to the right, taking them along the sloping inner flanks of Salisbury Crags so they wouldn't be ensnared in the bog that gave the valley its name. All eyes were fixed on the valley beyond the loch. It was an area about the size of a football pitch, enclosed at the far end by the rising lip of the bowl once more, and the site was ringed by a fence of flaming torches. More torches studded the hillsides above, their reflections dancing in the waters of the loch. The flames lit the central area, yet the natural tilt of the land hid this from the surrounding city.

On either side of the field were two wooden platforms, themselves lit with braziers. The one on the right, towards which the scouts were heading, bore the flag of Valhalla. The other displayed the standard of the Lion of Macedon. Punnr stared ahead as they approached. There was a knot of masked figures on the Valhalla platform. The column wheeled in front of it and dropped down through a gap in the fence of torches onto the brightly lit field. Punnr looked up as he passed and saw the lead figure in the knot step forward. It was dressed in long robes, but what entranced Punnr was the huge horned mask of silver that enclosed the head. He had seen an artist's impression of that mask on Oliver's iPad. Punnr thought the figure was looking back at him and he remembered his white apparel which shone like a beacon among the torches.

Orders were given further up the column and the Hersirs of each litter steered the Horde from order of march into line of attack. Freyja's scouts and Halvar's Wolves broke into two halves and deployed to the wings. The Hammer Regiment formed up in three lines of thirty-two in the centre, and Storm Regiment ranged behind and upslope. Surrounded by his Bodyguard and accompanied by his Thane, Sveinn strode around the Hammer Shieldmen and took up position ahead of the ranks, looking across the empty field to the opposite flaming fence line and the platform beyond with the Lion standard.

Punnr followed and stood just behind the royal group. He wished he knew which of the masked warriors were Calder and Brante. He felt hugely alone and would have given much to have them by his shoulder, just as they had been on that final summit in the *Sine Missione*. Since that day, Brante had settled well into the ranks of the Wolves, spending long hours in their company training, drinking and cajoling. When he had first learned of Punnr's selection as the White Warrior, he had joined his fellow troopers in raucous approval, but as he had come to appreciate the real risk inherent in the role, he had been more subdued and would watch Punnr with the proprietary eye of an elder brother.

'Good luck,' he had whispered earlier as they gathered in the tunnel.

As for Calder, she spoke little to Punnr, but he would catch her big serious eyes upon him and when she had passed him in the tunnel, she had also whispered two words: 'Be careful.'

Sveinn interrupted his thoughts and beckoned him to his side. 'An inspiring sight, is it not?'

'It is, lord.'

'Our foe always takes to the field last. Alexander loves to make a grand entrance.'

Radspakr spoke. 'I very much doubt Alexander has enough troops this year to make a grand entrance.'

'What do your calculations suggest?'

'A hundred and seventy, lord. Give or take a few.'

'Still a force to be reckoned with.'

'But much slimmer than when the Titans were in their pomp. We have the upper hand.'

'Perhaps.' Sveinn turned again to Punnr. 'The torches are fashioned from hazel. It's a small nod to an ancient Viking tradition. Formal duels or battles were known as Holmgangs and they would fence off the fighting area with hazel staves, a bit like a boxing ring. Blood could only be spilt within this enclosure.'

Movement on the opposite platform made him pause. Figures had climbed out of the night. Even at this distance, Punnr could see one of them wore long robes and a great golden mask with sunbeams bursting from the back of it. The Caelestis came to the near edge of the platform and stared out at the Valhalla Horde. Then he raised his arm and beckoned to the lip of the valley at the opposite end and all the Viking helmets craned to see.

There was a purposeful pause, as if the moment was being drawn out for effect, and then soldiers began to stream over the rim. First came another Lion standard of Macedon, surrounded by a troop of thirty and headed by a sinewy figure in burnished armour. They moved at speed, dropping down the slope and through the flaming fence towards the Horde. Scarlet cloaks whipped behind them, matched by great scarlet horsehair plumes atop their bronze helmets. They carried light circular shields and spears. They came at a run, pulling seamlessly out into a single line that stretched across the centre of the field. At a wordless order they came to a halt and brought the spears up vertically against them, butts on the ground. In moments they were motionless.

Sveinn leaned over to Punnr again. 'Menes and the Companion Bodyguard.'

'Cock-sucking pansies,' Bjarke grunted angrily from behind.

There were more figures approaching from the skyline. Again they numbered about thirty and came at a run over the rough ground, as agile as mountain goats in the darkness. They were dressed identically to the first group, but they carried bows. They broke into the flaming circle and split into two, deploying to each wing, then freezing motionless like the Companion Bodyguard.

'That will be Parmenion and his archers, peltasts and scouts. I had expected more of them. Radspakr is correct. The Sky-Gods are few in number this year.'

Now came a much larger mass of soldiers in disciplined

ranks. They approached in a concentrated square down the slope, around the front of their platform and squeezed through the gap in the burning fence line. They approached the Horde at a steady pace behind their shields. A solid wall of bronze and scarlet. The cheek pieces of their plumed helmets wrapped around their faces, leaving only their mouths exposed, as well as the black holes for their eyes. Punnr saw they each held a spear of enormous length. The weapons were elevated to marching slope and seemed to touch the stars.

'The eighteen-foot sarissas,' Sveinn mused to Punnr, seeming to enjoy describing his foe. 'Impossible to wield in battle without using both hands, so their shields are strapped to their forearms. How many do you count, Radspakr?'

'Eight rows of twelve, lord. Ninety-six.'

'Fewer each year. But are they still a match for our Hammer Regiment? What are your thoughts, Bjarke?'

'I'll cut off their balls and stamp them into the grass until they are nothing more than a stain.'

'Hmm, well, Punnr, you had better get a good look at them before Jarl Bjarke turns them into soup. The Brigade of Hoplite Heavy Infantry, the Titan Phalanx, led by their colonel, Nicanor.'

They marched with much greater order than Bjarke's Shieldmen. Precise strides even on the rough ground. This time there was a shouted order and the Phalanx halted behind the line of Companion Bodyguard. The sarissas were lowered as one until their butts touched the ground and once more stillness spread across the field. Then another, much smaller group shot from the lip of the valley and ran lithely into the arena. These bore blue plumes and cloaks.

They formed up as a unit on the rear left of the field, as far from the Horde as it was possible to get within the confines of the flaming fence.

'I count only sixteen, Radspakr. It is as well, I think.' Sveinn turned to Punnr and spoke quietly for his ears only. 'Those – my White Warrior – are the Titan elite. The Sacred Band. Beware them, Punnr. Each one is worth five of mine. You see the figure out front? She is Agape, Captain of the Sacred Band. What I wouldn't give to have her in my ranks.'

Punnr stared at the little troop. He remembered Leiv speaking of how they had appeared in the last Grand Battle just at the moment when he thought his Wolves could take Alexander. How they had come from nowhere.

His attention was wrenched back to the centre. From behind the mass of soldiers, four figures emerged and walked to the front of the lines. The foremost was tall, stately, dressed from head to toe in gold helmet, breastplate, shield, armguards and greaves. His plume and cloak were scarlet, trimmed with gold, and the Lion of Macedon was engraved on his breastplate. Punnr needed no telling that here stood Alexander.

Behind him came a robed figure, more simply dressed in grey, with a small silver helmet, and next to him was a burly soldier, bearing the red cloak and plume of most of the assembled Titans.

'Simmius, the Adjutant and Quartermaster of the Titan Palatinate,' mused Sveinn. 'The foe's equivalent of our very own Radspakr. And the stouter fellow will be Cleitus, Colonel of the Companions and Alexander's second in command. He is newly promoted since the death of

Timanthes last Season and I have a suspicion he may be their weak link.'

But Punnr wasn't listening because his eyes were locked onto the final figure at the back of the group of four. This soldier was slighter and shorter. He wore a plumed helmet, armour and shield like all the others, but every piece was fashioned in brilliant white. He waited behind the other three and Punnr had the sensation of hidden eyes staring back at him. The Titan White Warrior.

A snarl was growing from the ranks of Bjarke's Shieldmen. They hadn't appreciated the show put on by the Titans and they didn't intend to remain an obedient audience. The noise grew. It sounded like the deep hum below a pylon, like a vast power barely contained, and, indeed, the lines of Hammer Regiment were beginning to pulse. Individuals found full voice and hurled their own challenges across the divide. Warriors inched forward. Curses were spat and shouts became incoherent.

Sveinn and Radspakr turned to watch. Punnr thought the whole regiment was on the brink of breaking order and falling upon the foe. He looked back to the Titans and was surprised to see their ranks still motionless. They could have been statues of bronze, indifferent to the hatred being thrown at them. Now there were voices of order among the Shieldmen and a low beat started in their rear ranks. They were smacking their weapons against their shields. It spread. In seconds the entire Regiment was crashing in unison and their Hammer standard was wrenched in wide arcs above the rear ranks as every throat spewed curses until it was hoarse.

From within the body of troops three men emerged.

They carried no shields. One held an axe, one a hammer and one a broadsword. They had stripped to the waist and their torsos were black with swirling tattoos. They seemed unsteady on their feet, as though filled with liquor, and even in the fitful light, Punnr could see the wild stare in their eyes. They ignored the Royal party. They were groaning, growling and shouting incoherently and advancing slowly towards the enemy. They shook their weapons, postured and howled to the stars. The swordsman took the lead, swinging his weapon as he approached the front ranks of the Titans. Punnr knew of these men. Berserkers. In ancient days it was said that these Viking troops could stir themselves into such a frenzy that they were immune to pain. They led the carnage wherever the fighting was at its most fierce.

The three warriors were only metres from their foe. They planted themselves, legs wide, and roared their challenge at the silent helmets. Then, as one, the front row of the Titans – the single line of Companion Bodyguard – took a step back and swept their spears above their shoulders. For a moment Punnr thought they were about to loose them and surely riddle the Berserkers with holes, but again the Titans froze. The move, however, was enough. Bjarke gave a brisk order and the three warriors began to inch backwards, still yelling and never taking their eyes from their enemy. But the moment of crisis was over. The maddened Shieldmen were, in fact, still under order and they retreated to the ranks. Hammer Regiment had, however, made its point.

The noise subsided. The Companions brought their spears to rest again and Sveinn turned back to his counterpart. With a curt signal to his Shieldmen Bodyguard, he advanced forward without them. Radspakr followed him and beckoned for Punnr to do the same.

'Forgive my Shieldmen, Alexander,' Sveinn said, stopping just in front of the other king. 'Every year it's the same. Your boys seem to irritate them.'

'I'm relieved to see you have a modicum of control in your ranks, Sveinn. They were seconds from being skewered.' The Titan king's voice was cold.

'Just a little show. But you can hardly blame them if you insist on sending your troops onto the field like prancing ponies.'

Alexander ignored the insult and turned his helmet to Radspakr. 'Thane,' he said and nodded.

Radspakr bowed stiffly. 'My lord.' Then he also lowered his head to the robed figure behind. 'Simmius. I trust you are well?'

'I am, Thane Radspakr.'

Sveinn waved a languid hand towards the Titan ranks. 'You look few in number, Alexander. Not like the old days.'

'It is force enough.'

'I see you have used what few Blood Fund credits you received from last year to shore up your Phalanx and not your Sacred Band. A surprising tactical decision.'

'We are full of surprises. Ah, we have company.' Alexander's helmet swivelled as four figures emerged from a gap in the burning fence between the two armies.

The leader was Atilius, dressed in his usual purple robes and with a fur flung around him to keep out the cold. He was the only individual on the whole field not wearing a mask and he was escorted by three of his Vigiles, one filming.

'Good evening, gentlemen.' He was out of breath, no doubt fatigued from the walk up to the valley, and took a few moments to compose himself. 'Welcome to the Nineteenth *Agonium Martiale*. Tonight we acclaim the new Raiding Season and you will have seen that both the Valhalla and Titan Caelestes honour us with their presence.' He peered around at them all. 'They are expecting much from you this year. As are the Curiate and all the Pantheon's investors. I need not tell you that fortunes have been wagered on the outcomes. Empires will fall and rise as a consequence of your actions. Sums beyond the scope of our imaginings will change hands.'

He clicked his fingers and the rearmost Vigilis came forward, holding a golden flask and drinking bowl. 'Let us begin.' Atilius took the flask, removed the stopper, and poured the contents into the bowl which the Vigilis held. 'Alexander, as the losing Palatinate last season, it is for you to speak first.'

He held the bowl gravely towards the Titan king, whose eyes Punnr could just see flickering in the recesses of his helmet.

Alexander spoke clearly. 'By this sacred blood, I swear that I – Alexander, King of the Titan Palatinate – my officers and my troops will act at all times according to the laws of the Pantheon.' He turned to Sveinn. 'My lord Sveinn, High King of the Valhalla Horde, I challenge you and your warriors to draw blades from this night hence and to fight with courage and honour according to the rules of this Raiding Season. Furthermore, I challenge you to meet again in the Blood Season on the field of the Grand Battle and to face the wrath of my Titans. I give you my oath that if my life is ended by the sword arm of a Valhalla warrior, my Palatinate will surrender to you.'

Alexander dipped one hand into the bowl and splashed blood onto Sveinn's shield so that droplets ran across the Odin symbol and dripped onto the grass. Then Atilius proffered the bowl to Sveinn.

'My lord Alexander, Lion of Macedon, I accept your challenge. My warriors will draw blades from this night hence and fight with courage and honour according to the rules of this Raiding Season. We will meet you in the Blood Season on the field of the Grand Battle and face your wrath. I too give you my oath that if my life is taken by the sword arm of a Titan, I will relinquish my Palatinate to you.'

Sveinn dipped his hand in the blood and splattered it at Alexander so that the bronze features of the Macedonian Lion on his shield were spotted red.

Atilius spoke. 'You have given blood oaths, not only to each other, but on behalf of every one of your troops. It is done. The Raiding Season may commence.' He returned the bowl to the Vigilis, who disappeared to the rear again, then he seemed to notice the two White Warriors for the first time. 'And who have we here?'

Sveinn jerked his head to tell Punnr to step forward. 'This is Thegn Punnr, chosen White Warrior of Valhalla.'

Atilius' smile dropped and for a second he froze, looking at Punnr hidden behind his white helmet. 'Thegn Punnr? Yes, I remember. An unexpected choice, Sveinn.'

He said no more and Sveinn didn't reply, although Punnr sensed Radspakr examining him from the corner of his eye. Alexander broke the silence. 'And this is Lenore, chosen White Warrior of the Titans. She has proved herself worthy.'

Punnr stared at the helmet of his rival. He could just see the line of her lips between the cheekguards and a flash of eyes. She was a head shorter than him and only now did he notice the female curve of her hip.

'Excellent,' said Atilius. 'These identities will be confirmed before the Raids begin.' He clicked his fingers again and a second Vigilis approached, handing him two bound scrolls. 'Come forward, Punnr and Lenore.'

Punnr felt Lenore step next to him and their shoulders touched. Gravely Atilius placed a scroll in each of their hands. 'Take these and open them with your King. They are the clue to your first location. But whether I give you a clue to the same location – or different – is for you to find out.'

The Praetor waved them away and as they turned, Punnr saw long red hair dropping from the back of Lenore's helmet.

'Excellent,' Atilius said to himself. 'Now, I believe we have one more piece of business to conclude, my Kings? The Honour of Elysium?'

'Quite so, Praetor.' Alexander raised his arm to his Companions and Sveinn turned and signalled back to the ranks of Hammer Regiment. Two figures approached from each army. They carried shields, but no weapons. Ushered by their kings, the four of them formed a small row in front of Atilius.

'My brave warriors of the Pantheon, I understand you are ready for your journey to Elysium. You may remove your helmets.'

Elysium, Punnr thought. *The Paradise beyond the Pantheon*. Some thought it was in the Caribbean, others the south of France. Most, however, understood Elysium less as an exact location and more as an ideal, somewhere a warrior could grow old and lazy with the sun on his back. The four figures lowered their heads and pulled their helmets off. Punnr didn't recognise the two Valhalla troopers. They were both bearded, as opposed to the clean-shaven and shorthaired Titans. All looked older, grizzled and scarred, as men do who had seen much violence.

Atilius studied each of them before continuing. 'The Pantheon salutes you, my brave warriors. Each of you has completed ten Seasons. Each of you has fought courageously for your King and has defied the hand of death on many occasions. The gods smile on you and the Caelestia honour you. As is now your right, you have selected to leave the Pantheon. Hence you are no longer foe and you have no need of your helmets.

'You will journey far from here to the Elysian Fields, where you may live and prosper, funded by the Pantheon. You have earned the riches of your retirement.' From a pocket in his robe, Atilius produced four coins and placed one in the hand of each of the retiring soldiers. 'Charon returns your *denarii*. You are no longer in his debt.' In his high-pitched voice, Atilius spoke loudly enough for all to hear. 'Armies of the Pantheon! Behold your Heroes of Elysium!'

There was a roar from every throat and a clash of weapons on shields. Punnr realised that this must be the dream for all the warriors. To serve ten years. To survive. To earn the vast riches that the Pantheon offered. And then to live far away. At peace.

The noise died and Atilius pointed behind him to the gap in the burning hazel from which he had appeared. 'Go now. You will be delivered to Elysium forthwith.'

The soldiers bowed to their respective Kings, then marched towards the opening, their helmets still under their arms. Two of the Vigiles filed away either side.

Atilius turned back to the Royal parties. 'We are done, my Kings. The Caelestia and the Curiate watch and wait for your actions in the Raiding Season. There is huge anticipation. As always, live up to their expectations. May Zeus and Odin give you strength!'

He finished with a pompous flourish and waited while each king bowed to him, then spun on his heel and walked away.

'Thank the gods that's over,' said Sveinn and proffered a hand to Alexander, still red with drying blood. 'Good luck, Lion of Macedon.'

Alexander considered before accepting the hand, then gave it a peremptory shake. 'You too, King of the Vikings.'

XXVI

'Read it,' Sveinn commanded when they had returned to the Council Chamber deep below South Bridge. They could hear the hubbub of the warriors in the vaults off the Throne Room. They would drink until the first commuter traffic began to filter through the black hours of the morning and then change back into their arrival garb and exit in unobtrusive groups through the Five Gates to an Edinburgh miserably waking up to its first working day of the year.

Punnr opened the scroll and scanned the short message. The eyes of the Council were on him.

'Well?' Sveinn said.

Look to the North – where swimming tests are always fatal. You will find me beneath the gaze of the genius.

There was a moment's silence. 'That's it?' Sveinn demanded.

'Yes, lord.'

'What foolery is this?' Bjarke exploded from one end of the table.

Freyja leaned over the map. She had retrieved a marker pen, string and measure from a drawer in the table. Carefully she measured out from Tron Kirk, then attached the pen to the string and drew a circle that encompassed most of the map. 'Radspakr, you said one-mile radius from the Tron. So the arena for the Raids lies within this circle.'

Asmund came around the table to stand next to her. '*Look to the North. Swimming tests.* The only water in the northern half of the circle is a small stretch of the Leith at Dean and Stockbridge. As far as I'm aware, nobody swims there.'

'We don't need bloody riddles,' Bjarke grumbled. 'Just give me Titans to kill.'

'What about the southern half?' Sveinn asked.

'Not much,' Freyja checked. 'Duddingston Loch is just beyond the perimeter. The eastern end of Union Canal falls within.'

Bjarke swore and stalked away to a bench by the wall.

'What say you, Thane?' Sveinn turned to Radspakr.

'Lord, the rules forbid Simmius and me from taking a proactive role in planning the Raids. It is for your military minds to solve. However, the clue seems clear about looking to the north, so I would suggest we focus our attention there.'

A silence descended. Everyone except Bjarke stared blankly at the map.

'What about swimming pools?' suggested Halvar.

Freyja walked to a mahogany dresser on the far wall and retrieved a laptop from a drawer. She began a web search and the incongruity of the screen's artificial light shining on her silver chainmail was lost on everyone. 'Dairy, Warrender and Commonwealth pools in the southern half. Glenogle and Drumsheugh in the north.'

'I know those two,' said Asmund. 'Both fine Victorian pools. Beautiful heritage. They might fit.'

'But there will be any number of hotel pools as well,' added Freyja.

Sveinn stroked his grey-streaked beard thoughtfully. 'We have to be more specific than that.'

'If I may,' Radspakr spoke. 'Atilius would not send us to hotels. Too many prying eyes.'

Freyja interrupted him, still hunched over the laptop. 'There was a drowning at Glenogle three years ago. Pensioner. Heart attack.'

'This is a pile of goat shit!' fumed Bjarke from his bench.

'Jarl!' Sveinn's eyes flashed with anger. 'If you have nothing positive to add, you are excused from my presence.'

Bjarke bit back a retort and stomped to the door, knocking Punnr's shoulder as he passed. Sveinn waited until he was gone, then sighed. 'If truth be told, I don't like these riddles any more than our departed friend. If we cannot solve them, we will have lost the Raiding Season before my warriors have even launched an attack. Thegn Punnr, your silence is thunderous. You may speak.'

'Lord, I've little useful to add. I only wonder why the clue is so specific about swimming *tests*.'

Sveinn harrumphed and stared blankly at the map. 'The night is growing old and the troops call for our presence. We will adjourn. We have one week before the first Raid and before that, we must have this riddle solved and our approach plans agreed. Go now and share a cup with your warriors. We will meet again in three nights. Meantime, by Odin, solve this riddle and come to me with the answer.'

*

Punnr descended the steps with the others. A wall of raucous noise hit them, as well as a heavy stench of alcohol. Fighters were packed into the vaults and were spilling out into the Throne Room. They had already given their weapons to the Schola youths to return to the Armouries and the scene could have been any other rowdy city party. Punnr saw Brante, Calder and a group of Wolf Company sitting at one of the tables and his tall friend raised a tankard of ale and cheered as he approached.

'Hail the White Warrior! Come and join us.'

Punnr took a proffered drink gratefully. He needed one. He hadn't realised how drained he felt. He still wore the white armour and cloak, and other warriors came over to slap him on the back and push their beer-smelling faces into his.

Brante winked at him, but then leaned forward and asked more seriously, 'You okay?'

Punnr just shrugged and tried to muster a smile.

'You did well,' Brante said, then sat back and continued more loudly. 'Damn, those Titans liked the look of themselves.' The troops around laughed. 'Nice moving bastards. I thought I was at the ballet!'

More guffaws. Punnr recognised this as natural tribal bonding after a confrontation with the common foe, but he felt too tired to join in. He knew the Council members would look to him to solve the clue and then, if he managed to do so, the Titans would use him as target practice on the first Raid. He was damned if he did and damned if he didn't.

It was almost four in the morning and soon the Palatinate could stand down. He yearned to strip off his white clothing and go home to his flat and sink under a duvet. He was due to start his shift at the library that afternoon and the thought was ridiculous.

Calder was next to him. She was studying her wine, moving the glass in small circles on the table-top so that the liquid spun to the rim and threatened to spill. He looked at her profile and it struck him that he hadn't seen her smile since the *Sine Missione*. He wanted to say something, but could think of nothing.

Then he saw Radspakr crossing the hall towards his Quartermaster's office and anger shot through him, made rawer by the beer. He sprang up and paced after the Thane. 'Lord, may I speak with you?'

Radspakr scrutinised him then waved him into his office. He closed the door behind them, but didn't beckon Punnr further into the room. Instead, they again faced each other by the threshold.

'Have you shown my sister's photo to your colleagues?'

'My god, you're persistent.'

'Did anyone recognise her?'

'If you must know, I've not let anyone else see the picture.'

Punnr steeled himself. 'Then I won't be your precious White Warrior, not until I know the fate of my sister!'

'Caution, Thegn. Have a care for what you say.'

'Give me the photo and I'll show it to Sveinn himself.'

Radspakr's eyes flared. 'I will overlook your tone. You are understandably stressed after the *Agonium*, but you will not trouble our King with this matter or I will have you hung up and flayed until you scream for your mother. Do I make myself clear?'

Punnr was shocked into silence and couldn't hold the Thane's glare.

'Good,' said the other man icily. 'As it happens, I had no need to show the photo to others because I have discovered the fate of Morgan Maitland myself, after much time and energy on my part. It would seem you are correct, your sister was indeed a warrior of Valhalla, but I am sorry to inform you that she was killed last year. It was a quick death – a Titan javelin to the heart – so she would have felt no pain.'

Punnr gazed at the Thane and he felt the blood rushing from his head. 'Where are her remains?'

'Cleared as always by the *libitinarii*. Their methods are thorough. All traces of your sister will have ceased to exist.'

Punnr stood wordless, trying to understand this sudden news. Radspakr opened the door and gave him a firm guiding hand through it. 'It is a shock, I understand. But it is the harsh fate of many in the Pantheon. You will get used to it. Go home and rest. You have a critical role to perform.'

'When did she die? What date?'

'In the Raiding Season. But I will have to refer to my Day Books for the precise date.'

'What name was she given in Valhalla?'

'Go home, Thegn Punnr.'

He closed the door and Punnr stood unmoving in the tunnel outside. 'By what name was she called in Valhalla?' he yelled, but there was no response.

*

He exited by the East Gate through the Market Street vaults. The Gate Keepers checked the coast was clear, then let him out into the morning darkness. The starlit night had been covered by a blanket of cloud which gave off a thin drizzle, so he pulled up the collar of his coat and let the rain patter on his hat. His mind rolled in turmoil. Images of Morgan slipped in and out of his brain, followed by the masks of Odin and Zeus, and the noise of Hammer Regiment as the Berserkers threw themselves into a frenzy. Beneath it all, like a stone in his gut, he felt the empty weight of loss.

He let himself into his flat and collapsed on the sofa without even removing his boots. He must have slept, because the next thing he heard was a tapping on the door and he staggered up the hallway to find Oliver on the other side, holding a bowl of cereal.

'An all-night shift at the library?' he asked archly.

'Something like that. What time is it?'

'Eight.'

Tyler moaned and wandered back into the main room. It was stuffy and cold, so he cranked up the gas fire and put the kettle on. Oliver still stood in the doorway and Tyler was tempted to tell him to get lost. He wanted to be alone, needed to compute this news that his sister was lost forever. Perhaps needed to grieve, though his mind could not yet grasp that concept. Instead a jarringly different question struck him. 'You don't know about any swimming pools in New Town or Stockbridge, do you? The Glenogle maybe or the Drumsheugh?'

'Not really. Why?'

'Someone told me a riddle and I want to solve it.'

The lad stepped into the lounge, still holding his bowl. 'I *love* riddles! What is it? Tell me, *please*.'

Tyler debated whether to say more, then forced his brain to stumble back through its own labyrinths to recall the wording. 'Something like – *look to the north. Swimming tests are always fatal. Find me under the gaze of the genius*.'

Oliver's bottom lip curled out in puzzlement. 'What's that supposed to mean?'

'I've no idea, that's the problem. All I know is it's a clue to a location in a one-mile radius of the Tron Kirk and most likely in the northern half. I need an answer in three nights.'

'This is important, isn't it?'

Tyler stopped stirring his tea. 'Yes, it is.'

'Then leave it with me. I'll see what I can find.'

He marched out of the room and Tyler knew the lad would devote himself to the task day and night. He took his tea and sank onto the sofa again, staring forlornly out of the window and filling his mind with memories of his sister.

XXVII

The following day, in an attempt to process the sudden conclusion of his long search for Morgan, Tyler threw on his hat and coat and strode up onto Queensferry Road and across Dean Bridge, wandering towards the city centre. There was a greyness to the morning which was almost tangible, like Beijing smog, but when he reached the West End junction between Queensferry and Princes Street, he stepped into a churning mass of pedestrians fuelled by the New Year sales.

He began following the current east along Princes Street, dodging bulbous shopping bags and trying to marshal the confusion of thoughts spinning through his mind. But then his eye was caught by something ahead. It was only a glimpse, instantly obliterated by the swarming masses. He craned his neck around a fat man and then a gaggle of youngsters. There it was again. Long, blonde hair, straightened to within an inch of its life, over a body that looked so small among the crowd. A black coat, blue patterned skirt and grey suede ankle boots. He followed as best he could, but she navigated the crowds effectively and he was afraid she would turn unseen into a shop and he would lose her.

Could it be? If it was, he had only seen her hair

straightened like this the first time they met and he could never recall observing her in a skirt. And then he realised the detail that had caught his eye. It was the clasp she used to pull her hair back, square and bone-coloured. Calder.

On the first night he had ever seen her, Radspakr had said '*You do not converse with one another beyond these gatherings*' – followed by the even simpler statement – '*The Pantheon has eyes and ears everywhere.*' Tyler would do well to wheel away, but his feet kept him on a straight course and his eyes didn't leave the little blonde head.

She was approaching the corner of David Street and she glanced right. There she was. The pearl earring, the pale flawless skin and emerald eyes. *Don't let her see you, you fool. Walk away*. Without a pause in her stride, she swooped left and through the heavy doors of Jenners department store, and Tyler found himself following before he could stop himself. It was the cosmetic area and his lungs were assailed by a tsunami of perfumery. He wandered past the Clarins and Dolce & Gabbana counters, feeling gauche in his hat, and then he spied her again heading up the wooden steps at the rear.

On the second floor, he was just in time to see her disappear into the food department and weave through the aisles to the restaurant. He hovered uncertainly, staring at rows of Arran Oaties, Highland Fudge and Damson Gin Jelly, then peeked around the corner into the restaurant. She had paid for a tall latte at the counter and was walking to a table in the far corner with a view looking over Princes Street Gardens and the castle.

Was she meeting someone? He thought not. A person awaiting the arrival of a friend looks around occasionally,

CHRIS BARRINGTON

checks the entrance and delays sipping their beverage. Instead, she seemed immune to her surroundings. She was hunching forward with her elbows on the table and absently holding the latte glass below her chin.

The Pantheon has eyes and ears everywhere. He swivelled to take in the food hall. No one looked back at him, no face turned away. He retreated to the stairs, took four or five steps down, then dodged back up again. No one was exiting behind him. Cautiously he returned to the café.

'Pot of tea, please.' Once he had his order, he checked the room once more and advanced. She had her back to him. 'Can I join you?'

There was a split second as she turned when she was still somewhere in her thoughts, then her eyes widened. 'Oh my god,' she said looking beyond him and scanning the restaurant for the first time. 'What are you doing here?'

'I'm planning to drink tea.'

She continued searching the room. 'You can't sit here. We can't be seen together.'

He ignored her and placed his tray across from her. 'It's okay, I've checked. There's no one watching.'

'Oh my god, Punnr,' she said again as he sat, but less vociferously.

He made a play of serving his drink, pouring a careful amount of milk from the little jug and placing the strainer on top of his cup. 'Real leaf tea. Nice.'

She was staring at him, a hint of teeth beyond her open mouth. 'Punnr!' she whispered. 'You can't just turn up and sit with me.'

He poured his tea and finally met her gaze. 'That's what I kept telling myself. But then I thought, I'm here and you're

288

here, so what the hell.' He had never seen her made up for a morning in the city. Her mascara, eye shadow and lip gloss lent a severity to her natural radiance. A different type of armour.

She looked again around the café, then back at him. 'So what are the chances of this?'

'In a city of nearly five hundred thousand? Two hundred Valhalla warriors within a population of half a million. You know, it probably happens a lot more than the Pantheon would care to admit. But Atilius would need an army of Vigiles if he's going to have them following all of us.'

Finally she gave a nervous chuckle. 'Do you suppose Radspakr and Bjarke bump into each other at the olive counter in Valvona and Crolla?'

He found himself smiling and it felt good after the hours spent thinking about his sister. 'And Sveinn's always in my local Tums and Bums workout class.' They laughed quietly and went back to their drinks. 'It's Tyler, by the way.'

She studied him. 'I'm not sure I should know that.'

'Well, I've said it now, so we'll just have to deal with it. Tyler Maitland. I work at the university library.'

She stirred her coffee. 'Did you receive some money into your account?'

'I did. Riches do indeed await in the Pantheon.'

'Is that a monthly sum?'

'I think so.'

'I could give up my job.'

'That's probably the point. Easier to own warriors who don't have to be somewhere else at nine each morning.' It was his turn to examine her. 'How are you?'

'Why?'

'We've barely spoken since the *Sine Missione* and it wasn't exactly an easy experience.'

She looked down at her drink. 'No it wasn't. But we've sworn our lives to Atilius now. Cursed ourselves if we ever step out of line. I wonder if perhaps that was a very foolish thing to do.'

'I still don't know why I was selected by the Pantheon – why Radspakr and his Venarii party came hunting for me when they could have had their pick of the cream of Edinburgh. At the time I was a mess. I had a bad back, a lame arm, zero confidence and no plan.' He shrugged. 'But came for me, they did. So I'm running with it – even when they tell me I have to be their goddamn White Warrior and dress like a snowflake so every Titan can gut me. And why? Because I need to, Calder. Because I need to find something.'

'What?'

Tyler took a long breath and gulped his tea, peering at her over the rim of the cup. 'Last year, my sister, Morgan, disappeared. Just vanished into thin air. I'd suspected she was a member of the Horde for some years, but then something must have happened. So I spent six months wracking my brains for a way to follow her into the Horde, but deep down I knew it was impossible.'

'But then the Pantheon came for you, too?'

'Yes. Incredible as it seems. The answer to my prayers. *You never find the Pantheon – they find you.* So I couldn't believe it when Radspakr turned up and told me I'm in.'

'I thought no one could join if they already had a family member somewhere among the Palatinates.'

'That's the rule, although I was oblivious to it at the time. I assumed Morgan must have got me recruited and I'd see her as soon as we started training. When she didn't materialise, I focused on getting through the Armatura. Then I thought she would be there on the night of our Oath-Taking. But I was wrong. I asked Radspakr about her and he denied all knowledge and that's when he informed me about the rule.'

'So you must be mistaken. And, anyway, he would know her if she was part of the Horde.'

'You'd think so. But then the night before last – after the *Agonium* – he changed his tune. Told me she'd been killed by Titans in the last Raiding Season.'

'Oh… Tyler, I'm so sorry.' She reached for his hand, but he pulled away frustrated.

'But I think the bastard's lying. Nothing stacks up. First, he says he doesn't know her, even when he's supposed to be the guy with all the Horde's records. Then he wouldn't tell me the name she was called in Valhalla so that I could ask others about her. And finally he says she was killed in last year's Raiding Season. Correct me if I'm being stupid, but Raiding Seasons are six weeks long, that means they're over by mid-February.' He looked at Calder. 'My sister disappeared in March. So the whole thing stinks.'

Calder was silent. There were holes in Tyler's logic, but she could see he needed to believe in his sister's presence. 'Thank you for sharing with me. For trusting me.'

'I do trust you. Of course I do. You're the one I trust the most.'

She broke his gaze and peered out the window behind him, taking in the high outline of the Old Town on its spine of rock. 'I've discovered an uncomfortable truth. It's not the violence that scares me. The opposite, in fact. I'm scared because I *like* it.' She inclined her head to indicate the room.

'All this – everything – means nothing to me. It hasn't for years. Not since... not since I lost someone special myself. Yet now this new world of the Pantheon has opened up and I feel the sort of anticipation for life which I thought had deserted me long ago. I'm excited, Tyler. I'm actually excited that it all starts for real in five nights. No more training. No more ceremonies.'

'Only if I can find the answer to the bloody clue.'

'But that excitement scares me, because I wonder what it makes me.'

'It just makes you human. This world's lost its way somewhere. It's become ordinary. There's no risk anymore, no adventure. Everyone's pushed into their little bubble-wrapped slot and told to work till they keel over. You can die of stress – that's allowed – but on no account must you ever receive so much as a bruise. Today's weapons are mortgages, energy bills, council tax, health and safety rules. We're smothered with legalities, then bled of every penny. So maybe people look back at older times because they were kind of heroic. There's a kid in my block of flats and you should see his eyes whenever he talks about the Titans and the Horde. The way I see it – maybe we're lucky. We're Thegns of Valhalla and perhaps it's okay to enjoy it.'

She smiled sadly, displaying perfect teeth. 'I've never heard you speak like that. I had you down as the quiet one.'

He shrugged, suddenly self-conscious, and drained his tea. 'Perhaps I should be going. Better not to push our luck.'

She placed a light restraining hand on his. 'I'm glad you decided to sit with me, Tyler Maitland.'

'I know.'

'I'm Lana.'

'Hello, Lana.'

'Good luck finding the solution to the clue.'

He grimaced and stood. 'I'm going to need it.'

'And – Tyler – I value the trust you've placed in me by telling me about your sister. If there's anything I can do, you know you just need to ask.'

He sighed and nodded. 'Enjoy the rest of your latte.'

'I think I might have an answer,' said Oliver excitedly when Tyler returned. The lad was enjoying the last days of his Christmas holiday and his mum had gone to work for the afternoon.

This time Tyler was invited into his neighbours' apartment and Oliver took him over to a corner desk in the living room where a laptop screen showed a satellite map of central Edinburgh. Notepapers lay scattered across the surface, covered with Oliver's research and deductions. 'I quickly gave up on looking for swimming pools and focused instead on swimming tests. As you'd expect, an online search brings up every type of swimming class available, as well as water quality tests. But then I found a reference which took my thinking in a completely different direction and it all came together!'

The boy was loving his moment.

'And?' Tyler prompted.

Oliver zoomed the satellite image in on an area north of the castle. 'Princes Street Gardens, the site of the original Nor' – or North – Loch. It was drained as part of the city's expansion during the construction of the New Town. But in the sixteenth century, prosecutors used it as the site for witch-ducking, a practice they also termed "swimming tests". Those accused of witchcraft were thrown into the Loch with their hands and feet bound. If they sank, they were deemed innocent; and if they floated, they were found guilty and hauled out to be hung as a witch in Grassmarket.' Oliver looked at Tyler. 'Either way, it was fatal.'

Tyler felt a charge prickle up his spine. '*Look to the north. Swimming tests are always fatal.* And the second part of the riddle?'

'At one of the lowest points in the Gardens, probably right at the centre of the original Loch, there is now a sandstone statue of a female looking down on two male kilted children. Here – you can see it on the satellite if I zoom in again. That little blob beside the benches. Don't ask me why, but it's called The Genius of Architecture.'

Tyler's gloom was forgotten. He worked through the whole clue again in his mind, but he already knew the boy was correct. 'Thank you, Oliver. You're my saviour.'

XXVIII

Freyja led her scouts out at exactly one o'clock on the first night of the Raids. They went in four squads of four, disappearing into the darkness.

Calder's team slipped through the disused door below the steps behind the Divinity School which acted as the North West Gate and dropped towards Princes Street. Instead of taking the pavements, they hoisted each other over walls and trotted through private gardens. The night was cloudy, no moonlight to play on their armour and betray them. They moved onto the steep tree-lined northern slopes below the Castle Esplanade and one-by-one dropped into pre-arranged observation points.

It was as Sveinn had planned. To rush was to flirt with failure. Buses and taxis broke the silence. The occasional late-night resident walked unwittingly through the Horde's field of operations. There were rough sleepers in the shelters which were dotted around the Gardens and they could be seen by the flickering lights of their torches and cigarettes.

Punnr marked time as he paced the West Hall. Another giant map of Edinburgh had been hung from one wall and the King consulted it with his Thane. A platoon of Hammer Shieldmen under Bjarke's command lounged around the perimeter. They would be Punnr's bodyguard, tasked with keeping him behind their shields. Already waiting down the tunnels were the four Wolf Company Kill Squads. Halvar had directed two to the further South and East Gates, charged with emerging only if the Titan White Warrior was spotted. The remaining two, led by Halvar, were at the North West Gate. Brante was among them. He had clasped Punnr's hand before exiting the hall and gripped his shoulder.

'We've come a long way since that drum race.'

Punnr smiled weakly. 'You were the clear winner every time, so who'd have thought I'd end up being the poor sod in the white armour.'

'Like I said many moons ago, you were always the one who wanted it more than the rest of us.'

'Perhaps you can say that at my funeral.'

Brante play punched him. 'We've got your back. You go get that Asset.'

Word arrived from the southern scouts. Titans on the rooftops above Blackfriars and more over the High Street near St Giles'. But only small groups. Doubtless scouts themselves. As yet, there was no movement at ground level along the whole of the Mile, except for a few Vigiles patrolling in the shadows. The night was quiet. Sveinn studied the map and murmured with Radspakr. 'Send the Wolves. But keep one squad high, somewhere around the Esplanade. I want to know of the first sign of Titan activity in that quadrant.'

Brante's heart was thudding as he followed his teammates up the steps and out of the tiny door behind the Divinity School. Storm troop archers were stationed above and he followed Halvar as they took the same route as the scouts, over walls and through back gardens until they hit the steep slope below the Esplanade. Despite the cold, he felt sweaty in his mail and helmet, but his excitement had been replaced by a calm concentration. The second squad wheeled off up the hill to cover any approach from the Mile. Brante's team trotted after Halvar, down through the trees towards the Gardens. He passed Calder crouched by a tree trunk, forty paces from the next scout, but she didn't acknowledge him.

Castlehill and the Gardens were divided by the railway heading west out of Waverley. At the bottom of the slope there was a single wooden footbridge giving access to the Gardens and, as the Wolves descended to it, they saw six of Asmund's archers already covering this potential hazard. Halvar led his team across and they split around the perimeter of the Gardens. Below them was the main central lawn and the statue which, if Punnr had been correct, should mark the location of the Asset. The rough sleepers opposite hadn't spotted them from the confines of their shelters and the Wolves settled into dark places to wait.

Another despatch reached Sveinn in his Hall. The Titan scouts had dropped briefly to ground level and disappeared up onto the roofs further up the Mile, but they were still too distant to see any movement in the Gardens. This was the only change the Valhalla scouts had seen.

'It's inordinately peaceful,' Sveinn said to his Thane. 'It worries me.'

'It's possible they haven't managed to solve their riddle. In which case they will keep their White Warrior safely in their rooftop strongholds and rely on their scouts to spot where we go. That would explain the lack of activity.'

Sveinn growled his acknowledgement, but seemed indecisive.

'It's gone two,' Radspakr reminded him. 'We have but until four.'

The King walked over to Punnr. 'It is time. Stay well within the Bodyguard and they will follow the route already laid by Asmund and the scouts. The Titans are sleeping in their beds. You will be fine. God speed.' He spun around to Bjarke. 'Prepare your men. They go!'

Despite the surrounding bodies of the Shieldmen, so close their shields and arms knocked against him, Punnr felt horrifyingly exposed as soon as he emerged into the night. He thought half the city must be able to see his gleaming white armour and – heaving over the garden walls – he expected lights to come on in every house. How could he progress unseen dressed in this ridiculous gear? He was panting in his helmet and the men around him were breathing heavily too. They were the big men of the central shieldwall, built for smashing everything in their path, not for running through the night. Their mail clinked and their scabbards knocked against their legs, making him wince as the noise carried in the night. He couldn't see where they were going, he just ran between their shoulders, trusting they would spit him out in the right place. At the rear a Vigilis came with them, a GoPro camera fixed to his shoulder.

They arrived at the bridge and then they were in the Gardens. Calder watched the group proceed. Punnr stood out clearly and she strained her eyes for any foreign movement in the shrubs around the perimeter. A well-placed foe could take him out with an arrow from any number of positions. The run to the statue was exposed across wide lawns and the rough sleepers had spotted them. Some had phones and were starting to film the group, but it couldn't be helped. Blurry online footage was the least of the Horde's worries, even though the watching world knew this to be the start of the Raids and a good piece of filming might make the national news.

The shieldman in front of Punnr pulled up and spun around. 'We're here. Get on with it.'

Punnr found himself behind the statue that Oliver had shown him. *You will find me beneath the gaze of the genius.* The bodyguards ringed the statue and faced outwards, leaving enough room for Punnr to walk to the front and peer at the standing female. She was looking down towards one of the children and he followed the line of her gaze to the foot of the statue. Reaching to a bag tied on his belt, he pulled out a small UV torch and shone the light onto the sandstone. With relief he saw hidden words reveal themselves, invisible to the naked eye but illuminated by the UV beam. *Supplies* was written in capitals at the top, followed by a repetition of the clue that had brought them to this location. Underneath was a new clue, which Punnr spent precious moments memorising.

He was aware of the Vigilis kneeling only yards away, filming for the Caelestia and Curiate. Behind him the catcalls of the rough sleepers were growing in confidence.

'You have it?' demanded his lead bodyguard and Punnr nodded. 'Form up, we go!'

They ran back across the lawns. No arrows arched out of the sky. No cries of attack broke the night. Punnr was elated. All his tension had evaporated. He was bringing the first Asset back to Sveinn. *Supplies.* In the nights before the Grand Battle, the army of Valhalla would have food and water in its Highland wilderness.

They crossed the bridge once more and ascended through the trees. Behind them, the Wolves fell back and the archers peeled off from their stations. The first Raid was over. It had been easier than anyone had dared hope.

XXIX

'*Hark! It is the day of rest and all is at peace. You will find me beside the carts.*'

The Council was once more gathered around the mahogany table and again the sounds of jubilation floated up to them from the vaults below. The Horde toasted the ease of their victory, although there was a fragility to their celebrations for, after all the preparation, not a blade had been drawn in anger and the alcohol couldn't mask the anti-climax.

Punnr's elation hadn't lasted. Sveinn had congratulated him and given a few upbeat words to his warriors, splashing water from a jug to symbolise the water they could now drink in the field before the Grand Battle, but in the privacy of the Council Chamber he had grown serious. Halvar nodded appreciatively to Punnr, but Freyja barely acknowledged him and Bjarke and Radspakr glowered. Despite the excitement that had coursed through his veins, Punnr realised that by the standards of the Horde, the night had been nothing really. Barely worth its senior officers commenting upon.

'Any thoughts?' Sveinn demanded.

'The day of rest – Sunday. Everyone's peaceful on a Sunday,' Freyja responded. 'Could mean anything.'

Bjarke spat onto the floor behind him and Punnr saw a muscle twitch in Sveinn's cheek in irritation.

'I'm astounded the Titans did not come out to play,' he said to everyone in general, but directed to his Thane.

'If they were given a clue to a location that led them east or south within the one-mile radius, then it is possible we would not have seen them. Just as – events would seem to suggest – they failed to see us. It's also possible, however, that they simply couldn't solve their clue and had nowhere to take their White Warrior.'

'I know the feeling,' Sveinn said wearily as he considered the second riddle. 'Work your magic again, Thegn Punnr. Find me the answer before the second Raid, or we too will be sitting around on our arses with nowhere to go.'

'Let's start by putting "carts" into the search engines,' said Oliver, chewing on a cereal bar as he sat on the sofa in Tyler's lounge, his iPad on his lap. This time he was dressed in school uniform. 'If we need to we can also dip into the dark web with Pipl.'

Despite his exhaustion, Tyler had been pleased to see Oliver when he returned, and had wasted no time in reciting the next clue to him. Sipping on a mug of tea, Tyler leaned over the back of the sofa and watched Oliver scroll through the lists of search returns for 'carts'. The boy puffed out his cheeks. 'Go-karts, golf carts. Horse carts for sale. Old postcards of trams and carts. Milk carts. Airport bag carts. Pretty much everything and nothing.'

'And if the structure of the clue is the same as the first one, then the bit about *find me beside the carts* is the specific directional information once we've already found the location. We have to work out the first sentence about *day of rest* and *all is at peace* to know the primary site.'

Oliver finished his bar. 'Sunday. Day of rest. A church?' He searched for churches within the one-mile radius and brought them up on a satellite image. 'Well, that doesn't narrow the field much.' He looked at his watch. 'I've got to go. Time for school and Mum'll be yelling for me in a minute. Leave it with me, Tyler. I'll find the answer for you, I promise.'

After he had gone, Tyler showered, ate a light breakfast, smoked two cigarettes and drank a thumbful of whisky before falling asleep on his sofa dressed only in jeans. Later, as he ate noodles in front of the evening news, his fork was arrested midway to his mouth when the television screen filled with footage of his white-clad self kneeling beside the statue, surrounded by a bristling ring of shields and axes.

'This footage was taken at 2.30 a.m. last night in Princes Street Gardens,' a female commentator intoned over the film. 'It is believed to show members of the secretive – and illegal – Pantheon, known as Edinburgh's Valhalla Horde. The Horde is said to live like ancient Vikings, modelling themselves around the customs of this warlike people, and experts believe they inhabit long-forgotten tunnels beneath the Royal Mile in Edinburgh's Old Town.'

The piece cut to the reporter wrapped in an expensive coat and standing in the Gardens in the dull morning light. Next to her was an emaciated older man, with stubble and a woollen hat pulled tight over his head. He looked sullen, but when she turned to him, his face brightened.

'So, Iain, I understand you took the film and, indeed, witnessed much of the activity last night.'

'Aye, that I did. Aye. They just come down from the bridge, chum like. They had swords, shields, axes. So we not gonna mess with them, you know what I mean? Strong lads, aye. It were the Horde, I ken.'

'And did you see what they were doing?'

'Nah, it were pure shan. Sommat by the statue, but they were only there a few moments.' He grinned and pumped a thin fist at the camera. 'We canna believe we saw the Horde!'

The reporter turned back to the camera. 'A statement from Police Scotland says that they are treating this sighting seriously. But despite ongoing condemnation from both the Holyrood and Westminster governments, it seems the activities of the Pantheon continue unchallenged. Speculation is rife that the New Year marks the start of an annual cycle of violent activities and Police Scotland is warning everyone to take special care if out after dark in the city centre, although they also want to reassure both residents and visitors to the capital alike that there is no evidence of these activities ever jeopardising innocent members of the public.

'A brief survey among commuters this morning shows that this sighting – along with all other such sightings of the Pantheon – is being greeted with the usual mix of either excitement or complacent shrugs. The residents of Edinburgh are very used to these nightly activities during the winter months and sceptical that the government has the means – let alone the will – to do anything about them.

'In the meantime, the big question on many people's lips this morning is – who is the knight in shining armour? Shani Robertson, BBC News, Edinburgh.'

Tyler's blood ran from his face and the noodles were forgotten. There was a knock on the door and Oliver, back from school, pushed his way in. 'I just saw it. And it's all over the internet. They were by that statue. You know, The Genius of Architecture.'

Tyler stood and began to wave a placatory hand. 'It's not what you think.'

'I won't tell anyone, I promise. I won't tell a soul.'

Tyler studied him, took in the firmness in his eyes and the integrity in his young voice. 'You mustn't Oliver, you really mustn't. It has to be our secret.'

'Don't worry, I know. Not a word. Wow, Tyler. Amazing! The Valhalla Horde. I always thought so.'

'Please never say anything to anyone or I'm going to be in real trouble.'

Oliver nodded solemnly. 'You can count on me.'

Outwardly, Sveinn retained a regal calm, but few among the Horde were fooled. The first Raid, for all its ease, had turned out to be an almighty blunder.

'Well, thank you BBC,' he said acidly to his Council when they gathered four days later. 'Very kind of you to show the precise location of the Asset in such detail. Now the Titans don't need to spend any time solving that particular clue, they can just sit back and watch us stampede to it on the news.' No one dared respond. 'A few vagrants bedding down for the night, by Odin! They should have been rounded up and their phones destroyed. You are fools for the oversight! Asmund, we will need to split Storm Regiment for the next Raid to ensure you have archers in place if the Titans send their White Warrior straight to the Gardens. Or the next thing I learn will be that they've obtained the Asset uncontested.'

The King's mood wasn't enhanced by the news that no one yet knew the answer to the second riddle. 'Let me reiterate the importance of solving these puzzles. In the forthcoming Blood Season, we will face the Sky-Gods in the Grand Battle. Everything that has gone before dwindles into insignificance compared to this confrontation. Our army will find itself dropped into the wilderness of the northern Highlands, possibly several days march from the chosen battlefield. Our deployment, our tactics, indeed our very strength, will be hugely undermined by failure to collect these military Assets. So bring me the answer to this clue.'

But as the days passed, the combined efforts of Tyler and Oliver were not enough. Tyler spent lonely hours searching fruitlessly online, trying every variation of *Sunday* and *Edinburgh* and *day of rest* and *seventh day*, but he just ended up trawling through reams of websites for Adventists, churches and even seven-day weather forecasts. He cursed and anger pulsed through him.

He called in sick for three of his library shifts and spent the days locked in his flat, but during the nights he found himself drawn back to the underground stronghold. It was quieter between Raids, but Brante and Leiv were often to be found passing the hours in the West Hall or one of the vaults, practising their swordcraft, drinking beer or challenging others to games of Hnefatafl, the chess-like game adored by the ancient Vikings. Punnr joined his friend and they talked, but Sveinn had been clear that the riddles could be shared with no one beyond the Council of War, so he was unable to seek Brante's help. He would take himself off and pace the tunnels, listening to the light traffic above and to the music that sometimes oozed through the walls from bars and clubs that inhabited the vaults further south. Little did these establishments realise the Horde listened to their beats too. He didn't encounter Calder and he wondered if she slept soundly somewhere out there in the city.

Radspakr watched him. The Thane kept himself mostly shut in his administrative lairs, but Punnr knew the man's eyes were upon him. He thought about challenging his lie. He wanted to ram it down his throat, but he did little more than clench his fists and stamp down the tunnels.

Each night, Sveinn asked Punnr if he yet knew the answer to the clue and each night Punnr saw the disappointment in his king. Sveinn was different on these inactive nights. Quieter, more insular. Older. A man who had witnessed many troubled times and had perhaps lost the ability to find any peace. Punnr wondered what he did with himself up there on the streets during daylight hours. He must be a wealthy man for the Pantheon would have rewarded him generously. Did he idle behind the shutters of a central townhouse or the greenery of a Morningside mansion? Did he have a wife? Did he exercise a dog? Was there someone who called him father?

*

So came the day of the second Raid. Tyler waited in his flat until Oliver returned from school, but the boy was downcast and shook his head forlornly. This time there would be no breakthrough. They had nothing. Tyler shut himself in his apartment and slumped on the sofa. Well, Sveinn and the Council would have to accept it. He couldn't perform miracles.

He rose and walked over to the graduation photo. He unhooked his ivory Odin amulet from where it hung over the frame, squeezing it lovingly in his palm, and examined the three of them with their glasses of bubbly, laughing and embracing for the camera. They looked so genuinely happy. Not a care in the world. He ran his finger over his mother's image and then did the same to his sister's. He could feel his emotions rising and his eyes glazed over.

He took a deep breath to control himself. When he refocused he was looking at a face in the crowd behind. A face that must have been there all the time, but one he had never noticed among the celebrating throng. A face that was looking intently at his sister. A face he knew so well.

XXX

Sveinn needed only to look at the expressions of his War Council, at the eyes that wouldn't meet his, to know the solution to the clue had evaded them.

'A change of plan then,' he said in a voice so guttural it was barely intelligible. 'If we have nothing to go for, then we must hope the Titans will be fool enough to lead us to a prize instead. Housecarl Freyja, disperse your Ravens on the strike of one. Impress upon them the importance of what they do. Make them press out and up. Let them take risks. Tell them we must find the Sky-Gods tonight at all costs.'

'Yes, lord.'

'The rest of you will stand ready in the Throne Room until we receive news from the Ravens. All will remain armed and helmeted and ready to go at a moment's notice. Thegn Punnr, if you are lucky enough to get anywhere near one of the Assets tonight, it is vital you memorise not only the clue it gives you for the next location, but also the clue that determined the location of that Asset itself. Understood?'

Punnr dipped his head in acknowledgement.

'To your stations. Good luck.'

They dropped down the stairs to the empty Throne Room and dispersed to the Reception areas where their troops were preparing. Bjarke lingered, then double-backed to the Quartermaster's Office.

'Is there a plan for tonight?' he asked, having pulled the door to behind him.

'Only if the Ravens do manage to make contact with the Sky-Rats and only if the White Warrior is able to head out,' Radspakr replied from behind his desk. 'In which case, if your Bodyguard come into conflict with the foe, you are to brief them to fall back even if it leaves the White Warrior exposed. Is that clear?'

'Aye.'

'Get your head down, you fool!'

Calder felt Thurmond's hand on the back of her helmet as he pushed it below the parapet. There were three of them. They lay on a concrete roof above the main entrance to the Scottish Parliament at the far eastern end of the Royal Mile. They dared not move, for Titans had appeared above them on the steel and glass roof of the Main Debating Chamber.

'Looks like five. A scout party,' said Thurmond. 'They have a perfect view up there.'

'What are they doing?' whispered Runa.

'They've hunkered down, looks like they're staying put.'

'So we're trapped.'

'For now.'

Freyja had sent her scouts in groups of three in a wide arc, with orders for one from each detail to return to her command-post at the Tron if contact was made with the Sky-Rats. Calder had been deployed with Thurmond and Runa to the furthest eastern position to catch any movement at that end of the Mile. Runa was an accomplished urban climber and the post-modern architectural flourishes of the Parliament Building provided easy pickings, at least at the lower levels. She had dropped a rope for the other two and they had eased themselves into the darkest corner of their perch, pleased with their feat, until the Titans' appearance far above showed them what true Sky-Gods could achieve.

'We'll be pricked like three fat pin cushions if they see us.' Even as Runa spoke, there was movement from the road below. Half a dozen Hoplites streamed across the Parliament's entrance plaza and around the concrete ponds. They shot over the road and disappeared into the shadows under the outer walls of the Palace of Holyrood.

'Eyes peeled,' whispered Thurmond. 'This looks interesting.' Long minutes passed, then more Hoplites ran across the plaza. This time there were several dozen of them in two lines, moving fast as they swept over the junction with the Mile and streamed towards Calton Road. 'We've hit the main game tonight, ladies.'

'There,' hissed Calder. Another group had materialised. Ten in total, shields forming a tight perimeter, within which ran a ghostly figure. 'The White Warrior.'

These followed the first group and disappeared up Calton Road. Thurmond had his head half-turned to look above and he could see the five plumes on the high glass roof. 'Move, you bastards.' As though in answer to his prayers, the plumes shifted right and sank from sight.

'Have they gone?' asked Calder.

'Thor knows, but we'll have to risk it. Runa, get word to Freyja. Tell her to send the Wolves, but make them leave at the South Gate. If the Titans are heading towards Calton, they'll have the East Gate watched. So the Wolves should weave up from Cowgate, cross the Mile at Canongate Kirk and through the graveyard. One of us will meet them there. Calder, you're with me.'

They slithered across the roof, dropped their rope again and lowered themselves to street level. Runa ran a few metres up the Mile, hugging the shadows, and disappeared into one of the tight Closes.

'We'll cut across,' Thurmond said, steadying his bow across his shoulder. 'They'll have left rearguards along their actual route. Let's go.'

They bounded over the street and Thurmond led her down a dark passage, then across an empty courtyard and through gardens. He ran like the wind, his cloak billowing behind him. They reached a higher stone wall and he bent to take her foot. With a heave, she was astride it and dropped an arm to help him up. They jumped down onto Calton Road and pressed into the shadows, letting their breathing subside.

Nothing stirred. 'Where are the buggers?' Thurmond hissed.

A voice broke the stillness to their left and both of them sank to their knees as three men came down the road, but this group wore jeans and coats and sauntered with hands in pockets.

'She was like a fucking whale,' one of them said loudly as they passed, no idea they were yards from Vikings. They continued down the road, then made to turn onto a steep footpath that wound precipitously up the wooded slope to Regent Road high above, but they were stopped unexpectedly.

'What the fuck?' one of them exclaimed and there was a brief altercation in the shadows.

'Okay, okay,' another said in a more placatory tone. 'Keep your tits on, we'll go another way.'

The three of them emerged onto the road again and walked hurriedly away.

Thurmond looked to Calder with a twisted grin. 'I reckon they just disturbed a Titan. So the foe are climbing to Regent Road.' He thought for a moment.

'Under the rail bridge,' Calder whispered. 'Jacob's Ladder.'

'Full marks. We'll make a Raven of you yet. Let's go.'

They ran stealthily up the road, away from the hidden Titan and under a piss-smelling bridge. Beneath was a steep flight of steps disappearing up into the night. They squatted at the bottom, checking for any movement. None. Thurmond bounded upwards and Calder followed, taking two steps at a time. The climb seemed endless, but finally they reached the broad swathe of Regent Road. It was bright with streetlights and they hunched in the shadow of the top step, letting their breathing slow. A taxi drove by, followed by two cars. Then a moped roared the other way.

'There.' Calder had caught movement in the trees beyond. Only a shudder, but enough to tell her they were on the slopes of Calton Hill. 'They're going up.'

Thurmond nodded. 'Aye. And I'll wager a sack of weregild that the summit's their destination tonight. Somewhere up there will be the Asset.' He put his hand on Calder's shoulder. 'Get back down. You'll see an old yew tree we passed as we ran. It marks the back wall of Canongate Kirk graveyard. The Wolves will be coming over that. Meet them. Bring them here. Tell them the Titan White Warrior is on the hilltop.'

'What are you going to do?'

He nodded grimly across to the trees. 'Take down that sentry.'

Punnr fought his way through the melee of warriors gathering in the Throne Room. Halvar was briefing his Wolf litters, arranging them in one corner ready to exit any of the tunnels if the Ravens called. Punnr came beside him and waited impatiently while he completed preparations. Eventually Halvar became aware of his presence and turned. He was already wearing his helmet, but Punnr carried his, and the older warrior could see the heat in the other man's eyes. He placed a strong hand on Punnr's shoulder and guided him away from the Wolves. 'What is it?'

'Do you know my sister?'

'What are you talking about?'

'I have a photo of you, taken two summers ago, looking at my sister.'

'You're gibbering like a crazed fool.'

'Then let me be less ambiguous. You're standing on the lawn outside St James Church campus, part of Leith College of Art. It's the day of my sister's graduation from her foundation course. You're wearing a suit and holding a drink. You're in a crowd, but you're looking directly at my sister.'

'This is nonsense.'

'Her name is Morgan Maitland.'

Halvar leaned into Punnr's face, his eyes burning beneath

his helmet. 'This is the night of the second Raid. My Wolf Companies are standing to attention. *You* are the White Warrior. I'm bloody well not discussing this with you now.'

Even as he spoke, there was commotion from the South Tunnel. 'The Ravens have made contact,' someone shouted.

'Time to play,' Halvar glared at Punnr and then swung away.

'I'll not let this rest, Captain,' Punnr called after him. 'You have my oath on that.'

The Wolves were upon Calder before she even realised. One moment she was crouched in the shadows of an empty Calton Road and the next warriors were vaulting over the wall at the rear of Canongate Kirk graveyard. They fell around her like heavy raindrops and gathered under the boughs of the old yew tree.

Brante came beside her and she recognised him despite his iron helm. 'You okay?' he whispered.

She nodded. 'How many are you?'

'Three litters.'

'Who leads?'

'Halvar's with us. He should be arriving right about now.' As he spoke, the Housecarl appeared atop the wall and fell deftly among his troops. He saw Calder and slunk over.

'What's the position, scout?'

'The Titans are on the summit of Calton Hill. Thurmond's up there. They have sentinels posted along the eastern path, but Jacob's Ladder is clear.'

He swung around to one of his Hersirs. 'Two to remain here to guide the White Warrior party. Send a third back to bring Asmund's archers and tell them to cover a likely Titan retreat down the eastern path.'

Calder saw two more figures pull over the wall and recognised them as camera-toting Vigiles. Halvar turned his attention back to her. 'Lead on.'

The three packs followed her along the road and under the bridge, then took the long ascent of Jacob's Ladder at a silent run. She brought them to a halt when she reached the top step and peered across Regent Road. Thurmond appeared in the trees opposite and she knew he must have silenced the Titan sentry. He pointed west and Halvar understood.

'The Sky-Rats will have taken the direct route onto Regent Terrace, through the gardens and straight up, but they'll have scouts all over that. So we go around.' He drew his sword and Calder felt the Wolves follow suit. She started to inch forward, but he placed a restraining hand on her. 'You wait here. Punnr will need you.'

He checked both ways along the road and then loped west, bent double. Behind him streamed the rest of the pack.

They had barely disappeared around the bend when Calder sensed more warriors making the climb behind her. This time it was the Bodyguard. The Shieldmen were heavier on the steps than the fit Wolves and they came towards her breathing hard, but the lead warrior hardly paused as he closed the last few steps. 'Which way, scout?'

'West along the road. Then up the slope when you reach the trees.'

He pushed past her without a response and the other figures almost knocked her over as they flowed around her. In the centre, Punnr was carried past by the sheer force of their momentum. He came right next to her and she just had time to reach up and press her helmet to his. 'Look after yourself.'

Then they were gone and Jacob's Ladder was empty. She trotted across the road and went in search of Thurmond.

The ascent through the trees was steep and treacherous underfoot, and Punnr's heart was thudding against his armour by the time he broke out onto the bare summit slopes. His Shieldmen came behind in a ragged procession, sucking in the night air and stooping with hands on knees when they reached him, and he wondered how the Titans could have failed to hear their thundering approach. But his group was coming from the southern slopes and the foe were most likely on the eastern side.

He walked out onto the bare grass without waiting for the Shieldmen to form up around him and peered east across the summit plateau, past the Nelson Monument towards the colonnades of the National Monument of Scotland – the Parthenon of the north – silhouetted in the moonlight.

Titan Hoplites clustered among the columns, black against the starlight, and in their very centre he could see the white armour of Lenore. She was crouched at the base of the fifth column and he thought he spotted the beam of a UV torch. Below and surrounding the Monument was a line of Hoplites and to the left of the Monument were a group of Vigiles who had already ensured the hill was clear of unwanted spectators and identified the best positions to film proceedings. Even as he looked, Halvar's Wolves broke from the trees nearest the Monument. They drove in a pointed wedge aiming straight at the defence line closest to the group surrounding the White Warrior. Halvar knew his objective. Kill Lenore. *Sine missione*.

There was a moment when the scene could have been one of the tableaus etched in silver along the tunnels of Valhalla and forever frozen in time. Like their ancient forebears, the Titans defended their Parthenon, bronze shields and helmets alive in the moonlight, while the Viking mass hurled itself towards them, their swords high and their cloaks billowing.

Then the moment passed and all hell broke loose. Although fifty yards of ground still lay between the opposing sides, the excitement was too much for the Wolves and a war cry broke from their lips. At the same instant Titan orders sent the Hoplites into retreat. They had the Asset and this wasn't the time to meet iron with iron. The White Warrior vanished and her entire group disappeared the other side of the Monument. The single defence line broke as well, sweeping back over the summit of the hill, and the Wolves on their tails bayed in delight at the sight of lightly armoured backs to pierce. It was a dangerous decision by the Titan command: withdraw too slowly and the Wolves could slash them down at will; but gain the wooded eastern slopes and they would no doubt reach the cover of their own archers and it would be the Horde who had to check their headlong charge.

The Shieldmen joined Punnr and the leader yelled at him. 'Go, go, go!' He was right. Already the Wolves were disappearing over the rim of the hill and even the Vigiles were following with their cameras, having not seen the approach of Punnr's group. For a few precious moments the Monument was empty. Punnr ran between them, covered by their shields.

As they reached the base of the Monument, it became apparent that it was higher than it seemed. Punnr dropped his shield and had to use both hands to pull himself up onto the massive stone base from which twelve columns sprouted. The Bodyguard remained below as he ran to the fifth column and crouched on the spot where he had seen Lenore do the same. He took his UV torch and shone it up and down the column, gasping with relief as he saw words reveal themselves.

DISTANCE

I am first and last of the seven, though there lie fourteen leagues between.

You will find me on the fifth of the disgraceful twelve

Throttled by gunpowder in the old Kirk

You will find me where the lion's mouth drips

He recited the two clues feverishly to himself. Why hadn't he brought something to record them on? He must commit them to memory without error. Just as he thought he had them, there was a hoarse yell of warning from one of the Shieldmen and he spun around. Titans were bounding between the columns. Not many. No more than fifteen. But they came at lethal speed, shortswords glinting, and even though the colour of their cloaks was impossible to determine in the night, Punnr knew instinctively that they were the Sacred Band, the Titan elite.

He stumbled back along the Monument, ready to drop into the defensive circle of his Bodyguard, but he realised with dismay that they were falling back. The Titans themselves were leaping down and running across the grass towards the fleeing Vikings. Punnr watched open-mouthed. The Shieldmen were the huge hand-picked warriors of the central shieldwall. Every fibre of their being should have been screaming back a challenge to the smaller Titans, stamping their boots into the mud and shouting in defiance that they wouldn't retreat one single step. But instead they were running for the trees, leaving their White Warrior alone on the Monument and shining like a beacon in the moonlight.

Punnr looked around him in panic and decided the treeline to the south was closest. He had the clues and the Asset. The Titans had disappeared in pursuit of the Shieldmen. Calder's scouts and Asmund's archers would be lining his route back. All he had to do was get to the trees and he would soon be in Valhalla once more. His mind made up, he was just about to jump when he sensed another presence behind him. Jerking around, he saw her striding soundlessly through the columns towards him, sword in hand. He knew it was the Captain of the Band. The one Sveinn would give anything to count in his ranks.

Punnr was frozen to the spot, watching his fate come towards him with long hair shimmering in the light of the moon. He drew his sword and only then remembered he had left his shield below. He braced for the strike of her blade, but instead her booted leg came up and hammered into his stomach, driving him from the Monument. He fell like a stone to the grass below and lay stunned as the breath was driven from his lungs. He forced himself to his feet and tried to raise his sword again, but she was already at him. The pommel of her sword crashed into his helmet, then her shield punched him in the chest, sending him spiralling backwards. He had never been hit so hard, not even by the likes of Halvar.

He steadied himself and brought his sword up to parry the next strike. Their blades clashed and his entire arm buckled with the blow. Her sword came again, whipping against the other side of his helmet. He tried to stay upright, but it was no good. His head was spinning and his heels found no purchase on the muddy grass. He felt himself falling onto his back and his sword fell from his hand. The stars winked at him. The colonnades stood black and timeless. She reared over him and he knew this plumed and faceless soldier brought his death.

'Agape! No!'

The blow didn't come. He still breathed. He recognised the voice that had restrained her and he forced his head to one side. Halvar was standing silhouetted between the columns. He was alone and his sword and shield were both lowered. He didn't rush to Punnr's defence. He simply stood and watched the Titan captain. Punnr forced himself onto his elbows and stared through his helm's eyeholes at his would-be assassin.

She was motionless, looking back at Halvar, her sword still held for the strike. Then she broke the spell, bent down and roughly tugged Punnr's helmet from his head. He gasped and stared back at the featureless bronze visage. She was studying him. Debating with herself. Then she straightened, turned to Halvar once more, raised her sword in salute to him and swept away into the night.

XXXI

The two warriors hurtled down Jacob's Ladder. The Valhalla scouts had already pulled back and the Wolves were heading towards the Palace, nipping at the heels of the retreating Titans.

Halvar was furious. 'What a total balls-up! Every stupid bastard thinks someone else is doing their job for them. So I'm left to bring you back. Bunch of headless dog turds!' Despite his anger, he remained aware enough to grab Punnr and pull him into the shadows when they reached the road. 'Whoa, laddie. Slow down. You're still glowing like a Christmas fairy. Our lot might be witless morons, but I wouldn't like to bet against the Titans leaving a sting in their wake.'

They jogged back to the yew tree more cautiously, hoisted themselves into the graveyard and began to dodge between the headstones. Punnr's mind could barely keep up with the changing situation. One moment he had been certain of his own death, the next he was running behind a man he thought he knew, but one who had, over the course of a single night, insinuated himself into Punnr's most precious memory of his sister and then averted Punnr's imminent death by seemingly influencing the Captain of the Sacred Band.

Stubbornly, he stopped halfway through the graveyard and waited until Halvar realised and turned back. 'What are you doing, you prick? We aren't out of this mess yet.'

'What happened back there?'

'What happened?' Halvar was advancing angrily upon him. 'I'll tell you what damn well happened. Bjarke's Bodyguard fled like squeaky-arsed schoolgirls at the first sign of the foe.'

'I mean what happened with Agape? She listened to you. The Titan's most feared warrior took one look at you – and then at me – and let us be.'

'We're not going into that here! Move forward, Thegn, that's an order.'

'I'm not taking another bloody step until you start explaining.'

Halvar raised his sword. 'I'm warning you, Thegn, keep moving. I'm returning you to the South Gate.'

In response, Punnr lowered his shield and stood on the spot. He looked at the other man more calmly. 'Do you know my sister, Halvar? Don't lie to me.'

Halvar cursed beneath his helmet and aimed a hefty kick at one of the headstones. He stood with his back to Punnr, his weapon clenched and his shoulders heaving. 'Yes,' he admitted, finally.

Punnr stepped towards him. 'Is she alive?'

It seemed forever before Halvar answered. 'I think so.'

'Where is she?'

'I don't know.'

Punnr grabbed his shoulder and pulled him round. 'Tell me straight!'

Halvar didn't resist. The two men stood looking at each other through their helmets. 'Your sister left the Pantheon.'

'Left? What's that supposed to mean? When did she leave?'

'Towards the end of the last Blood Season, just before the Grand Battle.'

'Where did she go?'

'No one knows.'

'What do you mean, Halvar? Stop talking in bloody riddles. If you don't know where she is, how do you know she's alive?'

'She contacted me to say she was well. To say she would be okay.'

Punnr stared at him, trying to assimilate the answers. 'Why would she get in touch with you? Why not *me*, her own brother? Why you?'

Halvar took a slow breath. 'Because we were close.'

'*Close?* What the hell's *close* mean?'

'Lovers.'

The admission stopped Punnr dead and his questions perished in his throat. Finally, he found his voice again. 'Is that why you're in the photo?'

'Yes. It was a proud day.'

'But it was four years ago and she only disappeared in March. You've been lovers for *four* years?'

'Almost five.' Halvar sheathed his sword. 'I knew it was you from the moment you removed your blindfold in the vault on your first night. She used to show me photographs of you on her phone all the time and I even saw you through the windows of your flat one night when I escorted her home. By god, you surprised me when you walked into that vault. The Pantheon never recruits siblings, so I still ask myself what the hell you're doing here.' With this, Halvar remembered their current predicament and slapped Punnr on the arm. 'I've answered your questions. Now we go!'

'What? No. Wait.'

'Not another word, Thegn. Follow me!'

Punnr ran after the receding figure. They hurdled the graveyard gates and checked carefully before dashing across the Mile and dropping through the alleys towards Cowgate and South Tunnel. *Five years*. Punnr tried to make sense of it as they ran. *Morgan was Halvar's lover for five years and she never said a word to me?*

Another question came to him. 'If those four soldiers at the *Agonium Martiale* were being awarded their freedom after ten years in the Pantheon, how was Morgan allowed to leave earlier and midway through a Blood Season?'

'That,' said Halvar over his shoulder, 'is something I too dearly need to know.'

Valhalla was in uproar. A mass of warriors swirled around the Throne Room, shouting and demanding news. Men squared up to one another. There were shoves. Scuffles broke out. Fortunately weapons had already been deposited in the Armouries to be cleaned and oiled by the Schola youngsters. Sveinn sat on his throne and Radspakr stood by the stairs leading up to the Council Chamber. Their eyes met.

Calder struggled through the mob and pushed her way to Brante. The Wolves had chased the Titans from Calton Hill towards Holyrood and so, left on the southern flanks, she and the rest of the scouts had retreated from their positions unchallenged and bounded back to the stronghold.

'What's happening?' she yelled in Brante's ear.

'The bastards are claiming Punnr's fallen.'

Calder blinked at him and the tumult seemed to recede around her. 'Punnr? What are you saying?'

'His Bodyguard. They're back and they say they had to endure a fighting retreat against the Titan Sacred Band, but they couldn't get to Punnr. The last they saw of him, he was under the sword of the foe.'

She turned and looked towards the epicentre of the raised voices and only then saw the leader of the Bodyguards jabbing a finger at an angry line of Wolves. More Hammer Shieldmen were crowding behind him and pushing against the Wolf brigades. Her arms went limp and cold. Brante was yelling next to her, red with anger. She tried to make sense of everything, not daring to believe that the short moment when Punnr had run past her at the top of Jacob's Ladder might be the final time she saw him alive.

The scuffles were becoming too hostile and finally Sveinn rose from his throne. He remained calm, but his jaw was clenched beneath his silver beard. He raised a hand and gradually, despite the bad blood in the room, the noise dissipated and heads turned to him.

'My warriors, I understand your frustration. We had the foe in flight and if it is true that our White Warrior has been felled, then it is a bitter blow indeed. As I speak, the Vigiles are confirming whether he is dead or wounded.

Either way, we will be unable to claim the remaining Assets. But we must not turn on each other. The best plans always lie scattered the moment contact with the enemy is made, for warfare is ever in the hands of the gods. What's done is done. It was the foe who struck down our Warrior, so it is our duty now to focus our anger upon their heads. Two more Raids remain and we will dedicate ourselves to stopping the Sky-Rats and to the destruction of their own White Warrior. We will have our vengeance! This I swear by mighty Odin!'

He spoke well and the sound of assent swelled the assorted ranks. They shouted their support and swore their mutual vengeance on the Sky-Gods. Sveinn held up a hand to silence them so that he could continue, but as the noise dropped in the Throne Room cries could still be heard in the South Tunnel. Heads began to turn. Calder strained to see over the shoulders of the warriors around her. Sveinn himself looked to the tunnel, unused to being interrupted.

Now the men closest to the tunnel were starting to clap and excited shouts began to roll into the Throne Room. The crowd hummed and surged.

'Hail. The White Warrior lives,' someone yelled.

And Calder gasped, her hand coming up to her mouth. For it was true. From the tunnel came Halvar and Punnr.

XXXII

Tyler walked sluggishly past the shops of George Street in the dark hours of morning. The first signs of traffic were showing and the earliest office workers were opening up and switching on lights. He was drained to the point of exhaustion and his brain was as torpid as his limbs. He had showered mechanically in the Reception Area and was one of the last to leave through the North West Gate. It was bitterly cold and he clasped his coat around him and wondered why he hadn't felt the chill during the Raid.

He didn't even hear her speak the first time and she had to call again. He looked back to see Lana following him. She approached, watching him uncertainly, trying to read his expression under his hat. 'Would you like another coffee?'

He glanced around at the shops. 'I'm not sure we'll find one open yet.'

'Are you heading home?'

'Yeah.'

'Want company?'

He looked into her big eyes. 'Okay.'

They walked to Learmonth in silence. They didn't even check behind them, for they were past caring if the Pantheon was watching.

'This is me,' he said as they reached the corner outside his flat and she glanced around at the dark gardens.

'Nice,' was all she said.

The world was waking up as normal. A paperboy was making the early rounds. Fat Mrs Hendrie puffed by on her morning jog and gave Tyler a wave which he returned. Oliver's light was on, but his curtains drawn. They entered the building and the schnauzer went mad behind the Connaughts' door.

'Sorry. He spends every waking moment listening for me.'

At his front door, Tyler ferreted inside a pair of Wellington boots and retrieved a key, then led Lana inside. Food was still discarded by the sink and his duvet scrunched on the sofa. There was a full ashtray on the table and the place smelt, so he pulled back the curtains and threw open a window as the first hints of daylight leaked across the gardens. 'Make yourself at home. Sorry about the mess. I'll sort coffee.'

Lana folded his duvet and perched on the sofa while he busied himself in the kitchen. She took in the almost empty whisky bottle, the photos on the sideboard, the books stacked along the mantelpiece and the sheets of paper scattered around his laptop with notes scrawled across them.

Day of rest – a blog. Edinburgh Peace and Justice Centre. Edinburgh SDA Church. SDA = Seventh Day Adventists.

'Sorry,' he said again as he brought her coffee and then tidied up the papers.

'One of the clues?'

'The one we were meant to go for tonight. If I'd managed

to solve it, we wouldn't have needed to follow the Titans.' He settled into a saggy armchair opposite her and reached for the whisky. 'But I failed. And now I have two more.'

'Are you expected to solve them alone?'

'It seems that way.' He took a swig from the bottle and sucked his teeth. 'The War Council is privy to the clues, but the Horde is no exception to the rule that shit always falls downwards and guess who's at the bottom?'

'Let me help you.'

'It's not really permitted.'

'There's a lot of things that aren't permitted. It's not permitted for me to be sitting here.'

Tyler conceded her point with a shrug. Lana examined his haggard face. His hair was lank. His cheeks had not seen a razor for several days and purple blotches were livid beneath his eyes. 'Do you often start your day with that stuff?'

'When I've spent the entire night risking my life, yes I do.'

'How did you manage to be separated from the rest of the Horde? *You*. The White Warrior. The one we're all supposed to be protecting?'

'Bjarke's men deserted me without the slightest attempt to engage the enemy. Either they're a bunch of spineless cowards or someone told them to leave me. Whichever way, I don't trust them an inch.'

'That's a dangerous accusation. Blood was almost spilt in the Throne Room before your return, probably would have been if we'd still borne arms. How did you get away if they'd deserted you?'

'I wasn't meant to. My destiny was to die tonight when I had a Titan blade at my throat. She could have ended all

Valhalla's attempts at the Assets with one stroke, but she didn't. She released me.'

'Do you know why?'

'No.' Lana stayed silent. He was on the cusp of telling her more and she knew better than to push. He dragged his eyes from the mantelpiece and looked intently at her. 'But I have this voice in my head that won't stop telling me it all has something to do with Morgan.'

'Have you found out anything else since we last spoke?'

'Halvar thinks she's alive, but he can't say for sure. All I know is that it's now ten months since I last saw her, so something serious must have happened.'

'I'm sorry, Tyler. Do you have other family?'

He shook his head. 'Never knew my father. My mother's dead. It was just the two of us, and I thought we were doing okay. She used to be out most nights and I sort of guessed what she was doing, but we were okay. At least until the final months.'

'What happened then?'

'I think something – or someone – was really scaring her. But I'm probably only saying that now with the benefit of hindsight. I never saw her disappearance coming. Not in a million years. Just blew me away.' He drained the whisky bottle. 'So when I suddenly got a chance to join the Pantheon, I thought it was the golden opportunity to find her.' He laughed hollowly. 'Now look at me. She's buggered off and I'm the bloody White Warrior of Valhalla being hunted by every Titan in Edinburgh.'

'Not by one, from what you've just been saying.'

Her comment made him lapse into silence. He toyed with

the empty bottle and then stood. 'Do you want some proper breakfast?'

'That would be nice.'

He walked to the kitchen again. 'Just toast, I'm afraid.'

'Perfect.' She followed him and leaned on the work surface as he busied himself. 'I had a daughter,' she said quietly and he stopped to look at her. 'Amelia.'

'That's a lovely name.'

'She was the most perfect, beautiful bundle. She gave a crazy and intense new meaning to my life.' She picked at her lip and Tyler could see her fingers were shaking. 'She was born with acute lymphoblastic leukaemia. Her bone marrow was making too many immature lymphocytes. By two she was getting fevers and she would bruise at the slightest touch. But she was always happy. Always laughing.'

Tyler buttered the toast and pushed a plate towards her. 'Then, I think, she started to suffer more pain. She cried so much, yet it was always softly. Just her tears and the tortuous expression on her face. The doctors said it was her joints. Gradually she lost her appetite. That's when they started with the lumbar punctures. Oh Tyler, she submitted to all those tests with such *grace* for someone so young.'

She stared at him and he could see the pools in her eyes, so he moved awkwardly to hold her, but she brushed him away and forced herself to stay strong. 'I'm sorry.' She rubbed her eyes and took the toast back to the sofa. 'I didn't mean to get emotional. You don't need to hear all this.'

He seated himself silently across from her and waited for her to compose herself. 'She endured so much during those eight months after it was first diagnosed. And she did it with such dignity. Such... serenity. She left me just before her third birthday. Two years, eleven months and fourteen days.'

Lana bit into her toast and chewed, staring at the floor.

'What of her father?' Tyler asked. She blinked up at him and he immediately recanted. 'Sorry. That was crass of me.'

They lapsed into silence for a few minutes and then Tyler asked, 'Is Amelia why you're here? In the Pantheon?'

'You mean the reason I'm always so angry?'

Tyler held up his hands in defence. 'I didn't say that.'

She relented. 'Yes. Of course it is. One of the Pantheon's smart-arse research team will have gone – hey, look at her; the university dropout with a major chip on her shoulder, the loner with no family to speak of, the former national youth athlete, the girl kick-boxing her way through her grief, the woman defined by tragedy. Bingo, they'll have said, we'll have her. Send Radspakr and his *Venarii* party.'

She stopped, realising she had been talking too frantically, and went back to her cold toast. Tyler watched her. 'Thank you for the trust you've placed in me, Lana,' he said, echoing her words in Jenners, but she didn't respond.

Tyler must have dozed off, for he woke to a knock at the door and the sound of Lana clearing up his kitchen.

'Did they mind us not solving the riddle?' asked Oliver when he answered. The boy was about to depart for school and Tyler could hear Mrs Muir preparing to leave in the flat opposite.

'No, we got it sorted laddie. Thanks for all your efforts. But now I've got two more riddles.'

'*Two* more?'

'They're the last ones, I promise. Do you want to see them?'

'Of course.'

Oliver followed him into the lounge, but stopped when he saw Lana behind the work surface in the open-plan kitchen. 'Hi,' she said. 'I'm Lana.'

'Hi,' he mumbled shyly.

'Oliver's my neighbour,' Tyler explained. 'He's been helping me with my clues. Look at this one.' Tyler pointed to a sheet of paper on which he had been writing.

Oliver tore his eyes from Lana and came over to read the words. '*Throttled by gunpowder in the old Kirk. You will find me where the lion's mouth drips.*'

'Yeah. That's the important one, the one we really need to find. Along with the earlier one we still can't solve about the day of rest. Then there's this other one as well.' Tyler started writing beneath the first clue.

Once again Oliver read aloud. '*I am first and last of the seven, though there lie fourteen leagues between. You will find me on the fifth of the disgraceful twelve.* What's that supposed to mean?'

'I don't know, but we know the answer was on the top of Calton Hill below the National Monument of Scotland. You know the one I mean? With the columns?'

'Yes,' the boy nodded seriously. 'The Parthenon. It was supposed to be Scotland's monument to the fallen of the Napoleonic Wars, but funds ran out and it never got finished, so now it's known as Scotland's Disgrace. There are twelve columns, so I'm guessing your solution was by the fifth column.'

Lana came over. 'That's impressive.'

'It was the Distance Asset,' Tyler said without thinking and Oliver scrunched up his nose in puzzlement.

'What's that?'

'Oh, sorry lad, I never told you about the four Assets. Each location has something important for the Valhalla Horde.' Lana looked sharply at him. 'Don't worry, Oliver knows about my little nights out. So the first one at Nor' Loch was Supplies and this one on Calton Hill was Distance. The remaining two are Time and Field. It's too complicated to explain it further. Here,' he gave the sheet to Oliver. 'Do you think you might be able to make some sense of these?'

'Comprehension at school this morning. They won't notice if I'm concentrating on something much more interesting.' Oliver turned back to Lana and stared at her. 'Are you one of *them* as well?'

Lana glanced at Tyler, who inclined his head in the affirmative, and she nodded to the boy.

'Wow,' he said in hushed tones, not taking his eyes from her.

Lana brought the subject back to the matter in hand. 'Has it occurred to you that the Assets might be part of the solution?'

'How so?' Tyler asked.

'Well, I'm guessing Nor' Loch was once full of water, which is an essential supply for any armed force. And the distance clue says something about fourteen leagues. Just a thought.'

Man and boy looked at each other.

When Oliver had gone, Lana finished the dishes and came back to Tyler who had lost himself in the clues. 'I ought to be going.'

'Sure. Do you have work?'

'I threw in the towel last week.'

'Really?'

'The Pantheon pays twice as well and requires a lot in return.'

Tyler pondered this. 'I don't blame you. It does sort of make sense.' He led her to the door. 'Watch out for the schnauzer.'

She hesitated and then leaned in and gave him a peck on the cheek.

Bjarke was the last to shower in the Reception Area closest to East Gate and was alone pulling on his jeans, ready to emerge back into Edinburgh daylight, when Radspakr stole into the room. A fog hung in the air, scented by shower gel and deodorant. Radspakr sat on one of the benches, still dressed in his gown, while a bare-chested Bjarke pummelled his hair with a towel.

'What happened?' Radspakr asked.

'It was going just as we planned and the son of a whore should have been bled dry.'

'So I ask you again, what happened?'

'As agreed, the Shieldmen left him in the loving arms of the Sacred Band, so your guess is as good as mine. Perhaps there's more to this piss-stained whelp than I thought.'

Radspakr looked at the swirling tattoos that ran across

Bjarke's chest and throat. 'We can't rely on the Titans anymore. They seem incapable of killing our White Warrior even when we present him to them.'

'So give me his real identity and address and I'll pay him a visit.'

'Too risky, Jarl. It would raise too many questions.'

'It's easy to make it look like an accident.'

Radspakr considered. 'No. Not yet. I might return to your idea as a last resort. Meantime, we have two further Raids during which anything can happen.'

Bjarke pulled on a smart black shirt and buttoned the cuffs. 'You have a plan?'

'Confusing things, battles. People can lose their bearings. Make mistakes. End up skewering someone they did not mean to.'

Bjarke grinned. 'I'll have my Shieldmen prepare the skewers.'

'No, not them. They are too important. If the Vigiles saw anything untoward, your Shieldmen would be hauled in front of one of Atilius' tribunals and then have their skulls crushed until their brains came out their ears. No, I'm thinking more about your initiates in Hammer Regiment. What are their names?'

'You mean the new Thegns. Ulf, Erland and Havaldr.'

'Precisely. I watched the footage of their antics during the *Sine Missione* and could see they have no love for Punnr and his crowd. That one Ulf would slip a knife between his own mother's ribs if he thought it would benefit him. Can they be trusted?'

'All my Hammer Regiment can be trusted. They live in fear of me.'

'Good. And the brats are expendable if anything goes wrong. Have them admitted to the Bodyguard.' Radspakr rose. 'You will brief them before the next Raid.'

'I will.'

'Do not mention my involvement. They need know nothing except that the White Warrior must not return or they will answer for it with their own lives.'

Radspakr left and Bjarke brushed his hair, pulled on a smart, fitted jacket and strode out into a sunlit city.

XXXIII

Oliver was trying to maintain an aura of mystery, but the grin that split his face from ear to ear undermined him. It was two days since they had last spoken and he had been working relentlessly on the riddles.

'I'm guessing it's good news,' Tyler said, sitting in his armchair with a cigarette between his fingers.

'You could say that. You really owe me.'

Tyler chuckled. 'Hark at him.'

'I think my prize should be a tour of the Valhalla underground tunnels!'

'That's impossible, Oliver. You know that.'

The lad's grin faded. He was perched on the sofa opposite, his iPad in hand, but now he stared sulkily at nothing.

Tyler started again with a softer tone. 'But what about a virtual tour? When there's time – and your mum is happy for you to come over for an hour – I'll draw tunnels for you on a map and show you where the main rooms are and tell you all about them. Is that a good compromise? Please Oliver, I still need your help.'

'Okay.' Mind made up, the boy brightened. 'It's a deal. So do you want to hear what I've worked out?'

'Of course, partner.'

'Your friend was correct about the four Assets. They are all key to the solutions. Is she your new girlfriend?'

'No. But she's important to me. So it's also important to me that you like her.'

'And she's a Valhalla warrior like you?'

'Yes, she is.'

'Then I like her. The first clue was the witch swimming tests in Nor' Loch and it was for the Supplies Asset which includes water. We know that. The third clue was for Calton Hill and was the Distance Asset. It's not important now, but – *I am first and last of the seven, though there lie fourteen leagues between* – is a reference to Edinburgh supposedly being built on seven hills, like Rome. Once I knew to focus on distance, I soon found there's a Seven Hills race each year, which starts and finishes on Calton Hill and which measures fourteen miles – fourteen point three, to be exact.'

'Nice one.'

'You said the other two Assets were Time and Field. I *wish* you had told me that *earlier*, because now it all comes together. I went back to the clue we couldn't work out. *Hark! It is the day of rest and all is at peace. You will find me beside the carts.* Now I searched on "time Edinburgh" and got nothing. Then I tried "clocks Edinburgh". Mostly this just gave me shops and antiques, but then I saw something a bit different. The One o'clock Gun at the Castle. As most visitors know, at precisely that time each afternoon an L118 Light Gun is fired from the Castle ramparts as part of a tradition dating back to the 1860s when it was a signal for ships on the Forth, especially in foggy conditions. And get this, the only day it doesn't fire is a Sunday.'

'No one would solve that clue if they didn't factor in the time component,' Tyler said puffing out his cheeks.

'It's fired from Mill's Mount Battery, a platform on the north wall which sits below the coffee shop. Guess what this was before a coffee shop? A cart shed.'

Tyler grinned wolfishly. 'Brilliant, Holmes.'

'So that means the final clue must be for the Field Asset. This wasn't so simple. I used the search terms "field Edinburgh" and lots of irrelevant information came back. But as soon as you showed me this last clue the other day – *Throttled by gunpowder in the old Kirk. You will find me where the lion's mouth drips* – something rang a bell with me from a lesson at school. I remembered our class being told a famous story about Mary, Queen of Scots. How her husband was Lord Darnley and he was supposedly killed by an explosion in the lodgings he had been staying in somewhere in the Old Town. There was definitely an explosion under his bedchamber, but when his body was discovered there were marks showing he'd been strangled.'

'Throttled by gunpowder.'

'So I searched again using the "old kirk" reference in the clue and "field" and bull's eye! Kirk O'Field. The site where Darnley's body was found. None of it remains today, but the land was granted to the city in the 1500s to found a new university and it's generally believed that Kirk O'Field now lies under Old College on Nicolson Street.'

'I know the place. It's the university's principal site.'

'I'm afraid I've failed with the bit about the lion's mouth. I'm sorry.'

'Don't be stupid, laddie. You've done amazingly. I would never have solved these without you.' He stubbed out his cigarette. 'We'll find the damn lion once we're in Old College, have no doubt of that.'

'Supplies, Distance, Field and Time.' Asmund was leaning over the map in the Council Chamber and had his finger on the northern wall of the Castle. 'Clever bastard, whoever conjured that lot up.'

'It's as well we have our own clever bastard,' said Freyja, looking across the table at Punnr.

'Indeed,' agreed Sveinn, who hadn't taken his eyes from the map as Punnr had explained the solutions. 'So two Raid nights remain and we find ourselves armed with the answers to *both* the remaining clues. I believe we hold the advantage. Your thoughts on our strategy therefore, my Jarls and Housecarls. What should be our next steps?'

'We go for the Castle first,' said Freyja with conviction.

All eyes turned to her. 'Pray elaborate,' said the King.

'Because we were unable to solve the Castle clue before the last Raid, we had to track the Titans and follow them to Calton Hill instead. This means – in theory – that both Palatinates are now in sync. We both found the Calton Hill Asset on the same night and we're both now armed with the clue that directs us to Kirk O'Field under Old College. So we'll both be going for the same location on the next Raid night.'

'And this time the Titans will be expecting us,' Halvar said.

'Precisely. The full force of both Palatinates in the same place on the same night.'

'Bring it on!' said Bjarke. 'We'll feed them to the worms.'

Freyja ignored him and looked at the King. 'In my opinion, it would result in a scale of conflict not seen in a Raiding Season before and will put our White Warrior in immense peril. So the preferable option would be to avoid such confrontation and seek the Castle Asset unchallenged, leaving Old College until the final Raid when the Titans will be elsewhere.'

'You speak sensibly.'

'Bollocks,' Bjarke spat. 'I'm not running from a fight with those mini-skirted Sky-Girls!'

'And that is what makes you the great warrior you are, Jarl. Every time I have to face a Titan phalanx in the field, I give thanks to Odin that I have you leading my shieldwall. But on this occasion it's the Raiding – not the Blood – Season and we don't *have* to go shield to shield with the foe. We can obtain the next Asset and keep our White Warrior safe, all without the need for a full confrontation. I am decided. For the third Raid, we go for the Castle. Prepare your plans.'

'My lord.' It was Radspakr who spoke. He had been quietly observing the dynamics around the table.

The King turned to him. 'You wish to disagree, Thane?'

'Merely to proffer a slightly differing viewpoint, my lord, in the interests of robust debate.'

'Speak then.'

Radspakr produced a stick of chalk from his robe and

walked to one of the stone walls. 'If I may divert the Council's attention for a moment. I believe we can now deduce the order in which Atilius *planned* for each Palatinate to find the Assets as this….' He began to scrawl two columns down the stones.

	Valhalla	Titan
Raid 1	Princes St Gardens	Calton Hill
Raid 2	Castle	Old College
Raid 3	Calton Hill	Princes St Gardens
Raid 4	Old College Castle	

'If each Palatinate had solved the riddles in a timely fashion, they would have been sent to the locations in the order you see before you. Atilius was being punctilious about keeping us apart. However, the first two Raids have resulted in a very different situation, like so….' He moved along the wall and began to scratch with the chalk again.

	Valhalla	Titan
Raid 1	Princes St Gardens	Failed to solve clue
Raid 2	Failed to solve clue	Calton Hill
	Tracked Titans to Calton	

'So, if I may, I will take a moment to review the current situation. As Housecarl Freyja justifiably pointed out, both Palatinates ended the last Raid armed with the Calton Hill clue. So we know the Titans will be sending their forces to Old College next time. We must assume that they also believe we will be focusing on Old College.

'Additionally, thanks to our camera-happy audience at Princes Street Gardens, we should also assume the Titans know one of the Assets is located in the Gardens.

'*However*, the foe know nothing of the Castle. They will only gain that clue if they successfully find the Asset in the Gardens, as we did on the first Raid.' Radspakr turned back to his audience. 'So, the very sensible proposal on the table is that we leave Old College until the final Raid and go instead on this next Raid to the Castle, thus avoiding a direct confrontation with the foe and thus protecting our White Warrior. My lord, I contend that such a plan is flawed in the extreme and would risk throwing away the very tangible advantages that we currently hold.'

'How so?'

'Firstly, it gives the Titans a free run at the Old College Asset. Assuming they can solve the clue, it gives them a chance not only to find the Asset unopposed, but even to consider a further run on the same night for the Gardens.'

Halvar interrupted. 'Whether or not we send our White Warrior to the Castle during the next Raid, my Wolves will remain free to hunt the Titans at Old College.'

'But you will not be enough to stop their full force.'

Halvar held Radspakr's look for several seconds, then glanced at Freyja.

'Secondly,' the Thane continued. 'If we go for the Castle Asset next, as Housecarl Freyja proposes, we run a huge risk of being seen by the foe. It will take only one lone Titan scout on the rooftops of the Mile to spy just one of our warriors advancing on the Castle, and we will have presented evidence of the location of the final Asset right into the laps of the Titans.'

There was silence around the table for a few heartbeats and then Freyja spoke. 'My lord king, the Thane speaks wisely as a counsellor, but not as a soldier. The fight at Old College would be bloody and terrible, no quarters barred. Not only would we place our White Warrior at great risk, we would lose many others. And it might mean both Palatinates then meet bloodily again on the final Raid at the Castle. We will suffer many casualties before the Blood Season.'

Asmund concurred. 'Death would roam the streets of Old Edinburgh without constraint. I fear even the *libitinarii* would be hard pressed to eradicate all signs of such a bloodbath.'

'Aye,' nodded Halvar. 'The Pantheon still needs to act with some restraint during the Raiding Season. We can't unleash the dogs of war while still in the city. And be under no illusion, my lord, if you follow the Thane's advice, that is exactly what you would be doing. None of us could hold our warriors back in such a confrontation.'

Sveinn kept his eyes on the map, stroking his beard, giving himself time to hear his advisors.

Radspakr tried again. 'Lord King, we hold an ace in our hands. You have always shown us that wars are won by those who conceal their greatest strength until the moment of greatest need. We must hold that ace close to our bosom and the foe must never know we hold it until it is too late for them.'

'I note you won't be in the frontline at Old College,' Halvar glared at the Thane.

Radspakr ignored him. 'My lord, I should also remind the Council that the Castle Asset is Time. Even as a non-combatant, I can see that this must be the most important of all the Assets. Armed with it, a Palatinate will be given two weeks' notice of the date of the Grand Battle. Precious time to train, equip, plan and resource. Without it, a Palatinate will find itself deposited in the Highlands and thrown against the foe with no chance to prepare.' He leaned towards Sveinn and his voice became forceful. 'We cannot give the Titans even a sniff at this Asset. Have the courage to face them down at Old College, then play our ace on the final Raid.'

A silence fell across the room. The cases had been presented and the time for debate had passed, as Sveinn continued to stroke his beard. 'We have three nights until the next Raid. Let me think on this. In the meantime, you would do best to prepare your troops for either eventuality.'

The Council adjourned and Halvar stomped off to the Practice Rooms on West Tunnel. Each was already in use by warriors refining their fighting skills.

'Get out,' he snarled at two of them in the end room and as they hurried away, he picked up a discarded wooden sword and launched himself at the strike bag hung from the ceiling. He slashed in, left, right, left, right, again and again until he had almost ripped the bag from its chain. Finally he desisted and pressed his forehead against the heavy sack, panting.

'Something is amiss,' said Freyja from where she had been leaning against the doorway observing him.

'That bastard's bent on sending us into an all-out blood fight when there's no call for it.'

'He does seem surprisingly keen on that outcome.' She came into the room, her boots clicking on the flagstones, and circled Halvar to face him from the other side of the strike bag. 'Is there anything you should be telling me?'

'What makes you say that?'

'A raven's instinct.'

'It's Radspakr you should be asking. Why's he even throwing in his damn opinion? He said himself it's forbidden for him to involve himself in Raid planning. I swear, if we go shield to shield with the Sky-Rats it'll be a bloodbath. And Radspakr and Sveinn, and Atilius and all his bastard Vigiles cronies had better understand that. We can only hope Sveinn makes the correct decision.'

'He won't. I could see it in his eyes. Radspakr spoke well. He pressed all the right buttons. Sveinn won't be able to resist a chance to deceive the foe. He will withhold his ace and send us against the Titans in two nights.'

'Then I fear for Punnr, Freyja. We can't protect one man in a full confrontation. Not when every Sky-Rat aims to bring him down and he's dressed like a frigging snowman!'

Punnr spent the rest of the night drinking in the vaults with an expression that ensured he was left in peace. Then he dozed fitfully in a corner chair with his feet on a bench, until kicked by one of the Hersirs. There would be sunlight outside and the Horde's stronghold was already empty for another day. He showered, turned off the pump and began to pad across the floor, when he realised someone was sat on a bench opposite.

'Nice shower?' asked Ulf, grinning. 'You took your time and I didn't want to interrupt.'

Punnr faced him, hands on his hips. 'Have a good look, arsehole. See anything you'd like?'

Ulf's eyes flickered and his grin weakened. 'Now, now. I'm sure we can keep this on friendly terms.'

'What do you want?'

'I just wanted to say I'm delighted we'll be able to renew our acquaintance at the next Raid. It'll be just like old times.'

'What's that supposed to mean?'

'Accept my apologies. I had assumed our great White Warrior was included in all the Palatinate's planning these days now he's Sveinn's protégé. My, how your star has risen!' He glanced meaningfully between Punnr's legs. 'Many of us wonder what you must have done to so impress our king. He's really smitten.'

Punnr swung away and began to dry himself. 'Piss off.'

'Now that's no way to speak to your Bodyguard – we mere underlings who will sacrifice every cell in our worthless bodies to keep you safe and sound.'

Punnr paused. 'Bodyguard?'

Ulf rose and stalked towards him, this time grinning with malicious joy. 'Erland, Havaldr and I are being assigned to your Shieldmen for the next Raid. Our Jarl Bjarke believes we're best equipped to have your interests at heart, seeing as how we have such a shared history.' With an explosion of speed, Ulf grabbed Punnr's genitals, shoved an elbow into his throat and forced him backwards against the wall. He brought his face up to Punnr's and leered at him. 'So don't you worry your pretty head about anything, our lily-white dove safe behind our shields. We'll be there for you every step of the way.' He corkscrewed his hand, making Punnr gasp in agony. 'Whoops. Look what I seem to be holding.

I can't think how that got there.' He stepped away, giving a final wrench as he let go, which sent a shaft of white-hot pain through Punnr's guts, making him fold into the wall with a groan. 'Be seeing you, my Lord. Can't wait for the fun to begin.'

XXXIV

Tyler stepped out of the South West Gate into the brightness of Victoria Terrace. Clouds scudded across a blue sky and a low sun strained to reach into the closely knitted streets. He lit a cigarette and leaned on the balustrade at the edge of the terrace, which looked down on the rows of quaint shops on Victoria Street sloping away to Grassmarket square. It was almost nine and people already milled in and out the sandwich outlets or waited for the gift shops to open. A lorry struggled up the hill. A woman went by escorting four poodles. A group of foreign students argued about which way to go. Tyler watched them and blew smoke out across the drop.

Below him, ignorant of his presence, Halvar walked down the street towards Grassmarket. For a few moments, Tyler eyed him. With the exception of the train journey before Christmas, he had never seen any of the senior officers in the real world beyond the confines of the Horde and it took a while for his brain to register the Housecarl in his jeans and North Face jacket. Then he stamped out his cigarette and sprang to a set of steps that led down to the street below. Halvar was further down the road, beyond a group of customers exiting a coffee shop with takeaways. Tyler gave chase and caught the big man by the elbow just where the road flowed into the wide stone savannah of Grassmarket.

'What are you doing, you fool?' Halvar snarled and yanked his arm away.

'I must speak with you.'

'Get gone, maggot.' He strode out into the square, but Tyler wouldn't be shaken off.

'Bjarke's changed my Bodyguard for the next Raid. He's assigned Ulf, Havaldr and Erland.' Halvar kept walking and Tyler fell in beside him. 'Why would he do that? You saw what happened at the *Sine Missione*. They're the last people on this earth I can trust with my protection.'

'You're mistaken.'

'I wish I was, Halvar, but Ulf gave me the message loud and clear.'

'The little snake's just toying with you. Bjarke may or may not be aware of the bad blood between you, but he *will* know that Ulf and his crew are too inexperienced to be given such key roles during the Raids.'

'That's exactly why it makes no sense. God knows, I'm prepared to risk life and limb for Valhalla in a fair fight, but I'm not prepared to be struck down from behind by some treacherous bastard.'

'Go home, Punnr.'

'Nothing has felt right since I first spoke to Radspakr about Morgan. *Nothing.*'

Halvar came to an abrupt halt and stared at the younger man. 'You spoke to Radspakr about Morgan? He knows you're her brother?'

'He wouldn't believe me at first, but then he looked into it and told me she was killed by Titans a year ago.'

Halvar stared at him, then checked around the square and began to stride towards the south eastern corner. 'Follow me.'

Tyler trailed him out of Grassmarket, across Candlemaker Row and up a flight of steps beneath an arch. They emerged onto the peaceful greenery of Greyfriars Kirk and Halvar led him around the perimeter, passing the elaborate graves and tombs of Edinburgh's ancient elite. They swung by the Kirk itself and some distant part of Tyler's brain noticed a yew tree and guessed it was the spot where he and the other Thralls could once have deposited their Odin amulets if they had wanted to resign from the selection process. Halvar headed to the far corner of the graveyard, bordered by the ancient remains of the city walls, and stopped on the furthest patch of grass, hemmed in by tombs.

'Give me a cigarette.'

'Why do we keep having these conversations in graveyards?' Tyler quipped as Halvar bent to light the cigarette from Tyler's proffered flame.

They waited in silence until Halvar was confident they had not been followed. 'Since when has Radspakr known about your sister?'

'Since the night of the Oath-Taking, but I don't think he believed me until we spoke again on the night I first entered the Valhalla stronghold.'

'By all the gods,' Halvar swore under his breath and drew angrily on the cigarette. 'This is becoming a bloody mess! It explains your selection as the White Warrior.'

'You mean it was his suggestion?'

'What better way to silence you than to convince Sveinn to promote you to become the Titan's number one target?'

'Radspakr wants to silence me?' Halvar was looking at the ground and Tyler stepped closer, squaring up to him. 'Housecarl or not, you need to begin explaining things.'

Halvar pushed him back and leaned wearily on a tombstone as he flicked his cigarette away. He squinted up at the blue sky overhead. A blackbird was calling from the yew and there were snowdrops thrusting between the graves, peppering the grass with droplets of joyous white.

'I had five years of happiness with your sister. It began innocently enough in a bar and it was months before we realised we were both players in the Pantheon.' He laughed mirthlessly. 'We told each other tall lies about working night shifts. Then it began to dawn on us that we were always hurrying off at the same time on the same nights. We had a rip-roaring argument and convinced ourselves we had to end it. But we couldn't, despite the dangers, because we knew we were falling for each other. So we worked out elaborate rituals for ensuring we weren't followed. We would meet at my house mostly and sometimes I came to your place when you were at school.'

Tyler puffed out his cheeks, trying to picture Halvar in their little flat.

'And then we did something so bloody stupid...' Halvar reached out a hand. 'I need another.'

They both lit up again and he inhaled deeply, drawing in the smoke with his eyes closed. 'Like little lovebirds, we fantasised about being together in the Pantheon. We would lie in each other's arms during the long afternoons and whisper about how we could do it. I think perhaps it was just an irrational dream for me, but Morgan became more and more consumed by the idea. All she could think about was how she might join the Horde and fight alongside me. Such *stupid* lovesick fools!'

Halvar spat out the last words, but Tyler barely noticed. He was frozen to the spot, his cigarette burning forgotten between two fingers. 'What do you mean *join* the Horde...?'

The two men looked at each other and realisation flooded through Tyler. Halvar put it into words. 'Her name was Olena – *torch of light*. It took her four years to work her way through the ranks of the Titan Sky-God Palatinate to become Captain of Alexander's Companion Bodyguard.'

Tyler let out the breath he had been unconsciously holding and stepped sideways, reaching for a tombstone to hold. He gripped the granite, roughened with age, and tried to make sense of Halvar's revelation. He reached under his shirt and grabbed the Odin amulet around his neck. 'But she left one of these for me... I have it on my dresser. It was always the Horde.' But even as he said this, he was thinking about the tiny Star of Macedon etched onto the reverse of that specific amulet.

'Like I said, she became obsessed with the idea that she would join me. It was our stupid dream.'

'You mean I've come into the Pantheon to find Morgan, and I'm on the wrong bloody side?'

Halvar drew on his cigarette and didn't answer. He squinted at the yew tree and then continued. 'So I did something I'll always regret. You know how it is when a man's head is stuffed stupid with love and he thinks the maddest schemes make sense? I went to Radspakr and I told him of my relationship with a senior officer in the Titan Palatinate. I thought he would see the value and might know how to pull strings behind the scenes to bring her over to the Horde.' He grunted viciously. 'Aye, the bastard saw the value alright. Just not in the way we'd foreseen.'

'And by then he had you.'

'Aye. One word from him and the Vigiles would crucify me. A second word from him and they'd do it to Morgan. So the game changed to his rules. From then on, we were still free to engage in our secret rendezvous, but she always had to come armed with information. The Titan's numbers. Their deployment. Their plans. Their strongest warriors. Their weak spots. Where they would be and when. Everything we needed to know during last year's Raiding Season, she had to give it to us on a plate.' He stopped and gripped his fists to control his emotions. 'So fight by fight, skirmish by skirmish, we were always one step ahead of them, and one by one, they started to fall. The once great Titans, the unassailable Sky-Gods. Now every move they made, we were always there, cutting them down, paring their numbers.

'Then at some point, we started to realise that Radspakr was just as afraid as we were. He had told the Valhalla Caelestis of this prize and that changed everything. Odin used the secret to bleed dry the others on the Curiate whom he thought of as his rivals. New wagers were laid, bent wagers, against all the rules of the Pantheon. Sums beyond our imagining were won and lost on the information Morgan provided, enough to make powerful men enemies for life. If he had been exposed, Odin would have been stripped of his position and thrown from the Pantheon. Yet, if his secret was kept, he had the greatest opportunity in the history of the Pantheon to ruin his rival, Zeus, and perhaps even destroy the Titan Palatinate. It was the ultimate gamble that seduced him.' Halvar looked across at Tyler, who was still leaning on the tombstone. 'Your sister and I were embroiled in something far over our heads.'

'What did you do?'

'We thought it couldn't get any worse, but then Alexander began to ask questions. The Titans became suspicious. How could it be, they asked, that the Horde was always one step ahead of them? How could they be losing so many good soldiers so swiftly? They smelt a rat.

'Radspakr realised it wouldn't be long before the plot was uncovered and it would all come tumbling down around us. So he gave us an ultimatum – or maybe it came from Odin, I'll never know. One raid. In the weeks just before the final Grand Battle, Olena must lead the Titan elite into a trap. Not just any old ambush, but one that would suck them in so far that we could cut their best soldiers to pieces. Then, when we faced them on the field of the Grand Battle, their numbers would be so weakened that my Wolf Kill squads would have one incredible chance to take Alexander. The collapse of the Titan Palatinate! Imagine it. Somehow – in some stupid lovesick part of our brains – your sister and I convinced ourselves that it might even work out for the best. If the Palatinate collapsed then she really would be free to join me in Valhalla.' He growled in exasperation. 'What stupid bloody fools.'

'So what happened?'

'Olena did what was required of her. She risked everything for our love. She led her Titan comrades into the trap and we reaped their destruction and took the scalp of Timanthes, their greatest warrior.'

Tyler recalled Leiv's words at the feast of the Oath-Taking.

'But at the Grand Battle itself, you failed to kill Alexander. You sent your Wolves and they were close enough to see the fear in his eyes, but then the Sacred Band came from nowhere. Agape. And the attack was over.'

'Aye. It was still a victory, but nothing like it could have been.'

'And what of Morgan?'

Halvar took a few moments to answer. 'Olena wasn't present at the battle. At first I was relieved, but then a growing horror dawned on me. Had she been exposed? Was she even then in chains awaiting the justice of the Vigiles? Afterwards she didn't come to me at the house, nor answer her phone. I went to your flat, searched it while you were out. Returned and stared through the windows while you sat in front of the television. But I knew she wasn't there.

'I cornered Radspakr and almost took his head off, but I could see he was just as afraid as me and just as confused. If she'd been taken by the Vigiles all hell would have broken loose. But no word came from Atilius. No formal enquiry. Not even informal questions. Just silence. The Titans seemed none the wiser about their mole. The Season ended as normal. She had simply disappeared.' He drew the last millimetres from his cigarette and stamped the stub on the grass beside a gravestone. 'I could see that Radspakr was shitting himself. If Odin thought there was any risk of his illegal wagers coming to the attention of the Pantheon authorities, he would have silenced us all permanently and that would have included his greedy, ingratiating little Thane. But she was gone, so it didn't come to that and gradually the risk seemed to pass.

'Then one day last summer, I heard from her. A

handwritten note. She'd been to my house at night while I was in Valhalla, let herself in, left the note by the kettle. It said she was okay, but after the battle in the cellar she was so frightened that she confessed everything to Agape, and Agape told her to get away, hide, because others would be bound to discover her treachery and come looking for her.' He stopped and took a deep breath. 'She also said she blamed me for telling Radspakr and that I had to forget about her.'

Tyler slumped down onto the damp grass and leaned his bag against the gravestone. 'Shit,' he said to himself as the full ramifications of all this new information began to hit him. 'Does Sveinn know about you and her?'

'No. He guessed the Sky-Rats must have a mole because of our unaccountable victories, but he was too clever to delve further. In such situations, ignorance is by far the best insurance policy for keeping your head attached to your shoulders.'

'And the others?'

'I thought it was only Radspakr, but Bjarke's become the Thane's man and I suspect he's somehow in the loop. So beware of him. He acts the bellowing fool, but there is cunning beneath the bravado.'

'Hence his decision to send me into battle against the Titans in two nights with a Bodyguard packed with enemies.'

'Radspakr will be behind that decision, make no mistake. Your presence in the Horde will be terrifying the bugger. There'll be so many questions burning through his evil little skull. What do you know? Why are you here? Even more importantly, *how* are you here when it contravenes fundamental Pantheon laws? Think about it from his perspective. His Titan mole is allowed to disappear without any fuss coming from the Pantheon authorities and then her brother is allowed to join.' Halvar smiled grimly. 'Oh he'll be crapping himself. At least we have that thought to console us.'

'And what of the other player? Agape. Why would the Captain of the Sacred Band help my sister and then stay her sword at your command during last night's little show?'

Halvar mulled Tyler's question, staring at the graves beyond them. 'Agape and your sister, they were... well, they had a special relationship. With the exception of Timanthes, they were Alexander's strongest warriors and I think they recognised that quality in each other.'

'And that was enough for her to spare me?'

Halvar inclined his head. 'It would seem she recognised you.'

Tyler looked at the other man with a new resolve. 'This is too bloody complicated, Halvar. I can't take part in the next Raid. I *won't* do it. I owe the Horde nothing, least of all my life.'

XXXV

Agape stood upon the roof of the Court Houses, facing south, her back to St Giles' Cathedral. One o'clock precisely. Go, go go! Everything tonight was about speed. Already Parmenion's scouts and archers were rappelling down the ropes to street level from four separate rooflines south of the Mile. They would move swiftly along predetermined routes to converge on Old College and then take to the skies again. Each team contained the Titans' best climbers, capable of ascending almost every building the capital could throw at them, even the most modern minimalist structures. From their eyries they would drop ropes for their teams and then set about fixing further pre-agreed ascent points for the Companions who would follow.

Speed. Get to these stations before the Horde could deploy, then send the Titan White Warrior at once. Better to fight their way out of Old College with the Asset already claimed than to wait and have to fight their way in. The Horde were no fools. They would be coming from their South Gate on Blair Street even at that moment. Fanning out and aiming for the quieter routes to Old College. They would avoid South Bridge which would be crowded with people and traffic even at this hour, and would come instead up the back roads of Guthrie Street and Robertson's Close.

The rain soaked through her blue horsehair plume and cascaded from her helmet. Her hair was plastered to the nape of her neck and her cloak hung heavy. Behind her waited the Band. So few now. Only fifteen since the catastrophe of the raid last Season. Tonight they had a new role, not as the Titan's hunter-killers, but as the White Warrior's protectors, for tonight two Palatinates were coming straight for each other, shield to shield, and the price would be heavy. Her elite fighters would circle Lenore and give up their lives for her if the gods dictated. Lenore was standing with them now. She was a brave lass, thought Agape, dressed in her white regalia in the full knowledge this would be the Raid when the Horde's Wolves hunted her.

It was time. Agape extended a gloved fist and each member of her Sacred Band walked past in turn and smacked their right hand onto it. Then they followed her in two lines as they snaked across the Courts to the western side behind the Signet Library and jumped across to the eastern wing of the National Library. They would take an indirect route to Old College, coming at it from the rear. Ropes already waited for them at all the key places and squads of Parmenion's archers would now be covering their route. Zeus willing, the Horde would be somewhere further east.

The smooth, angled roof of the library was slippery in the rain, but they were all as sure-footed as mountain goats. They reached Cowgate, waited for the signal from the scouts, then flew down the ropes and crossed the road into the alleys behind BrewDog and the Three Sisters Pub. They passed through a hidden deserted car park and then up once more using waiting rope ladders. In minutes they were standing over Chambers Street and looking east towards the rear of Old College. The Band squatted and Lenore crouched between them trying to keep her bright armour as low to the roof as possible.

The College was dark in the rain. It was the traditional heart of the university, but at this hour there were no lights. Vigiles would already have taken out the cameras and temporarily detained the two gate porters, and Agape guessed the surrounding roads would also be liberally sprinkled with more Vigiles, for the Pantheon authorities knew the scale of confrontation threatening to take place and would be determined to block passers-by. Each Vigilis would carry a camera and more would have been mounted around the College, because the Curiate wished to miss nothing.

Agape spied a signal from the roof on the opposite side of Chambers Street. It meant the scouts had scaled the rear of Old College and the ropes were in place. It also meant Menes and his regiment of Companion Bodyguard would already be making the ascent. Thirty of them. They would secure the back of the College, while Nicanor brought his Hoplite Heavy Infantry storming down on the front entrance. That, at least, was the plan.

She signalled to her team and they moved across the roof in single file. A rope awaited them at the eastern corner and they dropped to street level. Facing them was the grand entrance to the National Museum, usually brightly lit, but tonight the lights had been taken out, the entrance porters rounded up, and the building sat in gloom. Cars were parked along the road, but they too had been checked and confirmed empty. The Band set off at a run, heading east along the street, using the cars in the central reservation as cover until they reached the junction at the back of the College where they peeled off.

There was a thud and a gasp from behind Agape. One of her Band had been thrown backwards against a car and lay propped with an arrow shaft through his arm.

'Cover!' Agape yelled.

Fourteen bronze shields came around the White Warrior like flower petals. Agape stared over the rim and could see their adversaries. A litter of Valhalla scouts. They had climbed the lower roofs of the buildings opposite and had set up station. They had an arc of fire which covered much of the rear of the College and, more importantly, they would already be sending a runner with news that the Titans were bringing their White Warrior from the west. Another arrow smacked into one of the shields, but now there were Titan archers atop Old College and they were returning fire. The Valhalla scouts hunkered down.

Time to go. 'Keep tight,' Agape hissed. 'Shields over Lenore at all times. Let's move.'

They were skilled at this. They went at a firm run without a single shield loosening from its position. In moments they were in the shadow of the College, tight against its dripping walls. The building reared high above them and even Agape marvelled at the skill of the Titan climbers to scale such an edifice. Window ledges, drainpipes, balustrades, even the cemented joins between the sandstone, there were finger holds enough but it was still a formidable feat on such a wet night.

At her signal the rope ladders dropped again and the Band fixed their shields on their backs and began to ascend. If Valhalla archers made it to street level below them, the White Warrior would be horribly exposed mid-climb, but Agape had to trust that Parmenion's own archers and the Companions of Menes were covering all approaches. The rungs of the ladder were soaked and treacherous and Agape had to cling for all her worth. The wind rose as they got higher, buffeting down the thin road below them and driving rain into their eyes.

Finally she reached the top and there were helping hands waiting to grab her. She stalked across the roof and looked down onto a grass quadrangle surrounded by sandstone terracing which formed the centre of the College. At the other end, the front wing rose above the main gate, up to a dome surmounted by a statue called the Figure of Youth.

She looked left and right. Companions lined the roof and others were already progressing along the north and south wings above the quadrangle. She spied Menes and he strode towards her. He was a warrior hardened by many Seasons, but had only been promoted to Captain of the Companion Bodyguard when Olena had disappeared. He would readily lead a Titan charge against a limitless foe, but she was less certain of his aptitude for strategic leadership. She wished Olena were still with them. *Agape and Olena, what a pair. We could have carried the night single-handed.*

'Nothing yet,' said Menes. 'But my arsehole's not relaxing until Nicanor's secured the front gate, and there's no sign of his mob yet.'

Agape stared at the main entrance. The lights had been shattered under the archways and nothing could be seen in the shadows. 'Anything could be happening under there.'

'And if Nicanor's made it along South Bridge without incident, then I'm a shrivelled goat's prick.'

Agape glanced back at Lenore, crouched in the angle of an elegant chimney and shivering with the damp. 'We can't wait. Have we identified the drinking fountain?'

Menes pointed. 'There, dead centre along the northern terrace of the quadrangle.'

'Show me to the ropes.'

As she spoke they both watched transfixed as a Companion fell from the northern rooftop, his hands together in front of him as though praying, but both knew he clung to an arrow shaft. He hit the terrace with a thud.

'Bastards must be under the arches,' Menes said and he was already swinging his arms to bring the Titan archers into place to return fire.

'And they know we've come from the rear, so there'll be a pack of them waiting for us down there soon. Get me to the ropes.'

'No need.' Menes pointed to where the building curved onto the northern arm of the quadrangle and Agape saw there was scaffolding clinging to the sides like a plank and steel creeper. 'They've got the builders in.'

Menes seemed pleased, but Agape knew while it provided them with a rapid descent, it also presented the Horde with the perfect apparatus to follow them if a fighting retreat ensued. 'Get your troops down there as well, Menes. We'll need support. Lenore, follow!'

They swung like armoured gibbons down the poles and

along the wooden platforms and were at ground level in moments. The Companion Bodyguard followed and fanned out along the rear terrace. Agape could see the water fountain along the north side. *You will find me where the lion's mouth drips*.

Menes came up beside her. 'Where the fuck are Nicanor and the heavy boys? We need them blocking the entrance three ranks deep.'

'I'll wager they're entertaining Valhalla's Hammers even as we speak.'

'It'll be a full-on battle if so. There'll be carnage in the streets tonight.'

Agape ignored him. 'Lenore, come.'

The Sacred Band streamed in two lines across the terrace and down onto the grass. Menes gestured to his Companions to advance along the terraces either side. The Band was within metres of the fountain and Agape was signalling for Lenore to approach, when there was a roar and the Wolves were upon them. The Viking killers poured from the darkness beneath the entrance arches and came at Agape's party in a diamond shape with its iron point aimed directly at Lenore. A shower of arrows accompanied them from the gloom.

'Form up!' yelled Agape and instantly her fourteen Titans broke from columns into line of attack in one fluid motion. They just had time to plant themselves and lock shields and then the Horde hit them with a crunch that rippled down the line and echoed off the ancient buildings. The Titan elite soaked up the impact by taking a regimented step back and bending the knees, then shoved forward in a single movement. It brought the Wolves' momentum to a halt, but their greater numbers meant they could round the flanks of the short Titan line. Menes exhorted his Companions to shore up the wings and the line held.

Agape faced a bearded heathen snarling at her from beyond her shield. He shouldered into her shield and she snapped back, making him stumble. A lightning strike of her shortsword into his exposed neck between helm and *brynjar* and he turned into a dying mass at her feet, but before she could advance again to seal the line, a taller man jumped over him. He held himself upright and she could just see his small manicured goatee beneath his helm. In the corner of her eye she was aware of Lenore huddled by the fountain, reading the clue in the light of her UV beam. The tall man attacked with a grace that surprised her and she had to parry his broadsword swipe. Iron clashed with iron. She rose onto her toes and began her dance of death and watched him do the same. He's good, this one, she thought. Their blades licked at each other as each attack was parried. He thrust high at her shoulder and she had to block faster than she could remember in many Seasons. She dropped her shield arm and hit hard against his own shield, unbalancing him and forcing him a step to the side. In the same moment, she stabbed him in the shoulder and felt her blade hit bone. He stumbled backwards with a gasp and she checked around her.

The Titan line was just holding. Where in Zeus' name was Nicanor? Lenore was rising and signalling that she had the clue, but even as she did a Wolf broke clear and surged towards her. Agape recognised the armour, knew the sword. Halvar. She ran to intercept.

*

Punnr made his way up Robertson's Close with his Shieldmen Bodyguard around him. There were eight of them, but all he could think about were Ulf and Erland just over his shoulder. He could sense them watching him behind their eyeholes, he could feel their iron spear points hovering close. Ahead was Havaldr, a blond man who spoke little and had an honest face, but always stayed close to Ulf and was swayed by his every word.

Valhalla scouts ushered the White Warrior group onto Infirmary Street and ran them west towards the junction beside Old College entrance. As they neared the agreed point, Punnr became aware of a commotion ahead and slowed. The junction with South Bridge was a battlefield. Bjarke's Hammer regiment had formed a writhing shieldwall, blocking the path of the Titan Heavy Hoplite Infantry. A hundred and eighty warriors surged against one another. Their war cries and the thunder of their pummelling shields cascaded around the streets. Arrows and spears rained from the rooftops and bodies lay trampled on the tarmac.

Freyja appeared in his face. 'Move. Get into the College!' She swung back and a row of scouts covered them with an arrow wall as they ran forward.

There was no traffic and Punnr could only assume the Vigiles had stopped everything, but there were people in windows on some of the higher floors, braving the missiles to film and photograph. He could feel the Bodyguard behind him and knew Ulf would be calculating, observing and employing all his cunning to seize the right moment. If Radspakr had indeed put him under orders to ensure Punnr was felled, he would have to do it soon. He wouldn't strike if the Titans could do the job for him, but he couldn't afford to wait until the seething mass of battle had ebbed away.

Punnr reached the iron gates of Old College and slipped into the cover of the giant arches, but any sense of shelter was transitory because another struggle was taking place ahead on the inner quadrangle. Arrows lanced from the roofs surrounding the quadrangle, but the Titan line on the ground was retreating. He thought he could see their White Warrior rising from a crouch beside a central drinking fountain and running for scaffolding in the far corner as the Wolf Kill Squads bayed at her heels. The fighting was rolling away across the lawn and the fountain was briefly left unattended. Oliver had been unable to pinpoint where the lion's mouth dripped, but Punnr knew it had to be there.

He waited behind a column and the Bodyguard grouped around him. Ulf and Erland were to the fore. They were looking up into the gloom of the arches and Punnr suddenly realised why. They were checking for Pantheon cameras. Without doubt Atilius would have set cameras above the quadrangle to ensure the Curiate could salivate over the bloody struggle from all angles. There would be individual Vigiles hovering in the corners as well, observing and recording. But in here, under the arches, it might just be the one place they couldn't see.

So his Bodyguard would murder him here.

Ulf's helmet ceased its examination of the arches and dropped to look at him. The others curled serpent-like around him, most looking outwards, but three staring in at him. An eerie silence fell and Punnr saw Ulf's elbow extend backwards to strike with his spear. But the man couldn't resist a final taunt. 'This is how a Perpetual says goodbye, Weakling. You won't be missed and you were never...'

Punnr smashed his shield boss into Ulf's helmet and threw a mailed arm into Erland's chest. In the same movement, he pushed himself around the column and ran out into the open.

Agape swung onto the higher platforms of the scaffolding and glanced back. The Horde were slower on the climb and she could pause for a few breaths. She was the last Titan to retreat, but they had left comrades slaughtered below and the wet grass had become slick with gore, the rain acrid with the metallic scent of blood.

Lenore was away safely onto the western roof, escorted by Companions. They would rappel back to street level and hope it was still guarded from a further Valhalla assault. The Band waited in a defensive line on the roof just above the scaffolding, along with the remaining archers who would cover the retreat. Menes came beside her, running his forearm across his nose where it bled profusely. Then he pointed with his sword and Agape saw the Valhalla White Warrior emerge from the entrance arches and tear towards the fountain.

'We can take him,' Menes stated flatly and without waiting for a response, he signalled to the archers. Agape watched the white figure, remembered him from the summit of Calton Hill and waited for the arrows to fly.

Punnr was ten yards from the drinking fountain and could just make out the bronze lion's head from which water would pour into the marble bowl below. He should be thinking of retrieving his UV torch from the bag on his belt, but he already knew he wouldn't be needing it. The battle had transformed into a hunt up the scaffolding and so the Wolves were too far from him. His treacherous Bodyguard were pouring from the arches and above him the Titans would be wondering how he could be alone and so exposed.

He heard a shout and thought he saw Halvar running back across the grass. He turned towards him and was about to respond when something smashed into his breastplate with such force that he staggered backwards. He tried to focus. There was an arrow shaft protruding from the centre of his chest and he let out a cry as pain shot through him. He could see Halvar bellowing at him. Then another blow smashed into his breastplate just to the left of the first and it lifted him backwards.

For a moment he saw nothing but the night sky, roiling black clouds above the high walls of the College. Then he was on his back and rain was sluicing into his helmet. His jaw hung slack and his vision was clouding like the heavens above. Halvar came beside him, and cradled his head, snarling at the Bodyguard to keep away and then shouting to him. 'Don't you die! Don't you dare die! Punnr, stay with me.'

But he could not. His mind was going somewhere, fleeing from the pain. The last thing he felt was the rain beating on him, relentless and cold.

XXXVI

The Valhalla tunnels were filled with confusion. Troops teemed back and forth, shouting for news, helping wounded comrades, stripping off armour and shoving each other to reach the water jugs. The air reeked of blood and sweat. Men cursed, others argued, some simply sank against walls and let it all flow over them. It had been a far more major encounter than any had expected. The heavy infantry brigades of both Palatinates had struggled shield to shield for almost an hour and neither had yielded a backwards step until news reached the Hoplites that their White Warrior had safely gathered the Asset and an orderly retreat could begin. Both sides had lost troops. Both had left corpses on the streets and the *libitinarii* were even now rushing to clear up in the last hours of night.

The wounded would go to the secret hospital where they would be afforded the best treatment money could buy. No one knew the location of this, but the healed who returned told how they were given every comfort, but kept under close watch and their private rooms locked. They were only permitted out at strictly enforced times and couldn't enter the opposite wing which housed Titan casualties. Within a stone's throw of one another, the wounded of each Palatinate would be restored and returned to fight another day.

Sveinn sat alone in the Council Chamber. He had been informed that his gamble had failed. His Hammer Regiment had been scythed, his White Warrior was dead, and now there was no value to the ace that Radspakr had been so keen to hold secret. The King listened to the tumult below and knew he should face his troops and rally them. But just at that moment he needed solitude. His bones ached and he was weary even though he had played no part in the conflict. What burden it was to carry the mantle of King. How he sometimes longed to be released.

In the East Tunnel, Radspakr stood in the doorway of his rooms and watched the swarming mass. He was shocked by the ferocity of the battle. Never had the Palatinates met with such force in the city during a Raiding Season and there would be bumpy times ahead. The media would descend into a frenzy of speculation, discussion and soul-searching. The internet would explode with images, soap-box opinions and gallows humour. Holyrood and Westminster would be forced to appear decisive and the security forces required to demonstrate success. Atilius would be obliged to offer them some placatory sacrificial lambs from both Palatinates and the Pantheon would have to ride out the storm with its usual diplomacy.

But ride it out, it would. These things always ebbed and flowed. People would shout and bicker about the horrors of a society in which the Pantheon could be allowed to prosper, but then they would subside into the same shared need to feed on the gory details and to gossip about the thrilling violence around them. In truth, they didn't want to live without it.

Radspakr picked at his lip. He should be looking on the bright side. The Horde would recover from its losses and this year it still held a significant numerical advantage over the Sky-Rats which should bode well when they entered the field of the Grand Battle in a few weeks. And the Valhalla White Warrior was gone without even the need for Bjarke's Shieldmen to carry out the deed. Three cheers for the Titan archers. Now just a little further mopping up was required, a cleaning out of the deadwood, then Radspakr could relax and the world could return to normal.

In South Tunnel, Calder let the tides of humanity ebb and flow around her. The Ravens had been corralled back to the stronghold at a run, shouted orders whipping around them. Stay ahead of the Titans. Get to the Gate. Once through, she had dropped her weapons and helmet and walked listlessly along the tunnel. She had witnessed the mass conflict on South Bridge. She had watched troops murder each other. She had smelt the blood and the fear. They were saying the White Warrior was dead, that much she understood. Men shouted the news and cursed the foe. Despite all their efforts, the loss of the White Warrior could only be interpreted as a defeat for Valhalla.

'Calder.' A voice called her, but she could barely recognise it among the commotion. 'Calder! Over here.'

It was Brante, being helped down the tunnel by Leiv. He was cradling his left arm. She ran to him. 'Are you hurt?'

'Sword thrust in the shoulder.'

'Oh my god, let me help.' She took the other side of him.

'It's only a scratch, I'll live. I guess I shouldn't be taking on the Sacred Band in my first Season.'

Leiv peered over at her. 'It's more than a scratch, but he's right that he'll live. We'll get him to the transport and then it'll be a few weeks in a hospital bed for our Wolf pup.' They eased him over to a bench by one of the vaults. 'I'll go for the medics, if you'll look after him?'

'Of course.' Calder sat next to Brante as Leiv disappeared down the tunnel. She looked up into his pained face. 'Is it true about Punnr?'

He grimaced and nodded. 'I saw it with my own eyes. Hit by Titan archers.'

'He's dead?'

'Halvar confirmed it. It would have been over quickly, at least there's no doubt about that.'

'It's not possible. I can't believe it.'

Brante found her hand and squeezed. 'I can't either. But it was always the risk once he took on the White Warrior role and he knew it. He played the part with courage right to the end.'

'He's not meant to be gone, it wasn't in the script. It was always the three of us, even from the start.'

'But now it's just the two of us and he'd want us to stay strong. He'd want us to honour his memory.'

She nodded weakly, but could feel the tears brimming in her eyes.

Brante squeezed her hand again. 'You're going to have to be strong on your own, Calder. I'm not going to be fit for the final Raid. Will you be okay?'

'Of course.' She wiped her eyes angrily and forced a smile

back up to him. 'You just get better, *Thrall II*. I need you back here soon.'

'I will, I promise.' He examined her face with concern. 'What are you going to do?'

'Go home,' she shrugged. 'Go to bed. What am I supposed to do?'

'Hang in there, Calder, and stay strong. He'd have wanted you to.'

'Would he? Do we really know what he'd have wanted? Did any of us know him enough to guess? I suspect he didn't do any of this for the glory of Valhalla. I think he had his own private reasons for putting himself at such risk and when he needed us most, we weren't there for him.'

A moorhen called from the reeds. Koi ghosted beneath the surface. After the wet night, the winter foliage hung heavy beneath a grey sky, but the air itself had a depth that clung in her throat. The silence was emphatic, just the timeless dripping of the plants and the sonant moorhen.

This was her special place. The place she had come in the weeks and months after she lost Amelia. She was glad it was deserted today and she sat staring into the depths of the ornamental pond. *The Chinese Hillside* was what the authorities at the Botanic Gardens called it and she sat within an oriental waterside pavilion, with koi before her and rhododendrons up the slope, but now it looked like any other bedraggled Scottish pond. She had been there hours and the afternoon light was already growing sombre. They would be closing the garden gates soon, but she barely cared. The pavilion kept the rain from her and she was long since numb from the cold. Her mind had taken her on long rambling journeys. Amelia always felt within touching distance when she was in this place and she had thought about her daughter for a while, remembering the sharp beautiful pinnacles within a fraying landscape of grief. She thought of her mother too and there were moments when she wanted nothing more than to be safe in her arms.

But her mind kept returning to Tyler. Ever since she had first seen him in the basement all those months ago, there had been something about him. Not good. Not bad. Just *something*. During the long hours of training with the other Thralls, she was always conscious of where he was, had always noticed him. It had bothered her and made her keep her distance. She wanted men to be an irrelevance because it was so much easier that way.

But somehow Tyler – Punnr – had worked his way under her guard. He had never been confident and generous like Brante, yet he contained a hidden drive that drew the other Thralls around him and she had found herself acting upon his word. Then the two of them had met over coffee in the real world and before her eyes he had become a real, sentient human being and she had told him about Amelia, something she had said to no one before. Dimly she realised she had been persisting in the Pantheon *because* of him and his loss meant she no longer knew what to do. He had been killed for some ridiculous token called an Asset, of no greater value than the paper money exchanged in *Monopoly*. So what *was* the Pantheon other than a stupid relentless overblown game?

At least Tyler had cherished a true reason for being in it, a true task to find his sister. Lana, on the other hand, had no credible excuse for being a part of this game, other than to keep running away from her life. Escaping, always escaping. No job, no relationship, in fact now she had no life outside the Horde.

She watched the moorhen bob across the pond and slowly, like the coming of the evening gloom, a conviction germinated within her. Perhaps his death had presented her with a new and unexpected reason to prosper in the Pantheon. She must continue his quest. She owed it to him.

Radspakr felt munificent. It was five days since the battle and the immediate crisis had passed, and he had become increasingly satisfied with the outcome. Now he sat with Bjarke at a table in his Quartermaster rooms and they ate slow-roasted lamb, the juices running from their mouths and greasing their fingers.

There was a knock at the door and he bid them enter, for he had invited them. Ulf stepped cautiously into the Thane's domain, Erland trailing behind him.

'Come,' Radspakr ordered. 'Join us.'

The two Thegns were dressed in linen tunics which made them look soft and young. They advanced obediently and sat on two chairs which Bjarke pulled to the opposite side of the table. Radspakr clicked his fingers and a serving girl brought two portions of steaming meat, already served into bowls. The scent made the Thegns drool. Bjarke poured them wine into beakers and Radspakr pushed a platter of bread towards them.

'Relax, eat. You deserve it. You did well.'

They bit into the succulent meat and gulped at the wine,

and gradually it soothed them and they loosened and ate more ravenously. Bjarke tore at the bread and mopped up the lamb juices, belching contentedly, and Radspakr sipped at his wine. He watched the boys, so young, but also so pliable. He had no doubt they would have killed Punnr on his orders without compunction if it had been necessary and that was useful to know. He might have need of them going forward.

But he also knew excitable youngsters like these could rarely be relied on to keep quiet. They could be too easily needled into bragging. A few drinks, a few hot words in the wrong company, and they might start talking about their mission to kill the White Warrior. He knew of only one way to ensure against such loosening of tongues. He must subject their impressionable young minds to an act of such abhorrence that they would forever dread him.

They were nearing the end of the meal and their chins glistened. Their cheeks had grown red with the wine and they were grinning, pleased with themselves for they were dining at the Thane's table and Bjarke was joking with them. They felt like warriors of merit.

'Have you read Herodotus?' Radspakr asked, twirling the stem of his beaker between his fingers. The Thegns looked at him blankly, still half grinning. 'He gives an account from the life of Astyages, King of the Medes, which always affects me. One night Astyages had a dream that his newly born grandson would soon take over his entire empire. Worried, the king tasked a kinsman called Harpagus to take the baby away and kill him. But Harpagus could not bring himself to do such a thing, so he left the baby with a lowly herdsman and thought no more of it.

'Years later, Astyages was travelling in the country when he came across the boy and, recognising his likeness, he guessed it was his grandson. He confronted Harpagus with the revelation and Harpagus broke down and admitted that he never killed the baby. Astyages feigned relief and said he was joyous that his grandson still lived after all.'

Ulf and Erland listened to the Thane, uncertain why they were being told this story. Bjarke drank slowly from his wine beaker.

'Now Harpagus had a son himself of the same age, so Astyages commanded that this son should visit the returned royal child. Harpagus readily agreed and went home mightily relieved, but when his son arrived at the palace, he was not welcomed into the presence of the royal child, instead he was taken to the kitchens where he was butchered and jointed and roasted and prepared for the table. That night his meat was given to Harpagus at a banquet. All the other guests had lamb.'

Radspakr drained his wine and then clicked his fingers again. The serving girl brought in a large platter covered with a lid and placed it in the centre of the table. Ulf and Erland stared at it as they started to piece together what Radspakr was saying. Erland had been chewing on a bone and now he stopped and placed it back onto his plate. Radspakr affected not to notice.

'Harpagus enjoyed his meal. Positively devoured it. Then, after he had complimented the King on the meat, Astyages called for the platter containing the feet, hands and head of Harpagus' son to be brought to the table. Then Astyages ordered him to raise the lid.'

For once, Bjarke was utterly silent, unmoving, not even

looking at the Thegns. Radspakr, however, now watched them like a hawk. Ulf's greasy face was pale. Erland was reddening and looking to his companion.

'So raise it,' Radspakr said quietly.

No one moved. Ulf stared at the platter as though willing it to disappear, then looked up into Radspakr's merciless eyes and knew there was no choice. Slowly he reached out, took hold of the lid's handle and lifted.

Erland exploded from his chair as if a charge had shot through it. His hands came to his mouth and he doubled over with a cry. Ulf didn't move, but every drop of blood drained from his face. Even Bjarke grunted in consternation. Just as Herodotus had described, the platter contained the neatly arranged feet, hands and head of Havaldr, glazed with their own steaming bloody gravy. Erland stumbled to the wall and retched, falling to his knees and sobbing. Ulf was shaking uncontrollably, but stayed locked to his chair.

Finally, when Erland's noises had subsided, Radspakr spoke again, calmly and quietly, as though he hadn't been interrupted. 'Harpagus did not break down. Instead he left the palace and accepted his punishment. He understood that any man – king or otherwise – who could countenance such an act, was a man to be truly feared. And absolutely obeyed. Jarl Bjarke, bring our friend back to the table if you will.'

When Erland was settled again, Radspakr continued. 'I'm sure you understand that I wished to illustrate my point this evening and your companion will not be missed amidst all the carnage of last night.' He fixed them with a cold glare. 'You are to be congratulated on your willingness to carry out my orders during the Raid. You have shown merit and I may yet call upon your assistance again. But let us tonight – around this table – be absolutely clear about my one message to you. Word of my orders to kill the White Warrior will never ever be spoken of again to anyone.'

He didn't prompt them for a response. He knew he had no need. He let the silence hang for a few moments and then waved them away. 'You may go.'

XXXVII

As Lana had hoped, Oliver was in his window seat, his face bathed in the glow of his iPad. It was eight in the evening and the drizzle had returned. She stood under the nearest streetlight and waved until he spied her. He peered at her in surprise for several moments, then disappeared and she sent a silent word of thanks when he opened the front door.

'Hi Oliver, remember me? Lana.'

'Sure. Where's Tyler?'

'He's had to go away for a while again and he asked me to collect a couple of things for him. Can I come in?' Oliver stood back and she got into the dry. The schnauzer was quiet for once. 'Do you know if he still has the key in his Wellingtons?'

'Think so.'

Once she had retrieved it and let herself in, Oliver followed and stood watching her at the entrance to the lounge. She looked around the room and had to clench her insides to retain her composure. His jeans were flung on the sofa. The laptop was discarded on the carpet beside the heater and a book was open where he had finished reading.

She picked it up and scanned the page, wondering which word had been the last he saw.

'How long's he gone for?' Oliver asked.

She wished he would leave her alone. 'I'm not certain, probably a few weeks.'

'Is he fighting Titans like on the news earlier in the week?'

'Not this time.'

The boy sidled further into the room. 'So what does he want you to collect?'

She dropped the book and tried to think. 'Um… some clothes…'

'Does he need my notes about the clues?'

'Yes! That's exactly what he needs. Can you get them, is that okay?'

'I'll load them onto a USB.'

Oliver disappeared back across the hall and Lana moved to the sideboard for what she really needed – the photograph of Tyler with his sister and mother. She had observed it when she was last there and if she was ever to find Morgan in the Pantheon she would need a picture of her. It was larger than she had remembered and an Odin amulet was hung over it. This was wrought from ivory and, when she turned it over, she found a tiny Star of Macedon painstakingly carved into the underside. Taking both the photo and the amulet, she checked around for something to use as cover before Oliver returned. She hovered in the doorway of his bedroom and felt as though she was trespassing on his private space. There were more scattered books, as well as a punchbag fixed to the wall and a set of dumbbells. His bed was unmade and she thought she could see the indentation where he had lain. Emotion bubbled in her, but she could hear Oliver coming back and so she steadied herself, yanked open a couple of drawers and retrieved a jumper, a pair of jeans and T-shirt. There was a sports bag tucked up behind the cupboard, so she placed all the items into it and returned just in time to bump into the boy.

'Everything's on this USB. I think you'll understand them, but do you want me to explain them to you?'

'No, no, that won't be necessary. Thank you, Oliver, you've been such a help and Tyler will be grateful.'

'He'd better come back soon. He was going to tell me all about the Horde's stronghold.'

She hugged him, which embarrassed him into silence, then she trotted back down the stairs and let herself out into the rain. As she opened her umbrella and began to stride towards Stockbridge, she didn't notice the figure watching her from the darkened gardens, nor see the glow of a phone as he made a call.

Radspakr listened intently on the other end of the line. Placing a trusted watcher on Tyler's flat had been his final precaution after the Raid to ensure everything was safely closed down. So often it proved to be the overlooked details that sunk great men. And it would seem he had been justified. So the girl knew where Tyler used to live. A quick night-time visit and a bag over her arm when she departed.

He left the caller waiting and stared ruminatively at the coals glowing in his hearth. He had hoped the dust would now settle, but such a discovery could not be ignored. What more did she know about Tyler Maitland? How often had she been in his flat? What had he shared with her?

With a sigh, he returned to the caller and gave his instructions.

Lana opened her eyes. There had been a noise and her heart was beating hard, but she told herself it was because she had come out of a dream so unexpectedly. She lay still and listened. She could hear the Leith flowing beyond the shared lawns and her radiators clicked, but otherwise her little house was silent. She squinted at her watch. 2.37 a.m. She sighed, rolled onto her side and tried to force herself to relax again. On the pillow next to her was the teddy which had been Amelia's.

But something felt different. Just a sensation. As though someone else breathed within her house.

She sat up, pulled on plimsolls, threw a gown over her nightdress and padded into the living room. The light switch was further along by the front door, so she just stood still and peered around. Everything seemed as it should. She took in the outlines of the television, the bookcase, the coffee table.

And then her heart froze. Beside her armchair, there was another shape. A figure.

In that moment it came for her. Two bounds and it was on her. She was flung against the wall and the breath forced from her, leaving her scream silent. A man's hand caught at her throat and his bulk thumped into her. All she could sense was hair and musk and raw power. He was breathing in her ear and she realised he wore a mask. She started to scream, but he threw her across the back of the sofa and she thudded onto the floor. She crawled to her knees, but he was already upon her. She felt him wrap his hand in her hair and tug her backwards onto the sofa. She struggled and he slapped her face so hard that fireworks exploded somewhere behind her eyes, but she continued to fight, rolling her legs up to kick and punching his chest as hard as she could.

Then she felt the point of a knife against her throat and froze, staring helplessly at his mask. He was breathing raggedly and she thought she caught the whites of his eyes. His grip on her hair was like iron and the knife played across her throat. For a moment everything was quiet and the river could once more be heard beyond the window.

Gradually the tempo of his breathing changed as his eyes moved up and down her, and she understood why. Her bare legs were exposed and her gown was open enough for her cleavage to be visible. He had been sent as a cold-blooded killer, but now something different pulsed through him. The knife travelled down her body and he lowered his head to sniff the skin between her breasts, but the mask prevented him from getting close enough to her, so he sat back and released his hold of her hair to yank the woollen mask from his mouth and nose.

It was the only chance she had. She had watched Punnr and Brante during the streetfight sessions in the vaults and remembered Halvar's teachings. With every last ounce of her strength, she brought her head up from the sofa just as he was once more lowering his and her forehead cracked into his nose. With a surprised curse, he fell back from her and brought his hand up to his face. With the other, he slashed at her with the knife, but she had already rolled her legs over her shoulders and dropped from the end of the sofa.

He staggered upright and she could see blood running on his hand and chin. As he came around the sofa at her, knife extended, she let her training take over. A tornado kick. In one seamless movement, she spun on the spot, her left leg raised tight at the knee. Then she pushed off with her right leg mid-spin, extended it, brought her left down for balance and smashed her right instep into her assailant's head. He fell sideways, stumbling against the coffee table, and she thought she heard the knife clatter across the table as he tried to arrest his fall, but she was already running for the door and out into the night air. The rain had stopped and her plimsolls splashed through puddles as she tore along the house fronts towards Glenogle. She dared not look behind. She just ran, a small terror-stricken sound bubbling in her throat. She reached St Bernard's and knew she was only moments from the main Stockbridge high street, where there would be lights and maybe taxis.

She burst onto it and stared wildly around her. He wasn't following her. She was alone. Tears were salting her lips as she sucked in air. Slowly she backed away along the street and then started running raggedly up into New Town, not knowing where she went, just letting her terrified legs carry her.

XXXVIII

Lana walked the wet streets for hours, keeping to the brighter lit areas. People stared at her, this pale, shivering, unkempt woman in her nightclothes and plimsolls. At least twice, night taxis pulled alongside and the drivers called to her to ask if she was okay. Did she need a ride somewhere? But she kept her eyes averted and wouldn't break stride, so they pulled away. Rough voices called sometimes from doorsteps and she hurried on. A man followed her along Broughton Street and she ran blindly into Hart Street until her breath rattled in her ribs and she was sure he was gone.

The rain came again and she huddled under shrubs near Union Street. She knew she needed to get somewhere dry, but her mind refused to focus. She couldn't return to her house, that was the only thing clear to her. Her assailant had been no random intruder. She knew he had come only to kill her and he would be back.

There was movement in the undergrowth behind her and she shot back out onto the pavement and stumbled away in the drizzle. Her legs took her south to Waverley and then up the hill to the towering claustrophobia of the Old

Town. She was numbed with cold and her body was close to shutting down. Before she even realised, she found herself heading to the Market Street Gate.

As the first light of a new day blossomed across the Forth, the Gate Keepers let her in. They helped her along East Tunnel, but didn't ask why she came at this hour, sodden, frozen and wordless. They left her in the eastern Reception Area with a tunic, leggings and boots. She sat alone in her nightclothes for an age until something inside her spoke of the steaming hot water so close to hand. In a trance, she showered, allowing the heat to wash over her. Mutely she dried and clothed herself, then stole to the Western Hall, where she warmed herself by the fire and one of the serving boys brought her bread and cheese.

Valhalla was quiet at this hour. Only a few warriors went about their affairs, but she found herself staring at each of them, searching for one with a freshly injured nose. What was she doing there? She grappled with the question and the only answer she could find was that there was nowhere else for her to go. Now she had no home, no family, no trusted friends. Even Tyler and Brante had left her. She knew her would-be killer had been sent by the Pantheon, yet she also understood that she was safest here in the halls of the Horde, where no weapons could be carried. It was, after all, the only place she now belonged.

She longed for Halvar. She didn't know why, except that Tyler had said Halvar thought his sister was alive. She was beginning to realise that Tyler's sister must be the key to it all. Was Morgan the reason she had been attacked? What had he said once to her? *I think something – or someone – was really scaring her.* Yes, and Halvar knew about Morgan

Maitland, so now she needed him, yearned for him to come striding into the hall.

But the day matured and more troops bustled to and fro, and he didn't arrive. She watched the activity in a daze. Warriors ate and talked and prepared for the final Raid that night. As the afternoon wore on, the place began to hum, and still she hunched by the fire and watched.

Later in the afternoon, Radspakr passed and he looked at her with his head held on one side. 'Are you well, my dear? May we get you anything?'

She said something in reply, but couldn't hear herself properly, and he smiled coldly, shrugged and departed.

Later it was Freyja who came to her and cajoled her into preparation. The final Raid was close and her Ravens were arming. Calder pulled on her armour and collected her helm and weapons from the Armouries, cleaned and oiled by the Schola apprentices since the last Raid. The touch of her sword on her hip strengthened her and her mind at last began to focus. Noise returned. Chatter. Urgent whispers. Grins from her comrades. Shared adrenaline. Perhaps she was among friends after all.

At precisely the appointed hour, the Horde streamed from the North West Gate. As always, Freyja led her Ravens in the vanguard and for the second time during the Raiding Season, they ran lightly through the back gardens of Ramsay Lane and out onto the wooded slopes above Princes Street Gardens, but on this occasion they turned uphill towards the black hulking walls of the Castle which sat squat and immovable on its cliff-top fastness.

It was an impregnable location and earlier Freyja had pored over maps with her Hersirs to identify the only possible place where the Valhalla climbers might be able to ascend. The Ravens now ran to this point, where the rear wall of the gift shop met the top of the wooded slope. Thirty feet of stone still stood above them, but it was the best option because fifty yards further along and the slope transformed into a loose, scrubby cliff which ran the entire way around the rest of the Castle's perimeter.

This time the elite climbers waited while grappling irons were swung at the railings on top of the wall. It took several attempts and the clatter as the irons came back down reverberated around the trees, setting everyone's heart pumping. *Where were the Titans?* They would throw their full force on the Castle as well, for they still hoped to claim the final Asset. The Horde had no such objective with their own White Warrior killed, so tonight their sole goal was to stop the Titans in their tracks and deny them the Asset.

The irons held at last and the elite climbers heaved up the ropes. Calder waited behind a tree trunk, straining her eyes to look for enemy movement. She knew Asmund's Storm archers would by now be taking up positions around the Castle esplanade outside the main gate, providing a covering shield for any full-frontal approach by the Titans. The Wolves too would be leaving the Valhalla Gate, followed by Hammer. All of them coming to this spot to ascend. It was a dangerous bottleneck.

The climbers were up and securing rope ladders. These came tumbling down and the rest of the Ravens started to ascend. Calder followed Freyja up the rungs. She was still not thinking clearly, but she knew with absolute conviction that she must stay close to Freyja tonight. She felt the strength of the other woman and trusted to it.

They reached the roof of the gift shop and fanned out, crouching and staring across the dark interior complex of the Castle as it snaked away above them. The Wolves were below and beginning to climb. It was vital that they caught the scent of the Titan White Warrior and took her down before she could retrieve the Asset. They came fast up the ladders, ran past the scouts and dropped into the courtyard below. She looked for Halvar, but it was too dark to make out individuals. Next came groups of accompanying Vigiles with cameras and Calder knew there would already be Pantheon cameras fixed at all the key points within the Castle.

At a signal from Freyja, the Ravens followed the Wolves over the edge. Calder found herself lining up with them at the bottom of a steep roadway, hemmed by walls, which ran up to a tower with a raised portcullis. In ancient days, this would have been a formidable second line of defence. Anxious murmurs passed down the lines. With the high battlements either side and the steep gradient ahead, this was no place to be caught.

'Let's go!' Freyja hissed and the Ravens ran up the road, followed by the ranks of Wolves. Calder looked back once and saw Hammer Shieldmen flooding across the roof of the gift shop. The Horde was in. *Where were the Titans?*

The first six Ravens reached the tower and raced under the arch, arrows notched and bow arms searching for the slightest sign of movement. They signalled for the rest to advance. The roadway began to widen onto Argyle Battery and there – a hundred yards ahead – loomed the cart shed coffee shop and Mill's Mount Battery where the One o'clock Gun would be found. Her mind was suddenly filled with an image of Tyler grinning as he finally understood the clue. It seemed impossible that he wasn't here tonight, running with them to claim the Asset.

To their left was a long flight of steps that ascended through the wall to the higher levels of the Castle complex. These would provide ideal viewpoints to cover movements around Mill's Mount, so Freyja signalled her scouts and they began to climb. Below them, the Wolves continued tracking up the roadway towards the cart sheds and the Hammer Shieldmen could be heard coming behind.

Calder followed Freyja, always keeping her shadow in sight, and the other Ravens were around her. They reached the top and it opened into a courtyard in front of the primary Castle buildings, the Royal Palace itself and the War Memorial. They were as high as they could go and Calder turned to see the expanse of Edinburgh winking below her. She could see the lights of New Town, Stockbridge, Comely Bank. Somewhere out there was her empty little house, trespassed upon and defiled. Further beyond were the darker patches of the Botanic Gardens and Inverleith Park. In the distance were the strident lights of the docks and then Fife. The scene was beguiling on this dank, cold night.

Her thoughts were interrupted by a sudden whirlwind of noise from below. A baying of Wolves. The Ravens rushed to deploy, but even as they did, arrows came lancing out of the sky from the top of the Royal Palace and struck the walls around them.

'Cover!' Freyja yelled. But there was none. Calder ran southward along the battlements, the yawning expanse of the courtyard beside her. Arrows clattered against the wall around her. She hoisted her shield and ran blindly. She felt a mighty blow and an arrow tip broke through the shield and sat peeking at her just inches from her face. She reached a place where the wall bent, pushed herself into the angle and curled under her shield.

She expected more hits, but there was a pause. She imagined Titan archers waiting for her to move, their bows already drawn back, but the seconds dragged into minutes and still no one fired. She forced herself to look out. The courtyard was empty and she could see no movement on the Castle buildings. Away to the north she could hear the sounds of battle, but around her it had become peaceful.

She pulled herself up and looked for the other Ravens. They were gone. They must have run in the other direction at Freyja's command. A panic rose in her because she had lost the one person she had sworn to stay beside. She shouldered her bow and unsheathed her sword, then returned the way she had come, heading towards the sounds of the conflict. She ran past the top of the steps and then saw a vast gun looming out of the darkness in front of a small, squat building. She realised it was the famous Mons Meg cannon and the building must be St Margaret's Chapel. Legend said it was the oldest structure in Edinburgh.

She rounded the cannon and gaped over the battlements. Below, the Titan Heavy Infantry had swarmed down from the opposite side of the Castle and the rival Palatinates were fighting a second great battle in just seven nights. To have entered the Castle from the other side, the Titans must have climbed the highest and steepest part of the cliff.

Lined across the roadway in front of them was Hammer Regiment, shoulder to shoulder, shields locked. Their line curved around Mill's Mount and anchored against the cart sheds, preventing any access to the One o'clock Gun. The Hoplite Infantry had smashed into Hammer's centre and Calder could see the rival lines ebbing and flowing as warriors pushed and kicked and stabbed. Behind them the Wolves were gathered on Mill's Mount watching for any sign of the White Warrior's party. She strained to see Freyja and the Ravens, but there were too many troops and the night was so dark.

She pushed back from the wall, suddenly afraid to be so alone on this high vantage point. She must return to the steps and they would take her down behind Valhalla lines. She skirted the giant cannon once more and ran back to the steps. Without looking ahead, she began to descend, peering through her helmet at her feet to ensure she kept her footing on the slippery stone. As such, she didn't notice the figures climbing towards her until she was almost upon them. At the last second she sensed their presence and looked up to see two Hammer Shieldmen. They were smaller and thinner than most of the brawny Hammers, and they carried spears, their swords sheathed. They stopped and looked at her through their helmets, but they didn't speak and she was seized by an instinctive dread. Her blonde ponytail was curved over her shoulder and one of them nodded knowingly.

'Hail, Thegn Calder. We've been seeking you.'

She would know that high-pitched whine anywhere. She gripped her sword and pointed the blade towards him. 'Take another step and I'll gut you.'

'Come and try it, beautiful.'

Courage failed her. The exhaustion of the last two days was too much. There was a wild crescendo of shouts from the battle and Ulf glanced in that direction. In the same second, she turned and ran for her life. She took the steps two at a time and flew onto the upper courtyard once more. She raced headlong to the great gun and along the battlements, where the battle was laid out before her again, hundreds of fighters oblivious to the cold murder planned above.

With a despairing cry she realised the battlements abutted the chapel and wouldn't allow her to pass. She ran to the chapel door and yanked at it, but it wouldn't budge. She turned and threw herself back around the cannon in one last effort to break out onto the wider courtyard, but her pursuers were already closing her escape. Hopelessly she ground to a halt and retreated until her back was pressed against the barrel of the gun. They spread themselves and approached with spears levelled.

Perhaps she had known this was to be her fate tonight. Perhaps this was why she had fled from her flat and washed up back in Valhalla. Perhaps the gods had decreed that she should make her final stand at the highest and most ancient point in the city, faced by the men who had hunted her so mercilessly in the forests of the Highlands.

Erland edged towards her and aimed his spear at her breast. 'Drop your blade and your shield, or I'll fucking skewer you right now.'

'You'll have to come and get them, little boy.' She braced herself into a fighting stance behind her shield.

They began to edge around her, breaking apart so that she could only defend herself from one of them at a time.

Her eyes flicked between them and gauged distances. Then she flew at Erland, smacking his spear aside and aiming a lunge towards his midriff. She thought she had him, but at the last moment he brought his shield across and her blade smacked into the hardened leather just above the Hammer symbol. She righted herself and was about to launch a follow through, when white-hot pain exploded beneath her extended right sword arm. Ulf had aimed his spear at the one place where she wore no armour, no mail and no protection other than her leather jerkin, and the iron point of his spear broke through to flesh and rib and shoulder-blade.

She staggered backwards, pinned by his weapon. Her arm dropped limply and her sword clattered to the ground. She stared at his helmeted face and could see the smirk on his tight little lips. He extracted the spear roughly and she collapsed against the cannon. Her vision lurched and her knees shook, but somehow the cannon's bulk kept her upright. She gaped at her assailants, words no longer forming in her throat. She could feel hot liquid spreading down her side and steaming in the night air.

'Nothing personal, you understand,' said Ulf. 'Orders are orders.'

Erland stepped forward and tore off her helmet. He peered at her through the eyeholes of his own, then forced his off as well. She took in his sallow cheeks and spotty immature skin, and remembered how he used to strut in the vaults in the first days. *Thrall VII*. He was leering at her, his eyes slits of black lust.

'I've always wanted to do this,' he croaked, then stuck out a long tongue and licked her slowly from throat to forehead.

She shrivelled at his touch and with one final effort tried to kick him. His desire turned to anger and he slapped her across the side of the head, sending her staggering around the cannon into a heap in front of the chapel door. Her face was in a puddle, but she had no strength to move anymore.

'Stop fucking about,' Ulf scolded. 'Just finish her and let's get out of here.'

She sensed Erland standing over her and knew he was raising his spear to spit her. A vision of Amelia came to her and somewhere the real her – Lana Cameron – smiled a greeting to her daughter.

And then the gods changed their minds.

The door of the chapel opened and two figures emerged. One huge and furious, the other swift as lightning and dressed in white. There were cries above her, the clash of iron. Something heavy hit the ground next to her and rolled to the chapel wall. Hazily she saw it was Erland's head.

Then hands were on her. Gentle ones. Turning her, cradling her head, wiping her hair from her face and she was looking up at a white helmet.

'It's okay, Calder. It's okay now. I'm here. You're safe. We have you.'

She tried to form a word. 'Punnr…?'

'Yes, it's me. And Halvar. He brought me through the secret tunnel. We have an Asset to collect.'

'But they said you died. They saw you hit with Titan arrows.'

'No, they saw me hit by Freyja's arrows, shorn of their iron tips. And they heard Halvar *claim* I was dead.'

Her vision was swimming. She tried to grip him so she would know he was no illusion. 'I thought you were dead…'

'It was my only option. There's nothing in the rules that says the White Warrior can't *pretend* to be dead. And if the foe fail to check, then that's their problem.'

'You bastard,' she croaked weakly. It was raining again, spotting onto her cheeks. Somewhere the noise of battle raged, but up here in his arms it was incredibly peaceful.

He leaned into her. 'Hush now. We'll get you to safety and then you must get well. Get strong. Because I need you with me for what is to come.'

★

Author's Note

Dear Reader

If you are here, then you have probably made it through the first months of The Pantheon with Tyler and Lana. You've toiled in the candlelit training cellars with them. You've travelled to the remote winter fastness of the Highlands and feasted alongside them in the Halls of Valhalla. You've run across the rooftops with Agape, wondered at the riddles with Oliver, then felt the shock of the arrow puncturing Punnr's chest. Thank you! After so long with The Pantheon locked in my head, it is amazing to know that you have shared these adventures.

Now, of course, you are left at the highest point in Edinburgh Castle on a grim winter's night as the shieldwalls of the Palatinates battle below and Calder lies wounded and broken in the arms of Punnr. Will she recover? How does he come to be there at the moment of her need? Will they escape and make it to the Blood Season? And what of Morgan? Does she wait for her brother somewhere deep within The Pantheon?

If you would like to connect, please visit:

cfbarrington.com

Facebook - @BarringtonCFAuthor

Twitter - @barrington_cf

Instagram – cfbarrington_notwriting

Meanwhile, here is a snippet from the opening of *The Blood Isles*: Book Two of the Pantheon. I hope you enjoy.

C F Barrington

THE BLOOD ISLES

Prologue

Pantheon Year – Eighteen

Season – Blood

He would never forget her face.

Sheet white. Ferocious. Streaked with rainwater and blood, a wisp of black hair plastered across one cheek and lips curled back in a snarl.

2.27 a.m. said the clock on his dashboard as he cruised down the Royal Mile hoping for a final customer on this miserable night. He had just bitten into a ham and coleslaw sandwich when there was a whump on his rear bumper.

'What the…!' He dropped the sandwich onto his lap, hit the brakes and peered into his mirror. A shadow flitted across his line of sight. Little more than a darker piece of the night, followed by a shout.

'Bloody drunks.' They'd get a piece of his mind. He applied the handbrake and was about to heave himself out, when he caught movement again in his sidemirror and froze, door ajar, cold air oozing into the stale interior. Only a glimpse. A flicker of bronze glistening rust-red in his rear lights. The whisper of a cloak and then gone.

He dropped back into his seat and closed the door. Not drunks. *Titans*. He stared again into his mirror and could now see them more clearly. Figures cutting across the Mile at a sprint, swords drawn, shields hauled onto shoulders. Others angled in front of the car and ran hard, uncaring if they were caught in his headlights.

'Okay, just keep it together. Nothing to worry about. Let them do their thing.'

There was something about the disarray of the figures. The abandon with which they hurled themselves across the street and disappeared into the shadows surrounding the High Kirk of St Giles'. These troops weren't attacking. They were fleeing. In moments they had vanished and he peered to his left, towards the tight opening of Advocate's Close from whence they had come. Rain arrived again, rattling on his roof, and it brought with it more figures from the Close. But these were different. Their helmets bore no plumes, their mail was iron, their blades much longer and they howled with glee, like hyenas with the scent of blood in their nostrils.

And that was the moment she appeared.

A thud on the bonnet spun his attention back to the front and her arms were spread-eagled on the hood as though she had run blindly into his vehicle. Her shoulders heaved, ebony hair hung from her helmet and she gripped a shortsword, but if she had carried a shield that night, she had already dropped it in her haste. She glared at him through the windscreen, then pushed back and became emblazoned in his lights. He gawked at her, his jaw slack.

He had never seen someone so magnificently desolate. So feral and untamed. She might wear the bronze of a Titan officer, but there was horror in her eyes. Tears mixed with blood. Rage broke from her lips.

For a moment, her eyes pierced into him, then her attention was torn to her pursuers. She hurled a challenge back at them, turned and fled. The Vikings gave chase, but they were slower and he watched her charge across the court in front of St Giles' and disappear under an arch beside the Signet Library. Some of the Vikings followed, but minutes later they returned and it was obvious from their frustration that she had given them the slip.

Good, he thought, though he knew not why.

The Horde loitered around the street. They yelled and hooted, swore at each other and swung their blades, but their noise was that of victors and they soon began to laugh and slap hands. He waited unmoving, numbed by the sheer incongruity of it all. The warm, air-conditioned interior. The mash of mayonnaise and bread between his legs. And the wild warriors of the night celebrating their battle honours.

When the last of them had gone, he eased the handbrake and slipped off the Mile onto South Bridge, but his mind was on the girl. Who was she? The last of the Titans to flee and a look in her eyes that would stay with him forever. He glanced at the seat next to him and swore when he saw his phone.

What a picture she would have made. What the papers would have paid for such a shot. A single image that summed up everything about The Pantheon. Its blood and its beauty.

★

Olena, Captain of Companion Bodyguard, ran. Her final look back had told her everything she needed to know. Timanthes, her Colonel and one of the Pantheon's most illustrious servants, would not be setting foot again on the pavements of Edinburgh and nor would so many of the Titan Palatinate's best troops. That hot, stinking cellar was their burial chamber.

She wept for them as she sprinted through the archway beside the Courts and on towards the parking areas at the rear of the buildings. A rope was hanging in a corner – one of many readied as an escape route for the Titan Sky-Gods – but she ignored it. Her Companions would already be on the rooftops and watching for the final escapees, but she did not intend to join them. As she passed, she glimpsed the rope being hauled up to prevent any Valhalla lout – high on victory – thinking they too could take to the skies.

She could hear her pursuers on her tail and she kept running. Across a yard, through a gate and then threading between vans parked at the back of the Court complex. A building blocked her way and she knew if the final rope had already gone, then she was lost. The Horde would trap her there, edge her into a corner and cut her down. One more of the Titan elite taken out of the game that night.

She charged to the wall and peered each way. There it hung beyond the last window, straight and still. She sheathed her bloodied sword and lunged across, grabbing the length and hoisting her legs up the wall in practised movements just as the first Viking pursuers came hurtling around the vehicles. They howled at the sight of her, but she was already out of reach. A young face appeared over the parapet, unmasked.

'Go!' Olena commanded as she dragged herself onto the roof. 'I can do this.'

The Rope-Runt nodded in awe and dashed away into the night while Olena began hauling in the length. The lead Viking arrived below and made a grab for the end, but he was too late. Then a slender female warrior danced across the parking area, allowed her momentum to take her up the man's back and leapt for the rope as it disappeared into the night. Olena felt the impact of the woman's hand on the other end, but the twine was wet and her grip failed. With a cry of exasperation, she fell back to earth and Olena yanked up the last few metres. Only when it was all safely coiled on the roof beside her did she peer over. Her adversary returned the look, pointed her blade, then stalked back between the vans and disappeared.

A hush descended and Olena raised her eyes to the sodden rooftops around her. Nothing stirred. A diffused glow from the streetlights created an eerie orange dome over the buildings, as though shielding them from the impenetrable blackness above. A breeze jostled across the roofs and searched for her exposed skin. Her arms were shaking – although whether from the climb, the cold or sheer exhaustion, she could not tell. Her troops would already be well on their way to Ephesus and Thebes, and when they reached the safety of the Titan strongholds, the Armouries would fill with cries of treason, for any fool could see the Companions had been led into a trap.

Carefully, she raised herself and found her legs trembling too. She searched the shadows for the slightest movement, then began to navigate along the roof. But not towards the Titan strongholds. Instead she went north, back across the Court of Session and the Signet Library, the steeple of St Giles' dead ahead. Then she cut west to the terrace over Lawnmarket where Timanthes had gathered his troops less than an hour before. She dropped to her knees and crawled to the edge. The Mile below was empty and resentful of her prying eyes. The Horde had gone and the entrance to Advocate's Close squatted sullen and black. *Timanthes, forgive me.*

She pulled her gaze away and slithered across to a chimney, where the southern side provided shelter from the breeze. She seated herself on the wet tiles and leaned back against the bricks. She was shaking badly now as she attempted to wrap her cloak around her, but the cloth was already sodden and her fingers were stiff and clumsy. She unbuckled her sword belt and gazed at the leather and ivory scabbard. The blade would already be sticky with drying blood. It needed to be drawn, cleaned and oiled, but instead she simply dropped it and removed her helmet. She shook her lank hair and rubbed her face, then propped her head back against the chimney, took a deep ragged breath and gazed up at the starless heavens.

A cynic might say her plan had worked. Sow a belief among her Titan commanders that they had an asset in the Viking Horde. Lead the cream of the Titan companies to a door which this traitor said led to the heart of the Horde's Valhalla stronghold. Walk them into an ambush. Watch them butchered. Then in the forthcoming Grand Battle the weakened Titan lines would not be capable of holding the Viking onslaught and Alexander himself might fall. A chance to combine the Palatinates. To be, at last, together with her lover Halvar.

She dropped her gaze. A stupid plan. A plan only love could make sense of.

It is the nature of things that you reap what you sow. The Vikings were supposed to feign surprise, but they had marched into that cellar in full battle regalia. It was obvious they had been expecting the foe and now every Titan still breathing knew they had been betrayed. At that very moment messengers would be flying between Thebes, Pella, Ephesus and Persepolis, tallying up the living, accounting for the dead and soon all inquiries would lead back to Olena. Then the hunt would begin. She knew she should run. Discard her armour and flee into the arms of the city. Find a haven and disappear.

But her limbs refused to move. Halvar himself had not been present in the cellar and she wondered if he already hung in Valhalla's vaults, helpless against Radspakr's instruments. Everything had failed. Their clandestine love had led inexorably to a bloodbath which had felled even the great Timanthes. And there would be no mercy.

She squeezed the cloak tight and hunched lower, but the rain would not ease and the cold was groping for her, burrowing into her core and dissolving her thoughts.

Acknowledgements

I first set pen to paper – or rather fingers to laptop – back in 2016. For some time I had wanted to find a way to bring the wonder and violence of the ancient world into a modern setting and during a series of dog walks in the Lake District the whole concept of the Pantheon came to me. I whisked off a first-draft of *The Wolf Mile* and, naturally, I was convinced there would soon follow a publishing bidding war over the rights, then a major film deal, and I would be boarding trains and finding half the carriage reading my work.

Reality bit sharply as I sent off letter after letter to agents and rarely even heard back. Months dragged and late summer found me sitting in a small rental cottage on the Mull of Kintyre. The place had appalling internet coverage, so it's a miracle I even discovered the email from Laura MacDougall at United Agents. She had read my first three chapters and wanted the rest. Uploading the script pretty much destroyed the Mull's entire internet – but just a day later Laura had completed the whole thing and wanted to sign me! I was over the moon. Since then, Laura has been my rock and the best agent any writer could wish for. She is so passionate about books and from the very start she totally 'got' the quirky story which is *The Wolf Mile*.

So I had a great agent. Now I needed a great publisher. Once again, it was my destiny to face many disappointments, but then – riding to the rescue from a distant horizon – came Hannah Smith and Holly Domney at Aries Fiction, part of Head of Zeus Books. *The Wolf Mile*, they said, was perfect for the adventure portfolio they were building at Aries. Since then, Hannah and Holly have been awesome at fine-tuning the story and guiding me through the various stages to publication. I am so thankful to have their wisdom and leadership.

Thank you too to some of the other team members: Olivia Davies at United Agents, who has so ably covered while Laura has been on maternity leave; and Dushi Horti and Annabel Walker, to whom I am indebted for such great copy editing and proofreading (I never knew you only put an *e* on the end of blond when describing a female – thank you Annabel)!

Through this whole turbulent process of giving life to the Pantheon and *The Wolf Mile*, I have been lucky enough to have the support of some amazing friends. Thank you to Mark Clay (markrclay.com) for the brilliant map of Edinburgh's Old Town and all the laughs and hill climbs along the way. A huge thank you to Mike Dougan, who always fizzes with such energy and believed in *The Wolf Mile* before he had read a single word. The evening he marched me around Edinburgh's backstreets is etched on my mind, crawling onto roofs, nipping over walls, lying in the middle of roads, to get the best photos for my website. My huge gratitude, as well, to Dave Follett, a friend since childhood, who has been my most stalwart reader throughout the development of Books 1, 2 & 3 in The Pantheon series and has provided such prescient advice and encouragement.

Much love and thanks to my family – especially my brother, Steve, who has been ready to read whatever I produce and give me the sort of honest feedback only kin can. Finally, thank you to Jackie, who has put up with me disappearing into a world of Vikings for what feels like half a lifetime and has always believed in me, even when the rejection letters were flooding in.

The Wolf Mile is only what it has become because I've been lucky enough to have you all on the journey with me.